Critical acclaim for *The Book of the Alchemist* and Adam Williams

'In *The Book of the Alchemist* Adam Williams brings complex history alive. He moves into Dan Brown's territory of archaeological and religious mystery with an epic sweep and brilliant story-telling of love, war and morality that touches all our lives.'
Humphrey Hawksley, BBC World Affairs Correspondent

'A thousand years go by in a flash as Williams spins a yarn uniting childhood camaraderie in the 11th century with the violence of the 20th-century civil war. Prepare to be captivated'   *Stylist*

'Reading this tale about Spain struggling to reconcile its identities is like opening a beautifully wrapped parcel to find a gift of equal wonder within . . . The parallels between past and present in this book, and again with reality, will touch the heart of any reader' ****   *Straits Times*, Singapore

'A true epic, spanning many decades and incorporating real events of magnitude. It is not easy to explain historical context entertainingly, but Williams pulls it off.' *The Times* on *The Dragon's Tail*

'Poetic and romantic in parts, harrowing and tragic in others' ****
Heat on *The Emperor's Bones*

'High drama, political intrigue, moral quagmires, and a healthy dose of romance are key ingredients for rip-roaring adventure. Adam Williams' new epic *The Emperor's Bones* has the lot.'
Time Out Beijing

'Full of love and loss and guts and gore and derring-do . . . this is as good as the adventure story gets . . . Williams is a master.'
The Times on *The Palace of Heavenly Pleasure*

'A sweeping tale of love, subtlety and courage . . . Rising passion meets passionate uprising in the Far East'
Sunday Telegraph on *The Palace of Heavenly Pleasure*

The Book of the Alchemist

Courage and redemption in war-torn Andalucía

ADAM WILLIAMS

HODDER

First published in Great Britain in 2009 by Hodder & Stoughton
An Hachette UK company

First published in paperback in 2010

1

'The Death of Lorca' by Antonio Machado, translated by Professor Paul O'Prey. Extract
reproduced by kind permission of Professor Paul O'Prey.

'The Gazelle' by Shmuel HaNagrid, translated by Peter Cole. Cole, Peter (trans., ed. &
intro.); THE DREAM OF THE POEM © 2007 by Princeton University Press. Reprinted by
permission of Princeton University Press.

Extracts of poetry by Abbas Ibn Al-Ahnaf and Abu Al-Ala Al-Ma'arri, from 'Birds Through
a Ceiling of Alabaster: Three Abbasid Poets' translated by G.B.H. Wightman and A.Y. al-
Udhari. Reproduced by kind permission of Penguin UK Ltd, on behalf of G.B.H. Wightman
and A.Y. al-Udhari.

A CIP catalogue record for this title is available from the British Library

B format paperback ISBN 978 0 340 89915 1
A format paperback ISBN 978 1 444 70028 2

Typeset in Monotype Sabon by Palimpsest Book Production Limited,
Falkirk, Stirlingshire

Printed and bound by
CPI Mackays, Chatham

Hodder & Stoughton policy is to use papers that are natural, renewable and
recyclable products and made from wood grown in sustainable forests.
The logging and manufacturing processes are expected to conform to the
environmental regulations of the country of origin.

Hodder & Stoughton Ltd
338 Euston Road
London NW1 3BH

www.hodder.co.uk

To Alexander, Clio and Sybil

The Gazelle

I'd given everything I own for that gazelle
who rising at night to his
harp and flute,
saw a cup in my hand
and said:
'Drink your grape blood against my lips!'
And the moon was cut like a D,
on a dark robe, written in gold.

Samuel the Nagrid (993–1056), translated by Peter Cole

From **The Death of Lorca**

Carve, friends, from stone and dream,
in the Alhambra a barrow for the poet,
on the water of fountains that weep
and whisper for eternity:
'The crime was in Granada,
in his Granada!'

Antonio Machado, translated by Professor Paul O'Prey

From **The Morte D'Arthur**

The sequel of to-day unsolders all
The goodliest fellowship of famous knights
Whereof this world holds record. Such a sleep
They sleep – the men I loved. I think that we
Shall never more, at any future time,
Delight our souls with talk of knightly deeds,
Walking about the gardens and the halls
Of Camelot, as in the days that were . . .

Alfred, Lord Tennyson

Contents

Prelude

A Matter of Conscience

Valencia, April 1937

The stench of bodies and urine was overpowering. He gagged before he reached the bottom of the iron stairs. Then, he saw the rows of faces caught in the torchlight: old men, women and children, hundreds of them. They were glaring at him, half suspicious, half afraid. He had read the reports and guessed who they were: refugees from the Aragón front. They were the forgotten, the unnamed, the human detritus of war.

There were curses as his chauffeur forced a path through the packed bodies. They had barely found a space to crouch before the German planes flew over for a second run, and the walls of the flimsy shelter began to shake, loosening chips of cement and plaster.

The bombing continued through the night, punctuated by screams and wails in the darkness. Sometimes the destruction was far away and they heard only faint whistles and distant thunder, but it was only ever a short respite before the air throbbed again with the noise of engines. Terror sucked away their breath as they imagined the black projectiles spiralling down towards them. Then all thought was extinguished as the walls shook and the crashing reverberated inside their heads, shrivelling their guts and unstringing their sinews. Lightning flashed through the cracks between the concrete ceiling slabs, illuminating white, maddened expressions. This was hell,

Pinzon thought, certain in the knowledge that the basement would be his tomb.

Some time after the shaking and the din stopped, he dozed. He blinked awake when he felt a soft touch on his shoulder. A little girl wrapped in a threadbare blanket was staring at him. She could only have been eight or nine. Her face, bluish in the faint light, was filthy and skeletal. Her eyes, deeply set, were both imploring and calculating. She was whispering urgently: *'Cigarrillo. Cigarrillo, por favor, Señor.'* He knew what the simpering smile meant. Tobacco was currency. It would buy food – and there were services even a little girl could provide that some men would pay for. Mother of God, she was only a couple of years older than his grandson.

'Get away, you little bitch!' snarled his chauffeur, who had risen beside him. His leather-gloved fists were clenched.

Pinzon caught his arm. 'No, Andrés.' He turned back to the child. *'Pocita*, don't be afraid. Tell me your name?'

'Carmelita,' she said, with the same coquettish smile, and he knew it was not her real name.

'You're from Aragón?'

'I come from a *pueblo*,' she said, confused.

'Does it have a name?'

'Pueblo,' she said, as if he had asked an idiot question.

'Where are your parents, Carmelita?'

She bowed her head.

'Then who looks after you?'

'Uncle, Señor,' she said. 'He takes us to the air-raid shelters at night.'

He felt sickened. He reached into the pocket of his overcoat. 'Buy some bread for yourself, *pocita*. And tell this man who calls himself your uncle that if I ever . . .' He saw how hopeless it was. For all his power, there was nothing he could do. There were thousands of Carmelitas in Spain today. 'Just make sure you buy a loaf and eat it before you give the rest of the money to your uncle. Do you promise me?'

Her eyes widened when she saw the silver coins on his palm. Then she snatched them and fled, hopping nimbly over the bodies. Eventually he lost sight of her among the shadows.

'Tread gently, Andrés. Try not to disturb them,' he ordered. He picked his way through the sleepers, trying not to step on a hand or a foot. They were near the door when he bumped inadvertently into an old man in a beret, who was raising himself with a crutch. It clattered to the stone floor and the man toppled. Pinzon caught him. Trying not to recoil at his stench, he steadied him, then reached down and gave him his crutch. 'I'm sorry, Señor. So sorry.' As he said it he noted that the old man was observing with hatred his expensive Homburg and the fur collar of his overcoat.

'Jackals!' the old man hissed, and spat.

They stepped into the street. An apartment block was burning, the road was covered with rubble and the air reeked of cordite and smoke. Shadowy black shapes were moving among the bombed buildings – old women, scavenging.

Pinzon pushed past the throngs of petitioners in the foyer and pounded up the marble staircase, ignoring the guards' salutes. He was in a cold rage.

'We were expecting you to come to the office last night, Excelencia,' murmured his secretary, stumbling after him with a box of papers. 'These are yesterday's releases for the newspapers. We need your approval of the wording.'

'Later,' snapped Pinzon.

He turned at the head of the stairs. 'Have you ever spent the night in one of our public shelters?'

'No, Excelencia. I have permission to use the government one under this building.'

'They're a disgrace,' he said, through gritted teeth, 'death traps. It's a total abnegation of responsibility. I'm going to speak to Largo Caballero.'

He paced down the corridor towards his office, his heels

clicking on the art-deco-patterned mosaic floor of what had once been a grand hotel.

'But you had good meetings in Barcelona, Excelencia?' said Gorriz, hopefully.

Pinzon looked at him scornfully. 'With the Russian general who wants to advise me on how we are to conduct our propaganda? What do you think?'

The secretary sighed, but made a last effort to be cheerful. 'Perhaps you saw your son, Minister? You told me Raúl's militia is back in barracks now.'

'There was no time.' He turned the brass knob. The door swung open and he froze. Behind his desk hung a portrait of Stalin. 'What in the name of the Mother of God is that?'

The old man in the shelter had called him a jackal, and, it was true. He had compromised his convictions too often in cabinet meetings to be able to deny it. When General Franco and his junta of conservative generals had staged their rebellion against the Republic he had been as supine and complacent as his colleagues, and overnight they had lost a quarter of the country. When the war began to go badly, he had voted with the others to ally with the Soviets. He had put aside his reservations because it had been pragmatic and expedient to do so – or out of desperation, because he had been as bewildered as his fellow politicians by the speed of Franco's advance on Madrid. And the inevitable had happened. First Stalin had bled the Republic of its treasury reserves, then Communists had infiltrated the army and the secret police. Now, with the backing of stooges like Negrín in the finance ministry, they were controlling the economy. The libertarian values he had espoused were being ground to nothing by a totalitarian machine. And he had never once stood up against it.

Once he had been a man of principle. He had abandoned his life as a country landowner because he wanted justice and equality for the people. The conservatives and the Catholic Church hated him: a cardinal had persuaded Spain's dictator,

General Primo de Rivera, to sack him from the chair of medieval studies at Salamanca University when he had introduced 'heretical' reforms into the curricula. The trade unions had backed the students, who had protested at his dismissal. Campuses throughout the land went on strike. His subsequent reinstatement had made him a Socialist hero. That was when he had decided to stand for the Cortes.

And what great things he had achieved. He had helped to create a new age. A new Spain! As minister of culture in the country's first truly liberal government, a coalition of all left-wing parties, he had presided over a glittering period of national renewal. He knew all the great painters, writers and musicians of the time – Unamuno, Manuel de Falla, Pablo Picasso, Antonio Machado, Fernando de los Rios. He had been the first politician to sponsor the young poet García Lorca and, one glorious summer, had accompanied his travelling theatre into the remotest reaches of the country. Together they had brought literature to the peasants and workers . . .

And nothing of it remained. Nothing.

Lorca had disappeared, probably killed by Fascists in his native Granada. Unamuno had pinned his colours to Franco, and died in disgrace after protesting against the brutal conduct of the war. Others had fled abroad. Only Pinzon was left, another compromiser in a fractious government that had abandoned, one by one, all of its ideals.

He had compromised enough. It was time to speak his mind. The sight of Stalin in his office had been the last straw.

But when he reached the prime minister's suite he found that his friend, the old Socialist warhorse Largo Caballero, in whose government he had served these last two years, was away. He was directed instead to the office of the finance minister.

Juan Negrín, the sleek playboy financier, the wheeler dealer, the compromise candidate, who in every government reshuffle had wormed his way closer to the top, and who, Pinzon suspected, had lined his Swiss bank vault with Soviet gold, waved him to a chair. Stalin watched balefully from a great golden picture frame behind the desk.

'I have a letter for the prime minister,' said Pinzon. 'Where is he?'

'In Madrid, I imagine, calling on his old unionist friends. Things haven't been going well for him lately. It'll be some time before he's back. Is this a matter I can deal with?'

'No, it wouldn't be appropriate,' said Pinzon, putting the envelope back into his pocket. 'I'm resigning.'

'My dear fellow, why?'

'This is no longer the government I agreed to serve. I do not support this creeping *coup d'état* by the Communists.'

Negrín laughed. 'The Russians are merely our allies – we need them to break Mussolini and Hitler's blockade. They bring us tanks, artillery, planes. When they stop being useful, we'll dispense with them.'

'So you're not concerned that bands of Stalinists are entering towns and villages in Old Castile and Aragón to break up Anarchist communes?'

'Far from it. Centralising production is essential to the war effort. It's a necessary rationalisation.'

'Not when it's imposed with guns. How many of our own people have been shot resisting your rationalisations?'

Negrín said nothing. There was a long moment's silence as they glared at each other. 'Perhaps you know that I was in Barcelona yesterday,' said Pinzon, quietly.

'Yes – seeing Popov.'

'Are you aware of the tension in the city?'

'Barcelona is always tense. Those Catalans need cutting down to size.'

'Is that what you intend to do?'

Negrín's eyes narrowed. 'What do you mean?'

'What I saw yesterday was an armed camp. Your Communist-led troops have taken control of all the forts. Catalan and

Anarchist militia have been instructed to hand over their weapons inside the city boundaries. They've refused, of course. I saw them marching in the streets – with the Trotskyites.'

Negrín snorted. 'They're insignificant.'

'Not for Stalin. He doesn't like opposition. Even in Spain.'

'What Stalin likes or doesn't like is irrelevant – I've told you so a hundred times. Our Soviet allies are only here in an advisory capacity. We are the government and we control policy.'

'Barcelona is a tinderbox, Negrín. Either you or somebody else has authorised the army's provocations.'

'That's nonsense.'

'I will not be party to the undermining of our democracy.'

Negrín stubbed out his cigar. 'This is a cabinet at war. You have a duty to protect the Republic.'

'I would agree if our Republic still existed, but you and your like have made us puppets to a foreign power.'

Pinzon went home for two days. He listened to classical music on his phonograph. At the weekend he requisitioned a car and drove to a government lodge on the Albufera lake. He took lengthy walks along its banks and once beside the sea, letting the soft waves of the Mediterranean lap his bare feet.

Three days later he heard a banging on the cottage door. It was his stenographer, Señora Aristzabal, who burst into tears when she saw him. 'Oh, Señor Pinzon! Señor, you cannot imagine what terrible things have happened.'

'So, tell me. What has Negrín done now?'

'I'm not talking about Valencia. It's Barcelona. There's been fighting – for three days and nights. Only yesterday did we get the full report, which was why I drove down immediately this morning.'

'Barcelona?' A chill was already running down his spine. 'So they did it? They tried to disarm the Catalan and Anarchist militias?'

'They arrested prominent Anarchists in the night. The secret police took them away in trucks, and nothing's been heard of them since.'

'And the militias?' he asked, unable to keep the urgency out of his voice.

'There was an insurrection, Señor. Street battles. They're calling it a civil war within a civil war.' She dabbed her eyes.

'And who controls the city now?' He was shouting in his desperation.

She stared at him. 'The Communists, Señor. I think they were prepared. They wanted them to come out in the streets – the Anarchists, the independent Catalans, the Trotskyites – so they could destroy them. They had tanks, Señor. They were waiting outside the city. And the militias only had rifles and makeshift barricades . . .'

He shook her by the shoulders. 'Raúl? Where is Raúl?'

'Oh, Señor.' She was weeping again.

Pinzon sank into his chair.

'He must have fought very bravely,' she said. 'They found him on one of the last barricades to be overrun. They – they reported it in the newspapers. They said he had been one of the ring-leaders of the revolt. He was so young . . . so young . . .'

'He would have been twenty-six on his next birthday.' Pinzon clasped the sides of his head and began slowly to rock backwards and forwards from his waist.

Pinzon made all haste to Madrid, but he arrived too late. His daughter-in-law, Julia, had been arrested in her apartment three days after the death of her husband. Her six-year-old son, Tomás, had been taken away by the secret police.

For the next month, as Communist control over the Spanish government tightened, Pinzon used all the ministerial influence he could bring to bear to find them. He failed with Julia. She was lost among the disappeared. He was more fortunate with Tomás. The trail led to an orphanage on the dusty plains near Albacete. And there he found him.

Pinzon had no desire to return to Valencia. In the wake of the uprising, Largo Caballero had been forced to resign and Negrín was prime minister now. For form's sake, he wrote to him, confirming his resignation. Then he made his way with Tomás to his old home in Agua Verde, in the foothills of the Seguras mountains in north-eastern Andalucía, where he sought out a long-time retainer of the family, Lupita. Together they looked after his grandson.

He had thought he might return to academic life. There was still much research to be done on the Reconquista, the wars that had brought the tolerant Moorish state of Andaluz back to Christendom. He still had his Arabic dictionaries and texts, some of which he had only partially translated when he wrote his first history – but now the books remained on his shelves. He spent his days cultivating the orchards that surrounded his house. As far as he was concerned, he had ended his life's journey and was merely tending his garden. Only his grandson mattered to him.

Andalucía, 1938

I

The Cathedral

Treading carefully so as not to wake his household, Pinzon left his hacienda before light and slowly made his way down the cypress drive, through the sleeping village and the olive groves to a rock that rose like an island lapped by waves of ground mist. He scrambled to the top, stretched his long limbs and settled his back comfortably against the smooth stone. He was glad he had brought his overcoat. A slight chill still persisted in these high regions even in the early days of summer. He was waiting, as he did every morning, for the sun to rise.

The Sierra revealed itself first, a white band of snow that ringed the horizon, a thin divider between the deep grey of the valley and the night's velvet cloak, studded by the single diamond of the Morning Star.

He was never able to pinpoint the exact instant when the silence was broken by birdsong. The chatter had swelled into full chorus before he was aware of it. By then, anyway, the miracle had overwhelmed him, the magic moment when the first pink glinted on the snow peaks and the world discovered colour again. Gradually, the bare slopes of the mountains took on identifiable shades. There were mauve slopes and purple gullies, turning to soft washes of amber and ochre when the sun's rim crested the escarpments.

In the darkness below, the forests remained for a while in

gloom, as also did the valley, hidden under its thick blanket of ground fog. Here and there, wisps and filaments of condensation rose, like smoke from campfires.

Clouds were forming: pink and insubstantial, not yet the cumulus castles that would dominate the day. The sun, a gold bezant on an azure shield, still had only empty sky to climb as it left the Sierra. Behind him he could hear the first signs of life in the village – the clattering of hoofs as Emilio led his donkeys out of their pen, the rattle of Jacinta's bedpan being emptied from her upstairs window, Francisco the shepherd whistling for his dog . . .

He waited for the second miracle of the day. The cloud ocean in the valley was dissipating. Now there were hundreds of campfire plumes, surrounding, like a besieging army, the shadow that was imperceptibly forming into the shape of a town. Then he saw it, the spire rising from the cloud, followed by the great vaulted roof and the leaping buttresses of the St Jaime Cathedral. For a few precious moments, the white marble shone in the sunlight, brighter than the star. It hung above the mist, as if it alone existed in the firmament, an illuminated manuscript of the heavenly city.

The vision faded. Other buildings took form, and the great church settled back into a drowsy provincial setting. Its transubstantiation had ended as quickly as it had begun. Ciudadela del Santo had reverted to being an unremarkable country town.

Pinzon felt the first heat of the sun on his neck. The watercolour took on the solidity of an oil painting. The valley below became a chequerboard of cornfields and fruit groves. The fresh perfume of dawn gave way to the sweet corruption of compost, dried dung and pungent black soil, and he reconciled himself to another harsh, hot Andalucían day.

He was thinking, as he often did, about Raúl. He kept returning to the day he had flown to Barcelona, just before the coup. If he had gone to his son's barracks, might he have warned him? Persuaded him of the danger? Cajoled him to leave? Might he still be alive today? Of course, Raúl would never have done anything dishonourable. He knew that, but that did not stop him wishing and imagining. He missed him. How he missed him.

The truth was that he had had time to see Raúl but, to his everlasting regret, he had shied away. He had felt dirty and compromised after his meeting with the Russian general. If Raúl had asked him about the conduct of the war, he would have been ashamed. And he had been preoccupied with his politics. His politics.

He remembered the day he had buried his wife, his dear, short-sighted, muddle-headed Manuela, after she had accidentally walked in front of a tram. He and his ten-year-old son had accompanied her body back to Andalucía so that she could be interred in the hills she had loved. Looking down at Raúl's brave, pinched face by the graveside, his little coat illuminated in the bright sunshine, he had made a silent vow to Manuela that he would bring up her boy to be as honest, as truthful and as principled as she would ever have desired. She had shared her husband's dream of a new Spain. Pinzon promised her that their son would exemplify its virtues.

It had not been easy because he was a busy man of affairs. In the early days, he had worked at home when he could so that he could oversee the boy's education. His office learned to adapt itself to his routine. Later, Pinzon would time his leaves to coincide with his son's school holidays, and together they travelled the length and breadth of Spain to visit its antiquities, or explored the mountains in their native Andalucía. Over the years the relationship between father and son developed into friendship.

At university Raúl had been involved in radical student politics. He had married a fellow activist, and become estranged from his father. Pinzon did not see him for three years. The reconciliation came during the long, hot summer before the war. They spent a month together on the family estate, and it was as if time had never passed. Pinzon learned to love his daughter-in-law, Julia, and his grandson, Tomás, and he discovered, to his joy, that every hope he had ever had for his son had been fulfilled. Every morning, while Julia played with Tomás on the lawn, Pinzon and Raúl would sit on the veranda of the hacienda, the morning sun reddening the young man's curly hair and glinting in his cornflower blue eyes as they argued the merits of Socialism against Anarchism.

'Come on, boy, libertarianism is all very well, but if the working man is to defeat the forces of reaction, he must create strong central institutions, with trade unions and constitutions based on the will of the majority to make his struggle effective.'

'And as soon as you do that, Papá, you create new tyrannies, new élites, and then where is the freedom for the working man or anybody else?'

They were politically apart, but Pinzon had never felt closer to him because he saw in Raúl his mother's generosity of spirit and unquenchable idealism, and appreciated for the first time the independent, fully formed adult he had become. While all his life he himself had been an armchair revolutionary, his son had evolved mysteriously into the real thing. He loved him the more for it.

He sighed. It was time for him to return to the hacienda, where little Tomás would be awake, playing with his toys, and Lupita would be cooking breakfast. But he remained where he was. Today not even the sunrise had been enough to lift his spirits. It had taken only a glance at the packet of newspapers the postman had brought yesterday evening for his pain to return in full force. As a former minister of information, he was experienced enough to decipher the truth behind the propaganda. And last night he had read the same tired slogans and recognised the formulae he had once authorised himself to disguise the painful fact of defeat.

'Brave troops valiantly maintain offensive positions,' declared the headlines. That meant there had been a massive enemy counter-attack. The assault on the Ebro – General Pozas's brilliant gamble – which was supposed to have surprised the enemy and forced Franco out of Catalonia, had failed. The victory that should have encouraged the liberal powers of Europe to come in on the beleaguered Republic's side against Fascism had not materialised. The chance of winning the war, or even a negotiated settlement, was now negligible. What would follow was the inevitable retreat of Republican forces to their starting positions and beyond, and the bodies of men they could no longer afford to lose would be left littered over the sun-baked Spanish soil they had tried to defend. It was Brunete, Jarama, Belchite, Teruel all over again, with the difference that, after this defeat, there would be no resources left to continue the fight. The Communists had squandered the Republic's last reserves of treasure, manpower and matériel.

He shuddered, as he envisaged the corpses lying on the banks of the Ebro. Each one had the same face: Raúl's. His remorse had not abated over time. On good days he was sometimes able to put it aside – but never for long, and then he experienced all over again the familiar guilt. How could he not? It had been his expedient actions and his neglect of his principles that had contributed directly to Raúl's death.

He and his fellow ministers had as good as pressed a pistol to his son's head and pulled the trigger. He was no Christian – he despised all religions – but he had not entirely lost his belief in the possibility of a God and, deep inside himself, he realised he had committed a sin – or condoned it, which to him was worse.

That fact paralysed him. It negated every positive achievement of his life. He had damned himself. His sense of honour, his charm, ability, intelligence, imposing manner and good looks weighed nothing when scaled against that involuntary murder.

He had tried to retreat from the world. But there was no escape from the Furies that hounded him in his mind.

Suddenly he became aware that he was being observed. A squat man wearing a beret was standing below the rock, looking up at him. He was not a farmer, although he was dressed like one. Bandoliers crisscrossed the sheepskin jacket that came down to his knees. Three hand grenades hung from his wide leather belt beside a huge hunting knife in a rawhide sheath and, on his other side, a revolver holster. Over his shoulder he had looped a rifle, and his stubby fingers were fiddling with a tin whistle that dangled from his unshaven neck. He seemed in two minds whether to blow it or not.

Pinzon stared at him. The man stared back. The tanned face was not unfriendly. The black eyes twinkled in the sunshine, apparently with humour, and the thick lips under the bushy black moustache curved into a wide, gap-toothed smile.

'Can I help you, Comrade?' he asked, trying to hide his unease.

'If your name's Enrique de los Reyos Pinzon, you can, Comrade,' said the man gruffly, but his tone was not unpleasant. 'Famous poet and scholar? Former politician? We were told to look for an old man sitting on a rock.' He waved a hand languidly at the empty landscape. 'You don't look that old but I can see no other.'

'And what if I am he?'

'Thank you. I take that as confirmation.' He blew three sharp calls on his whistle. 'My men are searching for you in other parts of the olive grove. I'm now calling off the chase.'

'The chase?'

'It's a sort of hunt, Señor, and you are, I'm sorry to say, our quarry. I must inform you that you are under arrest.'

'By whose authority? I believe I still retain the status of an ex-minister of the Republic, with the privileges due to the office I performed.'

'That's not the way I see it,' said the man. 'You resigned your post. When we poor soldiers have had enough and slink back home they call it "desertion" and shoot us for it. Anyway, fifth-columnists and traitors have no rights, whoever they may once have been.'

'That is preposterous.'

The man shrugged. 'They're convenient labels. Dig into anybody's past and you can always find some crime against the state, especially if your suspect is a so-called liberal politician, which, in my book, is a crime in itself. Your son was an Anarchist and took part in a rebellion. That'll do for a start. Fact is, I need you right now. Someone of your eminence might be valuable to us in our present circumstances.'

'My son was a patriot. He died bravely in Barcelona defending the Republic against those who were loyal only to Stalin. His wife was arrested afterwards and has since disappeared. I had to collect my grandson from an orphanage run by the secret police. Do you wonder I resigned from the government? But I am not a traitor or a fifth-columnist. I have retired. That is all. And you have no right to intimidate me. In fact, I'll see to it that you regret it.'

'Sounds to me as if you're a traitor and from a family of traitors. Couldn't have put it better myself.'

As he was speaking Pinzon was aware of figures emerging from the olive grove, dressed and armed like the man in front of him. They were grim-faced and stared at him coldly. 'Who are you?' he whispered. 'Is this a kidnap for ransom? Are you bandits?'

'No, Señor, we are regular soldiers of the Fifth Corps commanded by General Modesto but now we are on special duties. You may know there is a big battle going on in the north. We have been sent to create a diversion in the south. In Granada we were a little more successful than we anticipated and now our small company is being chased over the mountains by at least two divisions of angry Fascists. That is why I respectfully request that you climb down off your rock so that we can be on our way.'

'What have I to do with saboteurs? Partisans?'

'Nothing. It's just your misfortune to be in the wrong place on the wrong occasion. And we need a hostage, because the enemy will soon be on us and it's too late to get to the passes. Please waste no more time, Señor. We must be off.'

'And if I refuse?' Even to himself it sounded like pathetic bravado, but he was damned if he would be taken into custody without protest.

The man sighed. 'You will not refuse, because we have your grandson.'

He blew his whistle again. Another man came out of the olive grove. Unlike the others he was dressed in a brown military greatcoat and there was a red star on his forage cap. Sunlight flashed on a pair of round spectacles that dominated his thin, severe face. Pinzon's heart jumped with horror when he saw that the boy he was propelling roughly in front of him was Tomás.

'Grandfather!' It was a weak, plaintive cry.

'I beg you to consider wisely, Señor,' said the man. 'That is Levi, our political commissar. He is not reasonable like you or me. Obviously not, because he is a commissar. He hates anybody who deviates from the Party line. Anarchists, Trotskyites, liberals especially. His hatred extends to their families. Come with us quietly and your boy will not be hurt.'

Pinzon looked around him for help, but there were no villagers in sight.

The man was grinning at him confidently. He saw no way out. 'You don't need to bring my grandson into this. Let me take him back to his nurse and I will consider what you propose.'

'It doesn't work like that. We're not so trusting. Anyway, he doesn't have a nurse any more. The woman was a little too protective of your boy when we went to your house to get him. And, as I told you, Commissar Levi is inclined to hastiness . . . It was regrettable, but . . .'

Pinzon's temples throbbed and a chill ran down his spine. He thought of Lupita's fierce possessiveness of Tomás, remembered her short temper, and knew she would never have allowed anybody to take his grandson without a struggle. 'You've murdered her,' he said savagely. 'You *are* bandits.'

'No, Señor, we're not. For what happened to the woman, you have my apologies. It was an accident. As I said, a regrettable one – but these things happen when you're fighting a war. If people don't co-operate, they're liable to get hurt. If you're sensible, it won't happen to you – or the boy. Now, are you coming down from that rock or do I send somebody up to get you?'

Pinzon rose to his full height. 'I will personally see to it that you are court-martialled and hanged.'

'You do that,' said the man. 'But meanwhile we'll just try to get along, shall we? Oh, and by the way, in case you hadn't gathered, we're Communists. So you might want to consider more carefully next time you feel like badmouthing Comrade Stalin.'

With as much dignity as he could muster, Pinzon descended from the rock. In the valley below, an arbitrary spot of sunshine broke through the clouds and illuminated the spire of the great cathedral.

It took them the rest of the morning to make their way down the gullies, following the stream beds to the foot of the mountain. The partisans moved silently and professionally, sending forward scouts and leaving lookouts behind. The man with the whistle gave orders that were followed without question. They were disciplined Communists, nothing like the egalitarian militia his son had joined and whose trenches Pinzon had visited in Aragón on the only occasion that he had been to the front during the early days of the war. They were hard-bitten soldiers whose eyes were constantly watchful. They rarely spoke, which unnerved him until he realised, in a sudden burst of intuition, that they, too, were afraid. What their leader had told him was nothing more than the truth. The men who had hunted him were quarries themselves. The small company knew they were surrounded and that the enemy was closing in. They often looked up at the sky, cocking their ears for the sound of aircraft.

Their nervousness was both alarming and encouraging, he thought. It made them more dangerous but it might also cause a moment of inattention. If they were strafed from the air they would be distracted and an opportunity might arise for Tomás and himself to attempt an escape.

For the moment, though, he had enough on his hands with looking after his grandson. Tomás was shocked and silent, stunned by the murder of his nurse and the events that had followed. A seven-year-old boy who had only ever lived in cities could never negotiate on his own the high boulders and many streams they had to cross. In the easier stretches, Pinzon could perch him on his back, but when the going was precipitous, he carried him in his arms, murmuring encouragement. The man in command would sometimes come back from his position at the front to see how he was doing, watching with a smile his careful efforts to keep his balance.

'Need help?' he'd ask.

Pinzon would glare at him and press on.

He was a strong man with a constitution that belied his sixty years. As an Andalucían born and bred, he was used to mountains, but he had never done a route march at this pace, and after a while he began to tire. His shoe slipped on a wet stone, and he tumbled. Neither he nor Tomás was hurt, but the boy was scared and began to bawl. Pinzon hugged him and apologised, telling him not to worry, they would get to their destination soon, and then these bad soldiers would go away. When he looked up the man with the whistle was contemplating him solicitously.

'You've done well, Grandpa,' the man said. 'Proved you're a tough fellow. We all admire your *cojones*. You're not booted properly, though, for terrain like this. The boy on your back is slowing you, and that means you're slowing us.'

'I can cope well enough,' muttered Pinzon.

'A younger man can cope better.' He gestured over his shoulder. A loping, straw-haired boy was grinning amiably behind him. 'This is Privato Muro. I'm attaching him to you.' He smiled at Tomás, who was clutching Pinzon's legs in fear. 'You'll like Felipe, *pocito*. Not so long ago he was a schoolboy like you. Now he's a soldier. You're a brave lad, just like your *papá* from what I've heard. Maybe one day you'll join the army too. Felipe can tell you all about it. Would you like that? Meanwhile, will you do me a big favour and help your grandfather by letting him have a little rest?'

'You'll leave the boy alone,' growled Pinzon.

'Let him answer, Señor. What about it, Tomás? Will you help?'

Tomás's hand tightened in his grandfather's grasp but he nodded solemnly.

'Good lad. Knew I could rely on you. Felipe, meet my young friend.'

Pinzon, seeing no help for it, disguised his fury and lifted Tomás up, then fussed until his grandson's legs were wrapped safely round Felipe's neck. The commander snatched off Felipe's forage cap and placed it on the boy's head. 'There, you even look like a soldier.'

It pained him, but Pinzon soon saw that it was the best thing to be done in the circumstances. Without his grandson on his back, he could cover the ground at the same speed as the others. Tomás was apprehensive for a while, but the young soldier charmed him with his chatter and what rapidly emerged as a quirky imagination. As they moved down the hill, Felipe whispered stories to him. In that cave there lived a witch. The insects buzzing in that field of asphodels were actually fairies. Could Tomás see their long wings? The march became a game, and the boy began to enjoy the company of his new friend.

'Still coping, Señor?' the man in command asked him, when they were panting up a steep slope. The concern in his expression seemed genuine.

'As you can see,' said Pinzon, his attention focused on his grandson ahead of them, although by now he knew there was no need to worry – Felipe was scrambling up the hill as easily and surely as a mountain goat.

'Well done. Keep it up. We'll be on the plain soon and then the going will be easier. With luck, we'll reach the outskirts of Ciudadela del Santo by dawn tomorrow.'

'Why are we going there?'

'The cathedral precinct is a citadel. It will give us a position of strength from which we can negotiate a safe-conduct back to our lines.' He spoke as if he believed such a thing was possible.

'The Fascists won't negotiate with you. Why should they?' Pinzon spoke scornfully.

The man smiled. 'Because we can offer them you, Señor, as one of our hostages. A former minister of the Republican government. An enemy of their church. They'll see propaganda value in your capture.'

'Am I really so valuable?'

'You tell me.' The commander offered him his hand. The man had just scrambled over the steep lip of the escarpment. Pinzon hesitated, then allowed himself to be pulled up. He saw a meadow rolling down the other side to the plain. The commander was grinning. 'See? That wasn't so hard. Maybe we can co-operate after all.'

'Even though you intend to sell me to the Fascists?'

'It's not personal, Señor. You've impressed me. You're not the effete coward I expected. But you're expendable. You're of no use to the Republic. You've opted out of our struggle, while my men still have a role to play. Lesser necessity always has to give way to a greater one. So you're fair game.'

'That's your Stalinist dialectic, I take it?'

The man's face hardened. 'It's a fact of life.'

'You mentioned other hostages?' said Pinzon, seeing no point in continuing this line of questioning. Despite the apparent kindness he had shown Tomás, the man was clearly as doctrinaire as his fearsome commissar.

'There's a cathedral there. We'll fill it with civilians. Priests. Nuns. Landowners. Whoever they have in the town gaol. Not that the Fascists will worry over much about them, but you know the lengths those superstitious sons of whores will go to in protecting their religious monuments. Isn't this one also important to them? I seem to remember reading, maybe in your book – you are the same Pinzon who was once a medieval scholar, aren't you? – that it was one of the first cathedrals the Christians built in territory they took back from the Moors in the eleventh century.'

'The early twelfth century,' said Pinzon, surprised at the man's unexpected knowledge. 'It was built to commemorate the martyr St Jaime when Duke Sancho the Proud reconquered the Moorish state of Mishkhat in 1104.'

'Is that so? Well, if they refuse to negotiate, I'll blow it up. Make no mistake, Señor. If they choose to fight us, it will be costly for them. In every way.'

'As it will be for the innocent prisoners inside the cathedral, Comrade. Or is their murder for the greater good too?' Pinzon had raised his voice, repelled by the man's show of callousness despite his education.

'If it happens, it'll be the Fascists' atrocity, not ours.' The man's rumbling tones had turned into a growl, and Pinzon saw that he had touched a nerve. 'Don't tell me, Professor, that you have any objection to sacrifice. You were a minister in the war cabinet. You put your signature on orders that squandered the lives of ordinary soldiers in bloodbaths that gained us nothing. Think of it as your turn to put yourself in the firing line. For the war effort,' he added sarcastically. '¡Al carajo!' he swore, as he kicked a clump of wild daffodils. 'I told you. What I do, I do for necessity, and to bring my men home.'

So the man had some humanity, thought Pinzon. He decided to try a more conciliatory tack. 'I think I hear pain in your voice, my friend. You are perhaps not the murderer I took you for, although I understand why you are clutching at straws. Nor do I believe you're as ruthless as you pretend to be. I think you must be an intellectual, an officer, at heart a humane man used to civilised behaviour. I am sure what you are being forced to do is repugnant to you. Listen, perhaps the two of us can co-operate, as you mentioned earlier. I will willingly be your hostage. My life may, as you say, be worthless. Perhaps there is a case against me. As a public figure I must take responsibility for what I have done – but spare my grandson and the others you mention. Then you will gain your objectives without the blood of innocents on your conscience.'

His captor glared at him with sudden hatred. 'You do not know me, Señor. Don't presume that I am anything like you. I've read books – every damned philosopher you can name, until I found what I wanted in Marx – but I was never an intellectual, only a village schoolmaster. No better than the peasants I tried to teach. Neither am I an officer. Only a *sargento*. Plain Sargento Ogarrio of the Twenty-fourth Company of the Eleventh Division of the Fifth Corps. Party member two five seven five J. We do not have an officer any more, Señor. Our *teniente* died ten days ago when we were laying charges to a railway bridge outside Granada.'

'I'm sorry,' said Pinzon.

'Why? You never knew him, although you might have found him more agreeable than me if you had. He was an intellectual, a civilised man, a good Communist even. I considered him my friend. But he was stupid. He spared the life of one of the Fascist guards on the bridge because he was only a boy. He was high-minded, you see. Humane, too. Well, the boy pulled the pin of a hand grenade that he had concealed in his pocket, dropped it between them and attempted to flee. To protect the rest of us, our *teniente* covered the grenade with his own body. The boy didn't get far, of course. My lads caught him, stuffed another hand grenade into his trousers and threw him off the bridge. And I put a bullet into my officer's head because by then his intestines were coiled around the timbers and we couldn't move him off the railway track. That, Señor, was all the humanity we could spare for our beloved commander. I waited beside his body until the troop train came. You could call that a sign of respect too. It would have pleased him that he was still with us when we were inflicting damage on the enemy. Sadly it was also the Sunday train, when peasants from surrounding areas took their livestock to market. So when I pressed the plunger I sent women, children and cattle to the bottom of the gorge with the soldiers. We threw our own dead after them, including our *teniente*. What else were we to do with the bodies? Don't lecture me on civilised behaviour or bourgeois values. They no longer have relevance.'

Pinzon heard a man spit and saw a blob of bloody phlegm on his shoe. The commissar had come up behind them. He had been listening to their conversation and was examining him contemptuously.

'Spread out,' called Ogarrio, to his men, 'and keep your eyes and ears open for aeroplanes. From now on we'll be on open ground and there are still three more hours to dusk. When we get to the valley floor we stay as much as possible under the cover of the orange groves. We take to the high road when it gets dark.'

They set off in a straggling line down the hill. The only sound was the wind, and occasionally a burst of childish laughter, when Felipe pointed out a new curiosity to the seven-year-old on his shoulders.

There had been no chance to escape. When the sun set, Pinzon was given into the charge of Commissar Levi, who tied his hands tightly behind his back and prodded him along the road.

When, near midnight, they stopped at an abandoned farm for a meal and two hours' sleep, the commissar remained awake, his pistol on the table while, in his crabbed writing, he scratched his daily report in a little notebook.

Pinzon was too agitated to sleep. He sat on a broken chair by the fire, with Tomás, wrapped in Felipe's rough blanket, dreaming fretfully on his knees. From the darkness he heard the snores of the partisans, interrupted sometimes by the barked exclamation or moan of a nightmare. Once he thought he recognised Ogarrio's voice and turned his head. The *sargento*, who had lain down near him, had kicked off his blanket and was sitting upright, terror on his face, the firelight picking out the drops of sweat on his forehead. His features relaxed into an expression of puzzlement. He looked at his watch. A few seconds later he was asleep again.

Pinzon went back to self-recrimination. Ogarrio's words to him that day had been far closer to the truth than the *sargento* had perhaps intended. He had never stood up for the high-minded principles he boasted. He *had* put his signature to pieces of paper that had cost men's lives. Ordinary soldiers like Ogarrio had a right to believe he had betrayed them.

Expediency. *Conveniencia* – the word seemed to echo in the rumbling snores.

Perhaps there was justice in what had happened to him today. Ogarrio had appeared, like an executioner sent by Fate, to exact the penalty for crimes of which Pinzon had long ago pronounced himself guilty. He deserved the death sentence the *sargento* had handed down – both men knew that if he was passed to the Fascists they would shoot him. It would be an ignominious end to what had ultimately been an ignominious life.

If his death could save these partisans, who, for all that they were Stalinists, were soldiers like his son, he would be making some sort of amends for his ineffectual past. Perhaps he would even expiate his guilt in Raúl's death. But he knew in his heart that the Fascists would not negotiate. Franco was a modern-day crusader fighting a holy war. If the Republicans had rallied themselves with the cry *¡No pasaran!*, the Fascists' creed was 'unconditional surrender, with retribution to follow'. The atrocities that had accompanied every Fascist victory were evidence of their fanaticism. Fanatics did not negotiate. The truth was that Ogarrio would decide he had no option but to go ahead with his desperate plan to blow up the cathedral and his prisoners, for Ogarrio was a Stalinist, and therefore an ideologue, unwilling to compromise.

Expiation was not the answer. He had somehow to thwart the *sargento*'s plan, for it was not only his own life at stake.

He looked down at the tousled head of his sleeping grandson. How could he let Tomás – before he had tasted what life had to offer – become a victim of the pathological hatred that had overcome their country? He could not – would not – allow it to happen.

Suddenly an image of Raúl flashed in front of him. He was as he had last seen him, with Julia at the railway station on his second but last leave from the front. He remembered the certainty in his son's expression as Raúl had leaned out of the carriage window to say goodbye. He was going back to battle, perhaps to die, and his handsome features were set in proud confidence that he was doing right. For him any sacrifice was by the way. Somehow Pinzon had to discover the same fortitude.

He dozed a moment, and found himself back at the station. Raúl was still looking at him out of the dusty window. He seemed to be aware of what his father was thinking. His lips curved into one of his ironic smiles and his eyes shone, as they always had whenever he had bested him in one of their long political debates. And, with intense joy, Pinzon realised that Raúl had forgiven him, and was giving him a second chance.

But what was he to do? At the moment he and Tomás were trapped. 'Tell me what to do?' he pleaded, as the train puffed steam and began to move.

Raúl's face lit with a radiant, mischievous smile. Again Pinzon recognised the expression. It was when he knew the answer to a question and the great professor didn't. He was challenging his father, as always, to work it out for himself . . .

He snapped awake. The sleeping men were still all around him. Pinzon felt something tighten at the base of his stomach, and a throbbing in his temple. He recognised the sensation from his distant days on the campaign trail, usually after an opponent had pushed him too far. It was the first stirring of resolve. The next day the gloves had been off and invariably he had destroyed his challenger on the hustings. He looked down at Ogarrio and studied his enemy coldly. There could be no quarter between this man and himself. Ogarrio had murdered Lupita. He had threatened his grandson. Pinzon would have to be clever, because Ogarrio held all the cards, but he would watch and wait, he would dissemble as necessary and, when the moment came, he would have his revenge.

At the table, Commissar Levi shut his book. The pale, magnified eyes behind the round spectacles glanced coldly in his direction. He rapped the table sharply. The partisans shook themselves awake, and began to tidy their bedrolls.

In the Middle Ages Ciudadela del Santo had been an important city and, in Moorish times, a powerful emirate. The Christians who had taken it in the early days of the Reconquista had constructed a castle on an outcrop of the great rock that rose in its centre. In the sixteenth century Philip II had converted the cathedral that stood beside the castle into a Baroque treasure of the Spanish Church, a symbol in Catholic mythology of the crusade that had recovered Spain for Christendom, and the pilgrim shrine of the martyr, St Jaime. The top of the hill, dominated by the great domes, buttresses and spires of the cathedral, had become a cluster of monasteries, convents and a seminary, protected by stout, crenellated walls and a small fortress on the site of the old castle. A prosperous city had grown around it.

As always, Pinzon was saddened when he thought of its former grandeur. As the partisan band checked their weapons in the faint glimmer of pre-dawn, and Sargento Ogarrio peered up through a pair of binoculars at the shadowy citadel, he was thinking of how the bustling market town he had known as a boy had, with the coming of the railways and the near extinction of the mule-trade traffic, become an isolated irrelevance. The banks and mansions had fallen into disrepair, and the only people living there were the farmers who tilled the fields beyond the crumbled city walls. Ogarrio's thirty men should have no problem in taking it. The Anarchist council that had established itself at the beginning of the revolution had no militia to defend it. Opposition, if there was any, would come from a few aged policemen and the warders who guarded the corn exchange, now a makeshift prison, where the nuns and monks who had lived in the citadel had been sequestered since the beginning of the war. He hoped there would be no unnecessary bloodshed.

Ogarrio called his men into a circle and gave his orders. In groups of six they left the olive grove, disappearing into the darkness. Checking his revolver, the *sargento* walked to where Pinzon and his grandson were sitting. 'This won't take long,' he said. 'I want you to remain here with the commissar and Privato Muro. Your *amigo*,' he added, ruffling Tomás's hair. 'He'll look after you and play with you, won't you, Felipe? If you hear shots, don't be afraid, eh, *pocito*? It'll just be us grown-ups playing soldiers.' He drew Pinzon aside, and lowered his voice. 'I can't spare more men to guard you. Please don't have any foolish ideas that you can run away. Levi will shoot you both before you move a muscle. He's itching to do it.' He nodded and, with a hesitant smile, clapped him on the shoulder. 'Just don't give him a chance. *¿Entiendes?*' With a final backward glance, he ran after his men.

For a long time there was silence. Again, Pinzon failed to catch the first sound of birdsong that was now chattering around him. The olive grove filled with pink light, striped by shadows. Felipe and Tomás were playing a giggling game of hide and seek among the trees. The commissar, his pistol unwaveringly directed at Pinzon, watched them with a scowl.

31

The firing, when it came, was desultory, and over in five minutes, but the single, drawn-out scream was enough to frighten Tomás, who left Felipe and his attempts to calm him with a piece of dried sausage, and ran, weeping, into his grandfather's arms. Pinzon stroked the child's hair and murmured, 'It'll be all right. It'll be all right.'

'I want my *mamá* and my *papá*,' sobbed his grandson.

'I know,' he whispered. 'So do I.'

The commissar, a worried look on his face, had stood up and was staring at the town. They heard three long blasts of a whistle, repeated three times. Levi turned. For once there was a twist of a smile on his thin features. 'The place is ours,' he said. 'Get on your feet. You're about to see what happens when we liberate an Anarchist town.'

The cobbled streets were deserted. The doors of the houses were open. Some had been battered in or torn off their hinges.

They passed along a wider avenue lined with shops and cafés. At the top, by the barracks of the Guardia Civil, under the sign that read 'Buleva de España', they saw a body, a policeman's, crumpled into a contorted position on the pavement. His bicorn hat was resting in a pool of blood. Pinzon, too late, put his hands over Tomás's eyes.

Ahead, between two buildings that had once been banks, was the entrance to the Plaza de la Reconquista. This was where the townspeople had been herded. Men, women and children, some still in their nightclothes, were huddled on the ground. Ogarrio's men were positioned in a circle around them, covering them with their rifles.

In the centre of the square, the *sargento* was talking to a fat man wearing maroon pyjamas and nodding obsequiously to whatever Ogarrio was telling him. That did not surprise Pinzon. He had known Ramón Zuluaga before the war when he was the town's *alcalde*. It had not taken the conservative mayor long to trim his colours to new circumstances and he had quickly reinvented himself as the chairman of the Revolutionary Council, professing that he had been a secret Anarchist all his life. Now he was presumably trying to convince Ogarrio of his Communist credentials.

'Stop,' Commissar Levi called. He had a street map in his hand. 'We go this way.'

Felipe looked at him in surprise. 'But the *sargento* told us—'

'I am the commissar and represent the Party. You obey my commands.' He led them off the avenue into the Calle Jaime Santo.

Two of Ogarrio's men were lounging idly outside the corn exchange, smoking and enjoying the sunshine. They looked up curiously.

'This is the prison, right?' snapped Levi. 'Becerra, answer me when I speak to you. I want you to report the situation here.'

The two men looked at each other. 'What's there to report?' said Becerra. 'The wardens ran away before we got here. The place is full of monks and nuns praying in their cells.'

'Why are you not guarding them? They are reactionary elements. Fifth-columnists and traitors.'

'They looked harmless enough to me. They're all locked up. Here.' He threw a bunch of keys at the commissar. 'Go in and inspect them yourself if you're so worried about them.' His lean features curved into a wolfish grin. 'No hanky-panky, mind, Commissar. Some of those nuns are young, and one or two rather pretty.'

'Your insolence has been noted, Becerra. I advise you to be careful. Stay here with Muro and help him guard our two prisoners. Martínez.' He turned to Becerra's companion. 'You come with me.'

He entered the prison. Martínez, a younger man, about Felipe's age, shrugged and, throwing down his cigarette butt, followed him inside. Becerra made an obscene gesture with his finger at the departing commissar, then grinned at them. 'How's babysitting, Felipe? Enjoying it, are you?'

'Bugger off!'

Pinzon ignored the rest of their banter. He knew what the commissar would find inside. Shortly after the beginning of the war, when he had just been made minister for information and had come on an inspection tour of the south, Zuluaga had taken him round the prison. The clergy, as in all parts of Republican Spain, had been arrested as antisocial class elements, but Zuluaga had been at pains to explain that in Ciudadela del Santo the policy was not to punish but to reform. Pinzon had witnessed embarrassingly naïve lectures by young female schoolteachers who had been preaching the merits of communes. It had been worthy but essentially useless. Nevertheless he had been impressed that this one small town had somehow escaped the chain of vendetta, and was treating its prisoners humanely. He had wished that such tolerance could have been extended all over Spain.

But now he was worried about Tomás who, ever since he had seen the body of the policeman, had been white-faced and silent, gripping his hand tightly. To try to distract him, he pointed at an old house further down the street. 'See that building with the red roof, Tomás? When I was your age, that was where my old aunt Rosa lived. We used to go there for grand tea-parties, dressed in our smartest clothes . . .'

From inside the prison came the sound of a shot. The two soldiers stiffened. Thirty seconds later there was another.

'¡*Joder!*' muttered Becerra, grabbing his rifle.

There was another shot, and another, and another, then silence again.

'He's reloading,' said Becerra. 'Muro, look after the old man. I'm getting Ogarrio.'

As his boots clattered down the street in the direction of the square, the shots started again.

Felipe, his eyes round with fear, was pointing his rifle at them and fumbling with the safety catch. He was breathing rapidly. Pinzon saw a dribble of saliva trickling down his chin. He raised his palms upwards towards the frightened soldier. From inside the prison they heard two shots, fired in rapid succession.

'It's all right, Felipe,' Pinzon said, as calmly as he could. 'Look, we're going to sit on the pavement.' And to his grandson, who was clutching his knees, 'Gently now, Tomás. Felipe won't hurt us. See? There we are. We won't run away. It's going to be all right.'

Now the only sounds were Felipe's heavy breathing and the whimpers of his grandson. Pinzon was hoping it might be over, but the shots began again, at thirty-second or minute intervals, and he realised that Levi and Martínez were clearing another floor. He remembered his visit, visualising the faces of the occupants of each cell.

It seemed to go on and on and on.

He was already in a numbed state when he heard running feet and looked up. Sargento Ogarrio, pistol in hand, was pounding over the cobbles towards them, followed by Becerra and four other men.

As they reached the door, Commissar Levi came out of it, brushing the sleeve of his coat. Pinzon saw the twisted smile again. 'Ah, Sargento,' he said. 'I have pleasure in reporting to you that I have eliminated the fifth-columnist threat in Ciudadela del Santo.'

Ogarrio stared at him wild-eyed, then plunged through the door, brushing past a white-faced Martínez. A minute later his roar of rage could be heard from the street.

When he came out, he walked slowly towards the commissar, who had just borrowed Martínez's water-bottle and was wiping at a spot of blood on his sleeve. For a moment, Ogarrio said nothing. Then he grabbed the commissar by the collar of his greatcoat and hurled him against the granite wall. The round spectacles shattered on the pavement. Ogarrio punched his face and stomach, and kicked him when he fell, two hard blows to the groin. 'Those were my hostages,' he said softly. Then he yelled, 'Those were my pissing hostages!'

He turned his back on the commissar, and stood with clenched fists and closed eyes, his face turned to the sky. He pointed a finger at Martínez. 'You, you son of a mule and a whore. Why did you let him do it? Twenty-four nuns and eight damned priests, and you just stood by and let it happen.'

'He's – he's the commissar, Sargento.'

Ogarrio seemed to summon all his will power, and relaxed. 'I know,' he said. He patted Martínez on the shoulder. 'He's an arsehole. Forget about it.'

He looked scornfully back at Levi, who was crawling on the pavement hunting for his spectacles. Blood was pouring from a broken nose. 'Get him cleaned up,' he told Martínez. 'That's your punishment for being a donkey's turd.'

He noticed Pinzon. 'I'm sorry your boy had to see that,' he said. 'Are you all right?'

'Shocked. Disgusted,' said Pinzon. 'Ashamed that any Republican could commit such an atrocity. What do you expect me to say? Anyway, what are you going to do about your hostages?'

'I'll have to think of something, won't I?' said the *sargento*. 'Muro, bring your prisoners to the square.' He set off back the way he had come.

'Sargento Ogarrio!' It was a scream.

The commissar was tottering on his feet, waving his pistol. 'You have assaulted the Party's representative in the performance of his duty. You know very well that I take my instructions from the Servicio de Investigación Militar, and the SIM's standing instructions are to neutralise anti-revolutionary threats. That is the priority, overriding any strictly operational requirement. You have therefore defied the Party and the state. You have committed treason. By my authority I judge you unfit to command. I place you under arrest.'

Ogarrio barely glanced at him and continued on his way.

A shot rang out, missing him by a good distance and ricocheting off a lamppost. Ogarrio turned to his assailant. There was only derision in his eyes. Another shot hit the pavement at his feet, ejecting a cobblestone, which smashed a window. Wiping his forehead, Levi aimed again. This time it was two rifles that fired. The commissar staggered back against the wall and slid down it, leaving a red trail on the granite. Becerra and Martínez lowered their smoking rifles.

'That doesn't help me,' said Ogarrio, acidly. 'I need hostages. Hostages!'

Tomás began to wail.

The atmosphere in the square had changed. The townsfolk were no longer seated quietly on the ground. The men were yelling and waving their fists and the women were either screaming or weeping. Where Ogarrio was standing, in the centre by the fountain, three of his soldiers were manhandling an angry man to the ground. The council chairman was on his knees, tears running down his fat cheeks.

Ogarrio silenced the commotion by firing three rapid pistol shots into the air. There was an explosion of flapping wings as pigeons erupted from the elm trees and whirled in mad circles over their heads.

'Twenty women. Ten men,' he shouted. 'That's all. They won't be harmed. I'm only taking them as a guarantee of your good behaviour. You'll have them back within a few days when we leave. Don't resist, citizens, or we'll have to make examples, starting with your council chairman.'

The crowd stared at him sullenly. Some of the women were sobbing. A baby was bawling.

'That's better,' said Ogarrio. 'Now, I don't care how we do this. Either you give me volunteers or we take them ourselves. It's your choice.'

There was a long silence. An old woman in black widow's weeds stepped forward. The young man beside her tried to pull her back, but she shrugged him off. Becerra took her gently by the arm and helped her sit on the fountain steps.

'Thank you,' said Ogarrio. 'That's one.'

An old man with a white moustache and a beret walked proudly to the old woman and sat beside her, staring rigidly and impassively ahead while she took his arm. A younger man wearing a shepherd's fleece followed him. Several women in the crowd began to keen. The next to come was a red-haired woman in her early thirties. Her lips were rouged and she tossed her head nonchalantly. There was a murmur from the crowd. For a while nothing happened. Ogarrio paced impatiently. Then a middle-aged woman inched her way to the fountain, supported by her daughter. Others followed. After a quarter of an hour twenty-one people were sitting there.

'No one else?' called Ogarrio. He turned to Becerra. 'We need nine more women. Young ones preferably. Some of the nuns were in their twenties.'

'Most of those left have children, Sargento,' said Becerra.

'Then bring their bloody babies with them,' was the reply.

This led to more shouts and protests, but Ogarrio had his way after his men, marching forward to pull a pretty young woman out of the crowd, used the butts of their rifles to knock her resisting husband to the ground. The violence had the necessary intimidating effect. Eight more women, with six infants and toddlers between them, were taken without incident.

'Thank you, citizens,' said Ogarrio. 'As I told you, these people will not be harmed. In a while, my men will be coming to your homes to requisition food. We'll let you keep enough for your needs, then leave you in peace.'

Soon Pinzon and his grandson were following the thirty disconsolate hostages as they were marched up the steep steps that led to the citadel. Ogarrio came up beside him. 'I expect they'll be looking to you for leadership,' he muttered. 'You were once a grandee in these parts. Now you can exercise some of your political skills. They'll be frightened when the enemy comes.'

'I noticed that when you asked for volunteers you didn't think it necessary to tell them the town would be attacked.'

'What do you want me to do? Create unnecessary panic? They'll know soon enough.'

'What you are doing is morally despicable. These are not class enemies. They're peasants like you. Innocents.'

'Nobody's innocent, Señor. These people were happy enough to be Anarchists when it suited them. That fat *alcalde* was trying to tell me he was a Communist. Do you think they wouldn't raise the Fascist flag as soon as our backs are turned? As far as I'm concerned, everyone's an enemy unless they prove otherwise. My only duty is to my men. As I told you, I want to get them home.'

'It won't work, you know, this gamble with human lives. The Fascists don't negotiate. If you still had nuns and clergymen, well, perhaps, if the general attacking us had a conscience – but I've not heard yet of an enemy general who has. It's academic anyway. You've lost your religious hostages, and our opponents despise the peasantry, unless they're serfs on their own estates. They'll let them burn.'

'Who says I've lost my religious hostages?' said Ogarrio, belligerently. He stopped Martínez, who was struggling up the steps by his side, bowed under the weight of a heavy bundle. Ogarrio pulled his knife from his sheath and cut a slit in the rough sacking. Reaching inside he pulled out a coarse brown cassock, rummaged further and extracted a piece of blood-stained white cloth. 'What do you think this is?'

Pinzon had recognised it already. It was a nun's coif.

'I changed Martínez's punishment for shooting Levi,' said Ogarrio, coldly. 'I made him strip the dead.'

Pinzon shuddered. 'You're mad,' he whispered. 'You're mad and evil.'

A look of sadness crossed the *sargento*'s face. 'No,' he said softly. 'It's the world that's evil. I'm just a soldier fighting a war, and serving my Party and my country the best way I can.'

They walked on in silence. They crested the steps and Pinzon was dazzled for a second by the brilliant white facings on the battlements. They passed through a medieval gateway into a sloping square surrounded by ecclesiastical buildings, and to the left the red-brick parapets of Philip II's fort. Ahead, dwarfing the other structures, stood the cathedral of St Jaime. Its towering, sculptured façade shone brilliantly against a background of endless sky.

The citadel was already a hive of activity. The hostages were waiting in a resigned huddle while three of the soldiers were pulling back the bar of the heavy oak door, carved with the figures of saints. Others were carrying supplies to the fort, and lookouts were climbing the worn steps to the parapets.

'There's little point in arguing about it any more, Señor,' said Ogarrio. 'We're here.'

Although he was horrified that they had been included among the hostages, Pinzon was grateful for the other children. It meant Tomás had playmates. Felipe, who had been left to guard them, was ingenious in devising games for them. Their shrill exclamations of pleasure as they played blind man's buff in one of the side chapels, or hopscotch down the nave, was cheering and a welcome touch of normality in the surreal situation in which he and his fellow hostages found themselves.

It was remarkable, in fact, how quickly everybody had accepted the situation. There had been no panic when they were ushered inside the gloomy interior and the oak doors were slammed and locked behind them. The townspeople had separated, each to find a pew or an alcove that would be their territory, laying down the blankets Ogarrio had requisitioned for them. He noticed that a sort of social hierarchy had also developed, centring round the imposing old woman who had offered herself first, the kindly featured white-moustached old man who had followed her to the fountain, and the young man in the sheepskin who had volunteered third. The others appeared to look up to them. The old man busied himself with organisation, arranging a makeshift kitchen in a side chapel and a toilet behind some pillars, checking that mothers with infants had all they needed, generally making himself useful. The younger man sat sullenly by himself, but people passing him nodded respectfully. The greatest veneration seemed to be shown to the old woman. In ones and twos, townspeople would sit down beside her as if taking comfort from her presence.

Pinzon felt shunned. He wondered if it was because the other hostages had seen him talking to Ogarrio, or whether they were intimidated by his reputation as a politician in the central government. He guessed he appeared alien to them, and they were afraid of him.

'Do you mind?' It was the red-headed woman, who had elicited a murmur from the crowd when she had stepped forward to join the knot of volunteers. Without waiting for his answer she sat down beside him. 'We've met before.'

'Have we?' Pinzon was confused. 'I don't think I . . .'

She laughed. 'No, you wouldn't remember someone like me. It was when you came on an official visit. As minister. You stopped in the classroom in the gaol when I was teaching Anarchism to the nuns.'

'I do recall,' he said. 'Of course I do.'

'No, you don't.' Her freckles danced as she grinned. She waved a hand over her shoulder. 'Unfriendly lot, aren't they? Take it from me. I've been here since before the war – told you, came here as a schoolteacher – and they still consider me to be an *extranjera*, an outsider. Bastards. They think I'm immoral because I had an affair with one of the militiamen. Oh, they all espouse Anarchist politics here, but they don't accept the libertarian principles that go with them. I was left high and dry when my great lover went to war, leaving me pregnant with his child. Sorry. Do I shock you?'

'No,' he said, 'of course not.' He had been, however, a little surprised by her forthrightness to a complete stranger. 'Your child? Is he – she—?'

'It was a he. A beautiful boy.' A quiver crossed her face

before the smile returned. 'But he died of typhus before he was two, not that the villagers forgave me for that either. Wicked whore. Bad mother. Can't win, can you?' Her tone was hard-boiled but he caught the catch in her throat.

'I'm sorry,' he said.

She shrugged. 'It's life, isn't it? You learn how to keep going. Not that I wouldn't rather be somewhere else than Ciudadela del Santo.'

'You didn't think of returning to your home town?'

'Granada? It came out for the Fascists on the first day of the Rebellion. I'm stuck here, aren't I? Nowhere else to go.'

There was a moment's uncomfortable silence as she seemed to contemplate the frescos surrounding the altar. 'Tell me,' he said, 'who is the old woman dressed in black with the red shawl? She seems to be important in this community.'

'Her?' She paused. 'Yes, you ought to know something about our local worthies since we're all going to be bedfellows for a while. That's Grandmother Juanita. Her son commanded the militia that Ciudadela del Santo sent to the Aragón front and he died in the battle of Belchite. That makes her the mother of a hero and untouchable as far as the village is concerned. She's up there with the saints, or she seems to think so. Anyway, nothing gets by her eagle eye, so I'd advise you to be wary of her. Old man with her is Hector García. Used to be the *alcalde* before Zuluaga. He's decent enough, though Juanita has him in her talons.'

'And the man in the sheepskin?'

'That's Paco Cuellar. He sits on the council. He's a shit.'

'I see,' he said, confused by the venom in her tone. 'Well – thank you.'

'*De nada.* Welcome to Ciudadela del Santo.'

She laughed brittly, then narrowed her eyes in the direction of Tomás, who was playing near the altar. 'That's your grandson, isn't it?' She observed him thoughtfully. 'Want me to help you look after him?'

'That's very kind of you,' he said, 'but I think I can manage.'

'No, you can't. You're a man. Boy of that age needs a woman. Especially in a situation like this. It's no problem for me. I'd love it. He reminds me a bit of my own little boy. What's his name?'

'Tomás, but I couldn't possibly ask you—'

'Why not? You're on your own, like I am.' She indicated the other hostages. 'None of them will ever lend a hand. They've never helped me, any of them. All right, let's make a deal. I suspect you know a lot more of what's going on than anybody else. Maybe if things get bad you can watch out for me. And in return I'll look after Tomás. Does that sound fair? Mother of God, I'm scared,' she said, reaching into her skirt pocket for a packet of cigarettes. 'Want one?' she asked. She pulled out a tin lighter. 'Zippo,' she said, with a nervous laugh as she flicked back the lid. 'Boyfriend in the militia gave it to me.'

Pinzon smiled. 'Thank you, Señora. If you had a cigar, that might be a different story. Even so, I'd probably refuse. Being in a church . . . even though I'm not Christian. Prejudice and inhibitions instilled from birth. It's a bit foolish, isn't it?'

'Well, I'm no Christian, thank God. Oops, that's a contradiction in terms, isn't it?' She laughed self-consciously. 'But prejudice? Listen to them muttering.' She pursed her rouged lips and blew a puff of smoke over her shoulder.

'May I ask, Señora—'

'Call me María, please.' She sighed. 'Since we've been thrown together we might as well be informal.'

He nodded gravely. 'Then you must call me Enrique. But I'm curious, María. Why did you volunteer to be a hostage when you don't feel at home in this town?'

'To see the look on the sons of bitches' faces when I joined them,' she said, and gave him a radiant smile. 'Now, tell me, what do you think of my proposition? Will you let somebody so immoral look after your grandson?'

Pinzon laughed. It was the first time he had done so since

his capture, but this forward and obviously intelligent young woman had cheered him. 'I would be honoured, María. My grandson is fortunate. It will also be a pleasure for me to have the company of such a modern and unconventional companion.'

She looked at him slyly. 'I would imagine you were probably quite a charmer as a young man, Enrique. We'd better not let the tongues wag too much, or it will be you they start whispering about. I'll come back when Tomás has finished playing, and you can introduce me.'

It had been shortly afterwards that the aeroplane had flown over.

The first they knew of it was when the great doors burst open and Ogarrio, with twenty of his men, strode inside carrying the dripping cassocks and habits that Martínez had stripped off the priests and nuns. Pinzon supposed it was a small mercy that the blood had been washed out, but that was of small comfort to the other hostages, who had to wear them.

Ogarrio made them strip at gunpoint – even the old ladies. There was no allowance for modesty. Those who resisted had their clothes torn off them. They were barely given time to finish dressing before they were pushed, again at gunpoint, into the square, where they stood bewildered in the afternoon sunshine.

It was then that Pinzon, who had been herded out with them, heard the faint drone and, gazing up at the sky, saw a flash of metal reflected in the gap between two clouds. He recognised the engine sound. It was a Heinkel, the bomber flown by the German Condor Legion, sent to Spain by Hitler to support the Fascists. He remembered his night in the public air-raid shelter. This plane, though, was far too high to be a threat. Its circling flight pattern indicated it was on an observation not a bombing run – but he felt the familiar twinge in his stomach, the cold caress of fear.

Ogarrio had trained his binoculars on it as it circled over their heads. He noticed Pinzon. 'They have a camera,' he said, with satisfaction. 'You see, they will believe I have religious hostages. It also means the enemy is closing on us. Things are moving a little faster than I anticipated. I guess their troops will be outside the city by dawn. Then we'll be able to see who is right, you or I.'

'This is insane, Sargento. They will not negotiate. I beg you, let these people go before it is too late.'

'It might be better for your peace of mind if you convince yourself they will negotiate.' He strode off, shouting orders at his men, leaving Becerra to supervise their return to the church.

That had been two hours ago. The consternation that had followed the shocking and humiliating display of the hostages for the aeroplane had died down. The townspeople were sitting sullenly in the pews. Pinzon was interested to see that not a few were praying. Perhaps Ogarrio was right, he thought. Revolutionary politics in these out-of-the-way places was only skin deep. Peasants were peasants and always would be.

María sat down silently beside him. She looked fetching in her nun's habit, which hung loosely on her. She had removed the coif and her toss of red hair, her renewed lipstick and her exuberant freckles made her look vaguely decadent. She stroked Tomás's head. He was sleeping on the pew. 'Stretch your legs, Enrique,' she said. 'It'll be good for you. Don't worry about the boy. I'll look after him. We're getting on fine now.'

'You showed great tact with him after the aeroplane scared him.'

'Some introduction, wasn't it? Yeah, well, I like kids and we usually trust one another. Wish I could say the same about adults. Go on, take your stroll.'

He began to walk briskly up and down the nave, hoping the exercise would still the anguish in his heart. On either side rose the tall pillars. Leafy Corinthian capitals crowned the ochre and black striped marble of the base columns. From there, creamy white stone flutings fanned upwards into arches on the upper layers and, higher still, evolved into complicated tracery stretching over a vaulted ceiling that, in the dim light, was already swathed in shadow.

The rich reds and blues of the stained-glass windows had greyed in the darkness, except where a last pale shaft of evening sun shone through the magnificent rose roundel above the altar. A section showing the Annunciation was illuminated in the fading light. The exquisite colours blazed in the gloom like bright jewels. Behind the Virgin Mary and the Angel Gabriel, the gaily coloured palm trees, the mosque-like buildings and the bystanders in their turbans made Pinzon wonder whether this was a scene drawn from the old Moorish Andaluz before it had been recovered for Christendom.

He thought it ironic that a man like him – a hater of churchmen and tradition of all kinds – should end his days in a place like this.

The door opened. Ogarrio entered with three men. Martinez and Becerra had pickaxes and shovels on their shoulders while the other – he remembered he was called Rincon – was pulling a trolley on which a generator rested with some arc lamps, a coil of rope, tools and several white sacks containing explosive.

'You're going through with it, then,' said Pinzon, bitterly.

'Keep your voice down, Señor. Better these people don't find out what we're up to. We don't want a panic, do we, or anybody getting hurt?'

Pinzon saw that they were standing in dark shadow and only he had observed them.

'Becerra, go down to the altar and call everybody round you. Give them a speech or something so their attention's occupied. And send Muro back here to take your place.'

Becerra did not look happy. 'A speech? What about, Sargento?'

'Anything you like. Sanitary arrangements. Whatever comes into your head.'

'Sanitary arrangements!' the soldier muttered, as he put down his pickaxe and went off as instructed.

'Now, quietly, everybody,' said the *sargento*. 'Down the side aisle towards the steps by the western transept. Since you're here, you might as well come with us, Professor. As a medievalist, you may find the crypt interesting.'

The staircase was narrow, and they found it difficult to manhandle the trolley down quietly enough not to be heard. Pinzon followed them disconsolately.

They reached a small chapel where the effigy of a knight, a hound at his feet and a cross clasped in his hands, was carved on a stone tomb.

'Do we dig here?' asked Martínez.

'No,' said Ogarrio, flashing his torch towards the eastern wall. 'There's a grille over there, and more stairs that seem to lead down to a lower level.'

'Ai, that's probably where the skeletons of the monks and nuns are. I saw the ones they pulled out of the church in Barcelona in 'thirty-six,' said Rincon. 'Gave me the creeps. But it was funny, the way they put bishop's robes on them and positioned them dancing with each other.' He put his arms around Felipe and leered into his face.

'Get off me,' screamed the boy. 'That's not funny.'

Martínez's giggle was high-pitched, nervous, and somehow more eerie than Rincon's fooling around.

'That's enough,' snapped Ogarrio. 'Rincon, break that lock with your pickaxe, and, Muro, help Martínez with the generator.'

The cold intensified as they descended, and they became growingly aware of a musty smell of damp and decay. They passed through a trefoil arch into another dark space that their torches revealed was a corridor between layers of stone shelving on either side. Pinzon's cheeks brushed cobwebs, and he started when something cold scratched his cheek. He swung the torch they had given him upwards and the beam revealed a hanging, skeletal arm, held together by dried strips of skin. It was the ring on one of the fingers that had touched him. He raised the torch higher and stared into the leathery, shrunken face and empty eye sockets of a long-dead bishop, lying on the shelving. A mitre still rested on a bird's nest of grey hair. Rincon let out a howl, then he and Martínez laughed.

'I said, that's enough,' barked Ogarrio.

They heard a whimper behind them. Felipe had raised his torch to illuminate the top layers near the vaulted ceiling. The circle of light flashed over pyramids of skulls.

'It's a maze down here,' said Ogarrio. 'Better get the generator going to power the lamps.'

It took time and much fumbling before the machine whirred into life, and it was some moments later that the two lamps on their long leads began to glow, first a dull red, then blue, then a dazzling white that made them all blink. When they opened their eyes again they saw the extent of the charnel house. Along the corridors illuminated by the electric glare there were stacks of bodies and bones as far as they could see, separated at intervals by squat grey pillars. Now all three *privatos* were silent, staring with pale faces and clenched teeth.

'All right,' Ogarrio said. 'Let's find our way through this. Muro, you pull the trolley. Rincon and Martínez, take a lamp each. We want to head south-east to get ourselves under the chancel. That's where the steeple is, so we'll probably need to put the bulk of the explosives there. Muro, stop gibbering. It's live Catholics you'll soon have to worry about, not dead ones.' Carefully, he led them forward. They seemed to have forgotten about guarding Pinzon, who followed curiously behind.

The spaces between the platforms of corpses narrowed the further they went, and they had to move in single file, Martínez in front with the lamp. Ogarrio looked behind him at the capitals of the pillars. 'That's odd,' he said. 'They're angling out from a central point, like the struts of a fan.' He checked his compass. 'South-east. Probably from where we want to go.'

Rincon was eyeing the skeleton of a monk whose skull had rolled to the edge of its shelf and seemed to be ogling him at head height. 'Let's hope so, Sargento,' he muttered. 'At the moment I'm thinking back fondly to the attacks of the Condor Legion when we were fighting at Teruel. They were easier on the nerves.'

Martínez, ahead, cried out and almost dropped the lamp as he stepped backwards, bumping into Ogarrio. 'Sargento, I thought I saw one of them moving,' he hissed.

'Keep that lamp steady. Let me see.'

The *sargento*, followed by Pinzon, whose interest had quickened, stepped through an arch into a small semicircle, surrounded by a marble colonnade, from which the galleries of the dead indeed radiated outwards. The wall beyond was of solid black rock, glistening with damp and condensation. It was clearly the granite of the original hill on which the cathedral was built. In the centre there was a square block, also of carved black stone, probably a mausoleum or a sarcophagus. The side was incised with a gold inscription – but what had fixed his attention, as it obviously had Rincon's, was the life-sized alabaster statue that stood, or seemed to float, on top of it.

It was a clever optical illusion, thought Pinzon, after he had recovered from his surprise. The black base was almost indistinguishable against the darkness of the rock behind so the gleaming white figure of a man, in a long gown and a scholar's cap, appeared to hang in mid-air. The sculptor had also slightly extended the neck forward so the statue's sharp-boned features and intense stare challenged whoever approached and, in the play of light and deep shadow, it did seem, almost imperceptibly, to be moving.

'Who is it? Some king?' squeaked Martínez, nervously.

'I don't think so,' said Pinzon. Everybody was so absorbed

49

by what they were seeing that nobody questioned why their prisoner had suddenly taken the lead. 'He looks more clerical. No, this is interesting. Look what he's holding – a compass, a ruler and a hammer.' He moved forward to read the writing on the side. 'Yes, I'm right. This was an architect, probably the one who designed the cathedral. The dates fit. Listen.' He read the Latin quickly, then translated: '"Here lies Paladon, architect and mason. The greatest works of man are but shadows and vain shows. Yea, vanity, vanity, all is vanity. Yet may the Master Builder, the Prime Mover of the Celestial Spheres, the Lord of the Line and Circle, the True Form and the All-seeing Eye, still look kindly on his servant, who carved in rock and stone the mysteries that were revealed to him through his Craft, for the glory of the One God and in honour of His Creation, in whose Light may be found everlasting salvation. Ask, and it shall be given you; seek, and ye shall find; knock, and it shall be opened unto you." And it's dated "In this year of our Lord eleven hundred and twenty-one." This is all very unusual. The last sentence is a quotation from the New Testament but it's as if it's been tagged on. And the line and circle, the all-seeing eye. It reminds me of modern Freemasonry. Look.' He pointed to the carving of an eye in a triangle above the inscription. 'There's the symbol.'

'They say half the Fascists are Freemasons,' said Felipe. 'Even Franco.'

Rincon gave him a contemptuous slap on the head. '¡Idiota!' he snorted. 'Franco shoots masons. He also shoots donkeys like you.'

'This pre-dates Franco,' said Pinzon. 'It pre-dates Freemasonry, from what I know of it.' He stepped back and looked at the floor. 'See these white pebbles inserted in the paving? It's a pentacle inside a circle and the sarcophagus is in the middle of it. It's more a cabbalistic sign than a Christian one.'

'These squiggles on the back are pretty weird too,' came

Martínez's voice. 'Somebody else must have thought so too because they've tried to chisel them away.'

'Let me see,' said Pinzon. He shook his head in disbelief. The lettering was still visible, and he could make out a few words, enough to see that it was the same message as in the Latin – but in this inscription the architect's name was given as Yasin and the writing was Arabic. That was not surprising, he reasoned, although it was strange to find such calligraphy in the sanctum of a church. Arabic had been the *lingua franca* of Andaluz, used by everybody – Christians, Muslims and Jews – and 1121 was still in the early days of the Reconquista, but the date at the bottom read 515. The words preceding the date had been thoroughly defaced. He guessed they had read 'In the year of the Prophet'. And that made this message Muslim. In the vault of a Christian cathedral! No wonder some monk had tried to erase the heresy. 'Paladon? Paladon?' he muttered. 'Somewhere I've heard that name.'

'That's all very fascinating,' said Ogarrio, 'and I'm sure we're impressed that you can read Arabic, but that's as far as this historical lecture goes. We have work to do. Get ready, lads. I think we've come to the right place. The altar and the main steeple will be directly above the tomb. Since this Paladon has left a great granite box here, we might as well use it for the explosive. Can't think of a better shell casing. There doesn't seem to be a door in, so it's pickaxes, boys. Make a hole in the side. Then we'll pack the charges next to the man's bones. He said he wanted to get to heaven so we'll blow him there.'

Pinzon and Ogarrio sat with their backs to the colonnade while the soldiers worked on the sarcophagus. The enclosed space rang with the sound of metal against stone.

'I hope you're not too distressed that we're going to blow up this historical monument,' Ogarrio said softly. 'Your interest in a Roman Catholic cathedral is a bit strange, considering your anti-Catholic reputation. Maybe you've been working for the wrong side in this war and would have been happier with General Franco and his holy crusade.'

Pinzon ignored the gibe. 'I'm more concerned about the people you intend to blow up with it.'

'Let's hope it doesn't come to that. Would it surprise you if I told you that I, too, would be regretful if we had to destroy a thing of beauty like this cathedral?'

'No, you're an intelligent man, even if you're misguided.'

Ogarrio sighed. 'In your terms, perhaps. Not in mine. This is probably the most beautiful building I've ever seen in my life. *¡Puta de Madre!* The interior upstairs is dreamlike. It moves me. Believe me, it does. But it doesn't challenge what I believe in. This cathedral, lovely as it is, is an irrelevance. It's the eventual fate of all relics of the past, however beautiful, however much history they enshrine, to crumble into dust. More important is the historic task we have undertaken today.'

'Which is?'

'To defeat the forces of reaction and liberate the working man. That's something more beautiful and more significant to me than the Pyramids.'

'You seem to have no compunction about sacrificing the life of the working man you've come to liberate. That's what those people above us are, you know.'

'I do know, Professor. I probably know better than you do, but we must look to the future, not the past or even the present. To save my men, I'll sacrifice anybody I have to and it will be worthwhile. My men and I are no longer useful in Andalucía. We've done what we set out to do, but that's not the end of it. If I can get them back to the north, and the battle that is going on there, we can contribute maybe to the outcome of this war.'

'We've already lost the battle of the Ebro.'

'That's defeatist talk and doesn't become even you, Professor.'

'Even so, you think that thirty men can make a difference? That it's worth risking the lives of innocent peasants to get you there?'

'Everybody's efforts count. We are all pawns on a political chessboard, willing or unwilling. Our only significance is how useful we can be.'

'And if it's for nothing? If the Fascists won't accede to your hostage plan?'

'Then we die fighting and take as many of the enemy with us as we can. That's another reason for blowing the cathedral. I won't do it until the Fascists are right on top of us. So they'll die with us – and that will make it worthwhile. You think the Catholics have a monopoly on martyrs? If this is really going to be the end for us, I intend to make our deaths into a legend.'

'Including that of my grandson,' said Pinzon. 'I will resist you in any way I can. I see you as my enemy now, Ogarrio. You're as wicked as the Fascists.'

'Think what you like, but there's nothing you can do to stop me.' He might have gone on to say more but he was interrupted by a shout from Rincon. The three *privatos* were laughing as they pulled away the last rubble from the hole they had made. They were still laughing when they pushed one of the arc lamps inside, and stuck their heads in after it. Then they were silent. One by one they withdrew and stood helpless, clearly bewildered.

'What is it?' called Ogarrio. 'Scared by more bones?'

'There are no bones, Sargento,' whispered Felipe.

'What is inside, then?'

'Nothing, Sargento. It's just a hole.'

'There's another floor below,' said Martínez. 'A big one. We can't see the bottom but it's full of pillars.'

Ogarrio strode over angrily and looked inside. '¡Mierda! You're right. There is another floor. In fact, it looks as if there's a whole damned cathedral under there.'

Ogarrio set up the pulley, wedging it inside the sarcophagus. Rincon volunteered to be lowered with the lamp. They tied the end of the rope to one of the pillars. Martínez and Ogarrio took the strain, while Felipe let out the lead attached to the lamp. After a few minutes, he had reached the end. 'Stop,' Ogarrio ordered. 'Rincon, how much further before you reach the bottom?'

It was a tinny, echoing response. 'Not far. I can see the flooring. There must be three or four metres to the bottom.'

Still the height of a small house to go, thought Pinzon, stunned by this new development. How big was this new vault?

The *sargento* was shouting again: 'We have enough rope, but we've reached the end of the electric cable. I'm securing the end of it. If the lamp hangs free where you are now, will there be enough light?'

'It's a big space down here, but I think so.'

'All right, continue lowering him.'

It was still another minute before the rope slackened, and Rincon's now much fainter voice announced he was on the ground. 'What do you see down there?' Martínez called. 'More bones?'

The response was indistinct. Rincon must have moved further away, but Pinzon heard: 'No . . . empty except . . . pillars, hundreds of them . . . Beautiful . . .' and then distinctly: '. . . Mezquita in Córdoba . . .'

'I'm coming down,' Ogarrio shouted. He looked at Pinzon. 'You go first. I'll follow. I hadn't counted on there being two crypts. We may need to call on your expertise in medieval architecture after all.'

Pinzon's mind was whirling as they fitted the harness on him. Rincon had said, 'Mezquita.' That was the name of the great mosque in Córdoba. Could it be possible? This had once been a Moorish state . . . A subterranean church, not mentioned in any history, with access through the tomb of the architect himself, who had had inscribed on his sarcophagus words of Arabic? There had to be a secret here, something that had been buried and preserved at a time when Ciudadela del Santo was changing hands between Moors and Christians in the early days of the Reconquista, when loyalties were torn . . .

He knew before he reached the red and yellow chequered

terracotta floor that this was no Christian church. Even while he was hanging from the end of the rope between forests of pillars, the intricate inscriptions and sinuous arabesques carved on the tall columns were familiar from his studies of Arabic. When he saw the gold and white mosaics of stars covering the blue ceiling that had almost certainly supported a dome, he saw no images of Christ, the Virgin or the doves that would have decorated a Christian or Byzantine church. Around the edges, the floral patterns were merely more colourful variations of the carvings on the pillars – and in the centre, in swirling gold letters on a blue background, shone the simple message that 'There is no God but Allah and Muhammad is his Prophet.'

He found himself standing next to Rincon in what had once been a Muslim prayer hall. In the shadowy eastern corner he could make out the mihrab – the representation of the Prophet's house in Medina that is found in every mosque, an alcove set in the wall, again beautifully tiled with mosaics. He could not see the minbar, the preacher's pulpit. Perhaps it had been made of wood and had rotted away.

He stared around him in amazement, dizzy and awed when it struck him that probably nobody had been here for eight hundred years.

It was almost as large, and certainly as beautiful as the great mosque in Córdoba built by abd al-Rahman. The intricacy of the craftsmanship was extraordinary. Everywhere he looked there were carvings, above, below and around the imitation arches that lined the walls: Qur'ānic inscriptions, strange symbols and geometrical patterns, linked by tendrils of flowers and leaves, birds and animals, in a flamboyant tracery that made his mind spin.

He felt a crushing sadness. He had discovered an architectural and historical marvel, something of unparalleled beauty, a treasure of civilisation that belonged to the whole world – and the men with him had come to destroy it.

In some parts of the wall patches had fallen away. It seemed that the carvings were a surface layer of plaster or light stone. It took him a moment to appreciate what lay behind it. It did not look like the brickwork of most mosques of the Moorish period. Then he understood. The dank black walls were granite, like some of the pillars that supported the roof. The whole mosque was itself a carving, hacked out of the natural rock of the hill.

He had to support himself against a pillar as the implications dawned on him. The ambition of the architect who had designed it was breathtaking. Perhaps there had originally been a cave here, but artists had cut and shaped it into one of the most beautiful buildings he had ever seen. And what a concept! A mosque made of a mountain, constructed in the bowels of the hill. It had been an enormous undertaking . . .

He heard a thump behind him, and Ogarrio picked himself off the floor. He was staring wide-eyed around him.

Pinzon grabbed his arm. 'You can't put a bomb in the cathedral, Ogarrio. Look what we've found here. It's unique.'

Ogarrio shook him off, still gazing in astonishment. 'You're right,' he said.

'Thank God,' he breathed.

'No, we won't put a bomb in the cathedral,' Ogarrio continued. 'We'll put it here. This is the centre of the mountain. We'll fill the chamber with explosive. If this goes it'll blow up the whole hill, cathedral, fortress and all. It won't be just a few Fascists who'll die with us. It'll be a whole shitting division!'

Rincon, who had been wandering round the maze of pillars with his torch, was shouting excitedly: 'I've found a hollow column here, Sargento. I noticed a big crack in it, and when I touched it, the whole side came away. There's an urn inside, somebody's ashes, by the look of it. Maybe that architect who isn't in his tomb. And underneath there's a box. Shall I open it, Sargento? Maybe it's got gold inside or jewels.'

The *sargento* ignored him. He was already shouting orders. 'Muro, start lowering the explosive we brought. Martínez, go back to the fort. Gather enough men. Bring all the stock we found in the castle magazine . . . Yes, every bloody stick and sack . . .'

'*¡Maldita séa!*' Rincon cursed. 'It's just a book, a stupid, worthless book, and it's in Arabic.' Something thudded on to the tiles.

'Rincon, forget your fucking treasure and come over here,' Ogarrio shouted. 'I need your help.'

Pinzon wandered disconsolately around the great hall, sick at heart. His foot connected with something soft on the ground. He picked up the book Rincon had dropped. It was vellum parchment in a leather binding. The pages were handwritten in neat lines of Arabic script. It was a beautiful object, probably of great historic value. Not that it mattered any more. Absentmindedly he slipped it into his pocket.

Over the next two hours, he sat with his back against a pillar, hardly even aware of the frantic activity around him – the pulley moving up and down with bags of explosive material, the chain of men who were passing them from hand to hand, the piles growing in the gaps between the arches, later the lowering of a ladder, uncoiling of wires, the fixing of fuses . . .

He was thinking of Tomás. He had still not found a way to save him . . .

María was awake when he sat on the pew beside her. Tomás was lying with his head in her lap, asleep.

'Hello, you,' she said. 'You've taken your time. You were with the soldiers, weren't you? We saw them moving in and out of the cathedral, carrying things, but none of us was allowed near enough to see what they were doing.'

'They were shoring up the defences below the cathedral,' he said.

She raised her eyebrows. 'Oh,' she said flatly, 'and I thought they were laying down rat poison. All right, Señor Professor, don't tell me, then. I don't think I want to know, although the others are speculating madly.'

'Better they don't know,' he said. 'It won't serve any good purpose.'

'They plan to blow up the cathedral, don't they?' she whispered. 'It's all right, I'm a grown-up. I won't tell.'

'Only in the last resort,' he said. 'If they're forced to.'

'That was a Fascist plane, wasn't it? They expect to be attacked?'

'If the Fascists won't negotiate.'

'Negotiate? Is that why they dressed us up as nuns? Some sort of hostage exchange? Their lives for us? You believe the Fascists will fall for that?'

'I think there's good reason for believing so,' he said. 'Even if it doesn't work, I'm sure they'll release us before any fighting starts. Their *sargento*, Ogarrio, is a humane man.'

'For a politician, you're a terrible liar.' Her hands shook as she lit a cigarette. She took two deep inhalations into her lungs. 'You're right,' she said. 'We can't let the others know what's really going on, though we'll have to tell them some of the truth. They're not stupid and have probably drawn their own conclusions already. Maybe they'll believe the men'll eventually let us go if you and I act confidently enough. Damn. What a fix to be in.'

'You're a brave woman,' he said.

'A stupid one. Anyway, I'm more worried about your grandson for the moment. He's sleeping peacefully now, but he's been having nightmares and keeps waking up. We'll have to find some way to distract him. He's seen too many horrors. I tried to tell him stories, but I can never remember them, even the ones I told my little Pablo, although he was too young to understand, poor little mite. Anyway, I'm too frightened to think properly now. I wish I had a book,' she added.

'A book?'

'Yes, something to take his mind off things. You think you could ask your nice humane friend Sargento Ogarrio to give us a book of fairy stories?' She touched his arm. 'That was a joke, Enrique.'

He reached into his pocket. 'I've just found this,' he said.

She peered at it, and gave him a sour look. 'Well, that's no good. It's in Arabic.'

'I read Arabic,' he said.

She stared up at him, and slowly her lips curved into a smile. 'Fancy that,' she said. 'You're a man of many parts, aren't you? Well, when he wakes, let's give it a go.'

Pinzon ran his eyes over the text. There was a sort of dedication.

I, Sh'muel Ben Elisha, known as Shamal Ibn Eliazar or Samuel the Jew, also the Physician, the Mathematician and the Alchemist, have learnt that I am none of these things, only a healer who cannot heal, a conjuror of numbers whose calculations bring no illumination, an alchemist whose potions are wormwood.

I have lived hardly thirty-five summers but my heart and soul are already withered and my body is stooped with premature age. Only my memories survive. They are all that sustain me.

The dark philosopher Heraclitus saw the beauty that underlies all things, light in dark, good in evil, heat in cold. He believed in the law of Reason universal that exists despite the folly of mankind. I try to persuade myself that, despite the terrible calamities that overcame us, as long as the idea that impelled us survives, our lives may yet have been worthwhile.

In that vain hope, I have taken ink and parchment, and while it lasts, oil for the lamp. There is time, if the Prime Mover allows me, to make a record of what we attempted.

It did not look very promising – he feared it might be some dry philosophical text – but Tomás, awake now and wrapped to his chin in his blanket, was looking up at him with wide, expectant eyes, and María, puffing her cigarette, seemed to be signalling to him urgently that he should get on with it. Even Felipe Muro, who had been patrolling the sleeping nave, had sat on the altar steps near them, and was smiling at him, his rifle sloped between his knees, as if he, too, expected to hear a good story.

Worried that he might disappoint them, he looked further down the page. This was better, he thought. It was a touch gloomy, but never mind, at least it was about young people, children perhaps . . .

I will therefore write of the friends who live in my heart: of Aziz the Handsome, whom I loved; of Ayesha the Fair, whose fate I cannot think of without grief; and above all of Paladon who, more than any of us, strove to make material the dream that united us. I will write of the Craft that raised us almost to the heavens, then destroyed us utterly and scattered us, like the falling tower in the scriptures, leaving me, like the prophet, in the valley of dry bones.

Yet once it was not so. Once the sun shone on a youth of hope. It is those days that I now recall, when Paladon, Aziz and I were boys, living in a fair land surrounded by mountains, in a horizon of dreams . . .

He ran his eyes over what he had just read. Paladon? The name of the architect in the tomb! Now even he was excited.

'What's the story about, Grandfather?' asked Tomás, impatiently.

María gave him an encouraging smile.

'I'm not entirely sure, Tomás,' he answered, 'but I think it's about a boy of your age growing up in a country not so far away from here long, long ago. I think he may have been a sort of magician.'

Tomás's eyes gleamed in the candlelight.

Pinzon turned to the first chapter and began to read.

The hostages, in ones and twos, moved forward from the back of the nave until eventually a large group of adults, as well as children, was sitting on the pews and even the floor around him, listening to the tale.

Al-Andaluz, 1063–80
During the Period of the Taifa States

Codex I

The Alchemist

(I) In which I relate my father's travels with a prophet and how he was led to the perfect kingdom

It is difficult to know where to begin the tale of an individual life. As the alchemical process is a refining of essences defined in the dawn of Creation, so too is any human's brief existence on this earth predicated by what has gone before him, not to mention the astrological designs of the stars and all the other haphazard circumstance that brings the soul to a point in time when it can briefly define itself as 'I'.

And how do you define beginning anyway? My true life – the life that mattered to me – only commenced when I met Paladon and Aziz in a fig tree and I was already fourteen years old. But if it had not been for the education my father had given me earlier I would not have aroused in them the interest that I did. Nor would I have been sitting in a fig tree.

I do not know when anyone will ever read this book. Perhaps it will be some time in the future when the events of our own days are forgotten in the cataracts of history. They will ask, 'Who is this Jew telling me a story? In what age and in what circumstances did he live?'

I have therefore decided to start with an account of my father's life, and the improbable chain of circumstance that brought him to Mishkhat. He was certainly a remarkable man, who lived through troubled times, and in the telling of his adventures, the reader may appreciate a little of the background that shaped the story I am about to relate.

He died long ago, but I have vivid memories of him. He was nothing if not eccentric. To outside appearances, he was a respectable teacher of the Torah and a good orthodox Jew. As a rabbi, he was loved by his congregation, for his kindness as much as for his sermons, but I loved him for other reasons, and not only as a dutiful son: he would reveal to me, as he did to no other, a mystical side to his devotion, which was sometimes risible but always intriguing.

There was, for example, his rather embarrassing relationship with the Prophet Elijah, who was his constant companion, as real to him as the quill pen that now is clasped in my hand. It was unsettling growing up with an invisible presence in our household, but our family took it in its stride. My mother, when setting the table, put out a bowl for the prophet without thinking about it, and when I was very young I was always well behaved when I saw my father in earnest conversation with a shelf of books or an empty chair. I certainly did not wish to disturb a prophet, or my father for that matter, when they were discussing abstruse philosophy. Thankfully, the prophet absented himself when we had other company, or my father's successful rabbinical career might have been cut short.

My father gave me what I now realise was my first lesson in arcane knowledge when I was ten. I had just returned from the synagogue school after a turgid day studying the Torah – or, rather, sleeping through Rabbi Moshe's expositions on the Torah (my schoolmaster was a good man but an execrable teacher). I think I complained to my father that it was a waste of time. With a twinkle in his rheumy old eyes, he twisted his beard, then sat me down in his study and opened a random page of Genesis. He asked me to count the letters on the page. I did so and gave him a number. 'No,' he said. 'There are many more letters than that. You have only counted the black ones. What about the white?'

'There aren't any,' I said.

'Oh, but there are, hundreds of them, and each one is more potent than the black ones you see with your eyes.' Then he explained to me that when Jehovah revealed the laws to Moses on the mountain top, the totality of His divine knowledge was inscribed in fire on the tablets of stone, but Moses, when he saw the evil being done by the Children of Israel, realised they were not ready for the whole revelation, and cast the tablets at the sacred cow he caught the idolaters worshipping. Later, when he rebuilt them, he carved some of the letters in black, but others he left white so they were invisible. 'But they are still there if your inner eyes are opened to them, and if you combine them with the other letters of the Torah, you will find spelled out for you all the names of God. Now, you're a clever boy. Next time Rabbi Moshe drones on, you will ignore what he's saying and, with diligence and prayer, see if you can spot one or two of the white letters behind the words, for the light they reveal is the true secret of the Torah and the guide to ever-lasting life.'

Perhaps it was only a clever trick on his part to revive my interest in my schoolwork, for what boy of ten could resist such a challenge? In his way, however, he was pointing me towards what he considered were sacred truths. It was an intro-duction to philosophy, and led me towards the science of hidden causes to which I have devoted my life, and ultimately to the craft through which Paladon, Aziz and I sealed our friendship.

My father grew up in Córdoba during the last flowering of the Caliphate, when the wazir al-Mansur's armies ravaged the Christian states in the north and Andaluz was at the height of its glory. Not that this concerned him. He spent his time in the public library, studying, and was hardly aware of what was going on outside its portals.

Here one day he met a Mussulman philosopher, who took him under his wing because the young man, although a Jew, had impressed him. For a while, my father studied other books, unrelated to our religion, and it was perhaps these that later gave rise to his rather strange ideas.

Nobody knew it, but the days of the Caliphate were numbered. Al-Mansur's sons were not of the calibre of their father, and the mercenary troops that formed the army – Berbers from Africa and regiments of emancipated Christian slaves called Slavs – became uncontrollable. And one day everything fell apart.

My father lost his family and all his friends in the pogroms and butcheries that Córdoba suffered following the fall of the last Caliph. He was saved only because of his friendship with the Mussulman philosopher, who hid him in his house. Thus he was protected when the Berber mercenaries and Slavs, now suddenly leaderless, fell on each other and the people. Marauding armies repeatedly sacked the city in their attempts to impose their own candidates on the devalued Umayyad throne. Each time there was gratuitous slaughter of innocent citizens, whose relatives responded in turn by slaughtering the families of the soldiers, raping their women and looting their houses. The wheel of Fortune spun rapidly, and the country sank into chaos and civil war, in which no community was spared.

Certainly no one spared the Jews. We were killed by whoever temporarily took power, whether Berber, Slav or the enraged Arab townspeople with whom we had once been neighbours. The Jews of Córdoba, accustomed to peace after three hundred years of the caliphs' benevolent rule, were ill equipped for such calamities. We died like sacrificial lambs.

After some years, the Mussulman philosopher saw that he could no longer protect my father. The Berbers were in power again and were dragging even scholars from their homes. The two friends embraced before the Mussulman returned to his study to wait stoically for certain death among his books. My father, with nowhere to hide, decided he must try to leave the city that, for generations, had been our family's home. From every quarter he could hear the screams of those being murdered and the sky was red with fire as houses and palaces burned.

This was the first time that the Prophet Elijah came to him, or so he maintained. He cast a mantle of invisibility about him as he made his way along bloodstained streets in which soldiers rampaged like devils. His eyes tightly closed as he recited the Torah, my father followed his spiritual guide, and passed unchallenged all who stood in his way. The prophet guided him to a bark skiff tied to the bank of the river, and on this he floated away. Elijah's cloak deflected the light from the blazing buildings. Thus he escaped the arrows of the Berbers. Or so he said.

He spent many days on his skiff, paddling upstream against the strong current of the Guadalquivir. It must have taken some effort. He was a weak, scholarly young man more accustomed to handling books than oars, so perhaps there was some truth in his assertion that the prophet Elijah helped to propel him along. More probably it was the energy of desperation and fear. Be that as it may, the invisible cloak of Elijah was no longer effective when he landed on a sandbank somewhere near Granada, weak, exhausted and starving: he was immediately spotted by a troop of Berber horsemen, who arrested him. Not unnaturally, he believed that his hour had come. He fell on his knees in the sand reciting, in the mellifluous voice I heard so many times in the synagogue, the lamentations of Ezra and other relevant passages from the scriptures. He was astonished when he heard the commander of the Berber troop, a fearsome figure clothed in chain mail from head to foot, responding to his verses in better Hebrew than his.

That was my father's first meeting with Samuel the Nagrid, prince among Jews, scholar, philosopher, teacher, poet, statesman and soldier, the story of whose deeds ring in the annals of Jewry. At the time, he had just been appointed prime minister, or wazir, to the house of Zawi, the Berber tribe that had recently taken advantage of the troubles to set up a kingdom in Granada. The king, Habbus, had raised Samuel from his lowly position as secretary because he had recognised his excellent qualities. He so trusted him that he put him in command of his armies, a role no Jew had ever undertaken since Solomon's ancient temple was destroyed by the Romans. And he proved a master tactician who, in his long life, fought fifty campaigns. On this occasion the Nagrid was returning after inflicting a heavy defeat on a pretender to the Granadan throne. It was my father's strange fortune to arrive in the city that was to become his new home riding among soldiers in a triumphal parade. It was an experience rare, I imagine, for most rabbis, and certainly discomforting for my father who, only a few hours before, had been a wanderer, and destitute, and furthermore found it difficult to sit on a horse.

That was the extent of his brief flirtation with martial glory, for Samuel, after taking him to his comfortable house and interrogating him for several hours, was impressed enough by his learning to offer him a position as rabbi in a new synagogue he was building in the city. For the next twenty years my father lived in respectable obscurity. He married a good woman called Esther, originally from Elvira, who bore him two sons and a daughter, then settled into a quiet, contemplative life, benefiting from the patronage of Samuel the Nagrid, who always smiled on him. Those were indeed golden days for the Jews of Granada. Rarely has a person of our faith held such power and prestige, enabling him to become a shepherd to his people.

Sensibly, my father never presumed on his favours, as others of our tribe did, and thereby avoided the dangers that can beset the unwary at a princely court, for where there is power there is jealousy of him who holds it, and where there are several sons there are factions who strive for the succession. My father only visited the court once, and that was at the Nagrid's invitation to attend the wedding party of one of his nephews. He spoke of the banquet with horror, for he had never seen the dances of slave girls or heard the erotic songs of secular poets, and he left in agitation when he discovered that the comely boy who had been serving him wine all evening was the Nagrid's gift to him for the night. Later, when it was my fortune to be favoured at court, I smiled at this story, for I, unlike my father, had no such reservations, not when my friend was Aziz (my Gazelle, who is lost to me). Yet now I wonder, was my poor father, in his innocence, wiser than me?

I do not believe in predestination. I hold from my studies that God has willed it that we write the book of our own lives. But sometimes Reason is so challenged by the inexplicable malignity of circumstance that the mind is numbed. It is then that the hard tools of philosophy melt like wax in one's hand. Certainly, my father felt that the Fate that had stalked him since his youth, and spared him for so many happy years, had returned with a vengeance. This bright period of his life was soon to come to a savage end.

When King Habbus died and his successor was murdered, Samuel's son, Joseph, became the wazir, succeeding his great father who, too, had passed away. This Joseph, able and good man that he was, could not stem the rising tide of envy that was welling among the Arabs and the Berbers against the Jewish dynasty that had ruled their city. A polemical poem, written in the ink of hatred, stirred the anger of the mob, and Joseph was torn limb from limb while crossing the marketplace. So much is history, as also is the pogrom that followed the assassination of the Jewish leader: the loathing and jealousy of the Nagrid family extended to those who shared his religion. For the humble who are caught up in such events, a footnote in the annals becomes an eternity of suffering, scarring the memories of generations. It brought my father madness.

His synagogue was burned, his house ransacked. His two sons, Joachim and Mordecai, were slain when they tried vainly to defend his library. I once asked him what exactly had befallen his wife, Esther, and his daughter, Rachel, my half-sister, who was then thirteen years old, for about their fate he had always been reticent. It was the only occasion that I have ever known my father fail to answer a question. He stared at me with a quivering chin, he covered his head with his mantle, and his whole body shook with sobs. My mother took me aside and told me gently, 'They died too, Samuel. Mercifully. After a time. A long time. Do not ask him again.' Then I understood that my father had been in his house when it happened and had witnessed it all, and it was the greatest cruelty of his persecutors that they took pleasure in making him watch what they did, and spared him to live on afterwards.

Sick in heart and mind, he became a wanderer again, his crazed vision persuading him that somewhere he would find a land of peace. I like to imagine him as a stern prophet of the scriptures, striding with his staff into the desert where he lived on a diet of berries and wild honey, cursing the wickedness he was leaving behind him, but he was too mild and helpless a figure for that sort of heroism. He would not have survived had it not been for the charity of the Christian peasants and herdsmen in the high plains and pastures, who saw in his madness the touch of God and gave him food. Later, when he had somewhat recovered his senses, he sold medicines and charms. He had always had an interest in herbs, which he had studied in relation to the dietary laws of the Talmud. In his wanderings he became a skilled botanist, and I benefited later from that knowledge when, as a boy, I turned to alchemy.

He travelled through many kingdoms in his search for the paradise Elijah had promised him. Yes, his old companion was back again and accompanied him in all his wanderings through war-torn lands. I am grateful to Elijah for that, phantasm as he was. It was the reason my mother and I put up with him. If it had not been for this imaginary but stalwart friend I doubt that my father would ever have regained the elements of sanity that were left to him.

In those days the Christian princes remained in their northern fastnesses, not realising the opportunity which a divided Andaluz presented them. Thus, the kingdoms that the strong generals and magistrates had carved out of the ruins of the Caliphate were at the height of their power. These self-appointed kings maintained magnificent courts and warred constantly over perceived slights or insignificant fortresses on their borderlands. It was a far cry from the glory days of al-Mansur, who only ravaged Christians. Now Mussulman fought Mussulman, be they Berbers in Granada or Badajoz, or former Slav mercenaries in the coastal cities of Almería and Valencia, or true-born Arabs such as the al-Mu'tamids in Seville, who were already on their way to making a large empire by conquering their smaller neighbours. When my father travelled through these quarrelsome kingdoms he saw armies and devastation, and when he encountered communities of Jews, they complained about the heavy taxes imposed on them.

After many years my father found himself not far from where he had started, climbing a high, snow-peaked mountain. I believe he had despaired of his quest and was making his way back to Granada so that he could end his life beside the graves of his family, but that was not how he told it. As usual, he gave the credit to his spiritual guide. Elijah led him over narrow rock paths above gaping precipices, through wastes of snow and echoing gorges, on to a high ridge from which he could look down into a green valley. It was springtime and particularly beautiful. From this height, my father could make out flowering orchards and cultivated fields, a blue flowing river, neat villages and water mills, and under a high, dark rock the gleaming white of a walled city, its roofs touched with gold.

It was at this point that Elijah, his duty done, took his leave for a while, but as he stepped back off the ledge and began his ascent towards the sky, his long white beard and red robes already insubstantial in the morning mist, he stretched out his staff to the city below, and called, to his faithful companion, 'Lo, descend, for this is Mishkhat, the city of the holy cave in which there is light. Here, beloved, you will find the peace you seek.'

My father descended, with difficulty (I have no idea why Elijah chose to take him over the mountains when there was a perfectly serviceable road), and when he arrived in the city, he found a prosperous community of Jews, many of whom knew him because they, too, were refugees from Granada. As it happened, there was a vacancy in the rabbinate of a synagogue, which they offered to him. They gave him a house too, with a housekeeper, a widow named Tabitha. And my father did discover peace, and respect, and before long he was back to his old studies of the Torah as if nothing had happened.

In due course he married, despite his three score years against her two, the widow Tabitha, who became my mother. It was a difficult birth, yet I survived and so did she. I was brought up in a household of tranquillity, wonder and love. My father named me Samuel after the great Nagrid who had been kind to him. It was a choice between that or Elijah. On the whole, I am pleased he chose Samuel.

(II) *In which I describe something of the perfect kingdom and of how my life changed after climbing a tree*

So what, the reader may ask, convinced my father (and the prophet Elijah for that matter) that in Mishkhat he would find his land of peace? It was a Mussulman kingdom, like any other. It was a state afflicted by the same contradictions that beset many another – border disputes, diplomatic hiatuses, the games of princes. There were wars. I will later describe one because it affected our lives. Yet those who lived there – and I include all three communities, Mussulman, Christian and Jew – felt blessed and, above all, unthreatened. No matter what our faith or religion was, we considered ourselves first and foremost to be Mishkhatids. We were devoted to our king, Abu bin Walid al-Dawla, on whom we bestowed the affection and respect that a son owes his father. We rejoiced in his lavish public works, which brought honour and glory to us all. We even paid our taxes without rancour, because we believed he would spend the money for our benefit.

It was perhaps a little ironic, because anybody who had met the king – as I would many times – discovered that, though amiable enough, he was a selfish old rogue, with little interest in anything besides beautifying his palace, cultivating the finest of wines and accumulating slave girls for his pleasure. Indeed, it was a jest in the market – prideful because we wanted to believe it – that the palace contained beauteous creatures from every country in the world. Fortunes would be given, we were told, to a merchant who could sell him, say, a coal-black Nubian from the border lands beyond Egypt, or a flaxen-haired Viking from the snowy wastes of the far north, or any other kind of exotic flower. It was even rumoured that he had acquired a soft-skinned maiden from the land of Chin, or Serindia, as the Romans called it, after the silk that is reputed to be found there.

I was certainly impressed, when I became the court physician and was allowed to visit the women's quarters, by the range of physiognomies I discovered in his harem. A palace in itself, it was surrounded by exquisite gardens in which the barely veiled occupants, of all colours and hues, were its rarest blooms. There was indeed one woman, old when I met her (King Abu had been collecting for many years), whose like I had never seen before. She had eyes like almonds, hair like black silk, and a yellow-tinted skin of a pallor and softness I had never imagined could exist outside the celestial spheres. She spoke a strange, fluting language that nobody could understand, and was wasting away, perhaps out of loneliness because no one could talk to her. I assumed this was the maiden from Chin.

The others did nothing but chatter. It was a golden cage of canaries – but the goodwill in which they held their master was remarkable. There was none of the jealousy, as far as I could see, that poisoned most harems. Our king apparently shared his favours equally, and with extraordinary sexual prowess. That in itself was surprising because he was already an old man, and certainly not handsome, being completely bald, with sly, squinting eyes and a bulbous nose from his drinking. He was also, and this was a state secret for which I would have been decapitated had I revealed it in his lifetime, a eunuch – not of the kind produced by the slavers in their cutting shops in Gaul: in his case it had been a defect since birth, and of the nature that allows copulation but not generation. His sapling could stiffen into a mighty trunk, and many times a day, by his women's accounts, but no fruit hung from its branches and it was without sap or seed.

Yet they loved him, for he was kind to them, showering them with costly gifts, which women desire, but, alas, no babies, which they desire more. I doubt he cared. He was a confirmed bachelor, content to make his nephew his heir and happy with a hedonistic life in the beauty of the kingdom bestowed on him by his warrior father. Fortunately for the peace-loving people of Mishkhat, his father, a Syrian fortune-hunter in the ranks of al-Mansur's armies, had secured the throne bloodily during the time of troubles, then had the grace to die of chicken-pox immediately afterwards, sparing us the warfare that appealed to his cruel and rapacious nature. (May Allah be merciful to his soul because his death was certainly a mercy for us!)

I digress, but not too far, because certainly the magnificence of King Abu's palace made all of us citizens proud to bask in the reflection of its glory. Over the years the king must have collected as many rare stones as women. My father told me that when he first arrived in Mishkhat, not a day went by without him seeing a mule train straining its way up the steep path carved into the hillside, loaded with ancient Roman columns, or blocks of coloured Phrygian marble, Sicilian basalt, amber from the windswept Baltic, jet black obsidian from Lipari or the finest Egyptian alabaster to complete the great work that King Abu had begun at the start of his reign.

When I first visited the glittering palace, shining like a pagan temple on its outcrop at the side of the hill, I had expected in my intellectual arrogance that this magpie collection of expensive bric-à-brac would be tasteless in its final assembly. Instead I found, when I entered through the great gate, a maze of airy halls, with regular pillars variegated in hue, each fashioned from different stones. The rooms were separated, one from another, by horseshoe arches, their apses striped in reds and yellows. The effect was no less striking, I am told, than the famous doorways that once decorated the caliph's palace of Madinat al-Zahra. Stateroom led to stateroom, each wall carved in arabesques and more beautiful than the one before, until the visitor reached the breathtaking hall where King Abu received ambassadors sitting on his obsidian throne. There, the walls were of glass and polished steel. It was difficult to decide which were mirrors and which the real arches that showed the expansive horizon of the Mishkhat plain.

From a marble balcony one could view the king's gardens. They were quartered like the original Paradise by two ornamental streams, whose running waters reflected the heavens the garden represented. By their banks peacocks wandered among fountains, pavilions and rectangular flowerbeds, whose blooms in spring were as sensual as the colours of the Persian carpets in the king's halls. Scattered among the spacious lawns stood every kind of tree imaginable – cedar, maple, lime, palm, elm, willow, myrtle and poplar. The fruit in its spacious orchards shone like orbs in a green firmament. There were pomegranates, dates, oranges, lemons and figs. Hibiscus, vines, roses and other creeping plants tumbled in bushy clusters over the edge of the cliff. The effect brought to mind the mythical hanging gardens of Babylon.

It was a small palace – we were a small kingdom – but I

doubt that there was another so exquisite or well proportioned. It was the work of the master stonemason and architect Toscanus, whom the king had seduced away from the Christian king of Castile – that, incidentally, was how the young Paladon had come to Mishkhat, because the mason was his father. After he had completed the palace for the king, Toscanus decided to settle in our kingdom. Why not? It was not only we Jews who found this an agreeable place. Under the rule of such a gracious king, there was also much money to be made. Toscanus was quickly accepted into the Christian community, and one of the elders, a wealthy man who traded with Byzantium and other parts of the Christian world, commissioned him to build a small church. More of his relations arrived from Castile to help him in the task, and young Paladon, from an early age, acted as his father's apprentice. When I first knew him, he had already passed many of the degrees of masonry, as arcane a subject as any of the arts I ever studied. He was particularly admired for the delicacy of his carvings, and as a young boy was commissioned by the wazir to decorate the walls of his divan. That was how he came to know Aziz.

How I anticipate! It is as if Paladon and Aziz are jostling their way into my story before their time is due – but that was their nature. Their impatience, born of energy, curiosity and a zest for everything – everything – that life had to offer, was infectious. It infected me.

But it is time I spoke of the wazir. As I have said, our king, though benign, was indolent. The tolerant policies issued in King Abu's name were actually those of his capable nephew, Salim bin Yahya bin Walid, who combined the roles of wazir and qadi, controlling the king's cabinet of ministers as well as the state judiciary and religious courts. A thin, sombre man, always dressed plainly in a black gown, with a long grey beard and sunken, distracted eyes, Salim was a sort of Arab equivalent of the great Samuel the Nagrid, so revered by my father. Like the Nagrid, he was more than a brilliant statesman and, when it came to it, a competent general. He was a scholar, poet and philosopher, and to his house and its beautiful garden – it was situated near the old mosque at the bottom of the hill – came many of the most distinguished artists and intellectuals of our times, and not only Mussulmans: his interest in all ideas was broadly based and he had diplomatic contacts with other kingdoms in Andaluz and beyond, even among the Christian territories.

Yet it was not his brilliance or his philosophy that preserved the unique peace we enjoyed in Mishkhat. It was a much simpler virtue, one rare in great men. He was unambitious. He liked his exasperating royal uncle, and indulged him. He was in no hurry to take his place on the throne to which he was heir or to denigrate his uncle's glory. He was also a shrewd judge of men, and chose as his officials those of similar loyalty and character to himself. Uniquely, therefore, under his tutelage, our kingdom was spared what is perhaps the most divisive vice prevailing in any royal court, that of internal politics. The harmony between our rulers – more than the magnificence of our city, our wealth or our diplomatic achievements – accounted for the unity and peace in our kingdom.

For me, though, there was an even greater achievement to Salim's credit, which will make me honour and bless his name into eternity: he was the father of Aziz.

Of course, when I was growing up in the Jewish Quarter, we knew little of the goings-on among the great ones, except for the rumours we heard in the marketplace, which was a neutral ground in the city – as was the public bathhouse – where Mussulmans, Christians and Jews mingled indiscriminately.

Ours was a strict religious household. For all my father's idiosyncrasies, his intentions for his son were conventional. He imagined that I had no other desire than to follow him into the rabbinate. The result was that I led a protected life. The boundaries of my world were the synagogue, the school and my home. In addition I was of a solitary nature. I made no friends among my classmates. Throughout childhood, my companions were the books in my father's library. I must have read all of them before I was eleven.

The problem with my father, however, was that although he aspired to orthodoxy he was an intellectual enthusiast, and quite uncontrollable whenever any arcane fancy came into his head. I have mentioned his interest in the alchemy of plants. That is not encouraged in the Hebrew canon, frowned upon by the elders as one of the diabolic arts. Neither was astrology – but my father loved everything to do with it. I suspect they were sciences he learned long ago from his Mussulman protector in Córdoba, and which he used to support himself during his mad wanderings. He had not practised them in Mishkhat. Perhaps Elijah tipped him a word of friendly advice that they would be inappropriate, and consequently he restrained himself. But that was before he discovered that the son on whom he doted was intelligent and as curious as he was.

My first lesson in the arcane was followed in quick succession by others. It started with mathematics. I was always good at the simple arithmetic they taught at school but it bored me. One day I found in my father's library a book written by a Gonim of the great Jewish academy in Baghdad criticising on Talmudic lines the mathematics and philosophy of the ancient Greeks, such as Pythagoras and Ptolemy. It was the first time I had heard these names, or of neo-Platonism, for that matter, but I was fascinated. I ignored the religious objections of the great rabbi and lapped up the mathematical theory.

In one of the Arab bookshops in the marketplace, I found a second-hand university primer. It was months before I had saved enough of my pocket money to buy it but luckily it was still there. Before long I was making astronomical projections of my own, using Ptolemaic geometry. It came naturally to me.

When my father discovered what I was doing I thought he

would be furious, but he hopped from unsteady foot to unsteady foot, coiling his beard in delight. 'You have discovered numbers, my boy. Numbers! They also are secret illuminations of the essence of being, like the white letters I told you about in the Torah. How clever of you. And you are reading the stars as well!'

I think he had little understanding of geometry but he knew his astrology. Out came the books he had hidden in a box in the rafters, and thus it was, before I was twelve, that I mastered the art of reading the zodiac and making horoscopes. It was our little secret, which we kept hidden from my mother who would not have approved. Every evening we locked ourselves in my father's study so he could 'help me with my school work' and on summer nights we lay on the flat roof identifying the constellations. I don't know what Elijah thought of it. He was probably growling inaudibly into his invisible prophet's beard.

Astrology led in due course to alchemy. The distillation of medicines from the essence of plants, my father maintained, was the most practical and beneficial application of astrology because, as scientists know, the heavenly influences that control the four humours in a man's body have their correlation in the wider world of nature, including mineral and vegetable matter. Thus we abandoned horoscopy in favour of long walks in the countryside, gathering wild carrots, lavender, marjoram and dill on the Tuesdays when Mars was ascendant in the house of Aries, or burdock, columbine, mugwort and primroses on Fridays when Venus and Libra held sway. Our excuse this time was that we were seeking herbs my mother might find useful in the kitchen. She accepted our armfuls of vegetable matter patiently, although the sheer quantity of plants we brought back made her raise her eyebrows, and certainly challenged her culinary skills.

When my father judged I was ready, we set about our first experiments, seeking to separate the three essentials, the physical salt, the spiritual mercury and the sulphur of the soul, that are to be found in every living organism, having emanated there through the elements of earth, water, air, fire, and the celestial salt and nitre present in the Prima Materia. These essentials, mixed in the appropriate way, produce the magisteries and ens tinctures that make up the alchemist's medicines and potions. That is the theory, which is simple enough. The process, however, as anybody who has tried it knows, is complicated and laborious, involving distillation, digestion, sublimation, circulation and calcination. It requires steady fire at high temperatures and a maze of condensation pipes, vials, crucibles and other glassware, although at first we tried to make do with what we had in the house. More to the point, it is a very smelly operation. There was no keeping this from my mother.

When one day she returned early from her charitable work among the poor to discover that her kitchen had been turned into a wizard's laboratory, and a noxious one at that, she contemplated us with her hands on her hips, while we looked, shamefaced, at the rushes on the floor. 'Does your friend Elijah know what you're about?' she asked, after a withering silence.

My father had to confess that the prophet did not entirely approve of our experiments.

'Well, that's something to be thankful for,' she said. 'It's about time you showed a will of your own, my dear husband. I was wondering when you and Samuel would come into the open with your nefarious activities.'

We realised we had hidden nothing from her. She had been aware of our extra-curricular interests all along.

'One thing's for sure. You're not using my kitchen in future. You're lucky that we're living in a house that was built by a Christian with a pig pen in the cellar. If you have to be magicians, that's where you'll do it. And, my pretty Samuel, your punishment, for imagining that your mother's a blind fool, is to clear out the mess in there. No, don't flash your eyes at me, my dear. You'll not win me round this time with your good looks. As for you, husband, well, I'll let Elijah deal with you.'

It was indeed a terrible punishment for an orthodox Jew, as I then was. Nobody had been in the cellar since the original Christian owners had vacated the premises, but the sludge I had to wade through was evidence that they had kept many pigs. I persevered with brush and pail and made the room ready, then had to fast and pray for a week to cleanse myself of the spiritual pollution. Imagine our surprise when we went down there on the first day after my father judged me purified, to find already installed there every piece of equipment an alchemist might need. My mother had quietly bought them from an Arab friend who worked in the Mussulman hospital. (Oh, my dear mother! She was as remarkable in her way as my father, and I miss her still although she, too, has been dead these many years.)

For a year, my father and I worked together, but it was not long before I had delved into areas of the science that he could barely follow. The magician's apprentice had become more adept than the magician. He bore me no resentment. Rather, he could not conceal his pride. He would shake his head and sigh with wonder when he saw what I could do, and humbly pound the powder in the pestle, stoke the fire or perform whatever other menial task I required of him. I pretended all along, because I did not wish to wound him, that we were equal partners. I continued to make potions with the plants we had collected, and efficacious they were for palsy, liver complaints and the other ailments with which our townspeople were afflicted. My mother arranged for them to be sold by a Christian physician who offered prescriptions in the marketplace. He passed them off as his own and became famous. I used the money he gave me to buy books, when I could find them, and became even more accomplished in the art. By the time I was fourteen I had mastered methods of making potions with minerals as well as plants, and even dreamed of the philosopher's stone.

Meanwhile I maintained my interest in astronomy and mathematics. Yet all the time I sensed that I had hardly penetrated a world of knowledge that was still hidden from me. The more I achieved, the more frustrated I grew. How I also managed to spend full days at the synagogue school, and perform creditably when tested on scriptures that did not interest me, I do not know. I was filled with a fire for learning that hardly allowed time for sleep, but it affected neither my health, my concentration nor my desire to achieve more. I know my mother worried about me, but my father urged me on.

One day during the summer furlough, with a satchel on my back containing food my mother had prepared for me and another bag over my shoulder for my samples, I left Mishkhat to explore the hills on the far south of the plain to hunt for the flowers I needed for my potions. I hoped also to find antimony among the rocks. This rare metal, if processed correctly and under the right signs, can be refined into an essence that alchemists call the Seed of Gold, which in turn can be transformed into the Red Stone, sometimes called the Elixir, the universal medicine. It is important for any alchemist who wishes to attempt the transmutation of gold to master this art.

I wandered happily through the ripe fields, enjoying the sunshine and the open air. At night I slept under the stars. On the third day I was approaching the hills, making my way carelessly through a fruit grove and munching a stolen apricot, when suddenly I heard voices. At first I thought it must be the farmer and feared he would chastise me for taking his fruit. I sought vainly for somewhere to hide. Meanwhile the voices came closer. Whoever it was was not speaking the Romance language, the pidgin Latin adopted by the peasants, but pure, and cultured, Arabic. I became even more afraid: this was not the colloquial Arabic of the marketplace, but the rarefied version spoken by the faqis in the mosques or at the king's court. I knew I must hide, and so it was that, after a panicked scramble, I found myself cloaked by the dark green foliage of a fig tree.

Through the leaves I saw three figures approaching. The first, female, her head and her whole body wrapped in silk veils, was riding on a palfrey, legs astride like a man. She cantered into the glade, then easily, with a light pull of the reins, circled and brought her mount to a halt to wait for her companions, whom I could make out walking some distance behind. They were two young men of about my age, dressed simply in loose cotton jellabas, the skirts of which were tucked into their belts to allow their long legs freedom of movement. With their rough leather sandals and wide straw hats, I took them at first for the lady's attendants or grooms, until I noted, when they came nearer, the fine silk embroidery on their sleeves and under the necks of their costumes, not to mention the jewelled earrings, the gold chains that dangled from their necks and the bracelets on their arms. These were nobles. I tried to make myself even smaller as I crouched in a fork between the branches. I was puzzled as well as afraid. What were they doing there? And why were they carrying a thick coil of rope that trailed behind them as they walked?

It was the taller of the two young men who first caught my attention. His long hair poured in cascades of gold over his broad shoulders. His skin was pale like cream and his forehead and cheeks were flushed rose pink from his exertions. It was not a classically handsome face, but striking. The bones of his jaw and cheeks jutted like boulders, and his long nose appeared broken, but the energy in his expression, and a light in his eyes that was both stern and humorous, more than compensated for these flaws. His irises were of a bright blue that reminded me of mercury flaring in my experiments. He was like no native of Andaluz I had ever seen, for here even the Christians are of an olive hue, not so different from us Jews. But when he spoke, in a loud voice in which laughter echoed like bells, it was in fluent, stately Arabic. He was quoting a verse of a poem:

'*Though she soars the wind to flee her falconer
Love's jesses leash her, trembling, to my hand . . .*'

The other young man threw back his head and laughed. His straw hat slipped and I saw in the sunlight that suddenly illuminated his face flashing white teeth and the film of a moustache above pomegranate lips. His skin was smooth, like polished ivory, his features were perfectly formed, and his black, long-lashed eyes, now crinkling with mirth, were like pools of limpid pitch, pitch of the same lustre as his curling black hair that hung like bunches of grapes over a gold band round his forehead. Even then – yes, even then, at the first moment I saw him – I was smitten with delight, for he seemed half boy and half angel, and I had never seen any living form so beautiful.

'Oh, Ayesha,' he cried, and his voice was like music. 'Oh, he has you now. He has you now.'

The girl on the palfrey called back, and I heard from her voice that she was no lady but a child, perhaps eleven or twelve years old. 'Nobody will ever have me – certainly not a clod-hopping Frank like Paladon. If you two are going to be beastly to me again, I shall ride back to the tents and good riddance.'

At this, the tall young man gave a great sigh, clutched his chest and fell backwards into the undergrowth. A moment later he emerged, sitting up and laughing heartily.

'I hate you,' the girl cried, 'both of you. And what you're doing is boring. I'm leaving. Now.' But she didn't go. She sat on her palfrey, her shoulders slumped sulkily.

'It's not dull, sister,' said the darker of the young men. 'We're conducting an important scientific experiment. Come, Paladon,' he said, offering an arm. 'Get up. We must be nearly there. It can't be more than ten miles.'

'I just want to lie in the sunshine,' said the one called Paladon. He had lain back again and was sucking a grass stalk. 'We've been plodding for three whole days pulling that damned rope from peg to peg.'

'There isn't much sunshine here. We're in a fruit grove. And we need to get out of it so we can make proper bearings again. Come. Ibn Sa'id will be angry, and then we'll be in trouble with my father.'

'We should have gone up to the *meseta*. We need a desert if we're to do this properly, not stinking farmland. We need a big flat desert where you can see for ever. That's where the original scientists went. Some Godforsaken wilderness in Mesopotamia.'

'But we're not in Mesopotamia and we can't go to the *meseta*. It's Toledan territory and we're at war with them – or almost at war. Anyway, don't be so perfectionist. Ibn Sa'id says we need only to check the degree once, and our plain is extensive enough for that.'

Paladon groaned. 'It's pointless, Aziz. We're attempting to prove something that Abbasid philosophers in Baghdad confirmed a hundred years ago. And even they were imitating what some Greek had discovered a millennium earlier. We know the answer already from Ptolemy. It will be sixty-six and two-thirds miles. No more, no less.'

And that was the moment at which I gave a little cry. It was entirely involuntary, but I couldn't help my agitation: two things that Paladon had said had startled me. First, he had called the beautiful young man Aziz, and I knew of only one prince in our kingdom called Aziz and he was the son of the wazir. That terrified me. Second, when he had enumerated the distance, I realised exactly what they were doing. They were repeating the famous experiment of the Banu Musa Academy in the days of the Abbasid Caliph, Ma'mun. Several of the books I had acquired had mentioned how, from his throne in Baghdad, Ma'mun had instructed his House of Wisdom to confirm the Greek measurement of the circumference of the globe. The Arab scientists had gone to a desert and had extended a coil of rope from a point at which they had observed the elevation of the Pole Star to another point at which the elevation of the

Pole Star was one degree different, the distance travelled between these points giving them the length of one terrestrial degree. They had multiplied that number by three hundred and sixty degrees to give them a global circumference of twenty-four thousand miles, thus confirming the accuracy (or so they thought) of the Greeks' ancient calculations. Recently I had made my own astronomical observations, and I doubted the verity of this figure, which I thought was nearer twenty-five thousand miles – but I was excited that I had discovered others with the same astronomical interests as I.

This mixture of terror and excitement had caused me to bleat like a goat.

'What was that?' Paladon leaped to his feet.

'It came from that tree,' said Ayesha, composedly. 'In case you hadn't noticed, there's a Jew sitting in it. If you two philosophers weren't so absorbed in your important scientific observations, you might have spotted him.' She giggled and twitched the reins. Her palfrey executed a self-satisfied trot on the spot.

By then I was staring down at the faces of Aziz and Paladon gazing up at me with bemusement. I was shaking so much that I thought I'd fall off the branch.

'By God, she's right,' said Paladon. 'There is a Jew up there. A Jew in a fig tree. Never seen that before. Here, you, Jew, what are you doing? Why are you up a fig tree?'

I was stupid with fright. 'I won't tell, I promise I won't tell,' I managed to stutter.

'Tell what?' Paladon asked, with a smile.

'About the Banu Musa experiment you're doing. The – the circumference of the globe.' As soon as I said the words I knew I had made a mistake. They were still smiling but there was worry in Aziz's soft features, and suspicion in Paladon's.

'Aziz, did you mention the Banu Musa just now?' Paladon's voice was icy.

'I don't think so,' said Aziz.

'Neither did I. So how does a Jew in a fig tree know what

we're doing? You there, Jew, have you been sent by Aziz's father to spy on us?'

At this point I fell out of the tree. I banged my head on the trunk and slipped into unconsciousness. I woke to find the girl, Ayesha, bathing my brow with a towel soaked in perfumed water from her goatskin. Her veil had dropped from her chin and I saw that her face was as lovely as her brother's, but softer and rounder. Her skin was paler, too, like vellum, marred only by a single black mole on her left cheek that moved impishly when she smiled. Her eyes were flecked with brown, like those of a doe. I felt very weak. Behind her I made out Paladon and Aziz. They were examining my satchel. 'That's very odd,' I heard Paladon say. 'Why should he fill his bag with flowers and stones?'

'You can ask him. He's awake,' said Ayesha. She patted my shoulder to encourage me. 'Go on. Tell them. They won't hurt you.'

'They're for my alchemy,' I muttered. 'I make medicines.'

Paladon and Aziz exchanged a glance. It seemed that unspoken thoughts were passing between them. Aziz walked over and squatted beside me. 'Who are you?' he asked gently.

I saw only sympathy in his eyes. 'I'm a student at the rabbi's school.'

'And they teach you alchemy and astronomy there? We've found your astrolabe, by the way.'

'No, I study those things in my spare time. It's a hobby.'

'A hobby?' repeated Aziz, raising his beautiful eyebrows.

I nodded. I had a strange desire to run my finger down his cheek.

'And you know about the Banu Musa? And how to calculate the circumference of the earth?'

'Yes, but the Banu Musa were wrong,' I said. 'And so were the Greeks. They didn't take into account the movement of the celestial sphere on which the Polar Star rests so you should add another thousand miles to the calculation. Or nearly that. I haven't worked it out exactly. I lack proper tools. I had to make my own observation instruments, and they're crude, like my astrolabe.'

'You made that astrolabe? How old are you?'

I told him. He shook his head in wonder. 'You and I were born in the same year, yet you know so much.' The pools of his eyes were glistening like heated oil. I wanted to lose myself in them.

Paladon had dropped my satchel and was also crouching beside me. He and Aziz exchanged another glance, full of meaning. Aziz nodded.

'Samuel,' said Paladon, 'if that is your name – it's inked on to your satchel – Aziz and I think you're an extraordinary find. You're wasted in your little Jewish school, and you should join our academy. It's only an academy of two at the moment, but you can make three. If you're interested, of course. If your mind's not set on becoming a rabbi.'

'That's the last thing I want to be,' I said, with a passion and clarity I had never felt before.

Paladon and Aziz laughed, and Ayesha continued to bathe my forehead. She smiled at me, and when the two young men were out of earshot, she whispered, 'I think you were very brave, and Aziz thinks you're very handsome. I'm so pleased you've agreed to come and live in my father's home.' Then she leaned forward confidentially. 'You mustn't be afraid of Paladon. All my family think he's wonderful. And so do I.' Her last words were indistinct. A breath or a sigh, blown on the breeze.

And that was when I realised what I'd agreed to, and what sort of new world awaited me and how my life had been transformed, like antimony, into a seed of gold.

(III) *In which I tell how a Jew was educated among princes and how a neo-Platonist and a Sufi took two youths to heaven*

The man hired by Wazir Salim to be his son's tutor was a philosopher who had originally studied in Cairo called Da'ud ibn Sa'id.

He was the most unlikely-looking philosopher I had ever seen. He was enormously fat and his round, myopic face under a huge pink turban was fringed by a beard dyed with henna. Furthermore he was fundamentally idle, taking at least four naps a day and spending the rest of his time lounging on cushions and dipping unleavened bread into lentils, munching fruit or gorging himself on confectionery – but he was immensely learned, an Aristotelian of the school of ibn Sina, and he was also a syncretist, who had read and admired the works of the neo-Platonist physician and sage al-Razi. Ibn Sa'id's ambition was to write a work of philosophy that would reconcile the two canons of learning. Unfortunately, what with the naps and the confectionery, his great project had foundered because there were only so many hours in the day – and, in any case, he had to conserve whatever energy he could spare in the intervals between his sybaritic pursuits to educate Aziz, Paladon and, from now on, me.

He accepted me from the day that Paladon and Aziz had found me in the fig tree. I had accompanied them for the rest of their experiment: I sat on the palfrey because I was still weak from my fall. Ayesha tripped ahead with the reins, while the boys continued to haul their rope. Towards evening we came to a circle of gaily coloured tents, in one of which, chewing melon seeds for want of anything more nourishing, sat ibn Sa'id. He listened carefully as I explained my methods of calculation, and in the first hour of morning, when the Pole Star was visible, he tested my theories, nodding gravely.

'Well?' asked Aziz, eagerly. 'Is he correct?'

'His method of calculation is ingenious, but we will have to prove it further when we can consult the ancillary spheres and the mathematical tables in your father's house.'

'But can he join us? Study with us?' Aziz was more excited than I was.

'Oh, yes,' said ibn Sa'id, distractedly, his attention directed towards the shanks of a deer that two servants were carrying towards the blazing fire. 'He's a very clever boy.'

After we returned to the city, I had one more interview, a hard one because Wazir Salim tested me more severely than had ibn Sa'id. I could read nothing in his long, melancholy features and came out of the divan sweating. I sat miserably on the edge of the fountain in the courtyard, resigned to returning to my family, until Aziz, his eyes blazing, came to find me. 'He likes you,' he said. 'He likes you,' and he kissed me. That was the first time.

I doubt our neighbourhood had ever seen anything like it. When Wazir Salim went abroad, he did so in the full dignity of his office. There were trumpeters and drummers to announce his coming, followed by a detachment of cavalry, their long red cloaks bringing an air of martial splendour even to our little alleys. Four Nubian slaves, the skin of their bare torsos oiled, carried the silken canopy above the wazir's head. He walked because, being a valetudinarian, he liked the exercise, but Aziz, Paladon and I (in my new cream jellaba, with an Arab muslin headdress flapping about my face) were mounted on white horses behind him. A company of infantry followed us, their long mail hauberks jingling as they brushed the ground, their spears slanted on their shoulders, each with a pennant tied near the point.

And the purpose of this show? Wazir Salim, a punctilious and courteous man, felt it only correct that he should come in person to ask my parents' permission for their son to enter his household.

What did they feel, my mother and father, when they saw the ruler of the city, the heir to the throne, bowing at their door, while our neighbours hung out of every upstairs window to watch? I did not think about it at the time, so intoxicated was I with Aziz, so in awe of Paladon, so drunken with pride and arrogance in my new splendour – but I have thought about it often since. I imagine, when they understood I would be leaving them – how could they refuse a request from the wazir when he sat at our kitchen table? – that their hearts were breaking behind their strained smiles.

Meanwhile Paladon and Aziz were clattering behind me down the worn stone stairs to the cellar, for I had told them about my alchemical laboratory. Even Paladon was silent when he saw the extent of it. 'We shall take all of this,' he said, after a long pause, during which he had stared, open-jawed, at my arrays of pipes and retorts. 'This is better than ibn Sa'id has.'

And then – only then and for just a moment – I thought of my father, the hours we had spent in the pig pen together, he pestling or carrying wood, eyes gleaming with joy as he watched my potions bubble or observed my tinctures emerge out of the condensation, shaking his head in wonder as he contemplated his brilliant son. 'Can we not leave it all here?' I asked. 'We can surely buy new pipes, better ones?'

'That is up to you, Samuel.' Paladon shrugged. 'It seems a shame to leave it, though.'

'It's just that my father likes to experiment,' I said, knowing in my heart that he never would again.

'You made this?' Aziz was running his slim hand over my ancillary sphere. It was fashioned from wood, but serviceable – the proportions were correct. I was proud of it. He flashed me a shy smile, and I forgot my father as I basked in his approval.

My mother was fussing over a box of my clothes, remembering new items to put in while one of the Nubians waited patiently, and the wazir seemed to be studying with interest the shape of the beams. 'Your prayer cloth – how could I have forgotten your prayer cloth?' (When we returned to his house, Aziz gave the box to the kitchen slaves. I never saw it again.)

The last thing my father did before he embraced me, tears running down his old, worn face, was to thrust his little pile of astrology books into my hands. 'You'll need these,' he said, sounding the more tragic because he was trying so hard to be cheerful. 'You'll be studying diligently, because that's the sort of boy you are, and they may be useful.'

I took them, thinking of Salim's enormous library where I had been that morning. I never opened them again – not while I had the complete commentaries on the Tetrabiblos of Ptolemy by Abu-Ma'shar, al-Qabisi and Abi I-Rijal to study whenever I wanted – but something stopped me throwing those worthless volumes away. I kept them until only recently. They were the last of the possessions I burned to keep off the cold this winter, hiding in this cave. I felt my father's shade, and that of Elijah, watching me sadly when I did so. On that day, though, I merely handed the parcel blithely to a slave, before I gave my parents one last casual embrace. I did not look behind me after I had mounted my horse. I was concentrating too hard on keeping up with Paladon and Aziz.

The next two years passed like a delightful dream, for truly I was in Paradise.

Naturally I loved the learning. Each morning we would sit in a circle on the carpets in the library while our teacher lolled on a cushion. If it was a sunny day we would recline in the orchard under the shade of the orange trees. We had each our little pile of Córdoba parchment, and would take notes with peacock-feather pens while ibn Sa'id read sonorously from whatever tome he had chosen from the library, be it geometry or physics, astrology or natural philosophy. Then, as time approached for his mid-morning nap, he would set us exercises. They were easy enough for me, because there was little in the lessons that I had not already mastered on my own, but I took delight in helping Aziz, who, though eager and curious, was no natural scholar. Paladon's mind was as sharp as the awls he used in his masonry, and his memory was exhaustive. In practical geometry, he could make calculations faster than I. A good-natured rivalry developed between us – well, it was good-natured on my part. For him, though, competition was serious. He had the sort of temperament that made him fret if unchallenged for too long.

Sometimes we would spend the mornings in ibn Sa'id's well-equipped laboratory. There, I was in my element and before long, since the courses were simple alchemy and basic medicinal theory that I had learned when I was twelve, the philosopher began to treat me as an assistant, and then as an alternative teacher, and finally the only teacher because he saw the opportunity for longer naps and more prolonged snacks. Paladon and Aziz did not mind. I took the courses faster, and after a while extended the curriculum into the arcane, which fascinated them. That was the beginning of what later developed into our Brotherhood of the Craft. Sometimes, when we were way ahead of our work, we put aside alchemy, and then it was Paladon's turn to teach, for he was as advanced in the art of masonry and building science as I was in my chosen fields. I had something to add to his knowledge, however, because I knew from my alchemy the metaphysical qualities of the stones and metals that builders use as materials. So, we taught each other, and our relationship developed beyond friendship into mutual respect. Both of us helped Aziz, and by the end of the first year, he had successfully transmuted his first metal and had achieved the first degree of masonry, while I was already on the second.

Yet it was not the formal lessons I looked forward to but the long, free afternoons in the library, exploring at my leisure the vast collection of books that Salim had accumulated over the years. To me he seemed to possess everything ever written. There were the complete works of Aristotle and Plato, in the original translations of Hunayn ibn Ishaq; al-Farabi's *Catalogue of Sciences* (ibn Sa'id preferred ibn Sina's reclassifications: he had met the great man once in Bukhara and was still dazzled by him, but I thought al-Farabi's was the greater work and used it more); there was Ptolemy's *Almagest* in the original, as well as Thabit ibn Qurra's and al-Farghani's astronomical

compendia (I had dreamed of one day beholding these books
when I lay with my father on the roof looking up at the stars
– and here they were); there were the original manuscripts (how
had Salim acquired them?) containing all the complicated mathematical equations of Musa al-Khuwarizmi (after whom the
algorithm was named), there were . . . But I must stop, or this
memoir will turn into another great catalogue similar to that
of al-Farabi himself! Suffice to say, my wonder and joy were
probably comparable to Adam's when he first opened his eyes
in the Garden of Eden.

I had all this time on my own because when the wazir had
broached the idea that Paladon should become Aziz's
companion, the contract he signed with Toscanus stipulated
that every day after the midday meal Paladon should return to
his father's place of work to continue his apprenticeship. He
would return at nightfall when building ceased. Aziz's afternoons were anyway occupied with learning those other skills
necessary for a boy destined to be a ruler. They included the
arts of war – horsemanship, hunting, archery, jousting and
swordplay – and a thorough immersion in Qur'ānic law,
because his father had decided that he would take over from
him as qadi on his majority. Aziz would often, therefore, accompany Salim when he held court. He would be called away, even
from our morning lessons, when the wazir or the king received
ambassadors. Diplomacy is, after all, the secret of kingship,
and there is nothing like observing it in action, especially when
practised by somebody as subtle as Salim. And every evening,
whatever he had been doing for the rest of the day, poor Aziz
had to remain in the mosque after prayers, so he could be given
an hour's tuition by the chief faqi in the teachings of the
Qur'ān. The Mussulman kings of our day rarely exemplified
the virtues of Muhammad – ours certainly didn't – but they
had to know the vocabulary and appear devout in public, or
the Umma, their people, might become upset. Then riots would
erupt and dynasties fall. I would make sure when he returned

from those sessions that I greeted him with a goblet of wine, served by the handsomest of our retainers, having ordered the slaves to prepare a couch for him by the fountain where the tinkle of the water would be soothing to his ears.

One day, about six months after I had arrived in Salim's house, ibn Sa'id came into the library. He peered over my shoulder. I was reading Galen's correlation of the four humours and how they interacted between various parts of the body. 'Very good,' he muttered. 'Very good indeed.' He cleared his throat. 'Samuel, I'd like a word with you in my study.'

I followed his spherical mass as it rolled out of the library. He lowered himself on to his cushions, puffing, then waved a hand at his little table, which, as usual, was covered with dishes. 'Be a good fellow and pour some of that goat's milk over the strawberries and, yes, sprinkle a little sherbet on it. That'll be very nice. Thank you. Would you like some?'

I demurred, wondering what he had to say to me.

'I was having a talk with the wazir the other day,' he said, between spoonfuls. 'He's a little worried about you.' He paused to catch a drip of sugared goat's milk as it ran down his beard. I felt a susurration of alarm trickle down my spine. A week before I had moved my chest containing all my new clothes and jewels into Aziz's room. I feared he was about to tell me that the wazir disapproved. A prince having a Jew as a friend was one thing, but an acknowledged lover was something else.

'Yes,' he continued. 'He's worried about your relationship with Aziz. Are you sure you wouldn't like some strawberries? They're excellent. First of the season.'

'Have I offended the wazir in some way?' I could barely articulate the words.

Ibn Sa'id exploded with laughter, milk and strawberries flying everywhere. 'Certainly not. On the contrary, he is tremendously impressed by your achievements and the good influence you are having on his son. He's worried that you might want to leave our little academy.'

I froze in the act of mopping milk from the carpet. 'Leave?' It was as if the Archangel Michael had suddenly decided to expel me from heaven. 'But why? Why?' I was near tears.

'Oh, not now. In a few months, or a year, when you get bored. You're so knowledgeable already that he imagines it must be tedious for you to keep pace with our pedestrian lessons. He thinks you might go off to one of the proper academies in Kairawan or Cairo. They'd take you in the blink of an eye, you know. It's where you should be. You're a prodigy. Yes. Be a dear fellow and pour me a glass of that wine now, would you? Thank you.' He drank it, then lifted his big behind and farted. 'That's better. What was I saying? Yes. A prodigy. He's asked me to direct your studies on to wider things – in your spare time, of course.'

'What sort of things?' I was in a state of shock, comprised of bewilderment and relief.

'Well, take that Galen you were looking at. That's one of a total of sixteen books. Some we don't have, but the wazir has ordered a merchant travelling to Kairawan to buy the others. Dioscorides' plant catalogues, for example, and *The Aphorisms of Hippocrates*. You'll need those. Then there's al-Razi's *Comprehensive Book*. That's essential, and I have every volume here. I brought my own set from Cairo for my treatise, but you are welcome to consult it. Then there are al-Mashi's *Hundred Books*. And al-Majusi. Can't overlook him. And ibn Sina's canon. Marvellous work. Marvellous. I know it by heart. What else? Al-Jurjani's *Treasure*, perhaps? They're the basics, and they're in the library. So all I need to do is structure a course for you, and we can begin. No more floating round the bookshelves like a butterfly. Something more directed towards a future career. What do you say?'

'They're all medical works,' I stuttered.

'Of course. We shall turn you into a proper doctor. That's what you were born to be. Well, I suppose you consider yourself to be one already, what with your astrology and potions, but you're really only an amateur, a bit of a mountebank, aren't you? Yes. I shall make you into the real thing, and in return you can continue the good work you're doing in the mornings, helping Aziz with his studies. That will make the wazir very happy. Is that settled? We'll start tomorrow afternoon, shall we? I've talked to Dr Isa at the hospital and he's quite content for you to go along there to learn the practical side. Leeching. Moxibustion. Phrenology. Draining out the bad humours. Examining bodies. That sort of thing. After you know your al-Razi, of course. Now, please, before I finish these delicious strawberries, can I not persuade you to try some?'

And that was how I was given a career – but I never stopped being a butterfly, when ibn Sa'id was having one of his naps and I had the library to myself. There were too many treasures to ignore: by now, I was developing other interests, and there was valuable material on those shelves, which helped me when I was giving my secret lessons to Paladon and Aziz even before we had formally established our brotherhood.

As I said, those two years passed like a dream. So far I have only described our academic studies, but there were all the other things we did as well. We followed the parades, whether the festival was Mussulman, Christian or Jewish. A holiday for one part of our community was a holiday for all, despite the differences of religion. That was what Mishkhat was like. We always tried to partake in the feasts. Paladon was after women, who were likely to be more amenable after the wine. Aziz and I just enjoyed the atmosphere.

At other times we went hunting – not the complicated affairs involving armies of beaters and cavalry that constituted Aziz's formal education, just the usual pursuits of youths in the glow of health escaping the schoolroom for the countryside. We went after rabbits or partridges, and sometimes fox. Paladon taught us how to use a sling.

Within the city, after curfew, we became adept at avoiding

the night watchmen and climbed buildings, once the mosque itself, Aziz and I tottering behind Paladon on the ledges while he looked over his shoulder impatiently. He was a natural steeplejack – it was, after all, his profession. How I envied his daring and his wicked humour. He was unquestionably our leader. It was his idea to climb the walls of the *madrasah* to steal the chief faqi's jewelled turban. Paladon slid through the window and snatched it from a shelf, while the oblivious old man grunted over one of his students behind his bed curtain. On another occasion we crept into the harem of a merchant's house. Aziz and I kept watch as Paladon disported with a slave girl whom he had seen making eyes at him from a balcony. If he had been caught, the consequences would have been serious: he was a Christian. Fear, however, was never part of his makeup. He loved a challenge.

In the early days, Ayesha would accompany us on some of our jaunts, but after she began to menstruate she was secluded, as was the custom. We were still allowed to visit her in that part of the harem where Paladon and I, now considered members of the family, were sometimes allowed. Paladon and she continued their teasing relationship and I delighted in her company too, because she had been my friend from the moment she had bathed my head after my fall. It is perhaps those evenings with her that I remember most fondly. Then we three boys talked and talked, about everything under the sun, while Ayesha played her musical instruments or sang to us.

Best of all, however, were Salim's banquets. Being the man he was, the wazir's tastes were primarily intellectual, and we sat on the carpets listening in wonder to the discussions of the luminaries who attended. It sometimes seemed we were transported back in time, to the House of Wisdom of Caliph Ma'mun in Baghdad, or the Madinat al-Zahra of abd al-Rahman III. I will not even try to list the many poets, philosophers and statesmen who came as his guests. I would be cataloguing again.

I will just recall one night, which was representative and perhaps, in the light of what later transpired, significant. It was when the famous Sufi al-Gazali came to Andaluz, pausing in Mishkhat, at Salim's invitation. On the first evening he recited his mystical poetry, and we were entranced, because he was describing God in terms of a lover. Aziz and I held hands as we listened, and our bodies edged closer together, for we had always felt there was something spiritual about our love for each other, and these passionate verses seemed only to confirm what we already knew.

On the next night, al-Gazali and ibn Sa'id held a debate, in which al-Gazali inveighed against Aristotelianism, neo-Platonism and the natural sciences and ibn Sa'id defended them. Al-Gazali, displaying all the understanding of the sciences that he had mastered in his past existence as the leading scholar of the Mu'tazilah school of philosophy, which sought to reconcile the new learning with Islam, argued now from his new Sufi standpoint that there can be no knowledge of God but surrender of one's soul to His contemplation, abandoning intellect in favour of the communion of the spirit. Never had I heard such subtle or persuasive arguments. Here was Reason being employed in an attack on Reason. Paladon, Aziz and I were hypnotised by his power and conviction, seduced by the tanned, hawk-like visage, the ascetic fire in his eyes and the sheer beauty of al-Gazali's Arabic. Meanwhile the jelly-like ibn Sa'id reclined on his cushion and munched dates.

Then he wobbled to his feet and began to speak. We expected a polite and half-hearted rebuttal for form's sake and in honour of the wazir's guest, but instead, and after only a moment, we saw that he was no longer the rumpled teacher we knew. By some strange transmutation he had become a stern philosopher, an Aristotle, a Socrates, a Hermes Trismegistus with the knowledge of the universe at his fingertips. I can see him now, silhouetted against the fire, its light flickering on the bearded faces of the guests listening intently on their carpets, Salim with a wry smile, al-Gazali stony-faced, as he attempted to hide his surprise and mortification that anybody dared challenge him.

Coldly and clinically ibn Sa'id summarised the learning of our generation, starting with our knowledge of plants and animals and leading to a description of the heavenly spheres. He did not waste a word. He spoke matter-of-factly, but the effect was as seductive as the Sufi's rhetoric, for in the space of a few minutes he had created a vision of a cosmos linked through the humours and stars, all minutely and encyclopedically observed by man, and this he correlated with the indefinable essence of the Prime Mover. Then he turned al-Gazali's arguments on their head by demonstrating that any communion with God, even a limited understanding of God, could only be achieved by the rational intellect that God has given to us and by no other means, for only through the ingenuity of the mind can we penetrate to the hidden causes. In fact, he said, it would be blasphemous for man to reject the mental powers he had been granted, for those are the tools that God in His Grace has given him to observe the creation in which true divinity is reflected, and thus to be capable of worshipping Him. Seek God in mathematics, he said, for therein perfection lies. Let rapture and sexual ecstasy, to which al-Gazali seemed to compare his revelations, be left in the harem where they are appropriate. He would rather discover God in the laboratory, where truth can be ascertained through logic rather than intoxication. Then he imitated al-Gazali's technique by using the weapons of Theology to defeat Theology, rebutting every quotation that al-Gazali had made from the Qur'ān with another saying of the Prophet that seemed to imply the opposite. It was a titanic performance, which he ended with a jest, calling for a flagon of wine. He proposed to drink, he said, to the point of insensibility. By so doing, he added, he might have a better appreciation of al-Gazali's woolly thinking.

The evening ended with laughter, after Salim had said a few conciliatory words, praising both speakers, but we could see from al-Gazali's expression that he was insulted and enraged. Ibn Sa'id's last gibe had, perhaps, particularly galled him. Al-Gazali had ostentatiously refused the wine that Salim liberally served. In a country where vines grew in abundance there were few Andaluzis, particularly among the better classes, who were not partial to the grape – and this applied even to many Mussulmans, who observed the strictures of the Qur'ān in public: most toped happily at home or in private company. A man as devout as Salim might personally be abstemious (it was in his nature to be so) but he would have considered it the worst form of discourtesy not to indulge the pleasures of his guests. Such was the tolerance to be found in Mishkhat in those days – and it was clearly abhorrent to al-Gazali. He left the next morning, and later we heard he had returned to Africa and taken residence in one of the Berber kingdoms.

It had been an inspiring debate, however, and fuelled our own discussions over the following weeks, for we had not been entirely persuaded by ibn Sa'id, despite his splendid performance. We believed that mysticism and science were not irreconcilable. Even in our limited experiments with the arcane, we had come across phenomena that defied logic. What had left a chill, though, was the Sufi's fanaticism, which we had glimpsed in his eyes as he threw his shawl angrily over his face when he departed. We did not know it then but it was a sign of things to come. It had seemed only a momentary disturbance of the limpid air of a summer night. How could we imagine that in our lifetimes it might blow into a freezing gale from the north, to be answered by howling winds from Africa? If we had known, we would only have laughed, confident that our invincible intelligence would be enough to solve every mystery the universe had to offer, even the irreconcilable ones. After all, we were young and, being young, invulnerable.

The guests kissed Salim's hand in farewell. The courtiers

dispersed, and we made our way to Ayesha's quarters. There, on her balcony, lulled by wine, washed under the torpor of the stars by the scent of the orange trees, we watched the fire crackling in the courtyard and listened as Ayesha strummed soft tunes on her zither, her nightingale voice lilting in the melodies of haunting love songs, many of which she had written herself. Aziz and I, reclining on the couch, smiled at Paladon's stiff-faced attempt to persuade himself and us that he was charmed only by the music and not by the beautiful musician, and Ayesha's pretence that she was rehearsing ballads she had composed for her class, that the words were not directed at anybody in particular, certainly not at the big, sullen Christian sitting at her feet.

Aziz and I moved closer. He rested his head on my shoulder, and we relaxed in the sensuality of the perfumed chamber. Just as his face raised itself closer to mine, the night watchmen extinguished the lamps outside the walls of the mansion. The radiance of the stars washed the courtyard in silver, promising joy to come and freedom from care, and, yes, ecstasy, much as al-Gazali had described in his poems the night before.

Back in our room, we feasted like gods on each other's bodies, devouring each other with kisses. Our quivering flesh became perfumed ambrosia under our tongues, and we tasted nectar in the sweat moistening our hair and skin. When I entered Aziz or he entered me, the transubstantiation was complete. The seed we spilled burned like celestial fire. We had often joked that Aziz was Mars to my Venus. That night when I felt his cheeks scalding mine in the heat of his passion, or when I transported him by the power that had come over me and he shouted his joy, we were no longer two separate entities yearning for each other, like two planets condemned by immutable Fate always to be apart. We broke the restraints of mortality. We defied the stars. Our souls conjoined, and our tangled limbs on the bed coalesced into a universe born anew. He and I, and

God, and the cosmos, and every divine spark in every plant and tree and mineral were united and one.

That sweet blasphemy was his, not mine, for afterwards, mortal again, exhausted by the bliss we had shared, those were the first words he said to me: 'It's what you've always told me, isn't it? About the Prime Mover being inside us. That's the mystery we've just experienced.'

I smiled with pride as well as pleasure, for I was as much his teacher as his friend and lover. In the dawn light that was seeping through the curtains, I watched the exhilaration in his features as he leaned over me. 'Samuel, Samuel,' he muttered, and his tongue tingled on my chest, running down my belly to my loins. Under its soft caress, I began to stir again. He looked up once. 'It's you, isn't it?' he said, his eyes blazing. 'It's you. God's in *you*.'

'In us,' I murmured, rolling over him to find my place between his hips.

Later, naked in each other's arms, we lay comforted by the smooth touch of each other's skin. Our eyes, those shining reflectors of our hearts, gazed into each other's depths, as if by keeping that link, we might retain for a while longer the spiritual union we had just shared.

'Samuel, my Samuel,' he murmured, 'you will never leave me, will you? My heart would break if you did.'

I kissed him. 'Never, as I long as I breathe.'

'No, nor I you,' he whispered, his lips pressing each of my eyes in turn. 'With you I'm whole. Without you I'm . . . nothing. Oh, I love you, how I love you. Every hollow in your body and every muscle in every limb. Every curl of your hair. You're so beautiful, so beautiful.'

He hugged me, pressing his head against my chest while my arms circled his shoulders. 'I knew I was right to pick you as my lover. From the moment I saw you I realised you were the one.'

'When you kissed me by the fountain, I thought an angel had taken me to Paradise.'

'I was longing to ravish you even on that first day by the fig tree,' cried Aziz. 'And I *was* right, because I found you loved me too and now we'll be together always. Always,' he shouted, in exultation. 'Because we're one!'

The sound disturbed one of Salim's white doves, which had perched on the windowsill outside. Its wings flapped like my fluttering heart.

I had never known such happiness.

My Gazelle, with whom I shared an eternity of Paradise, in every second of every minute of every hour of every day of each of those two years, each a lifetime in itself, and in whose arms I died each evening to be woken to a new world at dawn, what has become of you? Where are you now?

My lamp is sputtering. There are only a few barrels of oil left. I cannot linger at this point of my story, even if it is here that my soul wishes to rest. I must write about the arrival of the Cid. That was the first disruption of our easy existence. It was when we went to war.

Codex II

The Idiot of God

(I) In which I tell how a scholar met a paladin and how a lover became a prince

It was an autumn afternoon like any other. Chill rains had puddled the courtyard, and the gardeners were sweeping yellow leaves from the fountain. I could hear them gossiping with the washerwomen, who were taking advantage of a patch of pale sunshine to hang out their sheets. Through the smoky panes of the library windows, I could see the tops of the cypress trees swaying in the wind, and I was grateful for the charcoal in the brazier. I was idling, indulging in a moment of melancholy, half wondering how I could translate my feelings into a poem for Aziz.

When one of Salim's Nubian slaves summoned me to the divan, I had no idea that Fortune had sprung one of her momentous surprises. I merely assumed the wazir required my medical services – for some weeks, at ibn Sa'id's recommendation, I had been treating him for chronic back pains. I sighed, because my pleasant reverie had been interrupted, picked up my bag of moxibustion bottles and ointments and made my way leisurely to his living quarters.

I was startled to find Paladon in the antechamber. He was wearing a workman's smock and his cheeks and hair were powdered with dust. He, too, had been plucked away from his usual activities by a Nubian slave. There was a brittle note behind his forced cheeriness. 'I was lying on the scaffolding, carving an archangel on one of the apses in that new church I told you about, when suddenly I saw this great fellow in court robes grinning at me from the top of the ladder.' He flashed his teeth, imitating the African's accent. 'Boy, the master's calling for you. You'd better take them wings of angels you're constructin' so fine there and fly to the palace as quick as a djinn.' He shrugged. 'So here I am.'

'What's it about?'

'I haven't any idea. It must be serious, though. I was escorted here by a troop of cavalry.'

We had no time to speculate further, because the curtain lifted, and Salim's secretary ushered us inside.

The wazir was sitting stiffly in a high-backed chair, examining a letter. He was dressed in the austere robes he wore on formal court occasions. Aziz, cross-legged on the carpet in front of him, half smiled when we squatted beside him. What caught our attention was the grizzled old veteran standing at Salim's elbow. He wore full armour and was holding a helmet under one arm. He was blind in one eye and a jagged white scar ran down his sunburned cheek to his chin. Of course I knew him. Who in Mishkhat didn't? He was General Abu Bakhr, commander of the king's armies.

Salim greeted us with a melancholy nod. 'Thank you for arriving promptly. I will come straight to the point. The Toledans have declared war on us. I have just returned from the palace. The king concurs with me that this time we have no choice but to fight.'

Paladon and I glanced at each other. The wazir had never involved us in a discussion of politics, let alone military matters, before.

'But the Toledans are in no condition to threaten us, Father,' said Aziz. 'Their king, al-Qadir, was ousted by his own people last year and Toledo is in disarray.'

'If you hadn't been dozing during the king's audiences, Aziz, you would know that al-Qadir was reinstalled on his throne three months ago.'

'I'm sorry, Father,' said the chastened Aziz, 'but I don't understand. Why are they suddenly declaring war? Our only quarrel with them concerns that little border castle you built to protect the passes. But you always told me it was a minor issue that could be handled through diplomacy.'

'So it might have been if al-Qadir had regained his kingdom on his own, but he was helped by a Christian army that bombarded the city with mangonels. And this is why I am worried. For the first time since the Caliphate fell the Christians have interfered openly in the internal politics of Andaluz. It also means that the Castilian king, Alfonso, has a puppet Mussulman as his vassal. Ostensibly we are being attacked by the Toledans, but Castile is stirring the pot. This is no longer an insignificant border dispute.'

We stared at him in silence. Behind Salim, Abu Bakhr was scowling. His one good eye seemed to revolve belligerently in its socket. The wazir sighed. 'The greater war that I have always feared is upon us. The enemies of Islam are growing in confidence.'

'But surely the Christians are not strong enough to harm us,' said Aziz. 'Their little kingdoms are impoverished. Al-Andaluz is rich with powerful armies.'

Salim shook his head in exasperation. 'Have you listened to nothing I've ever told you? Understand this, all of you. What was once al-Andaluz no longer exists. Since the Caliphate fell, we've been reduced to a motley set of kingdoms, warring on each other for petty profit. None of us individually can match Castile's force of arms. Our disunity is our weakness, and the Christians know it. Fifteen years ago Alfonso's father, Ferdinand, shocked all of Islam when he annexed Coimbra. It was the first time in three hundred years that Mussulmans lost any territory to Christians. We don't speak of it for shame.

Nor do we like to remember that the same year a group of Norman brigands, terming themselves "crusaders", blessed by the Roman Church, and with Ferdinand's connivance, crossed the mountains from Gaul and seized the city of Barbastro. They left with their booty but not before they had burned the mosques, slaughtered the men and packed the Mussulman women they had violated into boats to sell in the slave bazaars of Byzantium. It was disgraceful but it happened. We let it happen.'

There was no disguising the emotion and disgust in his tone. 'I had only just been appointed wazir but, inexperienced as I was, I saw the signs of things to come, and so did King Abu. No other king did. Instead of uniting against the Christian menace, as my uncle and I were urging, our proud neighbours did nothing. Worse, they agreed to pay the tributes Ferdinand demanded. One act of violence was apparently enough to make timid kings throughout Andaluz pay their monthly dues.'

He snorted and sipped water from his goblet. We must have looked as uncomfortable as we felt, especially Paladon, who was rubbing his hands as he always did when he was distressed. 'Paladon, I am not damning all Christians,' said Salim, in a more conciliatory tone. 'Those in Mishkhat are loyal and your father is my friend, but this is a crisis and as statesmen we must confront it.'

His mood became even more sombre. 'I had hoped that time was on our side after Ferdinand's death, when his sons fought for the succession and engulfed Castile in civil war – but, despite King Abu's and my pleadings, the other rulers in Andaluz failed to appreciate that this was an opportunity to rid ourselves of the Christians for good. Well, it is too late now because this new king of Castile, Alfonso, has reunited his kingdom, and proved to be even more formidable and devious than his father. The first thing he did was to revive the tributes – and our kings acquiesced without him even having to mobilise his armies.'

He banged his fist on the arm of his chair. 'Not us, by God.

Mishkhat will never pay an ounce of gold while my uncle is on the throne and I am his wazir.' He sipped again, angrily, before he continued. 'Last winter, my spies reported Alfonso's boast that he would play the Mussulman kingdoms off against one another. When the time was ripe, he told his knights, we would fall like apples into his hand. I made sure the other kings heard about this, but they laughed in my ambassadors' faces. Now Alfonso has begun to put his policy into action. His creature, al-Qadir, is weak, corrupt and terrified of his own people. He will do anything his new master wants.'

He waved a hand at Abu Bakhr. 'Tell them.'

'Yes, lord,' said the old man gruffly. 'Well, Prince Aziz, you've heard your father. Alfonso's coerced al-Qadir – may he burn in the land of Iblis – to wage war on us. We had his ultimatum last week. That in itself would be little to worry about. Prince Salim and I have seen off Toledan dogs before. But al-Qadir's made a pact with our eastern neighbour, the king of Almería, who has also long been eyeing our territory. So now we have two armies marching against us. That's why the wazir has called on his long-standing friendship with King Mu'tamin of Saragossa, who's agreed to send his forces to help us.'

'Albeit with a mercenary in command,' murmured Salim. 'And a Christian one at that. Mu'tamin should have come himself.'

'Oh, I can vouch for their commander, my lord,' said Abu Bakhr. 'There's no better soldier in all Spain. You boys may even have heard of Rodrigo de Bibar. He's better known as al-Sidhi or, as the Christians call him, the Cid.'

I sensed Paladon stiffening beside me, and even Aziz had an excited gleam in his eye. Of course we had heard of the Cid. His heroic victories, his valour, his nobility were legendary throughout Andaluz. Although for years now he had fought for Mussulmans, Paladon hero-worshipped him. Only a few months before, to Ayesha's annoyance, he had read to us an epic poem in the Romance language about his exploits.

Both the wazir and the general were smiling. 'You were right, old friend,' said Salim. 'They are as dazzled as you told me they would be. Go on, tell them the rest.'

Abu Bakhr rested his hands on his hips. His one eye twinkled fiercely. 'I have good news for you, lads. The king's granted permission for you to go to war. Prince Aziz is sixteen and of an age to fight. You others will accompany him as his squires. The major battle will be fought in the north, where the Toledans are besieging our fortress in the mountains. That will be a complicated affair. The Toledans may be reinforced by Castile. Wazir Salim, as our most experienced general, will lead the bulk of our army and smash whoever comes against him. You, Prince Aziz, because you too are a prince of the blood, will be the official commander of our smaller army in the east. The plan is to meet up with the Cid and our Saragossan allies to forestall the Almerians in the passes.'

'When General Abu Bakhr says "official commander", he means nominal commander,' added Salim, firmly. 'I am not having any of you, let alone you, Aziz, risking your lives in battle, and you will only be an observer in the war councils. Abu Bakhr is your guardian. You will obey every order he gives you. He's persuaded me that it will be educational for you to observe the art of war as waged by one of its most skilled practitioners – the Cid – but the condition is that you do so from a distance. Is this understood?'

'Yes, Father,' said Aziz, promptly.

His excitement terrified me.

'Then you will swear it on the Qur'ān. And, Paladon and Samuel, you will swear it on your holy books. You are to make a formal oath, all of you, that you will obey Abu Bakhr and take no action he has not sanctioned.'

Abu Bakhr had the books ready – a Qur'ān, a Christian Bible and a copy of the Torah – and we duly swore. We thought it was the end of the interview, but Salim kept Paladon and me behind and told us, in his quiet, precise manner, that if he later discovered that harm had come to a single hair on Aziz's head because of our foolhardy actions, he would crucify us and our families. He was looking intently at Paladon when he said this. I suspect he had learned about every one of our night-time escapades. Afterwards, he smiled at us in his enigmatic way, stroking his grey beard contemplatively, and Paladon and I left the room shaking, with no doubt that he had meant what he had said.

Our downcast mood lasted only the few moments it took to reach the garden, where Aziz was waiting for us, his face ecstatic. He grabbed our hands, and soon we were doing a little dance around the flowerbeds, the gardeners watching us curiously.

'We're going to war,' Aziz whooped. I had never seen him so intoxicated.

'We'll meet the Cid,' shouted Paladon.

My reservations were swept away by my friends' enthusiasm and, God help me, I whooped too.

For the next few days, while our troops gathered outside the city, there was no more schooling. Instead we prepared ourselves for war. We were measured for our new suits of chain mail (I found mine very scratchy) and scoured the library for accounts of ancient battles. Ibn Sa'id did not protest. Perhaps he saw an opportunity for undisturbed snacks and rest. He only murmured to me, before we departed, 'Wander round the battle-field afterwards, my dear boy. All that butchery. Best lesson in anatomy you'll ever get.'

We spent a last evening with Ayesha, who was in a contrary mood, scolding Paladon for trifles. 'My brother's going to war, which might be the death of him – and all because of your silly hero-worship of the Cid,' she rounded on him. 'How will I live if my Aziz doesn't come back to me?' And she beat at Paladon's breast with her jewelled hands while he stood there stunned and speechless. Eventually she ran out of the room, sobbing. None of us thought she was crying for Aziz. Not even Paladon could maintain the pretence this time. But we did not care. The drums were beating, the trumpets blaring.

Next morning at dawn we rode out of the city gates with a detachment of the palace guard. Townsmen lined the streets to cheer us. An hour later we were at the head of three hundred horsemen, all mailed as we were, jangling past the sedate water mills and neatly tended fields of the Mishkhat plain, following a muddy road that was beckoning us in the direction of battle.

Salim's careful plans for our safety collapsed on the afternoon of the second day. We were waiting while our troops crossed a stream when suddenly a snake coiled and hissed on the ground beside us. All our horses reared, including that of Abu Bakhr, the redoubtable old general who had spent his life in the saddle and was famous on his country estate as a breaker of wild horses. Because of a lapse in concentration, an accident of timing, he lost his balance. There also happened to be a jagged rock half buried in the sand, and when he fell, he landed heavily on it. An inch either way and he would have had a sore back, but it snapped his spine. He was dead before we knew anything had happened. Sheer mischance, a random spin of Fortune's wheel – and Aziz no longer had a guardian.

After we had buried him, leaving a cairn of stones and a flag to mark the place, we suddenly became aware that our troops were looking expectantly at Aziz. As far as the soldiers were concerned he was their commander. The form had become the reality. Aziz's immediate response was to look at Paladon. 'What do I do?' I heard the panic in his whisper and my heart ached for him.

'Be a prince,' said Paladon, coldly. 'Give an order.'

I was never prouder of Aziz than at that moment. I sensed his indecision, his doubt in his abilities and his fear, but he overcame them. He rose in his stirrups and commanded us to advance. Viciously he kicked his spurs into his horse's flanks and led us at a gallop up the hill. It took us some time to catch up with him. We could hear the thunder of three hundred horsemen behind us. Some were cheering.

A day and a half later, just before sunset, Aziz led us in column through the solemn Saragossan ranks that had lined up to meet us. The Cid was standing at the entrance to his tent, surrounded by a forest of flapping pennants.

There was no mistaking him. He was a head taller than anybody else. A scarlet cloak, its edges embroidered with gold tracery, was draped over one side of his hauberk. A gauntleted hand rested on the haft of a double-bladed axe. Behind him an Arab page, dressed in the finest court finery, held his helm on a velvet cushion. The Cid's face was obscured by a white turban, which he had wrapped, Berber-style, round his mouth and chin, but his posture exuded firmness and grandeur. He might have been a mercenary but he held himself in the indo-lent and assured manner of a king. And one of our own kings at that, for there was little of the Frank about him. Discounting his enormous size and the long nose, his appearance was that of Arab nobility, from the tarboosh peeping out of his turban to his curve-toed calfskin boots. The evening light glinted on the golden brooch that held his cloak, and rubies and emer-alds sparkled on the scabbard of his scimitar. He might have been our own King Abu reviewing his troops on his maidan after Ramadan, only the Cid was more magnificent. In our dusty armour and sweat-soaked under-padding we felt like shabby country knights come to a royal court.

Our hearts were thumping with anticipation at the thought that we were about to meet our hero, the Christian warrior, in the noble flesh – but I think that even Aziz, for all his military training, was uneasy at the prospect of sitting down with one of the most experienced tacticians of our age to discuss battle plans. We were uncomfortably aware of our inexperience and youth.

We were also a little scared. Approaching the Cid's camp we had seen the army of Almería darkening the hill opposite. Clearly we had arrived only just in time. The battle would be on the morrow. Without Abu Bakhr beside us, I suspect that we were all secretly relieved to entrust ourselves to the protection and guidance of the Cid, but we also knew that we represented Mishkhat and that Aziz, with responsibility suddenly thrust upon him, had to maintain the dignity of an independent prince.

We dismounted from our horses, trying to maintain the appearance of nonchalance and resolve. Aziz bowed elegantly, with appropriate courtesy but not so low as to diminish his status. I thought I observed a flash of grinning white teeth in the shadow of the Cid's turban, as he dipped his head at exactly the same angle. He rose to his full height and raised an arm. An attendant appeared with two goblets of sherbet on a silver tray. The Cid took one and the attendant proffered the other to Aziz. 'To the alliance of Saragossa and Mishkhat,' he shouted, pitching his deep voice so it could be heard by the assembled ranks. 'And victory tomorrow.'

He drained his goblet before Aziz had a chance to sip. 'Thank God that's over,' he muttered. 'Give me five minutes and join me in my tent.' Then he turned his back on us. 'Welcome,' he called airily, with a casual wave over his shoulder, as he disappeared behind the curtain.

Aziz's eyes were wide with shock. I put my hand on his arm. 'We must not presume discourtesy,' I said. 'This is a soldier's camp. Manners here are probably more informal than at court.'

Paladon was trying to smile. 'He's a bluff soldier, Aziz. That's his reputation. We all know of the noble deeds he's done. We must make allowance. He's – well, he's the Cid,' he ended lamely.

'And I represent the throne of Mishkhat,' said Aziz, softly.

It was in a mood of some discomfort that we entered the Cid's tent. Our first encounter with our paragon had not soothed our growing trepidation (and, in my case, now that I had seen the enemy, fear) and what we found inside did nothing to lessen our concern.

The Cid had already stripped off his mail coat. We saw his bare legs wobbling and stamping while he struggled to get his arms inside the folds of an Arab jellaba. He was cursing the scared servant who was trying to help him. Eventually a long red beard emerged, so prickly and tangled it looked like a thicket of holly from which robins might fly, then the long, aquiline nose, a pair of bushy eyebrows, and, finally, the close-cropped dome of his skull. The contorted features settled into shape, the jellaba straightened to his ankles, and two blood-shot eyes contemplated us blearily, while a gap-toothed mouth opened in a wide grin.

'It was as hot as hell out there waiting for you. Thought I'd get into something more comfortable. Excuse me.' He took a basin of water from the servant and poured it over his head. He shook his great beard, scattering drops in all directions. When he focused on us again, his eyes were slightly clearer, but his voice still had a slurred edge. 'Who are you? I thought some old general was coming to join me, but you're children. You,' he pointed at Aziz, 'you look Arab enough. You must be the wet-eared little prince I've been told to look after. But you,' the finger was shaking at Paladon, 'you appear to be as Christian as I am. You look like a Norman. Are you the bodyguard? God, you're not one of those damned Slav eunuchs, are you? That'd be a woman's loss.' He guffawed, then turned to me. 'You, though,' the finger was wagging, while the fierce eyes contemplated me as if I was an insect, 'damn me if you're not a Jewboy. *Very* rum. Can't be a money-lender. Too young. What are you? The prince's bum-cushion? Pretty little thing, aren't you?' He yawned, his broad chest stretching mightily as he flung back his arms. 'Never mind, never mind. Find yourselves a place on the carpet, and we'll have some wine.'

We looked at each other in further consternation as he

collapsed on to a couch, and the terrible realisation hit us. Our hero, the great general who was going to lead us into battle next day, the legendary Cid, whose name resounded through Andaluz as the paragon of nobility, was an oaf, and drunk to boot.

The next thing we heard was a rustling snore. He had fallen asleep.

'This man has insulted us,' said Aziz, his voice icy with rage. 'We should leave.'

'We can't,' said Paladon. 'We need his troops if we're to defeat Almería.' It was the first time I had ever seen him shamed.

'Paladon, he called you a eunuch, and me a little prince. If my father was here, he would have him beheaded.'

'He called me a catamite,' I said, 'but, Aziz, Paladon is right. Besides, I believe it would be a mistake to judge him so quickly. His words were disparaging, but were they not perceptive? Aziz, you *are* a young prince, and inexperienced. Paladon's no body-guard but he is your sworn friend. And I, well, I *am* your lover, aren't I? I think he knew everything about us already. Salim spies on Saragossa. We can assume that Saragossa also spies on us. How do we know he wasn't testing us? Firing us up to see what sort of reaction there would be? After all, to him, we're an unknown quantity. Perhaps he wants to find out before the battle tomorrow whether we are metals that will snap under pressure.'

We were startled by slow clapping. Turning, we saw that the big, bearded man was grinning at us. With agility and alertness in contrast to the drunken movements we had seen earlier, he raised himself to his full height. A gigantic shadow stretched across the carpet. He strode lightly to where I was squatting and ruffled my hair. All the while his eyes were on Aziz. 'Your Jew's a clever little bugger, isn't he? You're well served by your counsellors, Prince. That's encouraging. We might make some-thing of you after all.' He glanced at me. 'I've heard of you, Samuel, and your magic potions. Yes, we do have competent spies. King Mu'tamin's an experienced statesman. Honourable, too, like your father, Prince. That's why I serve him.'

Aziz was still angry. 'Do mercenaries know of honour? You treated us with disrespect, and you are still patronising me.'

The Cid smiled. 'I consider myself reprimanded.' He stepped back and bowed his head elegantly in the courtly Arab style, again as one ruler to another. Afterwards, he stretched out his hand in the Christian manner. I was willing Aziz to take it, knowing this was the right thing to do. He did, with great dignity. Then Aziz's face broke into a lovely, shy smile, and I relaxed, and so did Paladon, whose hand the Cid was now also shaking. In a moment my own hand was caught in a vice-like grip. The Cid's expression was solemn, but suddenly he winked at me, and I knew at that moment why people followed him.

'While we're being formal, Prince, let me say how sorry I was to hear about the death of General Abu Bakhr. I never met him, but once many years ago, before he went to Mishkhat, we were on opposite sides in a scrap near Valencia, and he handled his wing well. I was looking forward to meeting him because I think we would have been friends.'

'He had a high opinion of you too, al-Sidhi,' said Aziz. 'We grieve his loss deeply.'

I was amazed by Aziz's mastery of the high court style. We had always spoken colloquially. Now I realised that the boy I'd thought I knew had developed another side to him.

The Cid, too, impressed me, and not only because of his mastery of Arabic, which was as fluent as I had ever heard. With a sly smile, proffering a jest in apology for his earlier rudeness, he suddenly quoted Abbas ibn al-Ahnaf's famous love poem, skilfully altering the words to suit the occasion:

> *Give me your hand and let's be friends once more;*
> *And let's jointly curse whoever was wrong.*
> *Please answer my prayer; your reply will cure*
> *My depression. Oh, companion, I send salaams –*
> *As many as the stars, and birds flying.*

Even Aziz could not hide a smile.

I allowed myself to believe that we had been fooled by first appearances. This was no rude soldier, although it suited him on occasion to pretend to be. He was educated and intelligent, completely versed in our culture, and with a charm that he could bring effortlessly to bear in court society as well as the camp. He had easily won me over with a well-timed wink. I could imagine how the bluffness that had offended Aziz would bind to him the hearts of his soldiers.

The great man clapped his hands and sat next to us. Servants appeared, bringing viands, pastries, confectionery, fruit and wine. The centrepiece consisted of two roasted pheasants, stuffed with quails, inside which were wrens – this in an armed camp the day before a battle, with the enemy less than a mile away. Slave girls, fair, dark and brown, with light veils over their lower faces, and wearing hardly any other clothes, knelt beside each of us, offering us silver bowls to wash our fingers, refilling our goblets or serving morsels of food. The Cid reclined on his couch, eating heartily and drinking heavily. In his jellaba and the turban he had donned, he looked more Andaluzi than we did in our mail coats. It struck me again that this was no uncultured knight of the north. Clearly, during his years in Saragossa, he had absorbed our ways. He even belched in the appropriate fashion when he'd seen we had eaten our fill, announcing tactfully that the meal was ended.

We imagined that now would be the time to discuss tactics. Unlike the Cid we had picked at the food and only sipped the wine out of courtesy. We were still dreading the coming fight, but the Cid, after the servants had departed with the dishes, ordered the slave girls to remain behind. They huddled in a corner of the tent, making eyes at us until the servants reappeared with musical instruments. They began to play. Meanwhile the Cid settled into his cushions with a full flagon of wine and his goblet.

'I don't know what I'd do without music,' he murmured, as

we sat in eager, if rather puzzled, anticipation. This was not the strategy session we had envisaged. 'Probably go mad. Or die of boredom.'

'Your musicians are talented,' said Aziz.

'In bed too. I take the brown one usually, fiery creature, just right to wind you up before a battle. A Berber sold her to me, comes from some jungle beyond the great southern desert, but you're welcome to any of the others. The Frankish girl's ingenious, aren't you, my sweet?' He threw the blonde girl a grape, which she caught in one hand while continuing to play her flute with the other. Her eyes creased mischievously in the direction of Paladon. She lowered the flute. For a moment she rolled the grape provocatively between her sharp little teeth before her tongue flicked it quickly to the back of her throat, leaving only her smile, as she raised the flute to her mouth again.

'Al-Sidhi,' said Aziz, softly, 'shall we discuss the battle?'

'What about it?' He was paying us hardly any attention, tapping his fingers to the strum of the lute.

We stared at each other. Aziz seemed lost for words. Paladon, his mind still perhaps half on the girl, spoke nervously. Despite his earlier misgivings, he was still in awe of the Cid. 'We thought you would tell us the battle plan, sir. Your strategy. What instructions to give our men.'

'Battle plan? I'll make up my mind tomorrow when we see how the enemy's deployed. We'll have plenty of time to decide because it'll take them an hour or more to get down from that hillside.' He threw a grape at the lutenist, and laughed when she fumbled the catch.

'That's it?' asked Paladon.

'Well, I can't see that it will be much different from any other scrap. My men will hit them from the left, yours from the right. Or the other way round if you prefer. How many do you have? Three hundred? I've about five. Enemy's no more than nine, a thousand at the most. Half are infantry, whom we can ignore, so the odds are pretty good. I've fought the

Almeríans. They're a rabble. I spent an entire afternoon watching them set up camp. It's all over the place. No discipline, no good generals that I know of, so a single charge of cavalry will probably do the job. Perhaps a little sword and axe work when we've broken them. It'll all be over by lunchtime. We can spend a leisurely afternoon pursuing them. Grab a few prisoners for ransom and some plunder from their baggage train and be back here about sunset. How does that sound as a strategy? Warfare's pretty simple, you know.'

'It sounds a bit too simple,' said Paladon. 'When we studied famous battles of the past before we came here, Cannae, for example, when Hannibal—'

'Hannibal?' The Cid shook his head in derision. 'This is Spain, my lad, not ancient Rome. Tiny states having scraps over trifles, with little armies that are better at running than fighting. We haven't had a proper war since the Caliphate fell, and even then the armies were no more than a few thousand strong. About the size of a couple of Roman legions. Think about it. We haven't enough men to be bothering with tactics. It's head on and let the best man win. God willing, that will be us.'

He drained his glass, and sighed. 'Oh, I've a trick or two up my sleeve. I sent off my seneschal, Fanez, on a march round to the flank with fifty knights who've been with me since my exile from Castile. They're camping somewhere beyond those hills. They'll keep hidden until after the battle starts, so if necessary they can come thundering in if anything goes wrong, but I doubt we'll need them. I'd prefer them to stay fresh so that we can use them to chase the enemy afterwards and bring back more plunder. You'll like Fanez – he'll be at the victory feast tomorrow so you'd better try the Frankish girl tonight, if you want her, because he's enamoured of her and she'll be with him tomorrow. Unless he finds a better one in the enemy baggage train. You never know your luck. You look concerned, young man.'

Paladon's honest features indeed showed how disturbed he was, though I think it was partly because he was still distracted by the flautist, who was winking at him. I took over, guessing the question he wanted to ask. It was on my mind too – after all, we had both been at the meeting with Salim. But the Cid was in expansive mode, and the casualness with which he had described his battle plan disturbed me. I thought it would be better to clarify what he intended before we talked about Aziz. For me – Salim's instructions or no – his safety was paramount.

'With respect, al-Sidhi,' I said, 'I have a question. You used the term "God willing" just now. That surely implies some question about the certainty of victory. Yet you tell us it will be an easy one.'

'It's always "God willing", boy. There are no guarantees one way or the other. The battleground's a place of chaos. Arrows fly in all directions. Pikemen you haven't spotted may creep up on you from behind. Your horse might stumble on a molehill. I saw that happen once. Easiest victory I ever had. It was when I was a lad in Ferdinand's time, and still fought for Castile. We were campaigning against Badajoz, where there were Berbers. Good fighting men. They had a fine general too. Old fellow. Trained in al-Mansur's time. He led their charge. There were two thousand of them against four hundred of us. Hosts of hell bearing down on us. Could have gone either way – but the old man's horse tripped on a molehill as he was nearing our ranks. Down he came a-tumble and the men following him thought he'd perished. They turned, all two thousand of them, and fled. He was just stunned – not like your poor Abu Bakhr – and we ransomed him for a fortune. I used that money to restore my estate.' He sipped his wine. 'Not that I doubted the outcome. I never do.'

'Even against such odds, al-Sidhi?'

He laughed. 'I'm always certain of victory, boy. That's why I'm alive today. You see, when I go into battle I know that God is with me.'

The bald assertion surprised me. It was not in keeping with the rational tone of his earlier conversation. I picked my words carefully. 'Even if God is with you, He is with everybody else as well because He is everywhere and omnipotent, for such is the definition of God. How do you know that He will favour you, rather than anybody else? That today it will not be your horse that stumbles, if that is His will?'

He wagged his finger at me. 'You *are* a clever little bugger, aren't you? A regular little debater.' His face was slightly flushed. I wondered if the drink was getting to him. 'I've a mind to tell you a secret I've only ever told Fanez, and Jimena, my wife, who both understand me. You might, too, because of all that arcane law you study, and because of your capacity to love, which I've seen in the way you look at Aziz.'

Immediately Aziz's face paled and I was shocked, too, that he had mentioned our intimacy, but the Cid continued to smile. 'I'm not sneering at you. I've lived in Arab courts long enough to know of the spiritual qualities that exist in relationships between men and men. I tried a boy once or twice to please an Arab host and didn't enjoy it – but I know from those who've experienced it that love between two men can be quite beautiful. If you believe what the poets say, it's all unselfish devotion, union of souls. That's the point, you see, because I'm talking of oneness, as near as you can get to it on the earthly plane, when your own identity dissolves into another's. That's what a relationship with God is like. Am I making any sense to you?'

'You are,' I said, thinking of the poems of al-Gazali we had listened to a few months before, but I was surprised to hear such a thing from the Cid. 'I do not see what this has to do with battle, though.'

'Oh, but it has everything to do with it.' His eyes shone with growing intensity, as if a fire had been kindled inside them. I suddenly had the feeling that a different man was addressing us. 'When I go into battles, I feel this great power descending upon me, taking me over. I never remember afterwards what took place. And do you know why? It's because I've surrendered my mind and soul to my lover. I am absorbed into God and I am part of Him as He is of me. It is that oneness that makes me invincible. And it's all about love.'

I felt a curious urge to giggle, although the implications were terrible since he was clearly mad. The great Cid was telling me, if I was to credit it, that he was a sort of Sufi, one of the rapturous kind they call the Idiots of God.

Paladon looked crushed. He had sought a Christian knight, a warrior. The Cid's earlier crudeness, while offending Aziz, had reassured him, because he had seen in it the trappings of the plain-speaking man of action. This evidence of mysticism alarmed him.

Aziz, however, was angry. Circumstance had made him a general. He was mortally concerned about the day ahead, and the mentor he had sought had been at first, condescending and frivolous, and was now incomprehensible. I suspect also he thought he was being mocked. I could feel his icy stillness beside me and knew him well enough to fear an eruption.

Perhaps it was only I, the one the Cid had disparaged as a Jewboy, who understood, yet I had no chance to control the situation. Aziz was speaking in a tone of vicious sarcasm. 'You are referring to your Jesus, I take it? A carpenter, a fisherman, a prophet, but not a lord of battle. Like Samuel, I do not see the relevance of this line of discussion, or how it can be useful to us.'

But the Cid was oblivious. 'Yes, Jesus, and Allah, and Jehovah. It doesn't matter what you call Him. God. That's who I'm with.' He wore a radiant smile.

I was staggered by what he had just said. For a Christian this was blasphemy.

'You're saying you fight for God? Are you a crusader, then?' Aziz pronounced the word with contempt.

'No, no.' The smile was now almost beatific. 'I don't fight

for God. He fights for me. I love Him and He loves me. He desires victory for me.' Suddenly he frowned. 'What did you call me? A crusader?' He laughed. 'Oh, if only you knew how wrong you are. I loathe crusaders. They're – they're unspeakable.' And now his face was reddening with anger. I was watching these mercurial changes in mood with amazement. 'Don't talk to me of crusaders. They're bigots, hypocrites who want to enforce their beliefs on everybody else. Alfonso's as good as pawning his kingdom by inviting in those fanatical monks of Cluny – because their order's behind it, you know, urging the Pope to declare a holy war. Alfonso'll never get me back to Castile, not while those black-cowled droves infest us with new monasteries and urge a sort of Christian *jihad*, for that's what it is, murderous, intolerant, arrogant, sanctimonious, grasping . . . Eunuchs!' he shouted. Suddenly the beatific smile returned. 'No, no, no, no, that's not the sort of God I know. Mine shows His kindness to all. He doesn't want to destroy the Andaluz and Spain I love, where Mussulmans, Christians, even Jews live cheek by jowl and get on with each other. Where there are good clean wars and a man can make a living. Live and let live, that's what I believe, and why shouldn't it continue? I'll fight or kill anybody because that's the sort of man I am, but it doesn't mean I don't respect my enemy, whatever his faith. We're all brothers. I'm a Christian but I've been in these parts long enough to know that that's not the only road to heaven. All our various prophets come from the same damned desert, after all. We worship ultimately the same God – and it's He who is my lover, not His preachers, with their rituals and prohibitions. When I go to battle I am free, and He is with me. It is He who raises my arm to smite and destroy the enemy – or, rather, it is we who move together – yes, like lovers – because we are one.'

He beamed at us as if what he had said made eminent sense. Then he clutched his temples. When he looked at us again, his expression was rapturous. 'He's with me now. I feel Him. I feel Him.'

His voice rose in pitch. He had risen to his feet. 'Oh, God, oh, God,' he moaned. 'You are inside me. And it is beautiful. Beautiful. Oh, let us love. Oh. Let us kill, kill . . .' He was fumbling at his waist as if he was looking for his sword belt, which luckily was hanging with the rest of his armour on a pole by the door of the tent. 'I will love with Thee, Beloved,' he crooned, 'kill with Thee. Oh, Beloved. My Beloved.' He was swaying, lost in his fantasy. The music suddenly stopped. The women were staring at him in fear, as were Paladon and I. Aziz was on his feet, his brow darkened. I knew he had had enough and had decided to leave.

'It's a seizure, like epilepsy,' I pleaded. 'We can't just abandon him in this state.' I saw a disaster about to happen and I wanted Aziz and Paladon to understand. The Cid had gone into a trance, a bout of madness. I knew if we left him now, our alliance would be threatened. But I was also fascinated. He had talked in his warped fashion about a unity that could be found between conflicting faiths. He had even extended it to a tolerant view of humanity and society. 'It has something to do with the Prime Mover, Aziz. What the Persian sages term the demonstrable energy of God. The Cid goes into a kind of trance when he is in battle – he's in it now – and he's mad, but it may be caused by the divine power we are studying.'

'What's the Jew talking about? I hadn't noticed him drinking.' At the cultured, amused tones I froze. The fit, or whatever it had been, was over. The Cid was back on his couch, smiling amiably at me, the same worldly hedonist we had been talking to earlier. 'Where were we? I must have dozed off.' He looked at Paladon. 'We were discussing battle plans, weren't we?' He clapped his hands. 'Why has the music stopped?'

Discordantly at first, the slaves began to play again. We looked at each other, realising that everything he had been saying during the last half-hour had passed from his mind. Aziz sat down slowly, a wary glint in his dark eyes.

'Come,' said the Cid to Paladon. 'You had a question for me.'

Paladon looked at Aziz, who nodded. There was an expression of utter disgust on his face.

'Yes, sir,' Paladon said cautiously. 'You'd explained your plan of attack, and I was going to ask where you wanted us to be when you make your charge. Where the prince should be, I mean.'

'At the head of the Mishkhat troop. That's the usual place for a commander.' He frowned. 'But it's your first battle, isn't it? Better, then, if we merge your troops with mine and we'll all charge together. You stay close to me. I'll show you the ropes.'

I spoke for Paladon who had been stunned into silence. 'I think we need to know what the ropes are, al-Sidhi. The battle plan, if I understand correctly, is simply a charge against the enemy. I should tell you that the prince is under strict instruction from his father, Wazir Salim, to avoid danger as far as possible.'

The Cid was in the act of raising his glass to his lips, but his hand froze in mid-air. 'Then what, in God's name, are you doing here? The whole point of a battle is that it's dangerous.'

I knew then that, even when he was ostensibly sane, we could no longer rely on this man for protection. His whole life was one of sensual gratification, which included butchery, and he assumed that everybody shared the same appetites. I struggled to find a way out. If he insisted that Aziz fight, my lover would certainly do so out of pride. 'We might observe from the tent lines, perhaps? Or the baggage train?' I knew it would be demeaning, but I remembered our promise to Salim. Anyway, Aziz's life was so precious to me that I would risk even his displeasure to protect it – especially if the Cid was likely to go into a berserker trance as soon as the battle started.

The Cid, however, laughed. 'Clearly you know little about battles. The baggage train can be the most perilous place on the whole field. Rogue soldiers are always looking for loot and that's where they head for. How many times have I come back from a victory and found my crockery's been stolen? That's why I send these angels five miles behind the lines before the fighting begins.' A few more grapes flew towards the musicians. 'I don't want to come back for my bath and find my little peahens have been groaning in the mud all day under stinking enemy camp followers, or that their pretty throats have been slit. No, I understand why Salim's concerned about his son, but he'd be safer in the middle of the mêlée than up here. Anyway, how will he learn about war if he doesn't take part in it?'

'I will accompany al-Sidhi to the field, but at the head of the men of Mishkhat. There is no need for the great Cid to concern himself about my safety.' There was finality in Aziz's tone that brooked no opposition. I bowed my head. I could say no more.

'That's the spirit. Just keep your mind to the task, have some experienced old soldiers around you to show you how to slash and thrust, and you'll forget about the danger. You'll be too busy enjoying the experience. I killed my first man at fourteen and was a veteran by your age. Frightening, of course, before you set off for your first charge, but after the horses start galloping, it's heaven on earth.'

Aziz stood up again and, bowing, spoke the formal words of parting: 'I thank you for your hospitality, al-Sidhi, and your gracious welcome.' He added more curtly: 'Perhaps tomorrow morning when we meet you will honour us with your commands.'

The Cid lifted himself from his couch. 'Oh – going already? But the evening's just starting.' He tilted his eyes towards the musicians. 'Are you sure you wouldn't like to take one or two of them with you for the night?'

Aziz had reached the end of his patience. 'Thank you, al-Sidhi, but no. Perhaps your customs are different from ours. We think it more appropriate to fast and pray than to engage in revelry the day before a great killing.'

The Cid shrugged. 'Suit yourself. I prefer to get the revelry in first. If I'm to meet my Maker, I'd like to do so in the satisfaction of having enjoyed all the pleasures the world has to offer beforehand.'

'Then we are different, al-Sidhi. I wish you a good rest.'

As we lifted the curtain, I caught a last glimpse of the Cid. He had a flagon of wine in one hand, and he was beckoning with the other to the brown girl from the jungles beyond the great southern desert, ordering her to join him on his couch.

The night was cool. The sky was studded with stars. In their pale light I saw tears running down Aziz's cheeks. He turned to Paladon. 'What am I to do, old friend?' he said. 'What am I to do? The man is mad.'

Paladon's head was hanging. 'I don't know, Aziz. Try to be a prince, I suppose.'

'You are right,' he whispered. 'That is my burden now. I will talk to our captains. They will be waiting for my orders.'

'You'll be all right tomorrow,' Paladon said. 'Our men will form ranks round you, and I'll be at your side.'

'And I too,' I said.

'I know, Samuel. My heart will be naked if you are not beside me, but I fear for you, as well as for Paladon.' Aziz linked arms with both of us. 'Yet it may be that we will all three protect each other. And if we survive, we will do something remarkable. For surely we are a remarkable brotherhood.'

'I could construct a – a great monument – something the world's never seen before,' Paladon said. 'Something that puts together everything we've ever discussed.'

'Using all our knowledge and craft,' I added. 'That's what the brotherhood stands for.'

'The Brotherhood of the Craft,' said Aziz, tasting the words on his tongue. 'I like the sound of it. Come. It is late and we must prepare for a terrible day, whichever way Allah wills Fortune's wheel to turn.'

We visited the men of Mishkhat where they were camped and found them in good spirits. Aziz spoke confidently to them, praising the merits of the Cid whose brilliance would bring us victory. He said the words they wanted to hear. Paladon and I spoke quietly to some of the more reliable captains, who swore that they would protect their prince with their lives.

At the door of our tent, Aziz hugged me tightly and kissed me. 'Forgive me, Samuel,' he murmured, 'I'd rather you stayed with Paladon tonight. I must be alone if I am to prepare myself to lead my men tomorrow.'

I understood. He was telling me that I was the lover of the boy he had been, not of the prince he had become. Sadly, I had observed the change, as I had so often watched metals purifying in my pipes. The process had begun when Abu Bakhr died: over the last few days, kingship had distilled slowly into his being, and the final transmutation had taken place this evening during his encounter with the mad Christian knight. Yet he still demonstrated he cared for me and loved me. That was enough for now.

In the darkness of the tent I shared with Paladon we each lay quietly on our separate beds, thinking our own bleak thoughts. I doubted that either of us would sleep. Outside our tent we could hear the noises of the camp. The clink of metal as guards passed on their rounds. Occasional bursts of laughter from those still huddled around the fires. Once we heard the shrill scream of a woman and sat up, alarmed, but it was followed by silence. Paladon's bed rustled as he turned over. 'The Cid's enjoying himself,' he muttered.

I wondered if this would be my last night on this earth.

'Samuel.' Paladon's voice broke the quiet. 'Do you know

how to use a sword or a lance? I don't. I never expected we'd have to.'

'We could always try the Cid's technique and become one with God,' I said.

'I don't think so,' he said scornfully, and added bitterly, 'To tell you the truth, I'm a fraction disappointed in our great Cid.'

'I was reading in al-Razi about a strange disease of the mind in which a sane man can sometimes take on different person-alities, some of them touched by God. I was interested because my father showed similar symptoms – though mild compared to the Cid's. Al-Razi says it's curable with potions.'

'Well, don't try any on him before the battle. If his madness has brought him victory in the past we'd as well pray it does tomorrow. I can see no other hope for us.'

'I've brought the sling you taught me to use,' I said. 'It worked on rabbits.'

He chuckled. 'I have mine as well. What a pair we are.'

'David brought down Goliath with a sling.'

'So he did. So he did.' But he was no longer laughing.

There was a long silence. I could hear him shuffling under his cover.

'Samuel?'

'Yes.'

'If we win this battle tomorrow, I'm going to convert to the Mussulman faith. Salim's the qadi and can arrange the lessons.'

'Why? None of us believes in any one particular religion. As the Cid said, they're as valid as one another, all pointing to scientific truth. We believe in the Prime Mover, don't we?'

'You do, because you are the philosopher among us. But Aziz is still Mussulman at heart. He goes along with you because he loves you, but you've not really challenged his faith. And I'm probably still a Christian. That's how I was brought up. I've been building churches for as long as I can remember.'

'Then why do you want to become a Mussulman?'

'Because if I'm a Mussulman, and with Aziz's support, maybe I can persuade Salim I'll be worthy of marrying Ayesha.'

I did not reply. For a while I even forgot about the coming battle. I sensed doom.

The kettle drums began to beat just before dawn. We jerked awake and hurriedly Paladon and I helped each other don our chain-mail coats. Aziz was not in his tent. We found him standing on the ridge, fully armed, his crested helmet in the crook of his elbow. A servant held his shield and lance. His hair and cloak were blowing wildly in the wind and drizzle. He turned a pale face towards us, but his features were settled and his voice was determined. 'We have the left wing. The Cid was here earlier, still wearing his jellaba, gnawing at a leg of lamb.' His lip twisted in contempt. 'He is a brutish individual, but I suppose he knows his trade. There.' He pointed into the valley. 'There is the enemy.'

My stomach turned to water. The shadowy clumps covering the valley floor were not thickets and scrub but men.

'They don't number a thousand,' Aziz continued. 'It's nearer two thousand. They came down in the dark and are already in position. They're no rabble. They're in neat ranks. Not that the great Cid is alarmed. He still maintains that the odds are excellent.'

'Where is he now?' asked Paladon. The tremor in his voice belied his brave attempt to put on a stern front.

'God knows,' said Aziz. 'Getting into his armour, I hope, unless he intends to fight in his jellaba.'

I was amazed by how unperturbed he was. I wondered what sort of communion he had had with his soul during the solitary night hours. He was bitter, clearly, and still angry with the Cid, but I couldn't detect a sign of fear. Unlike me. I was shivering, despite the layers of silk and padding under my chain mail.

A pale shaft of early sunlight broke out of the clouds and

lit the valley. It was as if a river had flowed into it during the night, flooding its banks with silver reflections. Everywhere I saw the glint of armour. Pennants and flags undulated in the morning breeze. Three horsemen, princes or generals, were riding at great speed in front of the gathered horde, cheers erupting as they passed the ranks of their men. The infantry stood in the centre, their long spears quilling its mass like the back of a giant malevolent boar. On either wing, the mounts of the cavalry were jittery, stamping and circling, willing their riders to charge them up the hill.

Hoofs thundered behind us, and our captains appeared, leading our three hundred men. Now it was the turn of our horses to stamp the ground. Grooms brought our mounts. I sat on my restless animal, weighted to my saddle by the metal rings that draped me from head to toe. My feet sought balance in the stirrups, and my thighs were already chafed from pressing into my horse. The heavy shield suddenly seemed flimsy, the spear uncontrollable in my hand. My vision was narrowed to what I could see between the nose guard and the cheek flaps of a helmet that crushed my skull. I felt encoffined and helpless, while the force of events, mounting in escalating tension, dragged me powerlessly with it to whatever inevitable conclusion was in store for us.

I heard a harsh, brittle voice that at first I did not recognise. Aziz was circling his horse in front of me. His eyes were no longer soft and sensual. The pupils were dilated to twice their normal size. I struggled to make sense of what he was saying. 'Samuel, listen to me. Stay within the ring. There'll be men to protect us. Just stay within the ring.'

The Cid appeared, his red beard blazing under his helmet. He was riding an enormous white charger, more like a carthorse than our beautiful Arabs, and the colours of Bibar trailed from the end of his lance. A double-bladed axe hung from his wrist. His mouth gaped in a cavernous laugh, and his eyes were bright stars of madness. His red cloak cracked in the wind. His chain mail moved like a snake's skin over his giant body. I had never seen anybody so godlike. He was shouting something to Aziz about a surprise, and Greek fire, and 'Hold, hold on the ridge until you see me in the mêlée.' His horse reared, but he rode the movement easily. As he tightened the reins, he roared, 'Oh, God, it's a glorious day.' And he was gone, at a gallop, back towards the other end of the ridge where the Saragossans were massing.

There was a terrible sense of finality. Bile scoured my throat and nose. Yet at the same time I could feel the blood rushing through every vein in my body. My fingers, my toes, my ears were burning. I had never felt more alive. My heart, lungs, nerves and sinews seemed to be protesting the vibrancy of their health at a time when my mind and soul were convinced that in a few moments I would be dead. I had never sensed my mortality to such a degree. My fingers were twitching to pull the reins, turn the horse's head and ignominiously leave, but I could not have done, even if Paladon and Aziz had begged me to do so. Morbid fascination held me there, and excitement. I waited impatiently for something, anything, to happen.

When it did it was startling. A thicket of trees halfway down the slope below our ridge suddenly began to billow black smoke, and from it, seconds later, shafts of light issued, hundreds and hundreds of them, arching into the sky in the direction of the enemy. They were arrows, dipped in pitch or some burning material. I do not think it was Greek fire because that was a secret known only to the Byzantines and jealously guarded, but whatever incendiary material they were using, it had a remarkable effect on the massed infantry, who found that the shields they had held up to ward off the arrows had become blazing bonfires attached to their arms. The fiery shower had an even greater effect on the horses of the cavalry at the wings: they reared in fear and threw their riders. After only a few minutes, while the fire continued to rain down, the disciplined

Almerían ranks disrupted in turmoil. It was as if a stone had been hurled at a column of ants.

And the Cid charged. There was a tremor like an earthquake. The whole ridge on our right began to move, as five hundred horsemen poured like molten metal down the hill. The towering figure of the Cid was distinctly visible at the head, the power of his charger propelling him faster and faster forward so that soon he was riding alone, his red cloak and pennant flying behind him like wings.

Our excited horses were straining to follow and we had to heave on our reins to hold our positions. Aziz rode back and forth, screaming hoarsely, 'Wait. Wait. Wait for the order.'

Skin crawling, I watched what was happening below. The Saragossans had reached the enemy, scattering like thistledown the horsemen who had ridden out to meet them. The weight and speed of their attack drove them deep among the enemy cavalry. I found myself thinking of ibn Sa'id intoning one of his lessons in physics, 'When an irresistible force meets at great velocity an immovable mass . . .' But what was happening below was beyond any mathematics that my overstretched brain could bring to bear.

I needn't have worried. This was no immovable mass. The enemy cavalry broke on the first collision. Horsemen at the rear pulled away and rode for their lives, but most were still tangled in the chaos. And then the killing began. The Cid was head and shoulders above everybody else. He had dispensed with his lance and his great axe was rising and falling like a blacksmith's hammer, horses and riders tumbling around him. The Saragossans behind him were doing the same with their curved Arab slashing swords.

'They're in mêlée,' I heard Paladon cry. 'Aziz, do we charge?'

Aziz shook his head. He was leaning forward in his stirrups, staring intently at the battle. The archers were directing their burning arrows on to the wing in front of us and at the infantry, avoiding the part of the field where our own side was embroiled.

The Cid broke through. It had only taken him a few minutes to cut his path. Like a river reaching a fork, he and the men around him veered left, followed by more than half of the rest of the horsemen, while the others charged on, chasing the fleeing enemy cavalry. The demoralised Almerían infantry tried to swing their pikes and spears towards the threat on their flank, but the horsemen crushed into them, and the axe work began again.

'Aziz!' cried Paladon.

'Wait.'

The left wing of the enemy had somehow managed to regroup and were turning their horses in the direction of the Cid.

'Now!' screamed Aziz, and kicked his heels into his horse's sides.

With a jolt that almost knocked me out of the saddle I found myself hurtling down the hill. Faster horses overtook me, threatening to jostle me off, and it was all I could do to hold on. I dropped my spear and my shield in those first few seconds, just trying to keep hold of the reins and avoid the fat rump of the horse in front of me. I kept thinking, What about the ring that was going to protect us? I had no idea where either Aziz or Paladon were. Then I thought, What am I going to do for a weapon? I tried to unsheathe my sword, but I could not find the hilt. When I did I could not move it. Somehow the scabbard had become wedged between my leg and the saddle. Wobbling and bouncing, one foot out of my stirrup, I heaved. The scabbard upended, the sword slid out easily and was lost among trampling hoofs. I nearly tumbled after it. It was only by clutching on to the horse's mane that I regained my seat. In desperation I located the little dagger in my belt. I used it to sharpen quills. So it was that I charged into battle waving a penknife.

This was the point at which my memory fragments. I know from what they told me afterwards that Aziz had timed his charge perfectly and we smashed the flanks of the enemy cavalry before they were even close to the exposed Cid. Paladon and Aziz were at the front and the plan worked perfectly for them. They were indeed protected by a ring of steel as our skilful captains and their men closed around them when the mêlée started. I, however, was wedged among a group of our own horsemen near the rear.

On all sides I could see swords cutting and sparks flying when they met. I had no idea of what was happening. All around me were the faces of angry, frightened men, shouting, yelling, jostling for right of way. The press of soldiers and animals jerked me this way and that. I felt like the goatskin being pulled in all directions by polo players on the maidan in front of King Abu's palace.

Or I might have been a shard of coloured glass in ibn Sa'id's kaleidoscope. Impressions coalesced and disintegrated into patterns even more bizarre than the last. Two men, weaponless, rolled on the ground like lovers, seeking to sink their jaws into each other's necks. The scene shifted and a horseman, contemplating the point of a spear jutting out of his chest, pulled a silk handkerchief from his sleeve and fastidiously dabbed at the swelling blood. Here, a dislodged rider crawled through a maze of stamping fetlocks, dragging his hacked-off arm by a tendon gripped in his teeth. There, a pair of dismounted men, oblivious of the battle going on around them, squabbled with each other over the buckskin boot of a slain warrior. Two others, equally isolated from the chaos, were rhythmically battering each other's shields, pausing by unspoken agreement to get their breath, before pounding back and forth again. Another man, yelling and waving his arms, charged full tilt at a knot of enemy, though he seemed to have no weapon in his hand. He simply vanished, as swords and axes sliced him to shreds. It was as if I was moving from booth to booth in a market festival where an insane morality play was being performed in tableaux. Perhaps the only creatures more bewildered than I was were the horses. Their wild, maddened eyes stared accusingly or uncomprehendingly, the foam from their mouths pinkened by the clouds of spattering blood.

The tide of the battle rolled me like discarded driftwood on a wave. Once, I found myself facing an enemy soldier. He was not much older than me and was as panicked as I was. I screamed, and he screamed too. Somebody decapitated him. His neck spurted a scarlet fountain. After long seconds the body slid off the horse. Then I was galloping, I had no idea where. My horse was unsteady as its hoofs plunged into corpses. Only the staring, empty eyes were recognisably human in the abattoir of nameless body parts and ripped carcasses. Then there was another mêlée.

At some point – it must have been much later: I had lost all sense of time – a grizzled old soldier next to me noticed my penknife and laughed. I knew him. He was called Hamid and had once tended my horse. 'Here, take this,' he said, unsheathing his sword. 'But shouldn't you be—'

I don't know what he was intending to say because at that moment a mountainous white horse reared behind him, a flashing silver light descended, and his head split into two neat halves. I could see each side of the brain, nestled in the skull just as they were in al-Razi's drawings. The axe that had killed him rose again, and suddenly there were the bushy beard and staring eyes of the Cid. He had an an ecstatic grin on his face, and I remembered even then, as the axe was poised to strike me, that he had not exaggerated. In battle he was not there, or not in any recognisable human form. He had become a simulacrum, what my father used to call a Golem, a possessed killing machine. His chain mail was stained as red as his cloak with blood. I raised my penknife. There was nothing else I could do, and I suppose the sheer idiocy of it revived some dormant spark of reason in him, or at least curiosity, because the axe halted just above my head and he looked at me quizzically.

'You're the Jewboy, aren't you?' he said. 'What are you doing among the enemy?'

'They're not the enemy. You've just killed one of our men,' I answered.

'Have I?'

'A man called Hamid from Mishkhat.'

'What did he do?'

'He tended the horses.'

'Well, well.' He peered at me. 'What's that you're waving?'

'My penknife.'

'Killed anybody with it?'

'No.'

'Try a sword or an axe. Plenty lying around.'

'Al-Sidhi!' I screamed. 'Behind you!' A wounded infantryman had risen to his feet and was tottering towards the Cid's unprotected back with a spear. The Cid leaned to the side, allowing the spear point to pass him, and decapitated his assailant with a casual backhand.

'Thank you,' he said. I could see his eyes misting again. 'We'll talk this evening about— What was his name?'

'Hamid,' I said, as he galloped away, axe raised high, cloak flying.

It is extraordinary, the conversations you can have on a battlefield.

By then it was as good as over. Our forces had joined, and what remained of the enemy was fleeing. I found myself alone among corpses. I sat slumped on my horse, which was grazing a patch of bloody turf. Eventually Paladon found me and led me to Aziz, who embraced and kissed me. Both he and Paladon had thought I was dead. Paladon had been searching for my body.

It was as the Cid had predicted. We were back in the tents by sunset, already bathed and wearing clean clothes. It had been a spectacular victory. We had lost barely a hundred men but had killed eight hundred of the enemy and captured three hundred, whom the Cid ordered to be beheaded. 'We must be firm,' he explained to Aziz. 'An object lesson in ruthlessness is as good as a peace treaty.'

Aziz did not demur. He had killed his first man that day, spearing him during the charge (Paladon told me he did so elegantly; all those afternoon lessons in the tourney yard must have had an effect). I try to excuse his acquiescence in the slaughter of the prisoners by telling myself that the bloodlust was still on him, but in fact it was part of the change that had come upon him when he had put on the mantle of a king. It was a little shadow between us, although I said nothing.

Later, the Cid's seneschal, Fanez, appeared with booty from the enemy's baggage train. It included a beautiful Jewish slave girl who had replaced the Frankish girl in his affections. That meant the latter was free for Paladon.

There was another great banquet, a raucous affair that I hated. The girls played their music, but the brown girl from the jungles south of the desert was missing. The others appeared sombre and there was little of the liveliness they had displayed the night before, not that anybody noticed, except me – I was the only one not drinking. I hadn't the stomach for it.

The Cid was charming and civilised. The battle over, his madness had passed. He and Aziz got on well together. At the end of the evening, after Paladon had gone off with the Frankish girl and Fanez with the Jewess, the Cid urged Aziz to take one of the others. Without looking at me, he agreed.

I will not describe the feelings in my heart. Or the pain.

With nowhere to go, I found myself wandering in the moonlight. My steps took me to the battlefield. It was not to study anatomy. I suppose it was to indulge my grief. I looked at the white corpses washed by the moon and the stars. Most had been stripped of their armour. The scavengers had been, both animal and human. At that moment, I envied the dead.

As it turned out, there were still human scavengers on the

field, Christian peasants searching for what pickings remained. One saw me and must have been impressed by my costly clothes. He was a short, squat man in a conical cap who came at me with an axe, the second time I had been threatened with such a weapon that day. I ran, stumbling over the naked bodies, but I could not outpace him. I happened to have my satchel on my shoulder in which were my sling and some stones. It took some dodging and fumbling, but I managed to load my weapon. I hurled a missile at him at close range, and he dropped to the ground, another tiny corpse on the field. He was no Goliath. So I, too, had killed a man, as easily as a rabbit, and not even in battle. I never told Paladon or Aziz. I felt ashamed.

I slept in the captains' tent. Before dawn, Paladon roused me. His face was white with shock. 'What's the matter?' I asked, when we were outside. 'Didn't you enjoy the Frankish girl?'

'I did,' he said, 'but she's gone. I sent her away.'

'That's not like you.' I yawned. I was heavy with my own sorrows and not interested. 'Does she have a name?'

'Oh, Juliette,' he said distractedly. 'Anyway, she's not important. It's something she told me after we had made love.'

'What was that?' I was still yawning.

'You remember the brown girl – the one the Cid said came from the jungles? She's dead. He stabbed her with a dagger, through her neck, as he made love to her. While he was inside her, Samuel. He rode her death spasms like a bucking horse. Then he mutilated her. The others were there, and saw it happen. Theirs was the scream we heard in the night.'

I had nothing to say.

'She had a name too,' said Paladon. 'It was Ayesha – yes, Ayesha.' He paused, distressed. 'The Cid's a monster, Samuel. A murderer. Do we tell Aziz?'

I thought about it. 'No, he won a great victory for us. He's a hero.' I felt sick. 'We'll no doubt give him a big triumphal parade in Mishkhat. Don't worry. He's probably over his divine madness for now – until the next battle.'

There *was* a parade when we returned to Mishkhat. We passed through every quarter of the city on our way to the palace. Mussulman, Christian and Jewish women threw rose petals on our heads from their windows. Salim, who had won a greater and more difficult battle against the Toledans in the north, generously gave first place in the procession to the Cid. The mercenary left us a few days later loaded with treasure. Thankfully I never met him again, although I heard tales of his exploits. When, years later, he took the city of Valencia for his own kingdom, he boiled the governor alive in a cauldron. It has gone down in history as an object lesson, like his slaughter of our prisoners. I imagine, however, that he was communing with his lover, God.

There had been no disturbances during the Cid's stay. Even when he discovered that several of his slave girls had mysteriously escaped from his quarters in the palace, he did not become enraged (Salim sent his guards to search for them in the souks but they could not be found and the Cid eventually shrugged off such a small matter; by then he had been paid and could afford to buy new ones). I asked Paladon if he knew anything about it, and he denied it, but some months afterwards, he took me to a tavern in the Christian quarter, where four veiled women were playing beautiful music, and one flautist, with whom Paladon was on very good terms, had a fringe of blonde hair, just showing under her veil.

And Aziz, Paladon and I? We returned to our studies and our previous life, although now a shadow hung over our former paradise, not only because of the growing distance between Aziz and me: we had all, each in his own way, lost our innocence.

Andalucía, 1938

2

The Magic Book

'. . . We had all, each in his own way, lost our innocence.'

Pinzon paused, thinking of how the corrupting force of war had not changed through the ages. He looked up from the book, smiling to conceal his depression. The black hall of the cathedral had shrunk to the size of a small church. The faces of the townspeople he could see in the first few rows were yellow masks in the candlelight. It was hard to gauge from their blank expressions whether they wanted him to continue.

He had long ago achieved his purpose of putting Tomás to sleep. His grandson had had more stamina than the other children, who had faded during the early chapters. Only after ibn Sa'id spilled the strawberries, during the scene in which he had told Samuel to become a doctor, had Tomás, half chuckling, half yawning, laid his head in María's lap. There had been a sleepy giggle later, when Paladon stole the chief faqi's turban, and he hadn't stirred since.

It had been easier after that because Pinzon no longer had to doctor the more overtly sexual or philosophical passages for his grandson's benefit. He wondered what the hostages might be making of it all, especially Samuel's unsympathetic portrait of the Cid. Every Spaniard considered the Cid a national hero, the perfect Christian warrior. Samuel, however, had seemed to describe a paranoid schizophrenic. Pinzon had been grateful for the battle that followed. Blood and guts were safer territory and, from the sighs and gasps, much appreciated. Even so he had been surprised by the laughter when the Cid murdered the hapless Hamid on the battlefield. The mutters that followed had been just as disconcerting: '*¡Bueno! ¡Bueno!* Death to the Moor!' He wondered if they had noticed Samuel's lyrical descriptions of the tolerant Moorish society.

He was being patronising, he told himself. He had grown up among peasants like these in Agua Verde. They had little idea of and cared less about what went on in the outside world beyond their patch of hillside. In their closed, secretive society, even someone from a neighbouring village was considered to be an *extranjero*, an outsider, and never truly trusted. Neither had they much idea about the Reconquista. Nursery tales had informed them that Moors and Christian knights had played a part in their history, but they had no relevance to their own hard existence. They were stock figures from a story that never altered: Christians were good and Moors were evil. That was why the terrifying Moroccan colonial troops whom Franco had brought over fitted an ancient archetype. To them this memoir was just another fairytale, like the legend of Roldán and Oliveros, or the mad Quixote, no different from every other story that had been told and retold for centuries. The content didn't matter, only that he was reading to them. They were bewildered and afraid, and had taken what refuge and comfort they could in something ordinary they could cling to, the voice of the travelling storyteller. He had no right to be condescending. They were demonstrating an innate instinct for survival. After centuries of oppression, by the Church, by landowners, by grasping tax collectors, peasants like these trusted only in what they knew, and therein found their courage.

He glanced at María. She smiled at him and nodded encouragingly. It was as if she had read his thoughts. In the pew immediately behind her, he saw Grandmother Juanita leaning forward, her chin resting on her hand. Her eyes caught his and she gave a broad grin. 'Go on, Professor. *Es una historia hermosa.* A beautiful story.' There were murmurs of agreement from those around her.

Pinzon cleared his throat. He felt humbled. 'Well, we have reached the third section. The narrator, Samuel, says that he will tell us how a philosopher found light in a cave, and how a king became enamoured of a rock.'

He saw their faces light up with approval at the hint of romance and mystery. 'In earlier, happier days,' he read, 'long before we went off to war, we were sometimes allowed to hold our morning lessons in the king's gardens . . .'

His audience settled back into contented anticipation. He put his finger on the opening sentence, flicking through the first few paragraphs, preparing the translation in his mind. He faced the rows of expectant faces, ready to begin – but as he watched they froze. As one, their heads turned and startled eyes looked up in the direction of the darkened, stained-glass windows.

Then he heard it too: the rising whistle of a shell, followed a moment later, and far away, by the crump of an explosion. A memory flashed of his trip to the front line, when Raúl had proudly demonstrated his bank of mortars. He remembered that two of Ogarrio's men had been carrying these same heavy weapons on their backs – but barely had he identified the sound before the quiet space of the cathedral rang with the clatter of machine-gun fire, shouting, and a fusillade of rifle shots.

The townspeople were fixed in their seats with wide-open mouths and round, scared eyes.

The machine-gun rattled. Then there was silence again. It was as if a spell had been broken. Mothers clutched their children who, suddenly woken, began to cry.

Felipe had leaped to his feet. He had cocked his rifle and

was waving it foolishly in front of him. 'Stay where you are,' he was shouting, though nobody had moved. He looked more terrified than the hostages did.

Thank God the noise didn't wake Tomás, thought Pinzon. He turned to María. She affected a confident smile, but her shoulders were shaking. He reached out and touched her hand. 'It's probably just the men on the walls panicking,' he said. 'One of them may have seen an advance guard of the enemy.' He became aware of the warmth of the perspiring and slightly sticky skin pressed to his own. Suddenly embarrassed he tried to pull his hand away, but she clung to it. She was frowning. 'Enrique, we must tell them what's going on,' she whispered urgently. 'The Fascists, the explosives . . .'

'I know,' he said quietly. 'That thought's been in the back of my mind all the time I was reading. But it's important how we do it. We must avoid panic.'

'If you speak to them they will listen to you.'

He saw the anxiety in her eyes, and smiled. 'I'm still an unknown quantity. Best to get their leaders on side first. I'm thinking Grandmother Juanita might be able to help us.'

'Yes, everybody listens to her.'

'Good. Then we'll pick the right moment.' He was still conscious of María's hand in his. She was clearly afraid, but her response had been sensible and level-headed. There were depths to this woman he hadn't realised. She had impressed and surprised him. He was suddenly glad to have her at his side. 'We'll have to sit this out first,' he added. 'It's starting again.'

It was only the crack of a single rifle. The hostages listened expectantly, with indrawn breath. When the machine-gun began to fire again, there was a shrill exhalation from the women, followed by anxious whimpers of fear. Pinzon was relieved that most of the men remained calm. Still and tense, they were watching Felipe, who was strutting up and down with his rifle in front of the altar. Huddled in their pews, they looked like a real congregation waiting for a funeral service that was about to be conducted by a mad priest.

He listened carefully to the noise outside, trying to assess what was going on. This new bout of firing was more intense than the first. While earlier the shooting had seemed to come from their captors' side, now more distant volleys were accompanying it. The first contingents of the Fascist forces must be positioning themselves. He wondered how Ogarrio intended to effect his parley. He must have decided to make a show of strength first, so that the enemy would take him seriously. There was no reason for alarm yet. More worrying was the behaviour of their foolish guard.

Felipe was still yelling his ridiculous commands. When, after a few minutes, the noise of fighting stopped again, he was still screaming, 'Stay where you are.'

Grandmother Juanita, silenced him by banging her stick on the pew. Staring at him, she called derisively, 'What sort of soldier are you? Panicking like a chicken. You wouldn't have lasted long in my son's militia, that's for sure.'

Her outburst released a stream of angry questions from the others.

'Tell us what's going on!'

'Why are you keeping us here?'

'Who are they fighting? Is it the Fascists? Is it the Moors?'

'Why have you dressed us like clergy?'

'Why are we prisoners if we're on the same side?'

'What's happening to our people down below?'

Felipe backed two steps towards the altar, raising his rifle. Pinzon saw that he had to do something. The young man was a simpleton.

He stood up and lifted his hand in the commanding gesture he had used to still a crowd when he was a politician. Surprised faces turned towards him. 'Citizens,' he shouted, over the din. 'Let's not be too hard on Privato Muro. He's just a soldier, doing his job. Aren't you, Felipe?' He turned to him with a smile. 'Protecting us from harm. And for that we're very grateful.' He glanced humorously at the rifle. 'Keep that for the real enemy, eh?' He pointed at his grandson, who was peering fearfully over María's shoulder. 'Don't want to frighten Tomás and the other children, do you? They look up to you. You're their friend.' He broadened his smile. The young man looked as bewildered as a landed fish. Clumsily he rested his rifle by his feet. Pinzon clapped him on the back. 'Good lad.' Felipe grinned shyly, grateful that somebody else had taken the situation in hand.

Pinzon turned back to the suspicious faces of the townspeople. He might have been a storyteller a moment ago, but now he had become the *extranjero* again. He had still to win their trust. On the election campaign trail when he had faced a hostile crowd, he had gained their admiration by a display of *machismo* equal to theirs, but he sensed that humility might work better here. He fixed his eyes on the old lady. 'Doña Juanita,' he said, 'with your permission, I would like to say a few words to you in private.'

The old woman's eyebrows rose. She was about to reply when the young man in the sheepskin stood up. It was Paco Cuellar, the former shepherd who had a seat on the Revolutionary Council. Pinzon remembered María had called him a shit. His lips were turned down in a sneer and his eyes were squinting in anger. 'What have you to say to Grandmother Juanita that is not fit for the ears of the rest of us? And what gives you the right to lord it over us anyway? You're not of our town.'

Pinzon met his glare. 'No, I'm not, Señor Cuellar. And I have no right whatever to address your community. That is why I respectfully seek the advice of one of your elders, who will be in a position to judge whether I can be of help.'

'And I say, Señor Politician or Professor or whatever you claim to be, that I wouldn't trust you further than the door of this fucking church.'

'Pacito!' Grandmother Juanita admonished him. 'Wash your mouth.'

'Grandmother, with respect, I am the only elected official here, and you should hear what I have to say before you allow yourself to be tricked by a stranger. All of you!' He raised his arms to embrace the whole assembly. 'Has anybody here had cause to doubt me before? Is there anybody who's unaware of the hard work I've done on the community's behalf?' He curled the fingers of one hand into his lapels, and raised the other in an oratorical gesture. 'Day and night I protect our people. And now I share your danger. Why do you think I volunteered to be here with you?'

Grandmother Juanita snorted. 'Maybe so you can strut around boasting what a great hero you are.'

Paco looked as if he had been physically struck. His cheeks burned crimson with anger. Grandmother Juanita pulled herself to the end of the pew. She gestured to Paco to lean down and muttered in his ear. Pinzon could only make out the words because he was close to them. 'I know you, Pacito. Your mother was a friend of mine, and I held you on my knees when you were a little boy. You were full of yourself even then. Why this undignified behaviour now? Is it because you believed the *sargento* when he said we would leave unharmed? Now the guns are firing, are you panicking that you made a big mistake? Control yourself or you will cover yourself with shame.' Her tone hardened: 'And don't you dare try to browbeat me. We are not in the town hall now and I am not the pathetic Alcalde Zuluaga whom you have bent to your will.'

With an effort she straightened her back. 'Professor Pinzon,' she said, loudly so that all the hostages could hear, 'if you have matters to discuss with me I will listen to you, but I will bring with me Hector García, who governed us for many years and is my old friend, and also Paco Cuellar. He is young and, as he keeps reminding us, sits on our Revolutionary Council, so we must respect him. Together we represent the town.'

'By all means, Doña Juanita,' said Pinzon, sensing he had an ally. 'I would appreciate your advice.'

'If everybody's going to be represented, I'm coming too,' said María. She was standing proudly at the end of her pew, holding Tomás by the hand. Her eyes were fixed contemptuously on the young councillor, who was glaring at her venomously.

'Get back to your seat, woman,' snarled Paco. 'You have no standing here.'

'That's right, Paco, I'm not part of the town, am I? I'm the cuckoo in the nest. That's what you called me when you organised that witch hunt for spies and fifth columnists last summer. You'd have had me gaoled with the nuns if Hector here hadn't pointed out you hadn't a shred of evidence against me. He and Grandmother Juanita probably have as low an opinion of me as any of you, but at least they're fair-minded. They must be to allow a poisonous snake like you into their discussions. Grandmother Juanita, is there anything I have said that is untrue? We are equal now as hostages and that means even the cuckoo should have a voice when it comes to discussing our common fate.'

Grandmother Juanita shrugged. 'María, not all of us are Pacos and hostile to you. I do not know you well but I have seen you are prepared to help others and I admire that quality in you. If you want to join us, I have no objection.' She smiled slyly. 'Who knows? Your closeness to this professor, who stands in more danger of being considered a cuckoo than you, may help us understand him better.'

She stood up and faced the other hostages. 'Remain quietly where you are. And don't do anything to upset our lion-hearted guard. We will listen to what this politician from Valencia has to say.'

They gathered in the Lady Chapel. Grandmother Juanita perched on the priest's stool under the statue of the Virgin, whose benign face smiled at them in the glow of the candles held by Hector García, Paco and Pinzon.

They listened silently as Pinzon explained the situation. The old man, García, crossed himself when he described the murder of the priests and nuns, and Grandmother Juanita slowly shook her head from side to side. When he told them of the explosives in the mosque, Paco cursed and began to pace up and down the aisle. As he spoke, María sat silently, hugging Tomás.

'This negotiation, Professor? If there is one. Do you think the Fascists will agree to Sargento Ogarrio's terms?' asked Hector. 'That seems to be our only hope.'

Pinzon shrugged. 'It's possible, if Ogarrio can persuade the Fascists that you're the monks and nuns he's claiming you are. How he'll carry on with that deception once the Fascists agree to give him a safe-conduct, I don't know, but I'm sure he's thought of something. He's no fool.'

'You don't sound very confident,' snorted Grandmother Juanita.

'I'm sorry, I'm not. I think the chances of a successful negotiation are slim. The Fascists prefer unconditional surrender.'

'So there'll be a battle and Ogarrio and his men will blow up the cathedral with us inside it? Is that what you're telling us? Speak your mind. We're not afraid of the truth.'

'I'm not saying that negotiations won't take place,' said Pinzon. 'I'm only doubtful of their outcome. I think in all probability there will be a truce. After all, it is to the Fascists' advantage. A truce will give them time to deploy their men for the final attack.'

'But if Ogarrio fails to get what he wants, it won't matter to us if they've negotiated or not,' said Hector. 'He'll just blow us up later rather than earlier.'

'Yes, but that delay may be good for us, because it will give us more time to work out a plan to get out of here. It's also something positive you can tell your people, Doña Juanita. I believe that you should show absolute confidence that the negotiations will be successful. It's important your people believe that, because while hope exists they won't panic. And if they don't panic, they won't do anything stupid.'

'And what stupid things do you expect that my people will do?' Grandmother Juanita asked icily.

'I don't know. A riot, an attempt at a mass breakout. Anything like that would be suicidal. If we lose our heads and cause trouble, Ogarrio will retaliate. Some of us will be made examples of – he's a ruthless man and he'll summarily execute as many of us as he thinks necessary to cow the rest. The least he'll do is to add guards to watch us. That'll be the end of any escape plan. On the other hand, as long as he thinks we're docile, he'll leave us with Felipe, and we can take advantage of an opportunity if it comes. Look, I know you'd prefer to be frank with your people – but they're mainly women and children. The less they worry, the safer they'll be.'

'So we do nothing?' Paco's hands were shaking and sweat was running down his forehead. 'We tell our people lies – that everything's going to be all right? Is that the best you can come up with?'

'I'm saying we buy time, Señor.' Pinzon stared at him. 'We watch. We wait our chance.'

'There are thirty of them and thirty of us,' said Paco. 'And only one guard. Maybe we're not the cowards you think we are, politician.'

'I'm sorry, Señor. Not even bravery will open a door that's barred from outside. Or protect the women and children from the machine-guns they have on the parapet.'

'Grandmother Juanita, I told you we should be careful of this man,' snarled Paco. 'We've heard him out, and what have we got? Nothing, and excuses for doing nothing.'

'You have a better idea, Paco?'

'Maybe I have. What if we cause a diversion, some sort of struggle with our guard? We fire his gun to cause Ogarrio and one or two of his men to come in to see what's going on. Well, the door will be open then, won't it? One of us could slip out. I'd volunteer. It'll be dark so I could get to the back wall behind the seminary. There are goat tracks on the cliff there. We all knew them as boys. I could go down to the Fascists, tell them the real story about the dead nuns, that Ogarrio only has thirty men, maybe bring some of their troops back up the goat path to rescue us.'

'You'd do a deal with the Fascists?'

'Why not? It's these Stalinist bandits who are our enemy now. The Fascists are the only ones who can help us. Come on, it's a plan. Señor Garcia? Mother Juanita? What do you think?'

Grandmother Juanita observed him impassively. 'Hector?'

The old man shrugged. 'It sounds like a very good plan for saving one man – Paco himself.'

'That is also my opinion.' Her mouth twisted in scorn. 'You are lucky, Paco. First, because I promised your poor dead mother that I would look after you. Second, because my son Julio is not here, for if he was your throat would already be slit and your blood would be spilling on the floor for your treason. He did not sacrifice his life so you could hand our town over to the Fascists, who are murderers and rapists, our class enemies who would enslave us on their big estates as they did before our revolution. This Ogarrio is a fanatic and cruel but, for all that, he is prepared to fight our common enemy. Shame on you. I would rather die in his explosion than collaborate.'

'Well, that's what you will do if we listen to Pinzon. If you seek a traitor, you need look no further than him. I can prove it.'

'Go on,' she said, now looking at Pinzon as coldly as earlier she had regarded Paco.

'He talks plausibly enough, tells a good story, but none of what he's actually been doing makes sense. Take the explosives. All right, we can be reasonably sure they're down there. We saw the soldiers going into the vaults with boxes. But if he was just a hostage, why would Ogarrio show him what he was doing? And keep him with them for as long as he did. It's obvious to me. Pinzon was helping them. But maybe you still think I'm being overly suspicious. All right, let's take him at his word. For whatever reason, he was let into the secret of the explosives, and he comes up shocked with all this terrible knowledge. What does he do? Warn us? Help us plan an escape? No, he pulled out a book and read us a fairy story. A nice one, sure. It kept us all very quiet. Quiet as lambs. But why'd he do it? It wasn't perhaps because he had a *reason* for keeping us quiet? That those were his instructions?'

'I've already told you, Señor Cuellar. I didn't want to cause panic. I didn't then and I don't now. I think we're wasting precious time.'

'Wasting time, he says.' Paco had again adopted his orator's pose. He looked like an excitable small-town barrister who had made a clever point. Pinzon was puzzled by the man's malevolence towards him. It might be fear, as Grandmother Juanita had earlier seemed to be suggesting. Or perhaps he was worried that Pinzon was trying to supplant his influence. Whatever the reason, he was dangerous and Pinzon had to find a way to neutralise him, for Grandmother Juanita, despite her earlier scathing criticisms of him, appeared to be taking him seriously.

'Don't be bamboozled by his reasonable manner, Grandmother. Who is this Pinzon? What's he doing here? Who's to tell we're actually on the same side? Oh, yes, he calls himself a fellow hostage, but is he really one? None of *us* is chummy with the *sargento*, are we? But he is. We've seen them whispering to each other at every opportunity. Ogarrio didn't put *him* into fancy dress like the rest of us, did he? And now we've heard the fighting and want to know what's going on, what does he do? He spins us *more* fables, then tells us we should remain as quiet and – what was his word? – docile as before. How *very* convenient for our captors. Well, we've seen through his game now, haven't we? We may not understand the full extent of his trickery, but we know enough not to trust him.'

'And why should we trust you, Paco?' hissed María, her face red with fury.

'What's that supposed to mean – whore?' snapped Paco. '*Puta*.'

Her face paled. 'Forgotten, have you?' She was suddenly speaking in a tone of icy calm. 'That long night in your office when you employed me as your so-called "secretary". Cooking the books so you could cream off your percentage of the town's levy for the war effort. All those deals you made with the corrupt government collectors, which you needed my skills to cover up because you don't understand book-keeping. And – and the other things you made me do for you on the sofa afterwards. Favour for favour. Isn't that how you described it, when you told me your price for the medicine you said you'd get from your black-market friends to save my little Pablo?'

'That's a lie!' Paco shouted.

'What is? That my son was dying and you used the opportunity to buy your way into my skirts? Or the fraud I helped you cover up to save your hide when Hector here raised questions in the public meeting about your accounting as treasurer?'

'What are you saying, María?' Grandmother Juanita frowned. 'That Paco was stealing money from the municipality? That he . . . that he . . . abused you? These are scandalous charges. Why would you invent such falsehoods? You will apologise, or provide proof.'

María tossed her hair angrily. 'That's the trouble, isn't it? I can't, can I? Who would believe me? I'm an *extranjera*, even after all the years I've lived here. So's Professor Pinzon. That's why Paco can say what he likes about either of us and you'll believe him because he's one of your own and we're not. It was foolish of me, wasn't it, to do such a good job on the town-hall accounts? There's no evidence of his larceny there now. And as for the other, well, we all know what an upstanding figure of society he is. We see him promenading round the Plaza de la Reconquista every evening with his wife, like Señor and Señora Respectability. The big man. Who could conceive he was capable of— *Mierda*, what's the use?' She began to sob, hugging Tomás fiercely, and murmuring, 'My baby, my poor lost Pablo . . .'

'*¡Puta!*' hissed Paco again, and stamped out of the chapel. Grandmother Juanita and Hector García slumped on their pews, gazing at the floor.

'Doña Juanita,' said Pinzon, carefully, 'that scene was distressing, but this is not the time to lay blame on anybody. Whoever we are, whatever we've done, we are in this predicament together and we should support each other. I'd be grateful if we could return to what we were discussing earlier. I understand why Comrade Cuellar might be suspicious of me, but please believe me when I say that my grandson and I are hostages like yourselves. I – I refuse to give up hope. I swear this now. If I can find a way to bring all of us to safety, I will. Señor Cuellar was wrong to say I was proposing inaction. It is the opposite. We will probe their weaknesses. We will hold ourselves ready. We will not despair.'

Grandmother Juanita shook her head. Hector spoke bluntly. 'Your earlier words, before Paco interrupted you, were convincing. I agree that we should persuade our people to keep up their courage, if necessary by not telling them the whole truth – but now I think you're fooling yourself, Señor. From what you have described, there is unlikely to be any way for us to save ourselves. We must bear our fate with what grace we can. There is no cowardice in accepting reality.'

'Yet I don't and won't accept it,' said Pinzon. 'I bowed to what I considered to be fatalism and expediency once before. The result was that I lost my beloved son. He was murdered by the same kind of Stalinists who hold us captive. If Raúl was with us now, he would not give up, and neither will I. I will not lose my grandson, Señor. I will not let that happen.'

Grandmother Juanita was observing him curiously. 'You lost a son in this war, Professor?'

'Yes, he was killed in the street fighting in Barcelona, when his Anarchist militia was resisting the Communist *coup d'état* last summer.'

'I also lost a son last year, Señor, and he, too, was a commander in the Anarchist militia. My Julio fought for nearly two years with the Durruti Brigade in Aragón. He was killed in the attack on Belchite.'

'Then we share a common grief and pride, Señora.'

She nodded thoughtfully. 'You said just now that your son would never give in to Fate. I do not think that my Julio would be any different if he were here today. He, too, would be urging us to find a way to save ourselves.'

Her features quivered, then her face set hard. 'Thank you, Professor Pinzon. You have given us much to think about.'

She stood up and, followed by Hector García, began to hobble back towards the nave. 'We will keep in close communication,' she said, over her shoulder. 'I believe you are an honest man. Do not worry about our people. I will see to it that nobody does anything stupid.' She paused. 'Including Paco.' Then she turned. 'If you have it in your heart to do so, try to forgive him for his insults to you. As you say, it is not the time for quarrels. As for the other things that were said tonight . . .' She bit her lip. 'What María told us grieved me beyond measure. We have been mistaken about her these many years. As for Paco, I am . . . disappointed and I will not forget what I heard. If it is of any comfort, Professor, from now on neither I nor Hector nor any of us will view you, your grandson or María as *extranjeros*. There, I have spoken. Am I right, Hector?'

The old man shrugged and took her arm. 'Don't expect me to argue with you. You've spoken, haven't you?' His white moustache flicked upwards as he smiled. '*Buenas tardes*, Señor. Let us know when you have a plan.'

Pinzon sat back against his pew. The Virgin, flickering in the candlelight, smiled down at him. It had been his mention of Raúl that had saved them, he thought. In their shared sacrifice he had found a bond with Grandmother Juanita. He suddenly realised that it had been the first time since his son's death that he had mentioned his name without guilt – only with pride.

He turned towards María and Tomás, who were gazing at him with pale, wondering faces. He stood up and moved over to them.

'Will you be all right?' he asked her. Tomás was sitting on his knees, watching wide-eyed, while María was smoking a cigarette, erect and proud at the other end of the pew.

'Of course,' she said, her shoulders shaking slightly. 'I get over things. That's what I do. Give me a few moments alone, and I always come out smiling.'

'You were very brave,' he said. 'It took guts to say what you did, and I'm grateful. I would have had difficulty answering Paco if you hadn't discredited him.'

'You'd have done fine,' she said. 'You were magnificent. A rock of strength. I was a little in awe of you, actually. And proud of you. Very proud. You must have been fearsome in the Cortes.' She laughed shrilly. 'Fancy that – me on speaking terms with a great politician.'

'I think you were the greater politician tonight,' he said. 'And I am the one who is in your debt.'

Her quick glance was half smile, half suspicion and fetchingly vulnerable. 'You're only saying that,' she said. 'I doubt you think anything of me – after my confession. Anyway, you can't possibly see me in the same light as you did before.'

'That's true,' he said gravely. 'I never appreciated your nobility before. But tonight I learned how you unselfishly sacrificed yourself to try to save your son, and I saw with my own eyes how you were prepared to sacrifice your honour all over again to help me. You are remarkable, María, remarkable and courageous, and it is a privilege to know you.'

Tears bubbled in her eyes. Her voice broke. 'When I heard that bastard – that shit – that criminal, I – I – I don't know what came over me. I just wanted to stop him, to hurt him – and I was, I was— All I could think of was coming home to Pablo in the morning – I'd abandoned him all night with a woman who couldn't look after him as I did – and feeling so . . . so shamed and defiled . . . and . . . and guilty . . . Every morning he was weaker . . . weaker . . . and Paco never gave me the medicines. He never even ordered them . . . I'm sorry, I'm sorry . . . I'll be fine . . . just leave me a while . . .'

'Tomás,' whispered Pinzon, 'let's you and I wander round the cathedral. We can look at the paintings.'

Hand in hand they walked down the aisles. Many of the hostages smiled at them. Only Paco, slumped on his pew, looked away.

'Grandfather,' said Tomás, 'that man called Aunt María' – he hushed his voice – 'a *puta*. It's a very bad word, isn't it?'

'It is a very bad word,' said Pinzon, 'and he had no right to say it, and you mustn't say it either, and Aunt María is not – has never been – what you said.'

'I thought he was wrong. I didn't like him, Grandfather, not at all. And, Grandfather?'

'Yes?'

'Her baby. Pablo. Is he in heaven now with Mamá and Papá? That's where Lupita said they were. I suppose Lupita's there too now.'

'Let's . . . let's hope they're all somewhere like heaven, Tomás. If we always remember them, that's a sort of heaven for them.'

'Heaven must be getting crowded with this war,' said the little boy, thoughtfully. He paused, then added in a brighter voice: 'I'm glad you're going to save us, Grandfather. That's what you told the nice old lady, didn't you?' He looked around the great dark cathedral. 'I don't like it here. Will we be leaving soon?'

'As soon as I can find a way, Tomás. It may be difficult, but I promise you, I'll find a way.'

'I'll help you think of something,' said Tomás. 'I'm good with puzzles. Mamá always said so.'

'Thank you,' said Pinzon. He was almost choked with emotion. 'I'd really appreciate that.'

He felt the little boy tug his hand. 'Look, Grandfather. There's Jacopo and Emilia with Felipe. Felipe's organising a game. Can I go? Can I?'

'Yes, Tomás, enjoy yourself.' He watched his grandson run down the aisle towards the altar. His eyes were wet. He reached into his pocket for his handkerchief. As he did so, two figures stepped out from behind the pillars.

'What a touching scene,' said Ogarrio. The vulpine Becerra was grinning behind him. 'Who's the *puta*? I must meet her.'

'How long have you been there?' asked Pinzon, stiffly.

'A while. It's been quiet on the battlements after the excitement earlier. Thought we'd see how things are here. Slipped in just as the old woman and the old man were coming out of the side chapel where you must have been giving them a pep talk. Looks like I should thank you. What they told the other hostages was very upbeat. Negotiations for their release will start soon. Nobody's to worry. All will be well. They didn't even mention the explosive in the crypt. Maybe you told them not to. Very wise.'

'They don't know about it,' said Pinzon. 'You said I was to keep quiet on that.'

Ogarrio and Becerra grinned at each other. 'You owe me fifty pesetas, Becerra. You see? He didn't blab after all. Told you he was sensible, our professor. Shouldn't have doubted him, should you? And you'll continue to be sensible, won't you, Señor? That way we keep things happy. Felipe can continue to play with the children and nobody gets hurt. I'd hate to have to take disciplinary measures. Shoot a few – oh, not you, you're still much too valuable, but maybe that *puta* you and your grandson seem so fond of, one or two others. And there'd be a much tighter prison regime. Your grandson would have his work cut out thinking of ways to escape if that happened, wouldn't he, Becerra? Even if he is good at puzzles.' Both men laughed.

'Judging from your joviality, I take it that the Fascists have agreed to negotiate,' said Pinzon.

'Oh, it's early days still. Couple of parleys under the white flag of truce have taken place. We've told them our demands. Don't worry, we'll keep you informed of what's going on. They were very interested to hear about you, by the way.'

'I'm flattered,' said Pinzon.

'Famous man, aren't you? Wish I'd taken a bet with you. You were doubtful, weren't you, that they'd even negotiate?'

'Listen, Ogarrio, it's not too late, especially if you've been proved right and they're considering taking me. You don't need the others. Let them go, along with my grandson. Seek the humanity that I know's inside you.'

'Bit late for that even for our kind-hearted *sargento*,' said Becerra. It was the first time he had spoken. 'Fascists will hardly be pleased to find that their nuns and priests are really a bunch of villagers. Not much chance of an exchange taking place now, especially if they find the bodies.'

Ogarrio shrugged. 'So there we are. Shame we can't oblige. But look at it philosophically, Professor. It's just a historical process working itself out. Everybody has a role to play, the ends justify the means – and it's all good for the Republic.'

'The Republic is finished already. Politically, spiritually, idealistically, it died when the state was put into the hands of cynical Communists like you. I spit on your pseudo-philosophy.'

Ogarrio laughed. 'We'll never make a Marxist of him, will we, Becerra? Take comfort from your defeatism, then, Professor. Whether it's a bullet from a Fascist firing squad or an explosion in a cave, you won't be around to anguish about things much longer. Now, I'd love to stay chatting but we've got other things to do. Keep up the good humanitarian work. Maybe you'll get a reward in that heaven you and Tomás were talking about. You see? There's comfort every way you play this.'

He slapped Becerra on the back and both men disappeared into the darkness, laughing.

Pinzon stood for a long while where he was. Then he made his way back to his old pew by the altar, where his grandson was playing hopscotch with Felipe.

'You look depressed, Enrique,' said María, sitting down next to him. She had been queuing in the side chapel that Hector had organised into a makeshift canteen.

'Oh, it's nothing,' he said. 'I was thinking of my unpleasant exchange with Ogarrio.' He smiled. 'What have we got?'

She put the three packages side by side on the pew. 'A feast,' she said. 'Spicy Moruna soup, Trevélez ham, chorizo and sausages, Grandmother Juanita's finest Andalucían pottage. Only the best for Sargento Ogarrio's guests.'

'Cold cuts and onions,' he said, looking with distaste at the curled slivers of meat on dry crusts.

'And we have to wait for the gruel to come round and sip from the ladle because there are no bowls. But it's better than nothing,' she said. 'Shall I call Tomás?'

'Not yet, he's still enjoying his games. I'd like him to tire himself out.' He looked at her searchingly. 'You've recovered now?'

'I told you. I get over things. What did Ogarrio say that upset you?' she asked, her mouth full of bread.

'He mocked me. I found it distasteful, and a little worrying. He was courteous and rational before. He's become more fanatical, exhilarated. Inhuman. I don't think he cares any more what happens. He reminded me of Samuel's Cid, actually. There was a strange look in his eye, as if he was enjoying this. Feeling his power over us. It's one thing for us to stay calm and watch and wait – but if our captors begin to lose control of themselves, things may get out of hand faster than we're prepared for.'

'There may be an opportunity for us if they get careless.'

'Perhaps – but I think Ogarrio's beginning to tighten his grip, like an impresario planning every last detail of a great performance.'

'Men of blood,' she said. 'That's what my father used to call them. Communists. Fascists. Ideologues. They were all the same to him. He said anybody who believed in only one thing blinded themselves to life.'

'He sounds like a very wise man.'

'Yes, he was in his way. I miss him terribly, and I doubt I'll ever see him again even if I survive this. He was in Granada. The Fascists wouldn't have left somebody like him alive.'

'I'm sorry,' he said.

'It's all right. That's another thing I've learned to get over. Death is part of life. That's what my father told me. It's only the turning off of the lights before a long, dreamless sleep. I – I tried to tell myself that when my little Pablo died. That was . . . more difficult.'

'I wish I'd met your father,' he said, trying to steer her away from thoughts of her son.

She laughed. 'You're everything he most despised. Hidalgo, politician, pillar of the establishment. You'd have argued like cats. I don't know, though.' She scrutinised him. 'Maybe you would have got on. You're a bit of an idealist, too, in your way, and you're kind, like he was. He'd have liked Tomás. He loved children. He was a wonderful father to me.'

He thought of her looking after his grandson, the gentle way she anticipated his every need and knew what to say to comfort him – María had the same maternal qualities as his daughter-in-law, Julia. Even as they were talking her eyes were flicking to the boy, checking he was all right, with the early-warning instinct of every good mother. 'He's beautiful, isn't he?' she said suddenly. 'He'll have your good looks one day. Were you like him as a boy?'

'Perhaps there is a small resemblance,' he said. 'I've seen only one photograph of myself at his age, and it's a stiff family portrait, all the generations together in solemn rows. I look very bad-tempered and uncomfortable in my high starched collar, cross-legged on the ground in front of my grandfather.'

'I wish I'd known you when you were young,' she said. She chuckled and nestled closer to him. 'Though by the sound of it I wouldn't have been much welcomed by your family, except as a scullery-maid, perhaps.' She giggled softly. 'My father was a coalman on the railway, and an Anarcho-Syndicalist trade-unionist. Not your class at all – but maybe we might have smiled at each other when you passed me mopping the stairs.'

'I would certainly have noticed somebody as striking as you, and at that impressionable age I'd probably have fallen head over heels in love with you.'

'Oh, yes. I can just see it. The prince and the servant girl, like in all the fairy stories. My father warned me about people like you. He said all those tales were just ways to justify the feudal system and – what was it called? The lord's right to have any woman he wanted before her wedding night.'

'Ah, yes, the *dem'lio de pernada*. What the French call the *droit de cuissage*.'

'Yeah, that's it.' She was grinning wickedly. Pinzon was pleased to see she had begun to enjoy herself. 'You never know, though. Perverse as I am, I'd probably have led you on – to strike a blow for the revolution and corrupt a member of the ruling classes to our way of thinking. I'd have converted you to Anarchism instead of that anaemic liberalism you wasted your life on. We'd have eloped together and I'd have taught you how to throw bombs at the Guardia Civil. We'd have had the time of our lives.' She squeezed his hand and rested her head on his shoulder. 'If only, eh?'

'If only,' he said, 'but the fact is you're the one telling fairy stories now. I'm old enough to be your grandfather.'

'Flatterer,' she said. She peered at him. 'I knew you were a charmer.'

She darted her lips forward and planted a quick kiss on his cheek. The roundness of her breast touched his chest. He felt a flush of pleasure and embarrassment. He gently leaned away from her, sure it had been an accident on her part. There was not a hint of guile, only humour in her eyes. 'Did you really throw bombs at the Guardia Civil?' he asked.

'No,' she said. 'I'm a softie, really. I can't imagine myself killing people. Even shits who deserve it, like Paco. And I couldn't hate anybody simply because they believed something different from me. That's why I was drawn to Anarchism. It's not really about chaos and revolution. In its purest form it's about tolerance. Freedom. Live and let live. A bit like that old Arabic kingdom you were reading about. I suppose it's going to end badly in Mishkhat, just like our dream of an Anarchist paradise has fallen apart. Samuel's given one or two hints about fundamentalists and crusaders. It's like our own times.'

'History is the Cassandra of the liberal sciences,' he said, 'full of warnings that we're doomed to ignore. Sometimes I think we're tied to some implacable tumbrel that rolls on repeating the mistakes of the past. Did I tell you that above that mosque we found a statue of Paladon? If only he could speak to us. He might have some lessons for our age.'

'But he is speaking to us,' she said. 'Or, rather, Samuel is. Listen.' Her eyes were sparkling. 'We've nothing else to do for a while and you should read on. You never know – my experience has always been that ideas come to you when you stop thinking about problems.'

A shadow hovered over them. It was Felipe. He had brought back Tomás, who was now sitting on the pew eating his sandwich and swinging his legs.

'What is it, Felipe?' asked Pinzon. The young man's face was distraught and he was clumsily stepping from boot to boot, his rifle butt bumping the pew.

'If I can be so bold, Señor, er, Professor . . .'

'Tell me, Felipe. Don't be afraid.'

'I overheard some of the hostages, one or two of them . . . They were saying you had come up with a plan to save everybody.'

Pinzon felt the blood drain from his cheeks, wondering how much Paco, or whoever had spoken, had given away. 'You're muddling me with your *sargento*, Felipe. He's the one who's arranging a hostage deal.'

'But . . . yes, I know . . . but do you think they'll agree? The Fascists?'

Pinzon exchanged a glance with María. He sighed. 'We can only hope so, Felipe.'

'But what if they don't?' His expression crumpled. He looked like a grieving clown. 'We'll all die here, won't we?'

'We may. But I don't think we should despair yet.'

'But just in case. Do you think you might find a way to save us? I – I'm not sure Sargento Ogarrio's really interested in the hostage exchange any more. When he was here earlier, with Becerra, they kept laughing about blowing the Fascists sky high . . . But if you could think of a way, Professor, maybe . . . maybe . . .'

'I don't know, Felipe. I'd be the first to tell you if I thought of anything.' He was still taking in what Felipe had just said. It sounded like the opportunity he had been hoping for. Obviously, if they could somehow make the dim Felipe switch allegiance, all sorts of new possibilities might open, but he could not discount the likelihood that their guard was trying, in his clumsy manner, on Ogarrio's orders, to elicit information about a conspiracy. Amiable as he was, he was a Communist, one of the unthinking sheep. He had been brainwashed to obey orders unquestioningly. That he was experiencing a crisis was manifest – but that did not mean his conditioning had failed. This needed careful probing and, with Tomás and María beside him and the other hostages still awake around them, he had to be cautious. 'I'll put my mind to it, Felipe,' he said, 'but it may be difficult to come up with something quickly. Perhaps if you and I had a chat about it later, when we're not all so tired . . .'

'What about the magician?' It was a piping little voice. Tomás's eyes were gleaming with excitement.

'What are you talking about, you silly?' asked María, giving him a tender smile.

'The magician in Grandfather's book. The – the alchy-missi . . .'

'The alchemist? You mean Samuel?' asked María.

'Yes. Maybe if we look into that magic book we'll find the answer. Maybe he can tell us what to do.'

'That's a very good idea, Tomás,' said María, and mouthed to Pinzon over the child's shoulder, 'It'll put him back to sleep.'

'I'm not sure,' he muttered. 'The story's no longer suitable for a child.'

'Oh.' She seemed irritated. 'I think it's a wonderful idea. Felipe, you enjoyed the professor's reading earlier. You want to find out what happens, don't you? It'll help him come up with a plan. That's how professors get their ideas. Through books.'

Felipe looked doubtful. 'It's a good story,' he said. 'If, as you say, it will help . . .'

'Of course it will,' said María. 'Come on, Enrique, read on from where you left off.'

'Please, Grandfather.'

'Oh, very well.' He picked up the book. 'Where were we?'

'You said something about a philosopher finding a mystery in a cave.'

'Is it a magic cave?' asked Tomás.

'Probably,' said María, as they settled in a circle around Pinzon.

He began to read. As before, some of the townspeople

gathered round them, but it was after ten o'clock and few stayed the course.

María fell asleep before Tomás did, but soon afterwards he, too, began to nod and gradually his tousled head dropped on to her knees. Pinzon paused to lay a blanket over them. He looked up at Felipe. 'Do you still want me to continue?' he asked.

'If it helps you think, Professor,' said Felipe, eagerly.

Pinzon sighed and carried on. Only after a long period did he look up and realise that, some time during the last hour, the young soldier had fallen asleep, leaning against a pillar. His rifle had fallen on the paving. There was nothing to prevent Pinzon from picking it up.

But he left it. There was nothing he could do with it. What would be the use of one rifle even if they attempted a break-out? The men on the ramparts would turn the machine-gun on them and mow them down. He sighed, and closed the book.

He looked down at the faces of the two people who were now closest to his heart, his grandson and the strange woman who, in barely a day, had won his respect, affection, and – he had to admit it – perhaps more: what would he not sacrifice to save them? But it was hopeless. Hopeless.

Desperately he seized the manuscript again, hoping that the discipline of translation might still the screaming voices in his head. Tomás had called this a magic book. Felipe had believed that he would find an answer in its pages. Well, anything was better than nothing. Why not seek solutions to his problems in a story about an alchemist who had died eight hundred years ago? It made as much sense as anything else in this impossible situation.

Al-Andaluz, 1080–86

Codex III

The Mosque

(I) In which I tell how a philosopher found light in a cave, and how a king became enamoured of a rock

In earlier, happier days, long before we went off to war, we would sometimes be allowed to hold our morning lessons in the king's gardens, particularly in springtime when the flowers were in bloom. We would rise before dawn and walk briskly up the steep path to the palace. Ibn Sa'id trailed behind us, perched precariously on his donkey, while the Mishkhat plain shimmered in the first rays of sunlight that had crept over the mountains. When we arrived we would find carpets already laid out for us on the lawn, as well as an enormous breakfast.

The terrace had a view of the great granite rock that rose above our city. Near the summit was a cave that bored deep into the bowels of the hill, and under the overhang at its mouth was a Mussulman shrine. The common people considered it a holy place. From where we sat, we could watch the pilgrims in their white burnouses bowing in prayer or placing their petitions and flags in the gaps between the stones that blocked the cave's entrance.

Once, when we were still eager young students, not yet fifteen years old, ibn Sa'id had given us a theology lesson – or what passed for our eccentric sage's rationalist version of such a thing. His subject, since he perceived we were curious about it, was the shrine. I mention it because this conversation was

173

to have a significant bearing on the great enterprise that I will shortly describe.

I can see him now, lolling on his damask cushions, a glass of sherbet in one hand, a sesame bun in the other. Behind him was an explosion of red hibiscus and white lilac, their sweet scents mingling with that of the roses and the newly cut grass. A cuckoo was calling from a thicket, a comic counterpoint to our teacher's sonorous rhetoric, as he expounded on the Creation.

'Assuredly the Almighty is capable of accomplishing by a mere thought gigantic works of natural engineering,' *Cuckoo! Cuckoo!* 'but don't you think it more likely, in the case of this cave that the actual agent He employed to achieve His miracle was molten lava, which can dissolve the hardest of rock into liquid as easily as a flame melts a candle? Surely those smooth walls and round tunnels were bored as a result of a volcanic eruption?' *Cuckoo!* 'Paladon, wipe that insolent smirk off your face. You claim to be a church builder. Is there not a distinction between the grand plan in the mind of the master mason and the humble tools – chisels, pulleys and compasses – with which he achieves his effects?'

He belched happily. 'This is germinal to our discussion, boys. God's works are unfolded in scriptures that have been copied down to us over generations. No one denies their fundamental truth, but since they are the works of men, for such are scribes and even prophets, one must make allowance for the occasional metaphor, for deep mysteries are being described here, and words, even at their most eloquent, are inadequate to encompass the entirety of God and His works. We require Reason to interpret them.'

I could see Aziz bristling. 'The Holy Qur'ān is the literal Word of God.'

For a moment ibn Sa'id looked uncomfortable, aware that he had strayed into heretical territory. 'So it is, so it is,' he said. 'As revealed to his Prophet. You are right to point that out,

Aziz. Certainly the Holy Qur'ān must be taken as the exception to any rule, though much good work has been done by the Mu'tazilah School to reconcile the words of the Blessed Muhammad with the science that we have been studying. I was referring to some of the – ah – less reliable scriptures, not to mention folklore and mythology, which brings me back to the shrine over there. What do we know of its origins? What happened here three hundred years ago at the time of the Arab conquests? Aziz, you should be the authority on this. You attend the annual prayer meeting at the cave mouth in the company of your father and the king. Let us into the secret of its mysteries.'

Aziz glanced nervously at me – he hated being singled out – but this time I could not help him. 'We go to the cave to celebrate the miracle of our deliverance from Christian marauders,' he said sullenly. 'After the Conquest there were still a few Visigoth princes we hadn't beaten and they made raids on our villages.'

'Note "miracle", "deliverance", words of poignant association.' Ibn Sa'id smiled benevolently and popped a date into his mouth from the bowl of fruit the servants had just replenished. 'Go on. Go on.'

'One day the villagers who lived in these parts were visited by a wandering faqi – well, some people say he was an angel or a djinn. He warned them that the Christians were about to attack, and told them to take their women and children up the high rock where they'd find a cave to hide in. He said if they were to pray to Allah in this refuge, their enemies would be smitten and destroyed.'

'"Smitten". I like that. And?'

Aziz frowned, wondering if he was being mocked, but he went on gamely: 'They heeded his warning, but when they came to the mouth of the cave they were scared to go inside, so the faqi thumped his staff on the ground, and the cave was filled with radiant light. They went in and prayed, and down below in the plain, the Christians, who were burning the village, were swept away by a flood, because the river suddenly broke its banks, and the Visigoth prince and his army were drowned to a man.'

'Well told, Aziz. But the river kept rising, didn't it? All the way up to the cave mouth.'

'Yes, so the faqi had to go out and use his staff again to still the waves, and when he did they subsided, and the next morning, when the villagers went back to their fields, they found that the earth was dry, their crops were unspoiled, and the houses that the Christians had burned were restored, as good as new.' He shrugged. 'They were saved,' he ended lamely.

'And the faqi?'

'He'd disappeared. Oh, yes, and the rocks above the cave mouth had tumbled down, blocking the entrance, so, with the light of God sealed inside it, they ever afterwards considered it a sacred place – and that's why we pray there.'

'The light of God. Yes. That's what the cave is called, isn't it? Mishkhat. The Niche of Light. It gave its name to our city. A charming legend – but it has parallels with other stories too, doesn't it? Many are to be found in the scriptures. Samuel? Paladon? Identify some for me.'

'Noah's flood,' I offered.

'Moses' magic staff,' added Paladon.

'And you'll find more echoes if you look closely enough.' Ibn Sa'id was beaming broadly. 'The chariots of Pharaoh deluged by the Red Sea, perhaps. A messenger from God speaking to His chosen people. Even the divine light emanating from the Ark of the Covenant in Solomon's Temple. These are old tales . . . old tales, but dressed in new clothes.'

Aziz was looking furious. 'Are you saying it's all lies?'

'Certainly not,' said ibn Sa'id. 'I have no doubt that the early settlers were threatened by renegade Visigoths. Perhaps they did flee their village and find a hiding place. There may even have been a flood – but the details strike me as contrived, a story embroidered in the telling, borrowing from the scriptures with which even the common people are familiar. Yes.' He shifted his big behind.

'Consider another thing. These settlers had just arrived in a new land, which already had its traditions and holy places. Did you know that the Christians also have a legend related to the cave? In the pages of the Visigoth historian Isidore of Seville, I found a reference to a hermitage that had once existed there. It was rather famous. Why? Because of another local legend. It happened that a shepherd boy lost his lamb. He sought it on that very rock we're looking at, and when he came to the mouth of that very cave he was granted a vision of the Virgin Mary, who was standing in a shaft of blue and white light with his lamb in her arms. Well, that news spread quickly enough, and in the old days, Christian pilgrims used to file up the winding path to worship at the site of a miracle just as our Mussulmans do today – and for the same reason. The story, you see, is dressing, but the mystery is the same. The name gives us a clue. The Niche of Light. Light? What does that say to you? Godhead? Illumination? Enlightenment?' He paused. 'Knowledge?' He looked at each of us in turn, his little eyes twinkling behind his spectacles. 'Are any of you familiar with the word "numen"?'

'It's Latin. It means the spirit that inhabits a holy place,' I said. 'The presence of a god.'

'Correct. Has none of you ever felt such a presence? An otherwise unremarkable little valley that suddenly gives you the shivers and you can't tell why? Perhaps it once contained a temple. Or a chasm in the mountains that fills you with inexplicable dread? Was it once a place of sacrifice? A theory I came across in Egypt speculates there are nodal points in the fabric of the earth through which spiritual energy is released. The Pyramids are supposedly built on them, but these nodes cannot be unique to Egypt. Many of our mosques are sited on the foundations of what were once Christian churches, and those churches themselves replaced temples to pagan gods. Is it even strange that this should be so? The site would be holy to all religions if there was a numen there.'

'This spiritual energy – is it something like the celestial nitre that underlies the processes we use in our alchemy?'

'Perhaps, Samuel. We know from our studies that every aspect of science is conjoined – in the humours, in the spheres—'

'I don't see what this has to do with the legend of the cave,' interrupted Aziz.

'Let me tell you what else I found out during my researches,' continued ibn Sa'id, unperturbed. I noticed that he had become so absorbed in our discussion that for minutes now he had left his food untouched. A wasp was buzzing over the bowl of fruit and he did not wave it off. 'Would you believe me, Aziz, if I told you that even before it became revered by the Christians your sacred Mussulman shrine was an oracle dedicated to Apollo? A priestess lived in it who told fortunes. That was in Roman times, but they, too, had taken over an existing shrine. When the Phoenicians established colonies here, the cave had been a temple to the dark deity Cybele. The fact is that this cave has always been a centre of mystery and religion. I humbly put it down to the numen that people sensed there. That, surely, is the meaning of the invisible light in its dark recesses, not a flash from a faqi's staff. The light of mystery or arcane knowledge, if you know how to recognise it.'

I was suddenly reminded of the first lesson my father had given me, when he told me about the white letters behind the black ones in the Torah. I felt a burning desire to go inside the cave and see for myself.

'Of course, much of this must remain conjecture,' ibn Sa'id was rounding off his lecture, 'because nowadays nobody's allowed to go in. It's a perilous place, full of potholes. Wazir Salim's very wise to forbid entry. Too many disappearances. One unwary step and *poof*.' He swallowed a piece of bun.

That was enough for Paladon, for whom anything forbidden

was a challenge. A few evenings later, we slipped away with him from Salim's house after dinner and, as the sun was setting, climbed the steep path to the shrine. Roped together and holding torches, we clambered up the rocks festooned with prayer flags, through the gaps between the piled stones into the dark, ringing emptiness inside.

We marvelled at the size, the smooth granite walls and the well of shadows beyond the reach of our burning torches. I was awed by the aura of age and mystery. I hesitate to say sanctity because its numen was dark and forbidding. There was certainly no light inside the dank, wet cavern, celestial or otherwise, but it took little effort to imagine that those black recesses had once been inhabited by spirits or gods. I envisaged myself snatched back in time to the sanctum of Jove in Dodona, the Sybil's grotto in Cumae or the torchlight journeys of initiation in the underground caverns and tunnels of Eleusis. When the smoke from our torches disturbed a colony of bats nesting on the ceiling, I screamed in terror, thinking that the shapes fluttering round my head were Furies or sprites, and it was only Paladon's laughter that brought me to my senses again.

He did not suffer from an overheated imagination. Paladon saw the world in terms of physical spaces to be conquered. On subsequent excursions to the cave, he led us fearlessly into its depths, warning us of fissures and cracks in the sloping floor. He took us down tunnels to their dead ends, and often we were rewarded with wonders: subsidiary caverns spiked with stalagmites and stalactites, the colours of different minerals embedded in the walls – threads of silver and gold, the glint of copper, the black polish of obsidian (here was ample material for our alchemical experiments) – and once we made out insubstantial shadows behind the reflection of our torchlight on the dripping stone walls. Peering closer, we saw they were paintings of stick-like men with spears confronting elephants and antelopes, and realised that this extraordinary geological treasure had once provided shelter for our primitive ancestors.

That revelation, the continuity of sanctuary from prehistoric times to Phoenician to Roman to Christian and finally to our own, made the numen of this strange shrine even more powerful, and I began to believe ibn Sa'id's theory that there are indeed places on the earth where the life force of the Prime Mover resonates.

These were idle fancies then – we were engaged, after all, in schoolboy pranks – but two years later, after we had returned to Mishkhat, trying to renew our lives again after our traumatic experiences with the Cid, I remembered how Paladon, Aziz and I, on the evening before the battle, had talked of a Brotherhood of the Craft and Paladon had said he would construct a memorial to our fellowship. Where better, I thought, than in this cave? We could make it truly a Niche of Light, combining all we had been learning in a symbol of Enlightenment.

It was several months, however, before I was in a suitable frame of mind to broach the idea. I had first to overcome the devastation to my spirit when I discovered that Aziz no longer loved me.

Oh, my Gazelle. How it ended. With hardly a quarrel, just a silent fading away.

At first, it was as if nothing had changed. After the victory celebrations and the departure of the Cid, we left the army and its tents and moved back into our old quarters. I remember how my heart thumped with joy to see my box and slippers next to his in their familiar position at the foot of the bed. That night we lost ourselves in lovemaking.

Next morning we met Paladon for our lessons, and in the evening we visited Ayesha, who was overjoyed to see us safely returned, especially Paladon. Theirs was a touching reunion. Afterwards, while she played her music, Aziz and I reclined on our accustomed couch, but he did not nestle close to me as he always had before. He sat stiffly, lost in his thoughts.

I thought nothing of it. I put his introspection down to the news that his proud father had given him over lunch. As a reward for his heroism on the battlefield, the king had appointed him assistant qadi. He had much to study because in a year he would take over from Salim. It was a great responsibility. I nudged him to show my support. He gave me a lovely smile.

But when we retired to our room, he did not speak to me. The slaves doused the lamps, and he lay on his side of the bed and I on mine. I rolled over to be closer to him, but he murmured an excuse and turned his back to me.

For four weeks it continued in this way. In the daytime Aziz was friendly and charming, but no more so to me than to anybody else, and he rarely embraced me as he had been wont to do before. At night, we lay, like an old married couple, on the bed with a gulf between us. Neither of us spoke, neither of us slept much, in the heavy silence.

One evening I came back from the library to find him seated cross-legged at his small desk on the carpet. Our bedchamber was washed in moonlight and the flame of the lamp was flickering in the breeze that was rustling the curtains, casting soft shadows over his face. He was a creation of blue and gold, like one of the sketches of angels in Paladon's notebook. Half man, half boy. I recalled my first sight of him in the fruit grove and wondered again that anybody could be so beautiful and live on this earth. I watched him from the shadows. A ringlet of hair hung over his forehead and his lips were pursed in concentration. I suddenly noticed how tired he was, and felt a wave of pity for him. Softly I put down my books and moved behind him, reaching out my hands to massage his shoulders as I had done so many times before to relieve him of his strain and worries.

He shrugged me away, muttering, 'Stop it, Samuel. I'm busy.'

Something snapped. I paced the room angrily. He ignored me. I kicked his box of clothes. He did not even look up. I rounded on him. I asked what I had done to deserve his coldness. He continued to flip through the sheets of court records he had brought home to study.

I lost control. I threw my slipper at his desk, upsetting his pens and spilling a bottle of ink. 'Say something,' I shouted. 'You don't talk to me any more. We never make love. At least tell me what I've done wrong. How I've displeased you.' Eventually I ran out of words.

Silently he restored the ink bottle and pens to their former positions. 'You're making a fool of yourself, Samuel,' he said curtly. 'The servants will hear you. If gossip reaches my father's ears there will be a scene.' He paused, closing his eyes. When he opened them there was an icy glint in their pitch-black depths that I had not seen before – or it had never been directed at me. 'You might also remember your position in this household.'

I could not believe what I was hearing. I think my tone was also icy when I replied, 'And what is my position?'

He sighed. 'I'm very fond of you, Samuel. Really I am. You've served me well, and I believe I have always been kind to you.'

He might as well have kicked me in the face. Slowly I raised myself to my feet again and staggered back, sinking on to the bed in my misery. 'Is that meant to comfort me?' I croaked. 'You're also fond of your spaniel and you're kind to your horses.'

He rubbed his temple in exasperation.

I could not bear the silence. 'You told me that you loved me.' It came out as a half inarticulate gulp. I could feel the prickle of tears in my eyes. Soon I could not help myself. I was wailing, shaking in every limb. My heart was breaking. I wanted to die.

He rose slowly and walked over to where I sat on the bed. I thought he was going to embrace me, but he gave me his handkerchief. 'I need some time to think it over, Samuel,' he said. 'Things are difficult now. I'm in the public eye. So much is expected of me . . .'

'What? Are you suddenly embarrassed you have a Jewish lover?' I sniffed.

'That was unworthy of you,' he said.

He sat on the bed beside me and took my hand. His face was wreathed in an affectionate smile, but his eyes were detached. He was learning the politician's art of dissemblance. The kiss he placed on my forehead was perfunctory. 'You know I'll always be grateful to you, Samuel,' he said, in what he must have supposed was a kindly tone. 'You have done everything my father asked of you. I don't think I'd ever have got through my studies without you. You've opened my mind. Everything you've taught me will be useful to me when I become qadi. And,' he ran his hand down my cheek, 'there's also the tenderness you bestowed on me. Your poems. That sort of thing. You've been a wonderful lover. I have so enjoyed it.' He kissed me again.

I jerked my head away. 'But now it's over? That's what you're telling me, isn't it?'

'Did I say that? No, I'm not suggesting anything precipitate. It's the opposite. I like you to be near me.' He had begun to twist the handkerchief in his hands. 'But we must face it, Samuel. We are no longer boys with the freedoms that boys have. Who knows? There may come a day when both of us decide that it's time to put away childish things. Oh, we'll remain friends,' he added hurriedly. 'We'll always be friends, as we are with Paladon. We will still meet from time to time, and have those lovely conversations about philosophy and magic, and the Prime Mover, and the ideal world we dreamed of creating. I know how important that is to you. And it has been fun for me, too, though I don't always follow your complicated arguments.'

I was not sure what shocked me more – the casualness with which he had described our passion, or the way he dismissed the philosophy that I had always believed bound the three of us together. 'What about the Brotherhood of the Craft you wanted to establish? Was that just fun too?'

'No, I meant it. It's a fine idea,' he said. 'Why not? Paladon can build a temple. I'm sure he'll amaze everybody.' He chuckled and rubbed my knee. 'Though as qadi I'm not sure how far I can extend my approval to all your strange beliefs. I *am* expected to uphold the state religion, you know.' His arm was round my shoulders. There was a light in his eyes, and his lips were trembling. 'No more of this, Samuel, please. Quarrelling upsets me.' As he spoke he was untying the string of my jellaba. 'I'm sorry, it's my fault. I have been working too hard.' He pulled the robe over my head and with greedy fingers untied my loincloth, then roughly pushed me backwards.

He grabbed the pillow and wedged it under my behind. As he lifted my legs over his shoulders, fumbling with his own loincloth and the bottle of ointment, I heard his quick, rasping breaths. I struggled into the frontal position that was uncomfortable for me but it was what he enjoyed. I knew that his violence was only a momentary impulse of lust, yet I didn't care. After so long an interval, I was happy to be the object of any affection, in whatever form. I lifted my posterior into position so he could use me as he willed. I was beyond shame. I would let him do anything to me if it helped me to win him back. The more cruelly he treated me, the more I would abase myself. He could beat me for all I cared. As long as he noticed me.

I saw the hunger in his face as it hung above me. I closed my eyes, willing my body to shudder under his thrusts as it used to in ecstasy when we were united by mutual passion . . . But I felt only the chill of the night air on my legs and behind.

Aziz had stood up and was retying his sash. 'Forgive me, Samuel, I really am busy tonight,' he said.

I lay naked on the sheets, knowing for the first time how it felt to be a whore – worse, a rejected whore.

In the morning I quietly removed my box of belongings from his room. I know he was relieved. After only a few days, a woman took my place. To my mortification, I discovered that he had purchased a slave girl from one of the generals who had followed Salim into Toledan territory after his victory, and realised that his long absences into the dawn hours had not been because of extra work at his office but because he had been with his new paramour – even while he was still sharing his bed with me. And now that I had released him, he was not even content with her, for he and Paladon would often go out together on evening excursions, leaving me behind with my books.

Sometimes I thought I heard the servants sniggering when I passed them. Many had despised me at the height of my fortune and delighted in what they perceived to be my downfall. I ignored them. Oh, my friends were kind enough to me: Paladon was never good with words, but he always had a slap on the back for me and a sympathetic smile. Even Aziz tried to make amends in his own way. One night he sent me a beautiful, bejewelled Negro boy he had bought for me in the market. For a while I even considered dallying with his present – I was angry enough with myself and the world – but in the end I sent the lad back with my thanks. Nobody could replace Aziz physically or spiritually. No one ever has.

I don't know how I survived those first two months. I hardly slept. All I could think about was Aziz with one of his women only a few chambers away from me down the corridor. I barely ate. I found the morning classes with Aziz and Paladon difficult to bear. The proximity of my ex-lover was both tantalising and repulsive, and I was sometimes maddened by Paladon's cheerfulness. I was relieved when I could escape to the library to pursue my private studies. At least in books I could find some respite from my nagging misery. When I was alone in my new room I picked at my wound. Like all creatures spurned in love, I blamed myself, pondering uselessly what fault I had committed to cause Aziz to reject me.

It tortured me to see him roistering with Paladon. There

were several excruciating encounters when, on my way out of the library late at night with books under my arm, I came across the two of them drunkenly steering veiled and giggling houris along the corridors, and once I saw in the moonlight Aziz pulling a handsome soldier by the hand. That hurt me more than his dalliance with women. The young man bore a resemblance to me.

Aziz seemed insatiable, and no depravity, as he experimented with his new-found freedom, was beneath him. On another occasion I heard wild noises coming from inside his room and Paladon's loud laugh rising above the feminine squeals. I thought then that Paladon had betrayed me too. It was not their disporting that grieved me so much as what I believed was our broken fellowship. During those days we never met in Ayesha's pavilion as we had before to discuss ideas. I know now that if they were avoiding me it was because my bitter hatred of the world made me tiresome company.

One day Paladon, big-hearted as ever, took me aside to tell me that I should pull myself together. 'It's over, Samuel. Accept it. Move forward,' he said.

'You wouldn't say that if you knew how I feel,' I said. 'You can't imagine how he treated me.'

'Pretty brutally, I expect,' said Paladon. 'But isn't that a good reason to cut your losses? Hasn't he revealed what sort of man he is? Be angry for a while. It'll be healthier. Get your own back by finding somebody more good-looking and intelligent than he is. You know Aziz is not worthy of you, never was. He's like a brother to me but I can see he isn't as bright as you. He certainly doesn't have the same gentle sensibility that you have and, don't forget, he's a prince. All royalty are callous and selfish, spoiled rotten. It's in their nature.'

'But I love him, Paladon. I can't change that . . . and he feels a fondness for me still. I know it. Don't you see? I have to cling to the hope that he'll come back to me, when he's . . . when he's had his fun.'

Paladon shook his head, exasperated. 'Of course he still loves you – but not in the same way as before. For God's sake, Samuel. You're a philosopher. You usually see things more clearly than other people – and the reality of this is staring you in the face. He's a man now. He had his first taste of power during that battle with the Cid, and he's become addicted to it. I'm sorry to be the one to tell you, but love . . . Well, it just doesn't interest him any more. He can't help it. He's besotted by thoughts of his future and all the wonderful opportunities that lie ahead of him. All the pleasures, too, that power brings in its train. He's hungry to try them and – there's no gentle way to say this – you're in the way. Recognise that.'

My tragedy, of course, was that, deep inside, I did recognise it – but that was no help to me then. It has never been since for, as even the wisest philosophers will tell you, there is no Reason that can withstand the madness of love, and mine was no mere infection of the heart caused by a chance strike of Cupid's dart. To Aziz I had bonded my soul. The pledge I had sworn to him was eternal, and how could I make Paladon understand that? Or appreciate that if I ever relinquished the ember of hope, which was all that sustained me, my life would be over as surely as if I plunged a knife in my heart.

I could see the desperation in his face because he thought he was not getting through to me. 'I beg you, Samuel, grow up. It's the way of the world. First love can be wonderful, but it never lasts. I should know. I've been jilted more times than I can remember. I always manage to find another girl next day, though. You can get over anything if you put your mind to it.'

Then I became angry. 'Shame on you, Paladon. You don't believe that. Think of what you feel for Ayesha. You dally with others because you can't have her, but you know in your heart there's no one else. I may be a fool but you're – you're a hypocrite.'

I stamped away, hating myself. His voice came after me: 'Let

me help you, Samuel. You'll drive yourself mad if you go on
like this.'

And there, too, I agreed with him, for I had noticed the
signs of incipient insanity already. At times, when I rehearsed
my conversations with Aziz, seeking a hint – anything – that
might explain why he had rejected me, the voices in my head
seemed real, and on occasions I even saw him standing next
to my bed. Then I was terrified, imagining I had inherited the
delusions of my father. I would cower under my sheets, fearing,
if I peeped out, that I might see my own version of an Old
Testament prophet, with staff and tangled beard, rolling his
eyes at me accusingly. Yes, I was losing my senses.

And there was nothing I could do about it.

Ibn Sa'id said nothing but he hounded me over my medical
studies, perhaps thinking that hard work would relieve my
depression. He tested me severely on my understanding of al-
Razi, and, when he was satisfied I knew all the theory, he
insisted that I spend a few months in the hospital, working day
and night. Only thus could a young doctor learn his trade, he
said. I agreed to leave Salim's house, not because I was interested in becoming a physician but because I would be spared
the sight of Aziz.

At first it was easy. I assisted Dr Isa, setting broken limbs
and bleeding patients with fevers. After a month, he allowed
me to work with him in the ward for mental patients. I found
myself treating men and women whose minds were more fractured than my own. I found the bare cells of the manacled
insane, with their shaven heads, wild smiles and strangely
knowing eyes, curiously comforting. I sought in them the touch
of divine madness that I had glimpsed in al-Gazali and seen
in perverted form in the Cid. I was on a deranged quest to find
the Idiots of God and for some weeks I persuaded myself I
had discovered them. None could have been described as happy
– even those who raved and laughed – but neither were they

sad. They were humans levelled down to a vegetable state, free of care or responsibility, and for a while it suited me to believe that theirs was an enviable contentment.

Of course I kept such thoughts to myself. To all appearances I was Dr Isa's assiduous helper, and after a while, as no doubt ibn Sa'id had intended, the example of the hardworking Christian began to have an effect on me. Slowly, as the weeks went by, I learned to appreciate my superior's kindness and his unruffled sense of humour as he talked patiently to one impossible case after another, apparently taking their delusions at face value. He bowed to them if they thought they were the Caliph; he maintained a one-sided conversation with those who were locked in silence; he offered his shoulder to those who wanted only to cry. He was seeking in each the spark of sanity that he believed lay dormant inside the most shattered mind. I watched him administer his simple herbal concoctions, painstakingly copied from Dioscorides, until one day I saw that my knowledge in alchemy had far surpassed his and that I could help him.

At night, after the last medical rounds, I worked in the hospital laboratory, and within a month I had several samples, transmuted from minerals, not herbs. Nervously I offered them to him. He was sceptical, but when he appreciated that I understood the balancing of humours as well as, if not better than, he did, he let me experiment. I picked the most violent patient, a baker who was given to gnashing rages, believing he was a djinn from the land of Iblis bound on a burning wheel. In three days he had calmed to the point that he remembered his bakery and started to worry that rats were eating his store of grain.

I have since become something of an authority in the field of medicines for use on mental patients, and recently I heard that my theory of chemical imbalances, which I developed shortly after my sojourn at the hospital, is now being taught in one of the academies in Baghdad. Dr Isa is named as co-author. I am happy for him to be so honoured. It is small thanks to a man who, without realising it, was also helping me for, in a subliminal fashion, his gentle treatment of the mental patients under his care had cured me of my depression.

When I returned from the hospital, it was to find that the routine of our old lives together had changed for ever. Aziz had started his work as an apprentice qadi, and had no time for lessons in the mornings. He had enough to do with learning the complicated Mussulman laws. Wazir Salim had therefore closed our academy. Paladon now worked full time for his father. Ibn Sa'id finally had the leisure to labour on his abandoned book, and I – well, Salim, ever generous and thorough, had a plan for me too.

As a reward for my coaching and companionship to his son, he had secured for me a position as a junior physician in the palace. So, by an irony of Fate, as I lost the favour of one prince, I was elevated into the highest court circles, treating the numerous royal relatives and noblemen who served as chamberlains of the bath and honorary attendants of the bedrolls. I also treated the king's widowed sister, Janifa, who ruled benevolently in the harem. It was not long before I was appointed physician to the king's concubines. Janifa liked me, and I suppose the king and the wazir decided that the women would be safe with me. I might as well have been a eunuch. They knew my proclivities did not extend to the female sex, even the most sensuous blooms in King Abu's flower garden.

So the world I had known changed again but, thankfully, not the friendship we three had forged. Wazir Salim allowed Paladon and me to keep our rooms in his house, and once he and Aziz had seen that I was in control of myself, we met frequently in Ayesha's quarters. In time, Aziz and I got over our estrangement. He could see that I was no longer making demands on him so he relaxed again in my presence. I managed to persuade myself that neither of us had lost our affection for the other, even if our relationship was now to be Platonic. It satisfied me as much as anything could. Soon we had picked up the threads of the conversations we had enjoyed in the past, and any listener might have concluded that our academy of natural philosophy was as thriving as it had ever been. I think Aziz found our discussions soothing after a hard day's work in the courts, and for Paladon it was a welcome change from talking to workmen. No doubt he also wanted to escape the company of religious-minded cousins in his father's household, who took a dim view of his decision to become a Mussulman.

Perhaps they were sceptical about his intentions, and thought that his apostasy was driven by greed and ambition so he could marry a prince's daughter. They did not know Paladon as I did. He was a man of honour, incapable of half-measures. Desire for Ayesha may have impelled him to take this step – when he mentioned it first to me the night before our battle with the Cid I am sure that he had not thought everything through. It was months later that he approached Salim. He had already eschewed his flautist and all his other paramours. I once surprised him coming out of the mosque after Friday prayers, tucking his copy of the Qur'ān bashfully into his satchel. That was when I realised how serious he was, and I urged him then to talk to ibn Sa'id, who agreed to introduce him to the Islamic scriptures. I waited outside the curtain on the evening of his appointment with the wazir. He had been nervous. 'He'll never believe I'm sincere,' he said.

'Just tell him of your love,' I said.

'For Ayesha or Allah?' he asked.

'I think you have to persuade him, old friend, that they are one and the same.'

He nodded gravely. He was wearing only his jellaba but it seemed that he was steeling himself in chain mail. 'You taught me there is only one God.'

'And Allah is one of His names. Perhaps the finest. It negates no other if you are true.'

He nodded thoughtfully again and pulled back the curtain.

And Wazir Salim – who was not a man easily deceived – acceded to his request and offered personally to conduct the lessons Paladon had to undergo for his conversion. He warned him that it might take at least two years of study before he was fully accepted into the Umma. He also told him that ultimately it would not be his decision but that of the chief faqi, who was likely to test him thoroughly and probably not sympathetically. Then he smiled. There was the small matter of a jewelled turban, which had once mysteriously disappeared from the chief faqi's rooms. Might Paladon know anything about it by any chance?

Needless to say, within a day the turban was back on its peg in the *madrasah*, but that was no guarantee that the chief faqi's wrath had been appeased. Paladon persevered with his studies undaunted, and never missed the Friday prayers.

A month later Salim called our household together and announced that Ayesha and Paladon were formally engaged. We later learned of his conditions. First, Paladon had to convince him that his intention to convert to the Mussulman faith was sincere. (Well, half of that battle had been won in his initial interview.) Second, the young man had to prove his maturity: there were to be no more flamboyant night-time adventures, sexual or otherwise. If the wazir was to give away his daughter, he would accept only a man whose virtue and reputation were impeccable. Above all, he must be chaste. For the health of his body and to palliate the humours that affect young men, Paladon would be allowed to keep a slave girl, chosen by Ayesha, and otherwise eschew dissipation of any kind. To these terms Paladon acquiesced readily, as well as to the third: that he should devote himself in his profession to prove he was able to support a family. This was no hardship for Paladon, who loved his craft and was now acting master builder, since Toscanus was old, ill and thinking of retirement. The fourth condition was an eccentric one for a father to impose, for daughters ordinarily have no say in the matter.

Salim was insistent, however, that the marriage would take place only if Ayesha demonstrated that she still loved Paladon on the day his conversion went through. Finally Aziz, who would take over from Salim as qadi and one day wazir, must also approve the union.

None of us viewed the last two demands as anything more than formalities. Aziz was Paladon's greatest friend, as close to him as a brother: why should he object to a match that would bind his boon companion into his family? As for Ayesha, one would have had to be deaf and blind to doubt her adoration of her hero and champion. Aziz and I would sometimes joke about the transformation in our friend: the wild companion of our youth had become as gentle as a lamb. During our evening sessions we would often see the love-struck couple chastely holding hands, often entirely oblivious of us, whispering into each other's ears and gazing into each other's eyes. It was then we felt like interlopers.

Ayesha went to great trouble in finding a suitable slave girl. Swathed in her veils, she spent a month combing the markets – and the woman she mischievously chose for him, an Armenian Christian called Theodosia, was almost the image of herself, in colouring, features and figure, except that she had one boss eye and was mute. Paladon did not seem to mind. Aziz and I were sure he had only Ayesha's face in his mind when he hurried to his chamber.

Our life might have progressed quietly in this fashion had not King Abu, some eight months after the war with Toledo and Almería, decided that a monument should be constructed in thanksgiving for our victory. It would be a mosque, he announced, equal in magnificence to the Mezquita in Córdoba.

A planning committee was established to undertake the great task. The king appointed Wazir Salim as chairman, with Toscanus as his technical adviser, but since Salim was in the midst of negotiating an alliance against Castile and Toscanus was now almost permanently indisposed, Aziz and Paladon deputised for their fathers.

I saw my opportunity.

'But can you do it?' I asked Paladon. 'Is it possible?'

We were standing on the flat summit of the rock at a point that Paladon had calculated was directly above the cave. The noon sun was burning over the Mishkhat plain and the mountains were illuminated in such stark clarity that all perspective had flattened to the two-dimensional texture of a painting. I felt that merely by extending my arm I could touch the faraway snow peaks.

'Anything's possible,' he murmured. With a cloth wrapped round his head to ward off the glare, he was tapping the surface of the rock with an iron rod, occasionally getting down on all fours to press his ear to the hot stone. Eventually he stood up. 'I can't tell,' he said, wiping the sweat from his forehead. 'We'll have to bore a hole to be certain, but assuming my trigonometry is correct and the cave is as high as we think it is, its roof should consist only of a thin layer of stone.'

'So it would be possible to remove it? The gold and blue dome will rise above the rock to be seen from the plain?'

'Theoretically.' He sighed. 'Very well, it's possible. But can you even imagine, Samuel, how much work it would involve? Removing all those stones at the entrance, paving over the fissures on the cave floor, straightening and plastering the walls – not to mention the dome. We would be reshaping a mountain. I'm not even thinking of the complications you want to put into the design. Just to make the basic structure every mason in Mishkhat would be chipping away for years. God knows what it would cost.'

'If King Abu likes the idea, then money will be no object and neither will men. Salim brought back wagons of bullion and many slaves from his raid into Toledo after his victory, didn't he, Aziz?'

Aziz was idly throwing pebbles down the precipice, watching them bounce and echo from crag to crag. He shrugged. 'Your problem will not be King Abu. It'll be my father you'll have to convince.'

'But you're deputising for him, Aziz. You can go to the king directly. Didn't Salim say that he'd leave the decision to you?'

'And the rest of the committee, Samuel.'

'Placemen,' I said. 'Do you really think they will contradict the will of the king? Or yours for that matter?'

'No,' he said uncomfortably. His eyes flashed irritably under the hood of his jellaba. 'But what am I to say to Abu? You're talking of tampering with a holy shrine.'

'It's a shrine that commemorates the salvation of our city in the past. Now we've saved the city again. Where better to build a mosque to commemorate a miraculous victory? Wrought by God, as the Cid would have us believe.'

'Sarcasm and irreverence don't become you, Samuel.' He flicked another pebble over the precipice.

'No, Aziz, I'm talking about how legends are created. We're contemplating something that will be recognised, when it's finished, as one of the wonders of the world. It will accumulate its own legends. There is no heresy. It will be a Mussulman mosque, a shrine to Allah, but it will also be our own manifesto because it will contain hidden symbols that reflect the creation of the universe as the Prime Mover designed it, so it will be greater than any other mosque in the world, as mysterious and full of divine power as the Pyramids. If you are worried about King Abu's reaction, don't be. He'll be flattered. He half believes his own prayers influenced our victory. He'll love Paladon's design. A mosque set in the bowels of a holy rock? Where else in Islam has such an idea been conceived, or dared? Mishkhat will become the envy of Andaluz, and your name, and Paladon's, will be remembered in posterity.'

'I don't know . . .'

'Paladon, can it be done?' I turned to him.

'Yes, Samuel. I can build it, if it's what we all desire.'

'Aziz,' I said. 'The Brotherhood of the Craft. You coined the term. Are we to bow out at the moment we have opportunity and inspiration so combined?'

'You can really achieve this, Paladon?' asked Aziz.

'Yes,' he said.

Aziz bowed his head, and when he looked up, we saw the same determination written on his face as we had seen on the morning of the battle. 'Very well,' he said. 'I will talk to the king – but you must give me the materials to persuade him.'

That week an epidemic of African swamp fever broke out in the king's harem. Because the women lived together, they became infected. There was no longer the sound of chattering canaries in a golden cage. For two tense days all one could hear were wails and groans, and then a dreadful silence. Fear had given way to lassitude, as illness drained their last energies. The different pigmentation on the skin of concubines from across the world was now a uniform mottled yellow. From the hard trestle beds that had replaced the gaily adorned couches, pathetic wizened faces that, only a few days before, had charmed a king now gazed at me imploringly while I administered the bleeding bowl to their arms or placed moxibustion bottles on their sweating backs.

The great bathing hall, where in happier times the mischievous creatures, flush in their health and beauty, used to taunt me by disporting naked, was converted into my pharmacy, where I prepared potions and salves. The airy salons were darkened by blinds, and I had braziers burning incense to ward off the evil vapours in the night air that I thought might have brought the disease.

At my request, Dr Isa helped me. He had more experience with epidemics than I had. Of course, he had to tie a cloth round his eyes when we visited the women (harem rules applied even in this emergency) but he advised me of what to do. All the time Janifa, cowled and masked, not trusting the lives of her beloved charges to any servant, acted as our voluntary nurse.

It was a war, as intense and bloody in its own way as the battlefield from which I had recently returned, and sadly there were casualties, including, to my anguish, the sad lady of Chin, and one or two of the older concubines, though mercifully none of the king's current favourites – or not yet. The fitter ones could fight; the weaker died. When Janifa herself apparently succumbed, fainting as she washed towels on the steps of the bathing pool, I nearly despaired. Because of her advanced age I saw no hope if she joined the others in what had now become a death ward, but after a worried inspection of her burning body we found that it was not the swamp fever, only influenza brought on by exhaustion. We treated her separately, her fever broke, and in three days she was up and helping us as she had done before.

There were more deaths – young twins from Germania who had only recently arrived at the palace and were not even old enough to have been brought to the king's bedchamber, a fiery peasant girl from Mallorca and (to my own personal sorrow) a Jewess from Mishkhat. I knew her family a little. She had been too intelligent and sharp-tongued for the king to like her, although he enjoyed her body well enough. I had taken pleasure in talking to her after my clinics, and counted her among my few friends. In the morning, Janifa took me aside and told me to rest. I was in danger of wearing myself out, she said. As a special dispensation, and only for a day, she would allow Dr Isa to take off his blindfold.

After two weeks of reversals, we feared we would lose them all. Al-Razi's methods had been only moderately effective and I spent every spare hour synthesising new formulae, but progress was achingly slow. Then one bright morning, as often miraculously happens in epidemics, we went in and found that the temperatures of several women had fallen in the night. Some were sitting up on their beds, talking quietly to each other. More recovered over the next few days. In another fortnight they had all regained their health and most of them their beauty. Others, who feared the rashes on their skins left by the jaundice would permanently disfigure them, begged me for talcum and ointments, so I became a beautician as well as a physician.

At last came the day when I judged there was nothing more to do. I had just finished packing my equipment when suddenly I was grabbed by three naked houris, who pulled me into the pool with them and covered me with kisses. One after another, the others, giggling and splashing, climbed in too, while Janifa smiled from the side. I suppose it was their way of thanking me for saving their lives, but I was no Paladon and I can't say I enjoyed the experience. In fact, seldom have I been more mortified or embarrassed: I was immersed scandalously up to my neck in soapsuds, water and tawny flesh when a eunuch arrived – a real one – to announce that the king wished to see me forthwith. There was more laughter and a scramble of naked limbs to find me some suitable clothes.

In the glass throne room I found King Abu, his jellaba open to his round belly because of the heat, reclining on a carpet smoking herbs from a hookah, and Wazir Salim sitting cross-legged beside him.

The king grinned widely at me and, tottering to his feet, embraced me, scratching my cheek with his grizzled beard. 'The boy who saved my chickens for me. Thank you. Thank you.' He turned me. 'Look, Salim, so young and yet so learned, a Potiphar come to my rescue.'

'I think you're the Potiphar, Uncle,' murmured Salim, 'although you need have no fear for your wives from this young Joseph. That is the name you are searching for, by the way.'

'You can be irritatingly pedantic, Nephew. You know who I'm talking about – that brilliant Jewish boy who so impressed the pharaohs in the Hebrew scripture. What's it called?'

'Genesis,' said Salim, with a smile.

'Exactly. Look, I know you're teasing me in that superior fashion of yours, but I'm not a dried-up scholar like you are, thank the Almighty, so I don't give a donkey's fart if I muddle a name now and again. Anyway, I shall not let myself be angry with you today, because it was you who brought me this young genius in the first place.' He affectionately pinched my cheek. 'Well done, lad, well done.'

Then he frowned, his fingers tapping my shoulder. 'Salim, I've had a rather clever idea. Hassan's getting long in the tooth. He must have been my doctor for half a century at least, and he's clumsy now. He spilled my blood on a new Persian carpet last time he drained me, and his potions never seem to cure my headaches. I've a mind to replace him with young— What did you call him?'

'Joseph,' said Salim. 'And that is a very good idea.'

'I thought you'd agree. You probably planned it all along. Well, Joseph, what do you think? Will you be my personal physician? It's good pay and easy hours, because I'm very fit, aren't I, Nephew?'

'His name's actually Samuel,' said Salim.

'Don't confuse me. I'm the king. I can call him anything I like. Joseph, what's your answer?'

Still bewildered after my bath with his concubines, and now stunned by this unexpected honour, I could barely articulate my thanks.

King Abu clapped me on the back. 'That's settled. Find my chief chamberlain. He'll tell you what you have to do. I have a regular bleeding every second Thursday to keep the gout at bay. I shall see you then.'

Realising that the interview was over, I began to bow my way out of the door, but King Abu called after me: 'Joseph, come back. I want to show you something.'

Beside the throne stood what appeared to be a huge box, draped in a yellow silk hanging. With an excited gleam in his bulbous eyes, the king pulled the cloth aside, and I saw . . . a mahogany cabinet with a glass door, the leaves of which the king carefully opened, and stood back proprietarily to let me view . . . an intricate model, perfectly carved in oak . . . of the Mishkhat rock, and on top of it was . . . a golden and blue tiled dome!

'And look at this,' said King Abu, who could scarcely conceal his own wonder.

From the cave mouth he withdrew a drawer and held it at arm's length for my inspection. Inside I saw the mosque that Paladon and I had designed, perfect in every miniature detail. There were the three hundred and sixty-five pillars (the number of days in a year), there were the twelve apses in the walls (relating to the months and the signs of the zodiac), and there were the seven arches separating each row of pillars (representing the seven planetary gods, the days of Creation and the ages of man). Paladon had painted on the walls various arabesques and floral designs, hidden among which would be our secret symbols. The colours of the pillars reflected the different stones we would use, each with its own alchemical properties, and the tiny lamps, hanging in this model by a clever arrangement of threads and wires, would one day combine with the inverted cupolas on the ceiling to re-create the turning of the celestial spheres on which rested the planets and the stars. Finally, I saw that the mihrab and the minbar were set in the angles I had positioned them, best to channel the invisible celestial nitre.

'Is it not magnificent, my young doctor?' whispered the king. 'This is what my great-nephew and his friend, the Christian stonemason, have designed for me.' He glanced at Salim, who was watching us solemnly.

'The mason is called Paladon, Uncle. He is Toscanus's son.'

'I know he's called Paladon. I'm not senile. He's another brilliant young fellow, like Joseph. That fat ibn Sa'id of yours has taught his charges well. What do you think, Joseph? Will there ever be a more beautiful mosque in Andaluz or, frankly, in the whole of Islam? I gave my approval for it this morning. My sour-faced nephew over there thinks I will be squandering the resources of Mishkhat, but the son is wiser than the father, for when this mosque is completed, we will have achieved greatness, for ourselves and in honour of Allah. You are the first to see this design. Tell me what you think.'

'I think it will be counted among the wonders of the world,' I said. 'It is a marvellous enterprise, Majesty, worthy of a great king.'

'You see, Salim? There speaks an intelligent young man, and his view will be the common one, you mark my words. He is not even a Mussulman but he sees the glory of God that is reflected here. The Umma will be with me on this, Nephew. I am sure of it.'

'You are the king, Uncle. It is for you to make the decisions, and if you believe you are acting wisely for your people, then I am satisfied. Thankfully, my role is merely to obey your orders.'

'The hypocrisy of the man. Listen to him.' King Abu winked at me. 'You are joining my household at a glorious epoch in the history of Mishkhat, boy. Are you proud?'

'Yes, Sire,' I said.

'You see? He's sincere as well. Now, then, be off with you.'

Salim had risen to his feet. 'I will accompany Samuel, by your leave, Uncle, to the palace gates. I will return shortly.'

I don't think King Abu heard him. He was gazing at the model in his arms.

As we passed the guards, Salim murmured to me, 'That was not the first time you had seen that design, Samuel. You showed no surprise. Rather, you examined it as if you were checking for details that you knew already were there. You have played a leading part in this costly escapade, haven't you?'

'No, Wazir. How could I? I have been in the harem night and day for nearly two months.'

Salim observed me coldly. Then he smiled. 'I had always thought that Paladon was the leader of your little group. I see that I must rethink a little. Never mind. It is done. The mosque will be built. You have another triumph to add to your score. I congratulate you, because whatever I think of this mad scheme, which I now believe is your brainchild, I know you are a good influence on my son.'

He looked at me almost fondly, and there was an unexpected softness in his voice when he continued, 'He still loves and respects you, Samuel, even though your relationship has changed – in my view for the better, and I am speaking for the good of both of you, although you may not appreciate it now. I have been impressed by how bravely and quickly you composed yourself after the hurt he did you. I applaud you for that. You are extraordinarily mature for your years. And you are of a generous and forgiving nature. Those are good virtues to possess. Rare ones too, believe me. You may need them in the years to come, as well as the great intelligence you were born with.' He paused. 'I would like to think that Aziz, when he succeeds me, will be able to take advantage of them too. I have struggled all my life to preserve peace and prosperity in our kingdom, but the Christians, Samuel . . . This recent war . . . I fear we have not seen the end of it. Sometimes I wonder what sort of kingdom my son will inherit.'

'Of course, Wazir, I will always be loyal to Aziz. You and your family have treated me like kin and . . .'

He raised his hand to silence me. It shook a little. Suddenly he appeared to me to be an old, grey man bent by years of responsibility and care. 'You owe me nothing, Samuel. I am in your debt more than you are in mine. You earned this appointment to serve the king on your own merit, not by my favour. Your talent is such that, wherever you choose to go, you will be certain of fortune and fame – but I love my son, Samuel, weak inside as I know him to be. I fear for him. That is why I will ask you a boon. One day I will be gone and no longer capable of protecting him. Stay with Aziz, I beg you. He will need wise counsel. Be his friend, Samuel, however badly or foolishly he may behave.' He coughed. Perhaps he was embarrassed to have revealed his true feelings. 'I am not pressing you. I have no right. If you decide to follow your star to Cairo, or the academies of Kairawan, where ibn Sa'id believes you should go, I will be the first to support you, but think on what I have said. Now go home and rest after your labours. Your friends have missed you and so have I. Again, my congratulations.'

He turned sharply and strode back in the direction of the king's audience hall. I left the palace, blinking in the sunshine, and as I followed the road to the city, I forgot Salim's gloomy forebodings and thought of the mosque we would build together. I felt I was walking on air.

Within a month, the great work had begun. From the city, it appeared that the rock above us was infested with columns of ants crawling over its surface. These were the labourers and slaves marshalled by King Abu to assist Paladon. The tapping of thousands of mattocks on stone could be heard even above the noise of the market, and soon the citizens of Mishkhat became as unconscious of it as they were of birdsong.

Old Mishkhatids recalled the construction of the royal palace. Once again wagon trains streamed into the city from all parts of Andaluz and beyond, carrying blocks of the rare minerals I had chosen. Secretly Paladon gave me chippings, and in my spare time I began to process them in my laboratory for I had planned to bury a vial of pure essence at the foot of each pillar when the time came.

Meanwhile, the mountain sprouted strange mechanical contraptions that Paladon had designed to shift the enormous quantities of stone that were being removed from the cave mouth. The rock began to resemble a castle under siege surrounded by mangonels, but in fact they were complicated pulleys and interlinked towers, whose ropes and swings could manipulate large masses of stone, too heavy even for the myriad workers to carry, up and down the precipitous face of the hill.

On the summit there was an ingenious ram that Paladon had constructed using military technology. It took a month in the ironworks to cast the great steel bore, as heavy and almost as large as a house, another to lift it by stages to the top of the rock, and several weeks after that to attach it to its pulleys. The day came when the whole city started in terror: the huge, echoing crash of metal on stone sounded to the citizens like the prelude of an earthquake, but it was Paladon battering the strata of rock that separated the roof of the cave from the outside surface. Even granite could not survive such force indefinitely. The great machine rolled on several feet to its next assault, leaving the army of masons to exploit with their awls and mattocks the cracks it had left behind it. Within a year there was a sizeable rent in the canopy of the cave, and the workers who were chipping at the walls inside were able to see what they were doing by the natural rays of the sun.

At night, the eerie lights of furnaces and campfires, which burned incessantly, turned the rock into a ghostly apparition. The labourers worked in shifts, so at no time did the excavations cease, whatever the weather, whatever the season. After only three months enough stones covering the cave's entrance had been removed to allow easy access inside. Bright illumination was required for the masons smoothing the walls and stopping the holes in the floor, and so numerous were the fires and candles inside that their light leaked out into the darkness like a cloud of phosphorus, snuffing the glimmer of the stars. In those early days, Paladon would sometimes joke that he had already re-created the original miracle of the cave: 'You see? We have the Holy Light. Now all we must do is build a mosque to enclose it. And that, my dear Samuel, will be fiddlesticks compared with what we have already achieved.'

Sometimes even I was awed by the audacity of what we were undertaking, and I thought of the mythical Tower of Babel and wondered if we were challenging Fate, like the foolhardy and blasphemous king of old.

For Paladon it was merely an ambitious and complex exercise in mathematics and engineering. He had meticulously thought out his plans and schedules, and was confident in the outcome. His charts and drawings would have filled a bookcase in Salim's library, and the designs they contained would have dazzled any layman, including me. As far as he was concerned, he was working within tried and tested natural laws. He seemed to know instinctively what was feasible and what was not. I don't think he ever once doubted that everything would go to plan. He was not conceited, as anybody else would have been given such responsibility so young (the cave mouth was finally cleared when he was just two days short of his twentieth birthday). In fact, his modesty was sometimes baffling. He seemed far more impressed by my alchemical quackery than by his own technical genius. His pride in his work was enormous, of course, but it was professional. If any part of the project was overdue by even a day, his rugged brow would knit with concentration and he would pore over his drawings until he had solved whatever the problem was. Next day he would calmly issue new orders, sometimes not hesitating to don a workman's smock to demonstrate exactly what had to be done. His labourers worshipped him. He had always been a charismatic leader, as Aziz and I had known since our earliest youth.

As the work progressed, he seemed to grow in stature. His actions were more assured, his orders more precise. He had always been taciturn. Now he barely spoke unless it was to address with authority an issue at hand. His religious lessons with Salim had had something to do with it, for his conversion had evolved into a matter of deep gravity. His sense of honour and personal integrity had always made him the most loyal of friends, and it now underpinned his transference of spiritual loyalty to the Mussulman God. In the ideals of subservience that are the finest teachings of the Qur'a-n, he discovered something deeply satisfying. He never forgot that he was building a mosque for Allah, and this undertaking increasingly became a sacred duty. He approached it with humility: he believed he was building something that would transcend his own petty reputation.

Surprisingly, this made him even more committed to the hidden part of our project, for in the arcane philosophy based on science that had fired our Brotherhood of the Craft, he realised how the rational skills in which he excelled could contribute to the greater glory of the God he now worshipped. Paladon's conversion to Islam, rather than alienating him from me, brought him closer.

It also brought him closer to Ayesha, who was a creature of the air, fey and sometimes irresponsible. Paladon's increasing gravity was the earth she needed to ground her. Theirs was a love match of opposites, and it is a natural law for opposites to attract.

There was hardly a day on which she would not ride her palfrey, veiled, chaperoned and with her father's permission, up the steep path to where Paladon was working. She would unfailingly find a reason to tease him, mocking his great stone hammer as a toy or feigning boredom when he went excitedly into the mathematical details of his next project. Then Paladon's craggy face would blush with disappointment and concern, which made her laugh, and only then would he realise she was ribbing him, and he would laugh too, openly and heartily. Often, however, she would halt among her companions at a distance, so that Paladon would not be aware of her presence, and would watch him work, sometimes for hours. I, who regularly accompanied her (I was, of course, the chaperon), would notice the concentration in the eyes behind the veil. She could not disguise her pride, wonder, and adoration for her lover, who was achieving such marvels.

My deeper relationship with Paladon did nothing, however, to abate my grief that Aziz was moving further out of our circle. I had reconciled myself to losing him as a lover and it saddened me to think I might also lose him as a friend. His year of apprenticeship had passed and he had become the chief qadi, a position of great authority and dignity, with obligations that went beyond the law courts. Rarely did he attend our evening gatherings in Ayesha's quarters. There was always a banquet at the palace, or a tour of inspection of the provinces, or a meeting of the king's council at which his presence was required. When he found time for us, he was his usual sweet self, or seemed to be, but as time went on I detected arrogance and assertiveness in him and, increasingly, boredom with detail and ideas. He tried to hide it, but I suspect that he now considered himself rather grand for us, and viewed his presence among us as a favour he was bestowing on inferiors. By then, of course, I had become used to the ways of the court and, understanding him as well as I did, I knew how to flatter him.

Paladon, though, had never flattered anyone, except the women he had seduced in his younger days, and was confused. Sometimes he could not conceal his irritation or hurt. We no longer discussed natural philosophy: Aziz would lecture us on matters of state, while we were expected to listen in admiring silence. After a while, Paladon made excuses not to attend on nights he knew Aziz would be there. He was happier on his building site.

After only two years the clearing work and the foundations were complete and Paladon was ready to construct the mosque. It was a sad irony that while the great enterprise initiated by our brotherhood went from strength to strength the brotherhood itself was slowly dissolving.

(II) In which I recall how a philosopher discovered he was a devil, an alchemist became a devotee of the black arts, and a city lost its protector

Wazir Salim was single-mindedly pursuing his dream of establishing a confederation of Mussulman princedoms to counter the Christian threat. Failure only spurred him on to greater efforts, and as his health worsened under the strain of disappointment, I began to worry about him. He allowed me to treat him for minor ailments – a head cold, bouts of incapacitating diarrhoea, a return of his back pains or cramps in his fingers, anything that actively prevented him working – but cumulatively I saw these as symptoms of exhaustion, or perhaps something more serious. Whenever I advised him that he should rest, he impatiently waved me away and refused my repeated suggestion that Dr Isa and I should give his body a complete examination in the hospital. He had no time, he told me. There was this urgent letter to write or that ambassador to meet. His only concession was to change his diet, but since he ate like a bird, it had little effect. Day by day the liverish spots on his sallow cheeks became more marked, and he winced when he sat down. I suspected that he was hiding severe abdominal pain.

It was in this state that he received an embassy from Castile. King Alfonso, out of the blue, had volunteered to broker a permanent peace treaty with Toledo, and Salim, while he had no illusions about the Christian king's motives (he knew well enough the old saw about Greeks bearing gifts), nevertheless realised it was an opportunity better to understand our enemy. He overrode the objections of King Abu, who had never got over his disgust that these same barbaric infidels had asked him to pay tribute, and wrote back, under the royal seal, that Mishkhat would be pleased to receive Alfonso's emissary, Duke Estragon of Najera, on the second day after the end of Ramadan.

I knew this because King Abu complained to me about it one day when I was bleeding him. When I mentioned the matter to Paladon, I was surprised to hear that he was already aware of it. Salim had contacted Toscanus requesting that he house the Christian delegation in his mansion. Paladon was not pleased, since it would mean he would have to be away from building for more than a week – 'just at the time we will be putting up the first pillars'.

I asked him why he should even be involved. 'It's your father the king is asking, not you. And if your father's not well enough, can't those cousins of yours look after Estragon?'

'I'm his son. I have to be there.' He shook his head. 'He considers this the greatest honour our family's ever been given. He's already driven the household mad designing new liveries for the servants, ordering fresh wall hangings, grander furniture, plates, cutlery, carpets – the amount of incense he's bought is enough for a chapel and he's even thinking of gilding the beams. It'd be comic if it wasn't so pathetic. On any given day there's a permanent convocation of cooks on one side of his sick room deciding menus, and a circus of minstrels, jugglers and dancers on the other planning entertainments, while merchants wait greedily in the parlour for his orders. It's wearing him out before it's even begun. And he's ill, Samuel, and getting no better. This will probably be his last triumph. I must help him make it a success.'

I nodded sadly. Dr Isa had told me about the weakness of Toscanus's lungs, probably a legacy of the dust he had inhaled in a lifetime of constructing great edifices. I thought also of Salim. They were both stubborn old men, who refused to recognise their mortality.

'Anyway, it's my cousins who are the problem,' continued Paladon. 'Lucas and Jaime have taken holy orders, and Jaime's gone to be a monk at that monastery in the mountains. I attribute it to jealousy, because I didn't involve them in the mosque, and a reaction to my decision to convert. They loathe me and my father, and bitterly resent that we didn't give them advancement, but they'll jump at the opportunity to attend this mummery. The chance to meet a Christian duke? And in our house? That's another reason I must be on hand. I trust neither of them.'

'What do you mean?'

He sighed. 'They are not loyal to Mishkhat, Samuel. They're

still Castilians at heart.' He thumped a huge fist into the other hand. 'I'll handle them. All will be well – but if only it wasn't happening during the week we erect the pillars . . .'

It was not only Toscanus's house that was being scrubbed and polished. Salim wanted Mishkhat to be shining when the duke arrived. He had given orders that every building along the route that the Christians would take to the palace be whitewashed and painted and the roofs retiled. Scores of Paladon's workers were commandeered to patch the flaking gold leaf on the dome of the existing mosque. Seamstresses were occupied in sewing silk flags and banners, rethreaded with gold, to be hung over the streets. Meanwhile the army was trained in manoeuvres, and cavalry would line the roads from the border to the city. There would also be a demonstration of battle skills. Outside the city gate, a mock fort had been built that our army would bombard with mangonels, and from the veranda of the palace I could see the dust rising as tourneys, mêlées and charges were rehearsed. Salim intended Estragon to be impressed by our military power as much as by our wealth.

And, to my astonishment, I, too, was given a role. Duke Estragon had a son, Sancho, who was the same age as Aziz. Aziz was to look after him while their fathers were in conference and much of their time would be spent in the princely pursuits of hunting and tourneys, including a formal joust between Sancho and Aziz in the palace tilting yard. Sancho was also reputed to be something of a scholar. His father had sent him for his education to the abbey of Cluny, and his teacher, a monk called Elderic, would accompany the young man to Mishkhat. He had requested that Sancho be shown something of Arabic science. Ibn Sa'id was therefore called away from his studies to translate into Latin various philosophical texts, and I was deputed to prepare an alchemical demonstration and practical exercises in astrology and astronomy.

* * *

What impressed the Mishkhatids most about the Christians was their size and the pinkness of their skin, so much so that they called the sunburned men of the north, boiling in their metal cuirasses and heavy conical helmets, 'lobsters'. Estragon and his son were Spaniards and descendants of Visigoths. They were stout and swarthy, the father inclined to fatness, and little different from the Christians in Mishkhat, but their escort was comprised of Normans and Franks. To a man they were giants, a cohort of Paladons, and, like him, fair-haired. It was the first time that any of us had seen in large numbers the type of warriors we would later come to know and fear as 'crusaders'.

Ibn Sa'id and I watched the procession glumly from the palace terrace. It was lost on neither of us that these grim-faced soldiers sitting stiffly on their great chargers were meekly following a column of white-surpliced priests, singing psalms as they raised high their crucifixes and swung their thuribles of incense.

'It won't come to any good, you know,' murmured my teacher, 'everybody putting on vain shows to impress each other. It is at moments like these that I am inclined to follow the example of the great Diogenes and retreat from the folly of the world into a barrel.' His face became meditative. 'Of sardines, perhaps? Or anchovies? I don't know about you, Samuel, but I'm a little peckish. Shall the two of us have a splendid breakfast together – the condemned man's last meal before we meet the awful Elderic?'

Contrary to ibn Sa'id's expectations, the tall monk we greeted later that morning in the wazir's library was softly spoken, with an easy smile and features that exuded humour and curiosity. The grey-tonsured head tilting forward down the line of his finely chiselled forehead, nose and chin gave him a permanent air of intellectual enquiry. At the same time, he poised his still, muscular body in a way that indicated reserves of energy and will-power. Without the clerical garb, he might easily have passed for a lawyer expert at persuasion, a merchant formidable in worldly affairs, or even a soldier engaged in diplomacy. He charmed ibn Sa'id within moments of meeting him by saluting him in the most respectful Mussulman manner, and went on to speak in Arabic.

Ibn Sa'id's reputation, he told him, had reached the universities of Paris as well as the cloisters of Cluny. Even in the Christian world the names of Avicenna and Razes (he used the Frankish names for ibn Sina and al-Razi) were renowned as wise philosophers, though sadly there were as yet no translations of their works. Merchants, however, who had travelled in Mussulman territories, had identified the great Da'ud ibn Sa'id as being their most learned commentator. It was Elderic's most sincere hope that one day this body of knowledge might become available to Christian scholars. Meanwhile, putting differences of religion aside and in a common quest for scientific understanding, he had come as a humble pupil to sit at the foot of a true philosopher. Ibn Sa'id held the key to the treasure trove of God's mysteries, revealed to the Greeks in pagan times and lost ever since to the Christian realms. The wisest man in Christendom, compared to him, was nothing but an ill-educated child. It was an honour and a privilege to have a chance to discourse with him.

The monk's pronunciation was atrocious, and it was obvious that he was reciting a rehearsed text, but ibn Sa'id preened and his fat cheeks flushed almost to the colour of his henna beard. My poor teacher. Elderic had hooked his plump trout on the first cast, baited with a few words of flattery.

Afterwards we conversed in Latin, because Elderic's knowledge of the Arabic language was, as I suspected, as limited as his comprehension of the famed body of science in which he evinced such interest. I sat unobtrusively to the side making notes. I was impressed – who could not be by such intelligence and sugary skill with words? But I was also thinking, even during that first meeting, that this plausible spy (for what else was he?) was perhaps the most dangerous man I had ever encountered. While ibn Sa'id allowed himself to be lulled by the monk's eloquence and apparent humility, I was in a position to observe his eyes, which were cold, hard stones, glinting with the same uncompromising fanaticism that I had once noticed in al-Gazali's. They narrowed to serpentine slits of barely concealed triumph and avarice when the translated texts of Aristotle, Galen, Ptolemy and ibn Sina were placed before him.

Ibn Sa'id gushed enthusiastically about the content of each document. Elderic listened with his head cocked to one side, nodding gravely and murmuring polite formulae of appreciation. Then his long fingers snapped out of his habit. Briskly and efficiently, like a botanist on a field expedition who has just secured a rare flower, he smoothed the particular parchment that had just been discussed, pressed it between pages of calf leather and secreted it in a box he had brought for the purpose. 'Thank you,' he purred. 'That was extremely interesting. You are so kind. Did you also translate al-Farghani, by any chance?' And ibn Sa'id excitedly launched into a little lecture on how the new Arab star tables surpassed in accuracy those of the Greeks. 'Let me show you.' He would reach for a book or a chart from the shelves to illustrate his point or to offer a contrary opinion. The basilisk eyes watched hungrily, no doubt attempting to imprint an image into their owner's retentive brain to be recorded later in his room at Toscanus's house. Meanwhile the long fingers waited for the moment when they could emerge again to snatch yet another treasure for the collection.

After he had gone I asked ibn Sa'id if it was wise to reveal so much to so clever an enemy.

'Enemy? What do you mean? He is a scientist as we are. We were merely engaging in an exchange of knowledge and understanding, as scientists do.'

'The exchange seemed one-sided to me. I didn't detect any

sign of understanding, either. He struck me as more of a gold prospector than a scholar. Anyway, the Christians in the north don't have scientists. He's probably come here to gather evidence of our diabolic arts.'

'Samuel!' Ibn Sa'id harrumphed. 'I never expected to hear such prejudice from you. I thought Elderic was an excellent fellow, a very learned man. I've rarely enjoyed an intellectual debate more.'

I saw little purpose in pointing out to my intoxicated teacher that it had hardly been a debate since he had done all the talking.

I had thought long and hard about what to show them during my alchemy demonstration. The easiest thing would have been to prepare a potion from herbs, but I suspected that all they knew of the science were the tales of wizardry by which common stones were transformed into gold. Perhaps that was the secret Elderic was really after. I would not have put it past the credulous Christians to believe that Mishkhat's wealth somehow derived from occult practices.

I could, of course, have played the showman. A year or so back, to satisfy my own curiosity, I had mastered the art of making the philosopher's stone, and using it had transmuted silver into a few ounces of gold. I gave the minuscule nuggets to Paladon, who had smelted them into a small ring that now encircled Ayesha's finger. I toyed with the idea of doing something similar for Sancho but decided against it, for the exercise, while intellectually satisfying, is frivolous because the result is not commensurate with the amount of time and labour it takes. As I had told Aziz, who had been excited by my achievement, if you want gold in any quantity, pan a river or dig a mine.

I decided it would be more educational to show them something practical: the transmutation of antimony into an oil essence, known as the Red Stone or the Elixir. It had been antimony I had been looking for when I had met Paladon and Aziz in the fig tree many years before. I had since found it to be a wonderful agent in the transmutation of most other minerals, and I used it as my staple when making medicines for Dr Isa. I prepared the ground well in advance. I calculated the most auspicious astrological combination to initiate three different processes in my laboratory. The first of these, which was also the longest and most difficult, was to create the Elixir itself. Luckily I already had some in store, and I used it to start simultaneously on the transmutation of iron and cinnabar, which was the second process I wanted to demonstrate. The third stage was to make a potion out of the newly combined oil mixed with various other mineral essences. Again, I had material in store so this process could begin at the same time as the others. I had timed it so that by the time Sancho and Elderic arrived, all three operations would be at the point of readiness. I intended that my audience witness the various stages in the sequence. Finally, I had arranged with Dr Isa that he would provide me with one of his epileptic patients so that I could demonstrate the efficacy of the potion. This, I thought, would brilliantly demonstrate to the Christians that, far from being a diabolic art, alchemy was a benign and useful tool of modern medicine.

It all went – disastrously – to plan. I succeeded in terrifying Sancho, a morose, surly and – as it turned out – superstitious young man, during the first few minutes of my demonstration, when I snatched off the flames a sulphurous crucible in which purple smoke congealed before his eyes into the brownish-yellow paste that is the Elixir. I also noticed Elderic surreptitiously crossing himself. I thought wryly that he couldn't have learned much from his hours with ibn Sa'id if he considered what I was accomplishing to be magic. My explanations of both the second and third stages, simple as I made them, went entirely over their heads (perhaps they were not listening by then). When Dr Isa produced his madman, they shivered in fear because they thought I had conjured a devil, and their eyes almost popped out of their heads when I poured the vial of potion down his throat. The effect was instantly calming, which turned out to be the worst result I could possibly have achieved because, when they saw how their howling devil had transformed into a polite and rather mild human being, they believed that I had blasphemously imitated one of Christ's miracles – proof positive that I was dabbling in the diabolic arts. They almost battered the door down in their hurried attempts to escape my laboratory.

When I reported to Salim, he reprimanded me for lack of tact, but his heart was not in it: mine was only one disaster among many. The conference with Estragon had got off to a bad start when the duke had insulted King Abu at the welcoming banquet. He had refused to partake of the meal unless his chaplain was allowed to say a Christian grace. Salim had got over this embarrassment by arranging for the chief faqi to say a Mussulman prayer immediately afterwards, but nobody had communicated this plan to Estragon, who therefore did not understand that the white-bearded old man in the turban was intoning a quotation from the Qur'ān. While all the Mussulmans' heads were bowed in prayer, he proceeded to reach for a viand with his bare fingers, ignoring the fork at the side of his plate and tearing at the lamb with his teeth. This sacrilege, not to mention the bad manners, had caused King Abu angrily to leave the table, and Salim had to stay up all night negotiating the terms of an apology that the Christians might make without losing face. The argument carried over to the next day before a suitable formula was found, during which time the Castilian delegation remained in their lodgings and all the entertainments planned for them, including the military spectacles, had to be cancelled.

The delayed conference was eventually resumed, but it quickly degenerated into confrontation and mutual recrimination when it became clear that the treaty with Toledo proposed by Alfonso depended on Mishkhat providing tribute to finance a peace-keeping army of Castilians. Salim had to use all his diplomatic skills to prevent his uncle, when he heard about this further insult, from ordering the palace guard to fall on the Normans and Franks and massacre them. Somehow the two sides got back to the table to prepare an empty document that Salim and Estragon could sign. Clearly, there was no possibility of any treaty.

The only part of the programme that had so far been unaffected was the one that concerned Sancho. Aziz and he cordially disliked each other but they still went hunting every day as planned and occasionally Sancho accompanied Elderic to meetings with ibn Sa'id. The bored son of the duke dozed while Elderic continued his rapacious gathering of information. The final event on Sancho's programme had been the presentation joust against Aziz in front of his father's delegation and the king's court. It should have been a decorous draw – or that was how the heralds had choreographed it. Horses had been chosen for their taciturnity and lances had been prepared to shatter at first impact so that neither party would be harmed. Aziz, however, skilfully knocked Sancho off his mount at the first pass. Sancho fell badly and injured his head. It took an hour to bring him back to consciousness.

The Christians accused us of employing sorcery, saying that I had cast a spell on Sancho during my alchemical demonstration in the morning. Estragon apparently demanded that I be tried and burned as a warlock. This required more diplomacy from Salim: he eventually agreed not to a trial but to a discussion between ibn Sa'id and Elderic, to be held in the banquet hall following dinner. It was to be a repeat, in its way, of the debate that ibn Sa'id had once held with al-Gazali, in which he was to expound on natural philosophy and Elderic was to answer from the view of religion. I was the only member of the court not to be invited.

I heard about it afterwards from ibn Sa'id, whom I met in the moonlit courtyard on his return to Salim's house. I had never seen him so depressed. 'Oh, Samuel, you are truly as wise as the prophet after whom you are named, and I owe you an apology. How did I not perceive it myself? How could I have been so gulled? The man is a charlatan, a spy as you implied, not a philosopher. He as good as admitted it, boasting to his superiors in the delegation – the grim-browed duke and his dimwit son, and all those black-robed monks – that over the week he had elicited from me every one of my secrets and discovered they were only the lies that the devil uses to beguile men's thoughts. I am the black ram that leads the flock astray, and you, my boy, are a minion of Satan.'

'It didn't go well, then?' I said.

'Some of the more educated members of the audience might have found his quaint language amusing but it was no serious debate. He couldn't answer any of the rational questions I put to him, merely quoting apocalyptic material from the Christian Bible. Damnation and hellfire. The rest was a homily of the sort you might expect from an uneducated faqi in a country mosque. It was worse than offensive. It was tedious. Excuse me, I am too shaken and disappointed to say more. I might just briefly pop into the kitchens for a restorative – a pie or something – and then I am going to bed.'

The Christian delegation left at dawn. Far from negotiating peace, they had as good as declared war. Ibn Sa'id had not mentioned it, but Elderic had not stopped at attacking natural philosophy. He had insulted Islam, which he had referred to as something that might once have been a real religion, although inimical to what Christians held to be true, but now, from what he had heard during his stay, it was irredeemably tainted by the black arts it had superstitiously accepted into its tenets. Thankfully the king had not attended the debate or he might have ordered Elderic to be decapitated then and there. Salim merely told Estragon to return with his men to his lodgings and be thankful of the Mussulman rules of hospitality. At his orders, three regiments of cavalry escorted the Christians to the border. Next day Salim ordered the refortification of all our outlying castles.

I have since often wondered whether the devious Alfonso had not instructed his delegation to be offensive, thereby creating a justification for war in the future. Or whether he intended to lull the suspicions of Toledans with the promise of a spurious treaty at exactly the time he intended to move against them. Certainly the timing of the embassy had been carefully decided beforehand. Only a week later we heard that on the same day his representative had arrived in Mishkhat to discuss peace, Alfonso's armies in the north had converged on his vassal city of Toledo. Tired of operating through his creature al-Qadir, he had decided to annex the kingdom to Castile. There was no need for him to use mangonels this time: he had already rotted the state from within. He had also decided to make it his capital, at a stroke projecting Christian power within striking distance of the Mussulman south. We woke to discover that Castile, in the memory of our own lifetimes a tiny state, now ruled a third of the Spanish peninsula, and threatened the rest with its mighty armies.

When Salim heard that the event he had prophesied and feared had finally come to pass, he collapsed. The chancre in his stomach burst, and the poison spread through his veins. Perhaps his heart failed too. It was broken anyway. I did my best to save him, but he died three days later in his bed, without ever regaining consciousness. The great state funeral that followed passed under the very flags that had been strewn across the streets to welcome the Christians. There had been no time to take them down.

And the tragedy of Salim's untimely death – a devastating loss for those of us who loved him, and a calamity for the state he had protected through so many years – was not the only outcome of the destabilising Christian embassy. We did not know it, but Elderic had not restricted his serpentine plots to embarrassing poor ibn Sa'id. His most insidious mischief – although we did not discover this until a long time afterwards – had been wrought in the house of his host, Toscanus.

Aziz, my poor weeping Aziz, bereft of the guiding light of his life, clutched my arm while the chief faqi intoned his prayers and the great men of the kingdom, one after another, cast their flowers over Salim's grave. After they had departed, and while Paladon led away a stumbling and bewildered Ayesha, we two remained. He turned a haunted face to mine and implored me, 'Samuel, you won't leave me, will you? You won't abandon me?'

'Of course not,' I murmured, shocked and surprised, because he had rarely talked to me in the last year, and not once with the old affection.

He was squeezing my hand so tightly that his nails drew blood. 'You still love me, don't you?'

'You know I do,' I said.

'Thank you,' he whispered. 'I can't tell you how important that is to me.' He withdrew his hand and hugged himself, shivering with emotion. My heart went out to him. I wanted to enfold him in my embrace, press my cheek against his and kiss away his tears – but his guards were watching from the gate, the gravediggers were waiting under the elm trees with their spades and Aziz seemed locked in his own thoughts or fears.

'There will be lonely times ahead, Samuel. They frighten me a little. I'll need you more and more. Your wisdom. Your counsel. You've always been my truest friend. You alone know what my father's death means for me.'

I felt a lump in my throat and was overwhelmed by guilt as I thought of my own father, whom nowadays I only visited on the main Jewish festivals. I made a silent resolution to see more of him in his declining years. I was thinking as much about myself when I replied, 'I can guess how empty the world must seem to a son who has lost his father. I wish I had the words to comfort you.'

A flicker of what might have been contempt crossed his face. 'Of course I'm sad,' he said dismissively. 'Any son would be at his father's death, but I'm a prince and I must look at the larger picture.' He began to pace, and I sensed his growing excitement. 'This is my opportunity, Samuel, don't you see? The king must appoint another wazir. By right it should be me. I can't afford to make mistakes. I have enemies, jealous of my position, who will use my youth as an excuse to undermine me. They will try to poison the king against me. I need somebody trustworthy at my back who will protect my interests. My father always respected you, Samuel. With you beside me, what obstacles can we not overcome? We can rise together to greatness. Will you stand by me, old friend? Are you with me?'

I felt a chill run up my spine, followed by a wave of nausea. That the man I still considered in my heart to be my lover could be plotting his ambition within moments of burying his father! In my soul I was wondering what concatenation of Fate still drew me so helplessly to a man who so regularly disappointed me. But I was bound to him. He was my life. 'I'll always stand by you,' I said softly.

His expression transformed. He was grinning and clapping. I felt the eyes of the gravediggers on us but Aziz was oblivious. 'I knew I could count on you. And I have plans. As qadi, I've managed to identify some like-minded supporters. People who understand what the common people want. Clever men, with financial skills, who will . . .' He trailed off. He must have seen the expression in my eyes.

'You'll always have my loyalty and my love,' I told him. 'I promised your father I would help you, and I will, if you seek a path that is right and honourable. But it sounds as if you're contemplating conspiracy. Why? You are the heir to King Abu and everything will come to you in time. It would be dangerous and wrong to be precipitate.'

'It may be more dangerous if I wait,' he said, still smiling.

'Then I am not the adviser you need. I am a physician, not a politician.'

I knew, even as I said it, that I was dashing my last hopes that one day Aziz might return to me – but what could I have done? If I had encouraged him in his foolhardiness, I would have been breaking my oath to his father.

His cheek twitched. His fists clenched. Then, slowly, he let out a long breath. He smiled sourly and patted my cheek. 'All right, Samuel, be a physician, if that's the destiny you want. Mine is to be a king.' He flung his mantle over his head, obscuring his beautiful face from my view, and hurried away with sloped shoulders.

I stood alone by the grave. Outside the walls I could hear the lamentations of the crowd that had gathered at the gates to mourn Salim's passing. One of the gravediggers dropped his spade with a clang and a murder of crows croaked into the air.

With a bitter heart I made my way to the Jewish Quarter. My life suddenly disgusted me. In my despairing state, even our great enterprise on the rock seemed a vain enterprise, all show without substance. I wanted to be with my father and mother again. I craved an ordinary existence. For the first time since I'd met Aziz and Paladon under the fig tree I wanted to be with my own kind. To go home.

But when I did my parents treated me like a lord, deferentially serving me viands they could hardly afford, their eyes glistening with pride in the long silences that punctuated their eager and ignorant questions about life at the palace. The next day our house filled with strangers, seeking favours from the influential man at court.

Codex IV

The Tower of Babel

*(I) In which I tell how a prince charmed his people
and how a monk found eternal life*

For a week the shrill ululations of wailing women haunted
the streets. Mosques, churches and synagogues were filled
with sombre congregations praying for Salim's soul. Sack-
clothed processions filed past his house to the beat of a slow
drum. Mountains of roses piled at the entrance as a token of
affection.

It seemed an excessive display of grief. Although Salim's
firm government and brilliant generalship on the battlefield
had guaranteed peace, prosperity and order for as long as
anybody could remember, to the Mishkhatids he had been a
cold, severe figure, revered more than loved.

King Abu sensed that the hysteria was caused as much by
doubt and fear as sorrow for Salim. Like many kings, good
and bad, he had a bond with his subjects. His rule was distant,
he selfishly pursued his own pleasures, but his finger on the
popular pulse was as sure as Dr Isa's on the wrist of a patient.
In the fervency of their mourning for the departed wazir, he
had diagnosed the symptoms of a deeper distress.

The visit of the Castilians, followed by news of the loss of
Toledo and, in short space, the death of their prime minister,
had unsettled them. The rumours in the marketplace were of
imminent war. Abu sensed that what the common people craved
was a signal of reassurance from the palace that the peace,

prosperity and order they had become used to were not threatened.

He responded by inviting to his audience chamber his relatives, councillors, generals, faqis and even his more junior functionaries (which was why I was included). He made no speeches. He merely announced his decision. Aziz was to be the new wazir. 'Like father, like son,' he said. 'He has my full confidence. Mishkhat remains in good hands.' The young prince took his place beside the throne. We all bowed. Apparently Aziz had got what he wanted without having to resort to conspiracy.

I saw the sense of it from the king's point of view. Objections that Aziz was young and inexperienced could be overcome by pointing out that he was heir to the throne and had performed adequately in one official position already. The king had little to fear. If Aziz proved incompetent, Abu had enough loyal generals, backed by the palace guard, who would be able to 'advise' the young man appropriately. On the other hand, if Aziz demonstrated the wisdom and loyalty of his father, then the king could spend the rest of his life in the idle contentment to which he had become accustomed. He duly made the investiture and retired to his sybaritic pleasures in the inner sanctums of his palace.

Aziz was canny enough to appreciate both the opportunity and the danger. He had longed for power ever since he had first tasted it on our campaign with the Cid, but he was shrewd enough to know he had to prove himself first. His was no great intellect: his mind was more like his uncle's than his brilliant father's. Once Paladon had outraged me by observing that our academy of three was actually an academy of two with Aziz pulled along by our friendship; it had led to a short quarrel between us, aggravated for me because I knew that he was at least partially correct. Yet Aziz was never a fool. Like many princes of mere plodding ability, he had developed a capacity for guile as well as charm – it showed in his inauguration speech when he flattered every dignitary in the hall – and he had inherited an unerring sense of what was best for his self-interest.

So, for the first few months he played a waiting game. His task was made easier by the system of governance he had inherited, which almost ran itself. The treasury was full. The bureaucracy was hardworking and efficient. Modest taxes were enough to pay the kingdom's administrative expenses. Aziz realised that by initially changing nothing he could establish a solid reputation. He therefore concealed his ambition under a cloak of humility. He listened respectfully to Salim's experienced officers and rarely questioned their advice. Mishkhat continued to prosper – so much so that it became a common saying in the marketplace that the old wazir, in his concern for his people, had left his shadow behind him in the shape of his son.

After only half a year, Aziz felt confident enough to appoint his own financial adviser, as the king told me one day when I was massaging him. 'You should be pleased, Joseph,' he grunted, as I probed his back. 'My great-nephew's got it into his head to put a Jew in charge of the treasury. Not a bad choice. Ephraim of Seville. Do you know him? He helped Salim finance my mosque project. For a moneylender he gave us very reasonable terms. Existing tax more than covers the interest— Ouch! Well done, that's the spot. Keep pressing. Ah, thank you, Joseph. That's much better. As I was saying, Aziz was impressed and believes this Ephraim can help in other areas as well. Rather shrewd of him. We need clever fellows like that in the treasury. People who can think imaginatively about money— No, a little lower. Thank you. You Jews are good at that, aren't you? I gave the appointment my blessing. What do you think?'

I assented. It was none of my business and, anyway, I had troubles of my own to absorb me. I had still not recovered from the shock and remorse that had overcome me after my father's sudden death during the influenza epidemic that had swept the town's poorer quarters the previous month. By the time I had heard about it, it was too late to save him. I had been preoccupied with treating head colds in the harem and failed to read my mother's message, which she had sent to Salim's house. By the time I reached my father's bedside, there was nothing I could do except hold his frail, exhausted body in my arms as he died.

My mother had done her best to comfort me. 'He had no regrets, Samuel. You must believe that. It meant so much to him that you were with him at the end.'

'I wish I'd come earlier,' I said.

'No, Samuel. We know how difficult it is for you with all those heavy responsibilities at the palace. Goodness knows how you managed to get away as often as you did. It was very generous of you, but you always were a kind, good-hearted boy, so I shouldn't be surprised. Your father knew how much you loved him, of course he did, and all that talk about astrology and potions, and matters of court, and gossip about Prince Aziz, why, every time you came here you gave him a breath of new life. You made him feel young again, and when you were gone, he'd repeat everything you'd said and go over and over it, telling everybody who'd listen how important you are and how you'd achieved every one of his dreams. He was so proud of you. So proud. He'd never hear a word against you. He'd remonstrate whenever I complained that I didn't see enough of you. Then, I'm a mother and allowed to be a little selfish, aren't I?' She chuckled. 'Elijah said one day that he was tired of hearing about you. He accused your father of neglecting the scriptures. Your father grabbed him by the beard and kicked him out of the house, throwing his staff after him. Then he screamed abuse as the prophet ascended angrily into the skies. That was years ago and he's never come back. Well, your father didn't need him any more, did he? He had you.'

There had not been a hint of irony or accusation in her tone. Her sincerity and her love for me pierced my soul. I had, it was true, kept the promise I had made to myself to go home more regularly, and I was closer to both of them than I had been for many years, but my visits had still been infrequent, and they had not made up for the period when I had abandoned them. Now it was too late to make amends. It troubled me, which was why I was so disinterested in matters of state. For a while, I even forgot Aziz.

It was only after I had left the king's chamber that I realised the significance of what Abu had been telling me, for I recalled that I had met Ephraim before.

He had come to my father's funeral, I don't know why. Perhaps Aziz sent him so he would not have to be there himself. I was familiar with his reputation as a successful banker who had arrived in Mishkhat a few years before. I also knew that recently he had wormed his way into the wazir's circle. How could I not? The gossip in the marketplace was all about the prince's 'new Jew'. Ephraim had not stayed long after the obsequies. He had paused only briefly to tell us how much he had admired my father. My mother was quite taken with him. He was a handsome, self-possessed man of middle years and he had a silver tongue. He was also a dandy: he wore blue ribbons studded with discreet diamonds in his sidelocks. Afterwards she had scolded me for my shabbiness, telling me that Ephraim looked more like a courtier than I did. For my part, I had taken an immediate dislike to him. The most dangerous sycophants are those who can disguise their ambition. I experienced a moment of unease when I thought of this plausible fellow advising Aziz. Then I put him out of my mind.

In due course the two of them announced a new budget, Aziz's first as wazir. Aziz amazed everybody: he cut taxes by a quarter, yet the money he allocated for state expenditure increased by half as much again. The praise for the young prince in the marketplace subtly changed. Fortunate was Mishkhat, the traders pronounced. The father had been a David, who had built a mighty nation. The son was a Solomon, wiser than his years, who would enrich his people the more.

Aziz basked in it. He no longer saw any need for humility. His popularity manifested itself in ways that might have been more appropriate for a celebrated singer than a prince. His reputation as a lover was bruited in pamphlets, with portraits of the various Buthainas, Azzas, Lailas, Lubnas and other famous beauties whom he was supposed to have seduced. Verses reputed to have been written by him to his houris were circulated in the taverns. Once I had the mortification of hearing a poem I had composed for him with the names and sex changed.

An enterprising Arab potter, who had somehow obtained a verse written in Aziz's calligraphy, reproduced it on pewter tableware and made his fortune selling memorial sets for weddings and other celebrations. Not to be outdone, a Christian competitor commissioned a pictorial representation of the young wazir out hawking and made it the centrepiece of a silver banquet set. Christian merchants vied to buy them for their great occasions.

Aziz pretended to be embarrassed, but he made sure he was never out of the public ear or eye. He loved the trappings of his position – the band that preceded him, the cavalry behind him, dressed in new silver hauberks he had designed. Like his father, he would dispense with his horse, walking under a canopy, but in his case it was held up by nubile female slaves rather than muscular Nubians. His daily procession through the marketplace on his way to the qadi's court gathered enormous crowds. He would wave at the admiring throng and flash his big eyes at the ladies, charming them as he had done me when he was my Gazelle. Perhaps only Paladon and I knew of his inward vanity, but the people praised him for his lack of pretension.

Oh, yes, even then I had my doubts about his ability but, like the rest of the populace, I allowed my affection for him to drowse my judgement. Recent events had brought renewed fears of war with the Christians, but without a crusading army stamping on our border, the average Mishkhatid preferred to bury his head in the sand. The novelty of a boy wazir – capable, industrious and apparently cast in his father's image – one so attractive and glamorous to boot, allowed us to blind ourselves to reality: it was better for our peace of mind that we believed our charmed life in Mishkhat would continue undisturbed.

And that was how we became a kingdom of lotus-eaters, like all the other states in Andaluz who denied what Salim had tried to show them. It was a sad legacy for a man who had sacrificed his life to ward off the doom that was descending on us.

It is a well-known saw that the gods raise to great heights those whom they intend to destroy. So it was with the Baghdad of Harun al-Rashid and the Córdoba of abd al-Rahman in the living memories of our fathers. I cannot claim that in those last blooming days of our decadence and luxury I ever thought such a fate might also befall Mishkhat. I was as blind as the rest.

Every day we heard the comforting sound of hammers ringing on the mountainside above us. Every day brought news of marvels that Paladon, working with the fury of a madman, had achieved in his cave. We took the news complacently. We were so spoiled by riches that the remarkable was but common fare. So it must have been for the citizens of Babel, when they looked up idly from their pleasures at the great shadow rising inch by inch over their heads.

Fate had struck a cruel blow to Paladon who had already been deeply affected by Salim's death – his father, exhausted by the duties imposed on him during the Castilian visit, had quickly followed the wazir to the grave. What an evil combination of stars must have caused all three members of our brotherhood to lose their fathers within months of each other! Paladon and I had responded to our personal tragedies by burying our grief in work. In his case it took the form of more fevered activity on the mosque. He accelerated his timetable, and construction proceeded at a faster pace. Much sooner than expected, every pillar had been mounted.

One day Ayesha confided to me her concern for her betrothed. He hardly made time to see her any more, and she was fearful he had given way to despair. She suspected that Paladon was concerned about his conversion. With Salim gone, there was no one who could intercede for him with the chief faqi. 'But our marriage depends on him successfully becoming a Mussulman.' She begged me to talk to Aziz, having convinced herself that I would have more influence on him than she did. Little did she know. But she hugged me. 'Would you? I'll love you for ever if you do.' She sighed and kissed me, and I was putty in her hands. Next day I waited for Aziz among the many clients gathered in the antechamber outside his office in the palace. Of course my heart was beating fast: I thought only that I would see my Gazelle again.

Aziz was irritated when I accosted him. A clerk was following him, loaded with documents, and his acolytes, the elegant, blue-ribboned Ephraim among them, jostled behind. When I told him I was speaking at his sister's behest, Aziz surveyed me warily. 'Go on.'

I explained.

'Paladon knows about this?' he asked.

'Not that I'm talking to you about it,' I said.

He looked through me. Then he smiled. I think he relished the idea that he now had the power to help someone whom he had once looked up to for leadership. It probably also amused him that, having rejected his offer of advancement, I was now coming to beseech his favour. 'Very well. I will see what can be done.'

I left the palace sadder than I had come.

A few days later Paladon was summoned to the *madrasah*. He was led to the office of his old enemy, the chief faqi, who tested him sternly on his knowledge of the Qur'ān. Paladon told me that his face was colder and harder than the rock surface he was chiselling in the cave. The inquisition was followed by a long silence, during which the old man stared at the ceiling. Eventually he spoke: 'For a Christian, you have an impressive understanding. You even sound sincere.' So icy was his tone that Paladon felt sure he was about to dash his hopes. But he went on: 'Why should I be surprised? Your teacher was Salim. He was always a great judge of character, may Allah be merciful to him, so I will consent to be your teacher and, if it is Allah's will, in due course I will bring you into the ranks of the faithful. Who am I to question the wishes of two wazirs or, indeed, the grace of Allah, for how else could an infidel achieve such a holy work as the great mosque I see growing in stature and magnificence on the rock? I will be waiting for you next Friday evening in my private rooms.' His thin lips twisted into what Paladon suddenly realised was a grin. 'And I grant you permission to enter by my door rather than by my window.' That was the only reference he ever made to the stolen turban.

This conversation must have helped to chase away the devils that had haunted Paladon – but he did not slow the pace of his work. Artists and stonemasons were now carving his designs on the flattened cliff face that surrounded the mouth of the cave. When the scaffolding was removed, even I gasped in wonder at the depiction, in floral arabesques, of the Garden of Eden, where behind the plane-leaf and palm-frond motifs lurked every kind of animal and bird in Creation, and this was but the door frame. The final picture was completed when the great teak doors were mounted. Carved on them was the Tree of Life.

'You fashioned this?' I asked him breathlessly. 'Of your own imagination?'

'It was your idea, Samuel,' he said.

'But it is so beautiful. Every animal seems alive, every plant breathing. I never knew you were such an artist.'

He blushed. 'Come, Samuel, stop teasing me. I've been carving angels all my life. You learn a few tricks as you go along. I was worried, in fact, about what you'd think. That elephant looks like a plump crocodile, and the apples on the tree might be oranges. I'll try to do better with the interior.' His head twitched to one side as he heard a far-off cry and then he was running towards a pulley where the rope was fraying. All thoughts of art were forgotten as he jostled among a group of his workers, straining at a lever to stop the friction.

I watched him, amazed. He was totally unaware of his genius. I do not think there was an ounce of vanity in him.

The ordinary people of Mishkhat had no doubt about the miracle that was materialising in brick and stone before their eyes. Admittedly there was a modicum of self-interest. The Mussulmans were to receive a new and magnificent place of worship. The other members of the community, Christian and Jew alike, were aware that the extraordinary architectural achievement would bring travellers from far and wide to wonder at it, and with them would come revenue, business and trade. Mishkhat would become a Córdoba, as it had been in the days of the Caliphate, and everybody would prosper accordingly.

Yet there was something else too. I noticed it when I passed an artisan or a trader, a woman or a child standing silently in the street staring at the activity on the rock above them. I think they knew that something of remarkable beauty was being created there, and this brought a sense of purpose and meaning to their lives.

Seven months after Salim's death when Paladon, at the dispensation of the king, allowed groups of notables to view the nearly completed prayer hall, there were as many admiring rabbis and priests as faqis in the queues that wound down from the cave mouth. A half-year later, when the first bricks of the dome could be seen rising above the summit of the rock, the king asked Aziz to arrange a week of festivities. The high point would be Friday prayers in the new, as yet undecorated, mosque, and special galleries were partitioned off so that even non-Mussulmans could attend the service of thanksgiving.

One of the Christians who crowded in with the throng was a monk in a white habit. It was Jaime, Paladon's cousin, who had come down from his monastery in the mountains for the occasion. Nobody noticed him enter or raised an eyebrow when he elbowed his way to the front row of the gallery. Why should they have? All eyes were on the magnificent robes of King Abu, Wazir Aziz and the other courtiers, as they made their way solemnly to their carpets facing the mihrab. Here the chief faqi waited for them, also decked out in splendour, the jewelled turban settled on his bald pate. I was certainly not aware of the intruder. Standing in my place among the Mishkhat Jews, my eyes were blinded by tears, for I saw around me not a mosque but the fulfilled dream of our brotherhood.

There was much still to be done. The space above us was draped with canvas and shadowed by scaffolding. The dome and inverted cupolas on which the stars of the constellations would one day shine were as yet open to the sky. Nor had the walls been painted with our secret symbols – but under every one of the three hundred and sixty-five pillars, each fashioned of different stone with different alchemical properties, lay my little vials of essence, and every angle and proportion of every arch and apse had been erected according to my astrological specifications. It did not matter to me that the God about to be worshipped here was Allah, for to me Allah was just another name for the Prime Mover who had created on earth every man and beast, every stone, every plant, all that moved or breathed, everything animate or inanimate that had been brought into existence by celestial fire. I felt myself to be in a holy sanctum, a microcosm of God's universe. The lamp in the mihrab was burning. The cave had become once more the Niche of Light, filled with the flame of Knowledge and Science that is Reason's tribute to our Creator. I did not feel proud. I felt humbled.

There was a hush as the chief faqi raised his arms. The Umma dropped on their knees as one and bowed in prayer. The old man coughed, and closed his eyes, ready to make the invocation. He opened his mouth to say the beautiful words that would consecrate Paladon's master work—

And the monk, Jaime, leaped over the railings. There were no guards to stop him. Why should there have been in our peaceable kingdom on such a day of communal celebration? He strode forward among the kneeling Mussulmans, his straw sandals flip-flapping in the silence. Instead of the sensual words of the Qur'ān, the bewildered congregation heard the ugly rasp of mispronounced Arabic, as the Christian monk shouted his curse.

'Oh, damned are the heathen who worship the devil in the guise of a false prophet. Cursed be the name of the demon Allah. Cursed be the name of his incubus, Muhammad, the Antichrist foretold in the scriptures. May he burn in hell fire for eternity. Oh, Jesus Christ, our true Lord and Redeemer, smite down in holy wrath the blasphemy that evil has wreaked in our sacred shrine, for know ye that this cave, now polluted with shame, was where Mary, the Mother of Christ, appeared to a shepherd in a vision for the grace of her people. O Lord my God, and his servant, Alfonso, the true king of Spain, restore to us our lands and our sanctified places, stolen by infidels and devil-worshippers—'

Enraged Mussulmans wrestled him to the ground and began to beat him. Soldiers eventually came and took him away. The service continued, but the damage had been done.

Late that afternoon Paladon and I were summoned to the palace. It was the first time that Aziz, since his rise to greatness, had called us in to see him. We found him standing under the archway that opened from his office on to the king's marble patio. He appeared to be contemplating the peacocks on the lawn. He was still wearing his robe of state. Unlike Salim's austere black gown, Aziz's was of purple velvet embroidered with grey and studded with pearls. His gold-handled sword hung in its jewelled scabbard from his silk cummerbund. Filigreed silver slippers curled out from the brocade border of his skirt, and the large Indian ruby that adorned his turban flashed in the rays of the setting sun. I wondered if he had invited us there to admire him in his finery. Then I noticed the droop of his shoulders, and the limp, ringed fingers trembling on the balustrade.

It was no great prince who turned to greet us. The sad appeal in his eyes and the uncertain smile that flickered under his curled moustache were those of the boy we had once known. In a moment, he had taken the few paces that separated us and embraced us closely, his arms round our shoulders, lingering as he pressed his cheek against mine. There was a tear in the corner of his eye when he straightened. 'It has been so long since we three were alone together,' he murmured. 'I have forgotten what it is like to wile away idle hours with friends.' He looked intently at us, as if he wanted to persuade us of his sincerity. 'You are the only two men on this earth I can trust. Sit with me a while.' He gestured at the rich carpets. 'I would have you with me this evening. I would have the brotherhood meet once more.'

'What do you want us do for you, Aziz?' asked Paladon.

Aziz started, as if he had been slapped. 'So cold, Paladon?' His voice was gentle, but there was strain behind it. 'Must I have a reason for inviting you to see me? Can we no longer sit together as friends?'

Paladon blushed. 'Of course we're still friends. You're the wazir, though. I thought . . .'

'What, Paladon? What did you think?'

Paladon stared at him, his honest face showing his confusion. I cannot imagine he had intended to be rude. Blunt as ever, he had merely articulated the question that he and I had debated on our way to the palace.

Aziz sighed. 'All right, let us be businesslike if that is your will.' He stood up and walked briskly to his desk on which lay a piece of parchment covered with official Arabic script. It looked like a court order, but it was neither signed nor sealed. He picked it up and returned to where he had been sitting. 'Yes, there is something I wish to ask of you, my future brother-in-law, since I can officially call you that now. The chief faqi told me yesterday that he had decided to accept your conversion. Congratulations. You have impressed him as you seem to impress everybody. There are now no obstacles to your marrying my sister, except my approval, but how could I deny it to a friend? So, honour me with your advice, my brother, my fellow Mussulman. Tell me, what should I do with this?' He flung the document on to the carpet. 'You read it too, Samuel,' he added, in a softer tone. 'In a moment I will ask you for your wise words.'

Paladon read it quickly. I saw his face pale. He silently passed it to me.

'Oh, you're condemning him to death,' I murmured in shock.

'Don't you think he deserves it? The monk is guilty of sacri-lege, blasphemy and heresy, and since he is a citizen of Mishkhat, he has also committed treason.'

'Surely he's just insane, Aziz. You're the wazir and the qadi. You know the law better than I do, but isn't it the custom – it was certainly your father's practice – to make allowances for those touched by God? Dr Isa and I could examine him. In our hospital we have the resources to—'

'Touched by God?' interrupted Aziz. 'An interesting medical term. And in this case it's rather apposite, isn't it? It might depend on which God we're talking about, though – and, please, Samuel, don't give me your theories about a universal Prime Mover. Paladon, what is your view? He's your cousin. You should know him well enough. Is he insane?'

Paladon was gently thumping his right fist into his left palm. Eventually he answered, 'Jaime was moody, yes. Bitter, too.

Religious to the point of fanaticism, but always in control of his senses. I haven't seen him for more than a year, not since the Castilians were here. We're not friends. He's been in his monastery. It's possible he's become unhinged since he's been there – well, he must have gone mad. No sane man would walk into a Mussulman mosque and insult the Prophet.'

'A fanatic might,' said Aziz, quietly. 'That's what you just called him.'

He carefully folded the death warrant and slipped it into the fold of his gown. 'Your cousin did not restrict himself to abusing Allah and the Prophet, did he? He also mentioned the King of Castile. Is there anything you want to tell me, Paladon, about the time the Castilian delegation stayed in your father's house?'

Paladon did not attempt to conceal his bitterness. 'They were unruly and ill-mannered. Drunken Norman knights went to the kitchens and raped six of our servants among the pots and pans. The duke took pleasure in insulting my father, making him dance among the musicians, which contributed to his early death.'

'Oh, Paladon, you never said,' I gasped.

Paladon shrugged. 'Would it have brought him back if I had?'

Aziz had been watching us. 'You have our sympathies, Paladon. But at the moment I am more interested in your cousin, Jaime. And his brother, Lucas – another priest. Did they take part in this – revelry?'

Paladon's shoulders slumped. 'No. In truth, I was so occupied with trying to keep order that I had no time to monitor what they were about. They were with the monks in my father's private chapel and in the separate lodgings we gave them above the stables.'

'It's interesting that you use the word "monitor". Why would you feel a need to monitor your cousins?'

'I don't get on with them. They're Castilians at heart. They

never integrated into Mishkhat. I said as much to Samuel. I
didn't want them shaming our household.'

'If you suspected your relatives of disloyalty, shouldn't you
have told me or my father rather than Samuel? Was that not
a little negligent of you?'

Paladon was banging his fist into his palm again. 'Come on,
Aziz. It wasn't that serious. In fact, I stopped worrying about
them when it was clear that all they wanted was to spend time
with their fellow clergymen. I'd been afraid they'd complain
to the duke about our rulers in front of my father. What was
the harm in them praying and discussing religious matters? I
was relieved to know that they were closeted with the Cluniac
monk.'

'Which Cluniac monk? They were all Cluniacs.'

'The chief one. Sancho's tutor.'

'You mean Elderic?'

'Yes.'

'The man who, in our king's dining hall, insulted the
Mussulman faith during his debate with ibn Sa'id, in words
not so dissimilar to the ones used by Jaime today? It seems
their prayers and religious discussions were not as harmless as
you thought, were they, my old friend? Your monitoring was
not very efficient, was it, Paladon?'

In the silence that followed, Aziz paced the carpet by the
arch where we had first seen him. The sun was already over
the horizon, and in his dark robes he seemed just another
shadow against the velvet dusk.

'Do you remember, Samuel, after the battle against the
Almerians, I authorised the Cid to execute our prisoners? You
were angry with me at the time, yet I saw the logic of what
the Cid was advising. Ruthlessness, he said, is a deterrent to
others. My father, however, always advocated mercy because
that is in keeping with the teachings of the Qur'ān. Now I
have a choice to make. I can decide that Jaime is a madman
and hand him over to Dr Isa to spend the rest of his miserable

life in a cell for the insane, or I can make an example of him by dragging him to the market square, flaying him, blinding him, removing his ears, tongue, generative organs, liver and heart, then burning them with the rest of his carcass on a bonfire. That is what the chief faqi recommends I do. He says it's the appropriate penalty for blasphemy, and I've checked with the scribes in the qadi's court and they concur. Tell me, Paladon, how do you think that would go down with the Christian community?'

'They would support the wazir's decision,' he said. 'The Christian community is loyal to Mishkhat.'

'But they wouldn't like it, would they?' He turned to me. 'Samuel, what do you think? Bear in mind the circumstantial evidence that Paladon has somewhat belatedly supplied, which suggests his cousin was in league with Elderic, an enemy of our people and religion.'

I was so stunned by what I had heard that it took me a moment to clear my thoughts. 'Circumstantial evidence is not absolute proof,' I said eventually. 'We may suppose Elderic ordered Jaime to do this thing as part of a conspiracy by Castile to cause dissension in our state. We can equally well suppose that Jaime, because of his admiration for such a charismatic and seditious figure, decided to make a protest of his own volition, in which case it would not be a conspiracy but the action of a single, probably demented and bitter, individual.'

'And where does this tortuous sophistry leave us?'

'In the first case you must consider what Castile hoped to achieve by their conspiracy. A public burning might play into their hands if it antagonises a section of our community or causes civil disturbance. Dare you risk that? Might it not be better to defuse the situation by treating it as an isolated case of insanity? In the second instance, the probability is that Jaime really is insane, and I would recommend that you let Dr Isa and me examine him. I suppose I am pleading for mercy, Aziz. And – and statesmanship.'

'Statesmanship? What would you say if I told you that the king is expecting me to take a hard line so this will never happen again? That he wants to make an example of this creature.'

'I would ask for whom the example was being made. Earlier you said that ruthlessness is a deterrent. So it can be, if there is somebody to be deterred, but at the moment we know only of one, probably mad, individual who has committed a crime that has appalled every one of our citizens. Everybody is on your side. Why run the risk of alienating those who support you? What sort of example is that?'

'You are forgetting that a section of our community will demand revenge for the sacrilege this man has committed. The mercy you advocate will not sit well with the Mussulmans of Mishkhat. What do you say to that?'

'You are right. They will only be satisfied if you punish him. Oh, but, Aziz, that does not preclude mercy. A lifetime's confinement in either a mental ward or a dungeon would be a terrible sentence for any soul. It would be a judgement a rational man would approve – severe, but tempered by mercy. Appropriate to the crime. Worthy of a wise wazir. Paladon, I know he's your relative, but Aziz cannot let his action go unpunished.'

'I couldn't agree more,' said Paladon. 'The wretch deserves everything he gets. I'd light the pyre myself if Aziz decided to burn him at the stake.'

'Would you, Paladon?' asked Aziz. His tone was quite serious.

Paladon uttered a nervous laugh. 'I was speaking figuratively. I'm a stonemason, not a hangman.'

'Would you, if I asked you to?'

'What's the point of this? Why would you?'

Aziz stepped back into the light. His lips were pressed in a tight smile. 'Don't be too sure, Paladon. You and your family have embarrassed me. Maybe one day I will insist you make a demonstration of your loyalty, if only to prove that I was not mistaken in agreeing to let the cousin of a blasphemer marry my sister.'

Paladon rose to his feet, his fists clenched. 'You think I knew about this, Aziz? That I had something to do with it?' Before either of us could stop him, he had pulled his dagger from his belt. Aziz paled and grabbed the hilt of his jewelled sword, but Paladon had already pressed the blade against his own wrist. A thin trickle of blood curled down his forearm. 'You need a demonstration of my loyalty? I will cut off this hand, here and now, if I have offended you or Islam.'

Aziz smiled. Gently he unclasped Paladon's shaking fingers. He withdrew a white silk handkerchief from his sleeve and wiped the blade. He carefully sheathed the knife in Paladon's belt. Then he bound the handkerchief round the cut. 'Mishkhat needs those hands to complete their work on the rock,' he murmured. 'I'd be failing in my responsibility as wazir if I let you harm them.' He embraced him, rising on his toes to kiss the craggy cheeks.

He beckoned us both to sit down with him on the carpet again. 'Your great hands and Samuel's sharp mind – God help me, I need them tonight. The Christian monk's actions in the mosque today may have consequences that will affect the peace of our kingdom if I do not make the right decision tomorrow. It is already causing quarrels among friends. Samuel, give me your arguments again, and, Paladon, use your anger over your cousin's betrayal to help me. Put the argument against mercy from the point of view of the Mussulman you have become. Let us use the old methods of debate we have tried and tested so many times before – and with Allah's help we may come to the right conclusion.'

So, once more the Brotherhood of the Craft sat together long into the night. It was approaching dawn before we had finished.

Paladon and I left the palace. Far away below us, a man cried the third watch. A dog barked after each call.

'You're happy with what we concluded, Paladon? You put up a good argument against your kin.'

'I disown Jaime and also Lucas, wherever he is now. I wouldn't be surprised to learn that both brothers had a hand in it. They're no longer part of my family. They can hang for all I care – but that's just passion speaking. You were right to advise Aziz to be merciful. Salim would have agreed with you.'

'It was good meeting together again. Aziz has changed little underneath.'

Paladon was silent. Our footsteps echoed against the rocks. Then he said, 'He threatened me, Samuel.'

'What do you mean?'

'About Ayesha. He's had second thoughts about me marrying her.'

'Come, the two of you were just quarrelling. He's under a great strain.'

'No, it's more than that. He doesn't want me in his family. This Jaime business plays into his hands.'

I laughed, punching his shoulder. I told him he was the most gloomy, morbid, pessimistic fool I had ever known.

As we reached the bottom of the hill, the first rays of dawn shone on the peak of the rock. In its light, the white bricks of the first layers of the dome glinted like gold. We parted, Paladon to the old track that led to the cave, I to the hospital to rouse Dr Isa. I was intensely worried by the Jaime business but, at that moment, gratitude that Aziz had decided to speak to me again was uppermost in my mind.

We found Jaime in one of the dungeon cells under the palace. He had been manacled by his wrists to the damp rock wall. He had not, as far as Dr Isa and I could tell, been mistreated beyond the beating he had received in the mosque. We had our first proper look at him in the light of the candle on the table in the warder's room, where we were to conduct our examination.

He was tall, like his cousin, but otherwise in no way resembled him. His ragged brown tonsure framed a narrow, fox-like face, and he was skeletally thin. The white habit he wore, now torn and stained, seemed to drape him like a shroud, but for all his slightness, he was full of tense energy and strength. His black, beady eyes watched our every action suspiciously. When Dr Isa moved the candle closer to his face to examine his teeth and tongue, he jerked his head away, and the warder had to use all his force to keep him still.

'Malnourished,' murmured Dr Isa. 'I suppose it's that barley gruel the monks eat, or he's been fasting too long. Nothing wrong with his eyes, though. They focus well. No ophthalmia or dazed vision. Jaime,' he addressed the prisoner gently, 'do you see clearly?'

'More clearly than you,' he answered, in a composed, educated voice.

'Why do you say that?' asked Dr Isa, respectfully, adopting his hospital manner.

'Because you're a heretic, working for the heathen with this Jew, and I am filled with the Lord's holy light. You have an interesting predicament, Dr Isa. Yes, I know who you are. I've seen you once or twice at my uncle's house. You have two problems. First, you've come here to prove that I'm a madman, because that may save the state the trouble of executing me, as well as providing a convenient explanation for the embarrassment I caused in the mosque. Unfortunately for you, I am as sane as you are, as you will discover if you talk to me instead of prodding me. You will be breaking your Hippocratic oath if you judge me otherwise. Your second problem is a matter for your soul as well as your conscience. You are a baptised Christian, and if you assist my persecutors by collaborating with them in their attempts to silence me, you will be denying in the face of the Lord your God the truth that you know I uttered when I determined on a course of martyrdom.'

'A sane man is a rational man,' I said, noticing that Dr Isa had been taken aback by the fluency of his attack. 'Is what you call martyrdom rational? No creature on God's earth seeks death. In fact, there are the strictest laws in the scriptures of all faiths against suicide, including those written in the Old Testament.'

'Ah, yes. Rationalism, the broken shelter of the natural philosopher, who fondly believes that its pathetic thatch can protect him from the radiant light of Truth Revealed . . . I know you, too, Samuel the Alchemist, apostate of the Hebrew faith. You were the first to poison Paladon with your diabolical sciences, turning him on to the path of devil worship that he has now adopted to the damnation of his soul. Do you really dare to quote scriptures at me? But you are correct when you say that the Lord damns suicides. I have no intention of committing suicide. A soldier who engages in battle for his king is prepared to pay the ultimate sacrifice to attain victory. Nobody calls him a suicide if he falls in the fight. I wage war to ensure the victory of the King of Heaven. The sword I wield is truth. If my enemies slay me because I have declared the truth, who can speak of suicide? My death, however, will bring forward the ultimate triumph of my Lord, because my example will waken others. Draw your straw blinds around you, philosopher. Hide from the truth as best you can. Its light will find you on Judgment Day.'

'That is a pretty sermon, Jaime. Well reasoned, too, but it is the cavilling of a lawyer rather than anything demonstrable as truth, for the result is the same, whether you inflict the death you seek on yourself, or it is inflicted on you by another. A man who brings about his own death is a suicide by whatever means he employs. You use a military analogy, but no soldier seeks death voluntarily. You do. You are angry because you suspect we are trying to prevent the martyrdom you desire. Death, in other words.'

'Or life, Samuel.' Jaime smiled. 'Life eternal at the right hand of Jesus. A remission of sins. The company of saints.

What soldier would fear death if he knows that Paradise is his ultimate reward?' He grinned. 'Is that not also a rational goal to be desired? It's open to all of us, you know, who open their hearts to God. It's not too late for you to convert, even you, and join us in our fight.'

'Is that what Elderic told you?' I asked. 'Did he urge you to take up this fight?'

He frowned. 'It is the Lord who has instructed me to wage war on heresy. His commands are there for all to see in His Holy Book. Elderic is one of our captains, a great captain. He is marshalling the forces of God to combat the plague that the damned Muhammad has brought against Christendom. I am not God's only soldier. Others will come after me, in ones and twos, then in cohorts and armies. Can you comprehend that? I thank God. I thank Him for the privilege he has bestowed on me by allowing me to play even a small part in the great victory to come. Dr Isa, don't you see it? Are you blind? This is the hour, ordained by God, when truth shall be reborn, the Lord's enemies vanquished, and our inheritance restored. Wake up. Abandon the heathens you serve before it is too late. Put on the armour of God, man, that ye may be able to stand against the wiles of the devil.'

'And who will win this victory on earth for God?' I persisted. 'You mentioned King Alfonso during your rant in the mosque. If Elderic is a captain, is Alfonso the general? Did Elderic describe the chain of command of this holy army, which must also be a temporal one if it is to be effective?'

His face knitted suspiciously. 'Why do you keep mentioning Elderic?' Then he laughed. 'Oh, I see. He was, no doubt, the inspiration for my madness. He cast a spell over me, perhaps, when I was with him in Toscanus's house? Is that it? Gentlemen, please, make up your minds. What would you have me be? Mad, like the Gadarene swine entered by a host of demons, or an agent of Castile? Can you not understand that I merely follow the orders of a higher power? You have only to read the

Bible to see my instructions. Dr Isa, you must have a copy at your home. It's all in the New Testament and the Psalms. "And I saw heaven opened and behold, a white horse, and he that sat upon him was called Faithful and True, and in righteousness he doth judge and make war." Revelation nineteen. "And Jesus answered and said unto them, Take heed that no man deceive you. For many shall come in my name . . . and deceive many. And ye shall hear of wars and rumours of wars." Matthew twenty-four. "Let the high praises of God be in their mouth and a two-edged sword in their hand; to execute vengeance upon the heathen and punishments upon the people . . . This honour have all His saints: Praise ye the Lord." Psalm one hundred and forty-nine . . .'

Each quotation was like a shaft hitting Dr Isa in the chest. Suddenly he stood up. 'Excuse me,' he said, and hurried out. I motioned to the warder to keep Jaime secured, then followed him. The litany of verses continued implacably behind us.

'This man is not mad,' he said, in the corridor outside. 'He put it exactly. If I were to judge him so, I would be betraying my oath.'

'There are many forms of madness,' I said.

'None like this. It is his sanity that frightens me. His conviction. His calm. If we tried to demonstrate in court that he was insane, we would be mocked. He argues as fluently as you do.'

'I agree,' I said, 'but there is a difference. When I make a point, I base it on reasonable deduction. I use my reason. This man goes back only to his holy book. Is it not a form of unreason to guide your life purely by words written on a page? That literalism makes him dangerous to himself and society.'

Dr Isa lowered his head. 'Samuel, I also am a Christian. I read the Bible and find sustenance in it. Those words on the page govern my life too. Jesus talked of charity. I could not treat my patients if I did not have those precepts in front of me.'

'You talk of charity. Jaime talks of war. There is a difference.'

Dr Isa sighed. 'Maybe that's what the world's coming to, Samuel. All my life I've tried to be tolerant of others. I work in a Mussulman hospital. You, my best friend, are a Jew. But maybe a cull lies ahead. In the north, the priests from Cluny are urging the Franks to fight the infidel. Now they're in Castile. In Africa, the Mussulmans are becoming intolerant. Or so I've heard from travellers I've treated in the hospital. The Berbers in Marrakesh are preaching a stricter adherence to the Qur'ān, forbidding wine, closing the neo-Platonist schools. What's the difference? One Bible or another. Priests or faqis leading armies. A clash is coming. An Armageddon. I fear it, Samuel, I fear it. I'm a doctor. I can deal with madness. That's curable. I sincerely believe it. But this polarisation of belief that uses religion to divide us? It terrifies me. This Jaime terrifies me – not because he's mad, but because he's frighteningly, implacably sane.'

'He's only one man, Isa – a bitter, disappointed individual who has found a vent for his frustrations in an excessive display of religion. Lock him out of sight and he's harmless.'

'How do you lock up armies, Samuel? You heard him talk about Elderic. Didn't you see the Normans in the priests' train? Hatred is like those demons the Egyptian doctors believe live in noxious vapours in the air and cause plagues. Let one man breathe them in and soon everybody becomes infected. Didn't you hear him? He said others would follow him. No, I can't help you this time, Samuel. This is not a medical matter. I cannot commit this man. I wash my hands of him. Oh, God,' he groaned, 'what have I said?'

I watched him stumble down the corridor. I felt sick at heart. I saw no point in examining Jaime further. I ordered the warder to take him back to his cell. When he was shoved past me, manacled, he gave me a satisfied smile.

I climbed the steps to the palace, and waited outside Aziz's room. Eventually he had finished with his financial counsellor. Ephraim nodded unctuously at me as he left.

'Well?' asked Aziz, when I entered. 'Is he insane?'

'I believe so,' I said.

'Excellent.' Aziz rubbed his hands. 'I will enjoy examining him.'

'No, Aziz, you can't bring him into court.'

Aziz frowned. I suddenly felt extremely tired. 'You must try him *in absentia*. I – I can give you a deposition stating he's incapable. Mad. Anything you need. But don't try him openly.'

'I haven't a choice. The king has told me he will be there in person. He will want to see me interrogate him and pass judgement, the chief faqi, too, and important representatives of the Umma. We will be merciful – the king has agreed. It'll be imprisonment or committal rather than execution for the pragmatic reasons you argued. Why these unedifying histrionics?'

I tried as best I could to explain to him the dangers. I told him Jaime would not appear insane. He would quote scriptures fluently. He would repeat every insult he had made in the mosque. He would say anything and everything to antagonise every person in the court. 'He wants you to execute him. He will goad you into passing that verdict. The king will be incensed. The chief faqi. The Umma. You, Aziz. You will have no choice.'

Eventually Aziz lost patience and told me I was wasting his time. I should go back to my books and potions, and leave matters of state to him.

I stumbled back into the antechamber. Ephraim was waiting there. 'A difficult meeting?' he asked, with a benevolent smile. 'If ever I can put it in a word, please say so, my friend,' and he disappeared within.

I did not attend the execution in the square. Neither did Paladon.

Strangely, Dr Isa did. Its brutality upset him, and he did not come to the hospital for three days afterwards. I had to shuffle some of my palace appointments to stand in for him.

The Christian community was not as badly affected by it as I had feared. Most were ashamed of the monk and accepted the punishment that was meted out to him. They were probably relieved to be able to put the uneasy matter behind them. The Mussulmans did not hold any grievance against the Christians in general, preferring to believe that this had been the action of an isolated blasphemer who had been justly punished.

In any case, Aziz had taken no chances. After Jaime's eloquence in court, he had ordered that his jaw be broken to make him incapable of further speech. Humiliated by the other's oratory when he had cross-examined him, Aziz wanted to render him incapable of incitement from the scaffold.

That might have been the end of it, a shabby, bruising interlude in the life of the city, forgotten in time. But at the next Friday prayers in the old mosque, another monk, who had disguised himself as a Mussulman, threw off his cloak and he, too, insulted the Prophet. He was condemned to be mutilated and burned.

This time there was a rumble of anger and alarm among the Mussulmans. A small mob marched to the Christian Quarter and threw stones at shops until Aziz's cavalry dispersed them. Aziz determined on reprisals against what he believed was the source of the blasphemies. He sent troops to the monastery in the mountains. They found it deserted. They burned the buildings and came back empty-handed.

On the next Friday there were two more incidents of blasphemy in mosques on the outskirts of the city. A monk and a nun were apprehended. They, too, were burned. To prevent riots, Aziz positioned a line of troops around the Christian Quarter, sealing it off. The frustrated Mussulman mob marched into the Jewish Quarter and set alight a synagogue. Aziz imposed a city-wide curfew.

That did not prevent the stabbing of a Christian merchant in the main bathhouse. He did not die: Dr Isa and I operated on him successfully. Next day a Mussulman family who owned a laundry near the Christian Quarter were bludgeoned to death by a group of Christian youths. A larger, Mussulman mob broke through Aziz's cordon and burned a small oratory. The troops stood by and watched it go up in flames. Perhaps they were intimidated by the number of people on the streets. The mob's interpretation was that they had been given licence by the authorities. From that moment events spiralled out of control.

After dark, in defiance of the curfew, Christian and Mussulman gangs roamed the streets. There were more burnings, more stabbings. In the Jewish Quarter, the daughter of a rabbi was raped. The Christians blamed the Mussulmans, the Mussulmans the Christians. Nobody identified the perpetrators.

The king called the chief faqi, the Christian bishop and the chief rabbi to the palace. He ordered them to sign a joint declaration condemning the violence. There were stern injunctions to the separate communities to live in peace with their neighbours. Mishkhat had a tradition of tolerance, the notice stated. Religious hatred, manifested by a minority, was to be abhorred.

It was already too late. As the religious leaders were meeting, six Christian monks broke into a small mosque near the main gate of the city, tied up the mullah, and desecrated the mihrab. They took the copy of the Qur'ān from the minbar and defecated on it. They scratched an obscene representation of Muhammad, with phallus and horns, on the floor of the prayer hall. The mullah somehow escaped and called for help. A crowd gathered and two of the monks were torn limb from limb as they left. The other four surrendered to a patrol of cavalry. One of the monks was Jaime's brother, Lucas.

They were tortured in the king's dungeons. Aziz, presiding over the subsequent trial attended by most of the Mussulman population, read out the confessions. The finger pointed at Castile. A plot had been hatched, he told them, between

Alfonso's agent, Elderic, and the brothers, Jaime and Lucas, who had been spying for Castile for many years. Their aim was to foment rebellion in Mishkhat, using religious hatred to sow dissent among the communities. Jaime, the charismatic ring-leader, had spent the last year imposing his ideas on the credulous monks in their lonely monastery, promising them rewards in heaven and forgiveness for the crimes he was inciting them to commit on earth. These followers were to be the torches that Elderic and Jaime would use to ignite the passions of revolt. Their sympathisers within the Christian community were only waiting for a signal.

Aziz harangued the crowd. 'Don't think these four cringing wretches you see in front of you are alone. Their supporters within this city have been conspiring for years. Who knows how many Christians have been secretly plotting against us? Who knows how many crimes were being hatched behind closed doors while we in our innocence and our misguided tolerance slept? Oh, citizens of Mishkhat, beware. We have foes inside our own city walls. They are our neighbours whom we greet every day in the marketplace as friends. They are the merchants with whom we trade. They are the ingrates on whom we bestow our benevolence and our trust. We thought they were loyal Mishkhatids like ourselves, but they were working for Castile. Fellow citizens and brothers in Islam, we will not rest until we have found out who these traitors are, and when we have found them, we will punish them as we now intend to punish the four miscreants we have before us – with the knife, the disembowelling hook, the flames. We will continue to do so until we have purged our city of the Christian enemy within.'

Immediately the verdict was given, townsmen broke into the court and dragged the four monks away from their guards. They were hauled to the main square, where the mob did not wait for the executioners. They mutilated the monks and threw them on to the fire.

Aziz watched the whole thing from the roof of the qadi's

court. He refused the requests of his soldiers that they make an attempt to control the crowd that was massing towards the Christian Quarter. He stayed where he was and watched.

Whether he saw the opportunity himself or was advised of it, this was the moment at which he staged his coup. By appeasing the mob he assured his power. By a policy of calculated inaction, he brought the state under his control. From then on, Abu was only a king in name. His wazir ruled.

That night the sky grew red with the burning of churches and merchants' mansions. The first to go up in flames was Toscanus's house, now Paladon's, because that had been the home of Jaime and Lucas. (Paladon only escaped injury, or worse, because he was safely in his cave, working on the mosque.) As the night wore on, the devastation became indiscriminate, and no Christian dwelling, rich or poor, was left unmolested.

Only at dawn did Aziz send in soldiers to patrol the streets. There was never an official count of the bodies. At least a hundred Christian men had been beaten to death. They were the ones Dr Isa and I counted in the death room at the hospital. Probably there had been many more. Christian women had been raped. Not a shop or household had escaped looting. Mussulman citizens did to their neighbours what a victorious army does to a sacked city in time of war.

When it was over, Aziz went back to Salim's mansion and up to Ayesha's quarters. He hardly gave her time to pack. With only two of her slaves, she was taken to the palace, where Aziz had arranged for her to be housed indefinitely in the king's harem under the care of Janifa. She pleaded with him for a chance to see Paladon. He told her that he would discuss the issue of her marriage at a more appropriate time. Then he left her.

Paladon had his first inkling of what had happened that evening when he finished his day's work and went as usual to the *madrasah* for his lesson with the chief faqi. He had been looking forward to discussing the final arrangements for his conversion, now formally approved. He was barred from entry. He banged on the great gates that had been closed in his face. Eventually an old porter came out and handed him a letter. The chief faqi expressed his regret. Approval for his conversion had been rescinded due to the regrettable disturbances in the town. It was not considered appropriate that a relative of two criminals who had recently been executed for blasphemy and other crimes should be accepted into the Umma at this time. Allah, however, was merciful. Paladon had shown signs of sincerity in his devoted work towards the construction of the mosque. Let him continue with this task and in the meanwhile occupy himself in prayer. Later perhaps his application might be considered again. The letter ended with an invocation to the mercy and generosity of Allah and praise for His Prophet.

Paladon ran the half-mile to Salim's house. Pushing servants aside, he bounded up the stairs to Ayesha's rooms, and found them empty.

Then he knew what Aziz had done.

I came across him towards midnight, slumped by the fountain, staring at the moon reflected in the water. There was a bottle of wine beside him, but he had not opened it. He barely acknowledged me, just nodded when I sat down beside him.

The courtyard was full of shadows. No lights burned in the windows. The servants and slaves were huddled in their rooms, as were most other citizens of Mishkhat after the disturbances. The night air no longer rang with the banging of hammers from the mosque. Even the crickets were silent. The only occasional sounds, from far away, were the shouts of soldiers patrolling the empty streets, and the jingling of chain mail and harness when a squad of cavalry passed.

When the moon disappeared behind the clouds and the

surface of the water rippled softly in darkness, Paladon turned to me. 'Do you know where she is?'

'She's in the king's harem. I saw her when I did my rounds and she asked me to tell you she will always love you. She's – safe, Paladon. Angry. Sad. A little scared.'

'The king's harem, eh? Difficult to climb into those windows, I suppose?'

'I wouldn't recommend it,' I said, my heart breaking.

He threw a pebble into the fountain, and watched the ripples spread and fade. 'It seems you'll have to be the go-between, old friend.'

'Yes,' I said.

'You'll have to lie to Aziz. There's no point in you getting on his wrong side as well. That won't help anyone.'

I nodded.

'Better you and I quarrel, in fact. Show your loyalty to him by turning on me. We can meet secretly. Otherwise Aziz will stop you seeing her. Or move her somewhere where we can't find her.'

'I'll – I'll make a plan.'

He smiled. 'Dear old Samuel. Wherever would we be if we hadn't found you up that fig tree? Do you remember?'

'Always,' I said.

His brow furrowed. 'I won't give up. Ever. You do know that?'

'Yes,' I said. I drew my cowl over my head. I did not want him to see my tears.

'It's chilly. You could probably do with a drop of wine.' He did not reach for the bottle, and neither did I. We sat by the edge of the fountain in silence, waiting for the moon to come out from behind the clouds.

Codex V

The Go-between

(I) In which I describe how an African came to Andaluz and was offered a princess

As soon as he heard the news of Jaime's martyrdom and the massacre that followed, Elderic made hotfoot for Rome. His oratory incensed the cardinals, and a papal bull was read out from every pulpit in Christendom. The anger it aroused resulted in an orgy of pogroms against Jews throughout Europe (there were no Mussulmans to hand). Messianic preachers roamed villages and towns exciting the common people with promises of redemption if they made battle against the infidel. Frankish kings, who envied the riches of Islam, saw opportunity for territorial gain, and the Pope, pressured by fanatics like Elderic, began to ponder the merits of declaring a holy war. Vastly exaggerating the numbers of slain, the 'Mishkhat massacre' became a convenient rallying cry. It contributed kindling to the smouldering hatred that, in a few years, would conflagrate in a universal crusade that brought more Norman adventurers to Spain and great armies to the Levant. As I write, a Frankish horde of monks and knights is marching from Antioch, which they have sacked with great butchery, intent on taking Jerusalem.

Jaime, if he is indeed sitting at the right hand of God, would be immensely satisfied. Elderic's reward was on the earthly plane. He was given a bishopric and soon afterwards a cardinal's seat in the Vatican. In due course the Pope made him his legate to Spain with plenipotentiary powers.

Of more immediate concern to Mishkhat was how Alfonso and his armies over the border in Toledo would react. We were no longer a peaceful nation of merchants and traders. Artisans and craftsmen – even jewellers – were told to convert their workshops into smithies to make armour and weapons. Every boy over fifteen and every man under forty was ordered to report to the great training camps and barracks that Aziz was building on the Mishkhat plain. Younger boys spent their afternoons drilling in their schools. The *madrasah*s and even the synagogues resonated with the bark of military commands and the uncertain responses in reedy voices of boys who, a short while before, had been groomed to become faqis and rabbis but were now shouldering pikes. The Christian Quarter was sealed off and subjected to martial law. Every day we heard of new conspiracies, and the dungeons under the palace filled with suspected traitors. Many Christian families, some of whom had lived in Mishkhat for generations, slipped away in the night, leaving their possessions, hoping to find a new life in Toledo. The troops on the border looted what they had brought with them.

As the court physician I was exempted from military service. So was Paladon, because the king still wanted his mosque. Even so, he lost half of his workforce to the army and to the labour gangs who were being sent to the mountain passes to fortify existing castles and to build new fortresses. Dr Isa was less fortunate. Some of the junior doctors had sent reports to the qadi's office about the Christian who directed a Mussulman hospital. He was instructed to hand the keys to his deputy and was despatched to one of the army training camps to run a surgery. He accepted his demotion with good grace. It was better than being purged. At first I felt sorry for the mental patients who had lost their sensitive physician. Then I thought: In Mishkhat everybody is mad now.

The panic lasted about three months before it was understood that King Alfonso of Castile had no intention of invading

Mishkhat. He had already achieved what he wanted. Our kingdom was demoralised, our treasury depleted, and the harmony between our communities destroyed for ever. He could safely leave a small state like ours to its self-inflicted misery while he concentrated his efforts on bigger targets. He had sensed the time was right to declare war on the larger Andaluzi kingdoms. Eighteen months before, he had made a successful raid against Seville, reaching the sea at Tarifa before he returned with his plunder. Now he marched his army east to lay siege to Saragossa.

And then, at last, the kings of Andaluz woke up from their complacent sleep and grasped the extent of their weakness. Years too late, the confederacy that Salim had advocated was formed, but not, as it turned out, by any of our own kings. Al-Mu'tamid of Seville invited three of his fellow monarchs to his capital and proposed an alliance, but the rulers of Granada and Badajoz did not trust him to lead them. They preferred to look for help from a neutral power. They persuaded the Sevillian king, against his better judgement, to seek the aid of an African, Yusuf ibn Tashufin, a former shepherd who had spent the last forty years carving for himself a mighty empire covering most of Morocco and all of the Maghreb.

This Yusuf had just passed his eightieth year. Our fond kings believed his age would make him malleable. They did not appreciate that he still had the energy and intelligence of a man in his prime. Greed and religion had become an addictive combination in a conqueror who saw his allotted span on earth drawing to an end. Greed fuelled his appetite, religion justified his limitless ambition, and age made him impatient to win more territories before it was too late. As a boy, herding goats in the Atlas mountains, he and his tribe had been converted to an ascetic version of Islam. In a hundred campaigns since, he had imposed its joyless rectitude on every people between the southern Sahara and the Strait of Gibraltar. Prevented by the Fatimids from extending his power eastwards, he looked across the water to the fat, corrupt kingdoms of Andaluz, with yearning for their riches and disapproval of what he considered their immoral way of life. Al-Mu'tamid's invitation to wage war on the Spanish Christians was the pretext he needed.

King Yusuf sailed from Africa, landed at Algeciras and marched inland. The horde he led was composed of illiterate desert warriors who covered their faces with blue turbans, revealing only their eyes, which gleamed with lust for holy war. They called themselves the Almoravids, which was also the name of their fundamentalist sect. They had pledged their lives to *jihad*.

On his arrival in Seville, Yusuf showed no respect for his hosts and summoned al-Mu'tamid and every other king of Andaluz to meet him at his camp outside the city. He styled himself Amir, Sovereign of the Mussulmans, and none of our rulers dared gainsay him. Belatedly they had realised that the plank they had seized to save them from drowning was in fact a hungry crocodile.

I was with Aziz when King Yusuf's letter arrived in Mishkhat, so I saw at first hand the chilling effect his summons had on our own rulers.

On the surface, I was as close a friend to Aziz as I had ever been. After my grovelling apology for what I told him had been my stupidity when I had advised him on the Jaime affair, Aziz's anger with me had abated, especially when I blamed Paladon, saying that, despite his pretence of anger at Jaime's crime, he had been desperate to save his cousin's life. I told Aziz that that was why he had begged me to counsel him that Jaime was insane and not an *agent provocateur* of Castile, as Aziz had so cleverly discovered. It had been Aziz's decisive actions that had caused the scales to drop from my eyes, and now I saw Paladon for what he was: a selfish hypocrite, a place-seeker plotting to better himself by marrying into the royal family, tricking Aziz, his father and even Ayesha, because he had never truly loved her, only the fortune she would bring with her.

Oh, I knew how to flatter him. I had learned how to do it in all sincerity when I was his lover and sought only to delight him. I used it to good effect now that I had determined to become his toady.

Aziz, I said, had seen through Paladon: anybody unscrupulous enough to relinquish his own religion for material advantage was not to be trusted. I never wanted to talk to him again, and I had Aziz to thank: his brilliance had made me see the truth at last.

He lapped it up. Nowadays any criticism of Paladon was music to his ears. It is a common human trait that those who have harmed another justify their actions afterwards by intensifying their hatred towards those they have wronged, and such was the case with Aziz, who now loathed his former schoolmate as much as he had once loved him. It was galling to him that Paladon, because he was working on the king's project, was untouchable. Otherwise I am sure Aziz would have imprisoned him in the purge he was still conducting against the Christians.

He compensated by mocking his achievements to his shadow. Careful to remain wry and self-effacing, Ephraim had made it his business to provide each day a new criticism of Paladon's villainy. If he had not been a Jew himself, he told Aziz with a chuckle, he might have suspected there was a touch of the Hebrew in Paladon: he had just examined the project's accounts and found that Paladon paid skilled artisans even more meanly than Ephraim did treasury clerks. Yet the costs only mounted. Where did the money go? Or did the prince know of the latest shocking example of Paladon's overreaching vanity? He had been overheard asking the advice of one of the Arab stonemasons the best place in the mosque to put his own statue. The Mussulman had told him, of course, that graven images were not placed in mosques. 'Imagine the poor man's embarrassment!'

It was often only harmless innuendo, but Aziz would cry with laughter. I was on my mettle to come up with calumnious inventions of my own to match.

Ephraim soon discovered that Aziz was just as receptive to jokes about me. They took to referring to me as 'the philosopher' or 'the magus'. Ephraim would ask me in mock seriousness, 'Samuel, the wazir and I were discussing how to replenish some of the gold bullion in the treasury.' (They really were. Aziz's expenditure on the army was cutting into our reserves.) 'Of course, I can arrange one or two loans to keep us going, but perhaps there is a surer way. The prince told me you had perfected the art of the philosopher's stone. We were thinking of establishing a department of alchemy, using the granite that our dear friend Paladon is leaving in piles all over the mountain. Do you think you could head such a department, and turn some of it into gold bars?'

I would then, with equal seriousness, launch into a long, complicated explanation of how this scheme might be effected while they tried to keep straight-faced. Eventually Aziz would break into his shrill laugh and embrace me. 'He's teasing, you fool.' And they would laugh the more at my red-faced outrage.

I will leave the reader to imagine how I felt when my erstwhile lover made me the butt of his jokes, for even now I had not entirely sublimated my attraction to him. Like a sore that would not heal, it had survived my disgust for the terrible things he had done. Every day I had to remind myself that the scales had fallen from my eyes: I could no longer justify his actions or his follies, and if I was to be of any use to Paladon or Ayesha I would have to treat Aziz as my enemy.

Oh, but he was a sweet enemy. There were times, when I saw him bent contemplatively over his desk, his head resting on his hand, a smile playing on those red lips and sunlight gilding his black locks, that brought back in all its intensity the love and youth we had shared. If he had always been cruel to me it would have been easier, but sometimes, especially when we were alone together, he would amiably, as in the old days, question me about my mother and my personal affairs (he was ever generous when it did not threaten his own interests). On other occasions he would ask me to help him make sense of something that troubled him – a theological objection raised by the chief faqi to one of his new laws or a complicated matter of diplomacy – and then his brow would furrow and his soft, limpid eyes would gaze at me attentively as he tried to puzzle out my explanations. When his features were finally wreathed in smiles, revealing how pleased he was that he had understood my meaning, I could not help but recall the boy I had once helped with his mathematics.

It was then that I was tempted to give him the benefit of the doubt, to paint a picture in my mind of an innocent, impressionable young man who had been led against his true nature into wicked paths by his unscrupulous advisers. Then I had to remind myself that if Ephraim and his other counsellors were maggots preying on our kingdom, my prince had been their willing host. His vanity, selfishness, callousness and ambition were the breeding ground for their evil. He was to blame and he alone.

Every occasion caused a struggle within my soul. And afterwards I had to remain on guard, for I could not afford to let affection or sentiment blind me to the danger that surrounded me. Love, or pretended love, was a weapon for me now. As long as Aziz thought of me as his besotted spaniel, I could be close to him. If I ever allowed my heart to rule me, I would be lost, and Aziz – or, rather, the perceptive Ephraim – would penetrate my deceit.

So I encouraged them to humiliate me. Playing their fool was easier than betraying my one remaining friend, as I always felt I did whenever I traduced Paladon. There was another advantage in becoming their jester. Fools, like dogs, are invisible when they are not being petted. Sometimes Aziz and Ephraim would talk for hours, having forgotten my presence, and in this way I learned many useful things about Aziz's movements, as well as those of his creatures – for Ephraim's spies were everywhere and his 'secret' police patrolled the streets. They were never actually secret for Ephraim's intention was to keep our citizens cowed. Nevertheless, forewarned, I was able to arrange my rare meetings with Paladon in some certainty that we would not be discovered. Usually we communicated by a system of dead letter drops.

I passed messages between Ayesha and Paladon, if not daily, then at least four or five times a week. I was punctilious about not reading their correspondence, but I could see from the smiles and tears on their faces, on the occasions I was with them, when they perused each other's letters that their passion for each other, far from waning with absence, was increasing. To both of them I talked of hope. One day I would find a way for them to be together. This madness would pass. I saw no evidence of it but it was what they wanted to believe and, because they trusted me, I think the optimism I espoused helped them bear their enforced separation.

It was worse for Ayesha than Paladon. He could lose himself in his work, but she was condemned to sit for endless hours among frivolous concubines, whose vacuous laughter only intensified her grief. She looked forward to my visits as eagerly as she had once waited for Paladon because I was the only person whom she could trust. Even so we had to be circumspect. She was too proud to share her misery with the concubines, and wary, too, because the tittle-tattle of a harem can easily spread beyond its closed confines. The silent eunuchs, padding past with glasses of sherbet, and the slave girls, kneeling by their mistresses' looms while they wove their tapestries, had receptive ears, and a whispered secret had often become the next day's gossip in the marketplace. For years Mishkhatids had enjoyed the stories of palace jealousies aroused by their king's sexual prowess. Abu never minded. He knew it kept him in his people's affection. In the new atmosphere prevailing in Mishkhat, though, innocent remarks could easily be blown into evil rumour with fatal consequences. Even in King Abu's palace, there was no way of knowing who had been suborned by Aziz or his spymaster, Ephraim. We usually spoke elliptically in Greek. I was pretending to give her lessons.

In the end we were not discovered by a secret enemy but by an unlooked-for friend. One day after my rounds I was politely summoned to attend Janifa. The king's sister was lying on her bed being fanned by her ancient maid. 'Give it to me,' she said.

I pretended not to understand her.

'The letter, Samuel. Where did you put it? In your medical bag? In your sleeve? Or the fold of your gown, perhaps? You and Ayesha both have dextrous fingers and my eyesight's not as good as it was or I'd have known where you concealed it.'

I blustered. I told her Ayesha had given me a harmless shopping list of fruit and confectionery she wanted me to buy for her in the market. It was nothing to bother the Lady Janifa with.

'Samuel. Give it to me. If you'd rather I called one of the guards to search you, I could do that with a clap of my hands – but it's too hot. Anyway, don't you think it's better for all of us if we're discreet? Mary has been with me long enough to know when to be deaf and dumb.' The old Christian woman fanning her gave me a toothless smile. Janifa watched me composedly as I reached down to pull up the skirt of my gown. 'Ah, your slipper. How clever of you.'

She read the letter silently, holding a magnifying mirror close to the end of her nose. I watched her in trepidation, alarmed when her lips twisted in displeasure, and terrified when her cheeks burned crimson in anger. 'The wretch, the utter wretch,' she muttered. 'If he was still a little boy, I'd have him spanked.'

And with a flood of relief I deduced she was angry with Aziz, not Paladon. I also noticed tears in her eyes.

'That poor sweet girl,' she continued. 'She can write, I'll say that for her. Oh, this is dreadful. If Salim knew, he'd be rolling in his grave. He gave his approval for the marriage, didn't he?'

'If Paladon converted to the Mussulman faith and if Aziz agreed,' I said.

'The shit. The little shit. I'm amazed Abu lets him get away with all this evil he's brought on our kingdom. I suppose he hasn't any choice, though, because Aziz is so popular with the Umma. He and the chief faqi are hand in glove. It makes you want to weep.'

I stared at her in amazement. I had found an unexpected ally in the highest quarters.

'Take the letter back, and give them both my love. No, better not. Better they think I don't know.'

I felt emboldened. 'Is there anything that can be done?' I asked.

She sighed. 'Not yet, Samuel. There's little use in my talking to Abu at the moment – he's too concerned with the state of his kingdom to take any interest in his great-niece's amatory problems. Anyway, Aziz is trying to persuade him that he should marry Ayesha to a king who can form an alliance with us. They haven't found any candidates yet but it makes sense to Abu. Men have never cared about a woman's heart. Oh, I'm so angry I feel a fever coming on. You'll probably have to bleed me again. Thank God for you, Samuel. Keep watching and listening, and if I can ever help I will. But be careful. I noticed you today so others might. Keep me informed. You have my blessing, for what it's worth.'

'I wish only that there was a way for them to see each other.'

'Now you have taken leave of your senses.' She snorted. 'How do you expect me to arrange that?'

'It doesn't bear thinking of,' I said.

'No, it doesn't,' she said. She observed me quizzically. 'Why do you even mention such a foolish idea?'

'I'm sorry, Lady Janifa, I shouldn't have. It can't be done.'

'But you suppose I can arrange it?'

'No, Lady Janifa, it's impossible, as you said.'

Her eyes had narrowed suspiciously. 'Then there's no more to be said, is there?'

'Certainly not, Lady Janifa. It would be irresponsible and dangerous for anybody in their right mind even to contemplate such a thing.'

'There's something dangerous about *you*, young Samuel,' she muttered. 'You'd better be off before I think you're trying to charm me.'

I was delighted to see she was smiling.

I left her, fortified in the knowledge that we had a champion at court and, more, that there might be hope. I was alarmed, though, by what she had said about Aziz's marriage proposals for his sister. I determined not to tell either Paladon or Ayesha – they were miserable enough already. I also knew that I had to push myself even closer into Aziz's confidence to get early wind of his plans. By the time Janifa found out about any impending marriage it would probably be too late.

So I played the fool the more, and continued to damn Paladon with innuendo. I also became an informer, taking care, however, that the elaborate Christian conspiracies I invented never brought anybody real harm. I chose as my perpetrators those whom I knew had just fled, or pointed to mythical Castilian agents whom Aziz's secret police spent fruitless days trying to discover.

Sometimes when I made these allegations I caught Ephraim smiling at me with amused contempt. I am sure he knew I was fabricating evidence in an attempt to ingratiate myself – he was doing the same, but the charges he brought against innocent citizens invariably cost them their lives. I hoped my clumsy sycophancy would earn his grudging approval, at least his tolerance, for it certainly allied with his own purposes. The more fearful his master remained of threats to the kingdom, the more Ephraim, in his capacity as head of security, strengthened his hold on him. And, as both of us knew, Aziz was prepared to believe anything. His inner lack of self-confidence made him fear that he had overreacted during his *coup d'état*, so any corroboration his toadies could feed him, however fanciful, justified the extreme actions he had taken.

The greater my lies, I convinced myself, the more the prince would trust me. And the more transparent they seemed to Ephraim, the less of a threat I would appear to him. Like many evil men, he judged his fellows by his own stamp; by his standards I was merely an amateur – and therefore harmless.

It was flimsy protection, but I had dug myself in too deep to retreat. I spent every hour I could spare with Aziz, only leaving his office when I had to treat the king or visit the harem.

Nearly a month had gone by before Janifa called me again to her chamber. As the last time, Mary was sitting quietly behind her.

'I'll come straight to the point, Samuel. You may not have noticed, being so bookish and hardworking, but we've been blessed with some wonderful autumn weather lately.'

'Indeed, Lady Janifa,' I said, somewhat bewildered.

'I may arrange a picnic tomorrow afternoon for some of my favourite girls. In the fruit orchard in the south-east corner of the garden, where it abuts on to the rock, just above the old pilgrim path to the cave. We don't go there very often. The cliff is not so precipitous in that section, and our guards tell me that after the landslide in the summer they are concerned there might even be access to the palace grounds. The fence is not very high, as you know, so recently it has been strictly off bounds and well guarded.' She paused. 'Against prowlers and the like.'

'Then – then why should you choose such a spot for a picnic, Lady Janifa?'

'There are such lovely persimmon trees there – a whole forest of them. You could get lost among them. The fruit is ripe and delicious, hanging off the boughs. The girls may like to pick it.'

'It sounds delightful,' I said, my ears burning with interest.

'Since I'll be taking the king's ladies with me there is no question that soldiers or gardeners – or any men, for that matter – can remain in the vicinity. I've had tedious discussions with the captain of the guard and the keeper of the king's orchards to ensure that we will be left to our own devices there between the fifth and sixth hours of the day.'

She rummaged among a pile of parchment next to her cushions. 'The captain has kindly left me a map of where he'll be placing his guards – as you can see, far out of sight. If a prowler were to get hold of this, he'd know exactly how to avoid them. But I don't see why you shouldn't look. If you're interested.'

I pored over the crude drawing, memorising the dots and crosses. 'There'll be no security at all?' I asked, hardly able to believe what she was telling me.

'Oh, we'll have security,' she said. 'The captain insisted. I'll be taking Sebastian and Asif with us. They're eunuchs but hefty fellows. We will be quite safe. Their task will not be easy for them because, of course, my girls can be very mischievous.'

She observed me closely. 'No, security is not a problem. My worry is that one or two of the girls may wander and, as I told you, the trees are many – a veritable jungle. Inside the thicket nobody would be able to look outside or in. I would feel much more comfortable if I had somebody reliable to keep an eye on any strays. In case of prowlers. Perhaps you will be free tomorrow afternoon – to help.'

My heart was pumping with excitement, but I was careful to keep my voice even. 'I would be honoured,' I told her.

'Good. Shall I see you there tomorrow afternoon? I would so appreciate it.'

Her expression suddenly became serious. Behind her, Mary had lost her habitual smile and was also staring at me intently. 'Samuel, you will be careful, won't you? You know how dangerous prowlers can be, especially if they're caught. Even worse if they should kidnap one of our girls. Dangerous not only for the girl in question but for all of us, including me.'

'You have my assurance, Lady Janifa, and my thanks,' I said.

'You'll bring her back safely. That's all I ask.'

'I promise,' I said.

I left her chamber with my head spinning. I had no idea that the seed I had planted in her mind would sprout so quickly. I hurried through the rest of my medical chores in the harem, then made post haste down the hill to the secret place where I left messages for Paladon, pausing halfway to write a note and transcribe the map I had memorised.

Janifa had been right about the girls' mischief. After a scramble with their baskets to gather persimmons at the edge of the thicket, they returned giggling to the carpets, where they settled, lifting their veils flirtatiously in the direction of Sebastian and Asif, licking the soft pippy flesh and reciting suggestive verses, while Janifa pretended to scold them.

'Blind man's buff,' one of the concubines shouted and – as they had once flung me into the harem bath – they mobbed the two hapless eunuchs and tied silk scarves over their faces.

All this time I had kept my eyes on Ayesha, who was sitting quietly by herself. Suddenly I, too, felt soft hands scrabbling at me and a scarf being pulled over my forehead. 'Girls,' I heard Janifa call, 'leave the poor doctor alone.'

When I had extricated myself I saw with shock that Ayesha was gone. Frowning, Janifa slanted her eyes and chin towards the trees. I pretended to be caught short and rushed into the thicket. For a few panicked moments I stumbled through the branches and bushes. My heart was thumping with fear that I would not be able to find her. The squeals and laughter grew fainter behind me. At last, to my relief, I stumbled into a small clearing and observed through the leaves her veiled figure, right in front of me, under a tree.

She hadn't seen me and was looking anxiously around her, a slim hand clasping the brooch of a blue cloak. The hood shook from her head, and her brown hair tumbled over her shoulders.

I suddenly remembered the little girl I had first seen, riding on her palfrey, also in a fruit grove. I had subconsciously thought of her as that child ever since, but in the chequered light that filtered through the leaves, I noticed, for the first time, how much she had matured during her incarceration. When Aziz had taken her from her home, she had still had the plumpness and vivacity of a young girl, but now she held her tall, slim body with a sad, natural dignity. Meeting her every day, I hadn't appreciated the incremental changes, the nobility and courage that hardship had wrought in her character. She had always been beautiful to me, and she was even more so now, but I also saw suffering in the speckled brown eyes that peered above the veil. The expression in them was tragic, and my heart ached for her.

'Samuel, is that you?' she called hesitantly. 'Aunt Janifa said you had something to tell me.'

I was about to step forward when I saw she was looking in an entirely different direction. I heard the crack of breaking wood and the rustle of undergrowth. A huge figure stepped into the glade. Ayesha gasped and her hands flew to her mouth. 'Paladon?' she whispered.

At first he made confident strides towards her, but suddenly he seemed to lose control of his limbs. He gazed at her, still several feet away from her, his big hands hanging loosely by his sides. His shoulders were shaking. Then I saw tears rolling down his cheeks. 'Forgive me, my beloved, I . . . I had prepared so many words . . . I felt so strong, but now I can't . . . You're so beautiful, so beautiful . . .'

It was as if a spell had been cast on them. Her lips parted, she gazed back at him in wonder. Like a sleepwalker she moved forward. Her arm shook free of her cloak and pulled away her veil. Her copper bangles tinkled in the silence as she raised a finger and touched his cheek. 'You're . . .'

'Yes,' he whispered. 'Yes. And you, my love? Are you . . .?'

'Yes.' She sighed, her eyes filling with tears. 'I'm safe here. Your letters brought me such joy.'

'I've missed you – I – I—'

'I know,' she said. 'Hold me.'

His arms gently enfolded her and she pressed her head against his chest. His lips touched her hair. Now she began to shake. 'I'm sorry,' she moaned, through her sobs. 'I just can't believe that you . . .'

In my hiding place, I felt like an interloper but dared not move. I, too, was entranced. I hardly dared breathe. It was only when they kissed that I turned my head away.

Occasionally one would speak, but the other would reply after only a few words had been uttered, knowing the thoughts before they were put into words. It was a language of lovers I could not follow. They spoke also with their hands, running their palms over each other's limbs as if to communicate by touch the messages that were passing between their hearts.

Their stumbling utterances and silent gestures were more eloquent than the songs of a thousand poets. I recalled the lovers in the romances of all the ages, and could think of none more beautiful than Paladon and Ayesha, or of any love so pure or a story so tragic. The persimmon glade had suddenly become a holy place. I was awestruck. I felt like a mortal who had inadvertently trespassed in a realm of spirits. And I was afraid, because it seemed that the two together were an emblem of the hope and happiness of mankind, and if their union should be prevented, all the joy in the world would be eclipsed and there would no longer be suns or moons in the firmament.

Suddenly Ayesha stepped back, her eyes wide with fright. She beat his breast and cried, 'What am I thinking? You must go! If they find you here—'

'They won't. They can't. Samuel told me where the guards are. I'm invisible. There's only you and me . . .'

'But if he's been deceived, if it's a trap?' Her fists continued to pound his chest. He kissed her and she slowly relaxed.

Then I heard the words I had feared.

'Come with me,' he said. 'Come with me now. There's a way I know. Nobody will ever see us. Once we're out of Mishkhat and free . . .'

She was hugging her shoulders, shaking her head. There was terror in her stance.

'My darling, we'll be out of your brother's power for ever . . .'

'Even if it is possible, your life is here. Your mosque. It's everything that you . . . I can't allow you to . . .'

Paladon was pacing over the fallen leaves, thumping his hand into his palm. 'My mosque means nothing. I only want you.'

'And I want you, my dearest. You are my life. But our friends . . . Janifa . . . I think she must trust me to have arranged this meeting . . .'

'She's the king's sister. No harm can come to her.'

Her lips trembled. 'Then there's . . .' She was silent.

His shoulders slumped. 'You're right,' he said, and his voice rang with grief.

'We owe him so much. And if my brother were to . . .' She clasped his hand in hers and leaned against him. Her face was white and stricken with sadness.

I stepped into the glade. I felt quite calm. I had made my decision. They looked at me, startled. I took their hands. 'Go,' I said quietly. 'Take her, Paladon. It'll be for the best.' I smiled at Ayesha. 'Paladon's right. Nothing else matters but you two being together. You'll be safe away from Mishkhat. Go.'

'You can come with us, Samuel,' said Paladon.

'No,' I said. 'Better I remain. They'll be hunting you. I can tell them stories. I'll keep them guessing for days.'

Paladon hugged me fiercely. Ayesha kissed me.

'What are you waiting for?' I said. I heard my voice break, felt the first tremor of fear. 'Go.'

Paladon and Ayesha remained where they were, arm in arm. 'No, Samuel, old friend,' he said softly. 'We couldn't live with the knowledge that you'd sacrificed yourself for us, though we'll never forget that you offered. Just knowing what you were prepared to do for us . . .' He shook his head. 'I'm humbled.'

'But I—'

'No, Samuel.' Paladon's voice was firm. 'We're brothers and we look after each other. We'll find a proper way out of this. And we will. I'm sure of it.'

Ayesha was smiling at me through her tears. 'How much longer do Paladon and I have, Samuel?' she asked.

I bowed my head. 'We should be getting back.'

'Give us five minutes, friend,' said Paladon.

'I'll come back in ten,' I said.

I stumbled back into the thicket, found the bole of tree, slumped against it and began to weep. Faintly I could hear the laughter of the picnickers outside the wood. Sparrows chirped gaily in the branches above me.

Ayesha was alone when I returned, waiting by the tree. Carved into the trunk were two hearts, enfolded in the talons of an eagle. The noble bird's wings were poised for flight. It was roughly drawn but I recognised the elegance, movement and sureness of Paladon's craftsmanship.

'Our two hearts are bonded for ever, Samuel,' she said softly, 'and one day we'll fly away together like this eagle. Paladon left it for me as a sign of hope. Thank you, dear, dear Samuel. I will never forget what you have done for us today – and what you would have done had we asked it.'

'We must go,' I muttered.

The two eunuchs were folding the carpets when we returned. The girls were lying on the grass, basking in what warmth remained of the afternoon sun. Janifa came up to us. I nodded and her lips twisted briefly into a smile. She turned and clapped her hands. 'Ladies, pick up your baskets, please. It's time to go back.' She crooked her arm into Ayesha's. 'You, my dear, can walk with me to the harem, and tell me about your ramble in the wood with Samuel. No, don't. I'm too exhausted, and I really don't wish to know.'

I made my way back to Aziz's office. I discovered he had been called away to see King Abu. I was grateful for the solitude and a chance to nurse my bitter thoughts.

I was sitting quietly on the carpet when he returned, Ephraim bobbing behind him. Aziz was shaking with anger. He was holding the summons from the sovereign of the Mussulmans, King Yusuf, in a shaking hand.

'Abu blames me,' he raged at Ephraim. 'As if I had anything to do with it. He scolded me as if I was a schoolboy. It was my fault, he told me, for not continuing my father's diplomacy. If my father have still been alive, he shouted – he actually shouted at me – Mishkhat would have been at that conference of kings and we might have had a chance to persuade them that this jumped-up African – that was what he called him – is more dangerous to us than the Christians. As if al-Mu'tamid or King abd Allah of Granada would have listened to me if I'd tried to argue such nonsense.'

'It's outrageous,' agreed Ephraim, 'and unfair. You're the one prince in Andaluz who's taking on the Christians.'

'That was not what he said. He accused me of depleting the resources of our kingdom and imposing a reign of terror to combat a monster of my own imagination. Does he not understand that I've built an army to protect Mishkhat from enemies without and within? That I'm preserving his throne?' Aziz threw a cushion at the wall.

'I'm sure he does,' murmured Ephraim, 'but – ah – he is old and . . .' He shrugged suggestively, opening his palms.

'Senile is what you mean,' muttered Aziz. 'He – he insulted me, then asked for my advice on how to respond. I told him we have no choice. He had to meet King Yusuf if all the other kings were going. We'd be isolating ourselves if he didn't.'

'Quite right,' said Ephraim. 'Wise counsel.'

'Then he said he wouldn't humiliate himself by fawning on a desert nomad if wild tigers dragged him there. I'd created the mess we're in so it was up to me to deal with it. He wants me to meet King Yusuf, taking my army with me. If I go, who's to look after Mishkhat?'

Ephraim cleared his throat. 'With respect, Prince, your great-uncle may have handed to you a priceless gift.'

Aziz looked at him suspiciously.

'You and I have often discussed how your efforts have been unappreciated. Everything I have heard about King Yusuf suggests he is a good Mussulman. A *jihadi*, even. He'll know of the decisiveness with which you've tackled the Christian menace and should look favourably upon you. No other Andaluzi prince has shown such fortitude and resolve. Your father tried to throw back the Christians with talk. You have done it by action. He'll be impressed. And he's powerful. He seems just the sort of friend you should have. Good for Mishkhat and good for you. If he is going to lead a coalition against the Christians, then surely the magnificent army you have created should be in the van. You could quite easily make yourself indispensable to him. Once he returns to Africa, which he certainly will, he will continue to consider you his friend. Who then will be able to withstand you, knowing you have the Almoravids at your beck and call? Mishkhat may become the pre-eminent state in Andaluz, and you would be recognised as its greatest prince. Forgive me. I am only a humble merchant and no expert in great affairs, but I have, as you know, a little experience in finance and banking, and in that trade one learns to appreciate people's true character. I saw the qualities of leadership in you, Prince, the first time I met you. I am sure that King Yusuf will too.'

Aziz's eyes were following Ephraim's lips as a snake's are fixed to the flute of its charmer. 'But how to make sure?' he whispered.

Ephraim shrugged again. 'You have other assets, Prince. One in particular. King Yusuf is old but still, I am told, virile. If he were to be offered a young, beautiful and highly intelligent wife . . .'

'Ayesha,' breathed Aziz.

Ephraim sighed. 'You did say that you were looking for a worthy match for her . . .'

'Yes,' Aziz murmured. 'Yes.' He began to pace. Suddenly he saw me. 'Samuel, I hadn't noticed you were here. What do you think of Ephraim's idea?'

I felt numbed. Scarcely more than an hour ago she had been with Paladon and the chance of flight had been open to her. I cursed myself for my weakness. If only I had persuaded them.

Suddenly I recalled a night long ago, when we were still students together. Ayesha was sitting cross-legged on her stool, with Paladon, as usual, at her feet. Aziz and I were curled on our couch. Aziz had the excited gleam in his eye that I saw now: he had been enjoying their lively banter about marriage. Paladon had been teasing her, telling her that probably Salim would sell her off to a rich old man, and that would serve her right because she was such a shrew. She had rocked back on her couch with laughter and told him, 'If he were rich, I would marry him,' and then she had suddenly looked serious and picked up her lute. The music was her own but the ironic words were those of the famous Syrian poet, Abu al-Ala al-Ma'arri. She sang softly, and her eyes never left Paladon's:

> *His silver hair appeared like day*
> *But not like the dawn, or stars at night.*
>
> *He speaks the words she doesn't want to hear,*
> *The old man is nothing but phrases.*
>
> *She wishes she could say to him,*
> *'Take the dowry and be content';*
>
> *Then she prays God will let him die,*
>
> *But what young man will have her now?*

We had sat dumbly not sure how we should react. We had been laughing at the comic thrum of the strings with which she had highlighted the protagonist's scorn for her aged husband, but the tragic fall of the last line silenced us. The song had ended in a throb of despair. She had surveyed Paladon sardonically, then Aziz and me. 'I will never – ever – marry a man I do not love,' she said, and with her five fingers flicked the frets of the lute causing a jarring sound that haunts me still.

'Well, Samuel?'

I wanted to tell him that what Ephraim was proposing was madness, as well as being monstrous, cynical and cruel. That Aziz would achieve nothing by sacrificing his beloved sister. King Yusuf had hundreds of wives: one more or less would mean nothing to him. He would view Aziz's offer merely as tribute from another weak kingdom trying to buy his favour. He would accept her, ravish her and exile her to his harem in Africa to eke out the rest of her life among his other neglected concubines, content that at no cost to himself he now held a hostage to Mishkhat's good behaviour. Meanwhile Aziz would be so compromised that he would be little better than Yusuf's creature.

My soul was screaming to shout what seemed so obvious to me, to warn him that his flattering counsellor just saw another means to line his pockets. Ephraim had never had Aziz's interests at heart as I did for, God help me, I still loved him even after all the evil he had done. Above all, I wanted to tell him that he would break Ayesha's heart, and crush Paladon's hopes – and also shatter my own poor heart, for it had been beating for the three of them since childhood. But I knew it would be useless. His vanity would make him deaf to my pleas. I would succeed only in losing his trust and making an enemy of his powerful acolyte, and if I did that, there would be nothing I could do to help Ayesha or Paladon.

'I think it would be a very political match,' I said.

Aziz leaned forward and kissed me. 'Dear Samuel. Always so loyal.'

By the time he had risen he had forgotten me again and, shortly afterwards, I slipped away. I left Aziz eagerly discussing with Ephraim what dowry would be suitable for Ayesha to bestow on such a conqueror, and Ephraim was suggesting another loan.

I wanted to report the matter straight away to Janifa, but the gong of the curfew had sounded. Not even I would be allowed into the harem now. I spent a sleepless night and rushed there at first light – but Janifa was still at her prayers and I was ordered to wait. It was two hours before I could broach the subject to her. She listened silently. At last she shook her head. 'King Yusuf's old enough to be her great-great-grandfather. Does Abu know of this?'

'I don't believe so. Aziz will probably tell him at tomorrow's council. I fear that he will agree because on the surface a match with such a powerful king might appear beneficial for Mishkhat. But if you were to talk to him first, indicating some of the dangers . . .'

'And how am I supposed to have heard of this? From you? You'll become an enemy of Aziz if he finds out you were the informer. Are you prepared for the consequences?'

'If it saves Ayesha and brings her to Paladon.'

'No, you're too valuable to sacrifice. Let me think. There's a slave girl in the harem called Yasmin, a pretty little thing. Aziz has been dallying with her recently. He thinks I don't know, but Yasmin tells me everything. He usually has her during his afternoon nap, about now in fact. What if he were to talk today in his sleep? He often does. Many girls have told me. It's a habit of his.'

I lowered my head. 'I know,' I said.

'Eh? Oh, yes, I'd forgotten. Well, what do you think?'

'That it would be hard on Yasmin because Aziz will punish her.'

'She's only a slave. I can probably protect her from anything worse than a whipping, and make it up to her afterwards. Anyway, if Aziz can have his spies all over the palace, why can't I? I'll wait for her to return, then go to Abu. Where will you be later?'

'Here, if you like. There is a small operation I was going to perform tomorrow. I could bring it forward to this afternoon.'

'Ah, yes, that horrible carbuncle on Zubayda's cheek. Abu will be pleased if you make her pretty again because she's his favourite at the moment. I'll tell him. Yes. It might put him into a good mood and make him more receptive.'

As I was leaving, she stopped me. 'Don't raise your hopes too high, Samuel. Even if we scuttle this particular match, it won't stop Aziz trying to find another husband for Ayesha.' She laughed. 'Just look at your long face. We'll deal with that, too, when it comes. We achieved the impossible yesterday, didn't we? What's to stop us doing it again?'

Somehow, through that long afternoon, I managed to perform my regular duties competently, though it was not the prettiest operation on a carbuncle because my hand was shaking. It was dark when Mary found me and brought me to her mistress's bedchamber. Janifa was huddled on her cushions.

'Abu was angry,' she said flatly. 'He agrees with your analysis. The idea is foolhardy. It would give more to Yusuf than anything we would gain in return. He believes it would be dangerous. Yusuf, he said, is as much of a predator as King Alfonso of Castile. He – he also thinks it would be a tragedy for poor Ayesha.'

'It's good news then, Lady Janifa?' I asked, alarmed by her tone.

'It isn't. He plans to let Aziz go ahead.'

I stared at her incredulously.

'He says he's already authorised his wazir to undertake this mission on his behalf, and the wazir should be allowed to conduct it as he thinks best.'

'That's – disappointing,' I said.

'It's a lot more than disappointing. It's a calamity. My poor dear Ayesha. Thank God she doesn't know about it. She mustn't, Samuel. I want your word that you won't tell her in the few days left before she must leave with Aziz. She'd probably attempt to hang herself if she found out. I know I would if I faced a half-life in some aged African's seraglio. She'll probably be a widow before she's twenty. And then what? They're fundamentalists over there. No wine. No music. She might as well be locked in a tomb. Oh, it's too bad.'

'But why has the king agreed?' I expostulated.

'Politics, Samuel. We women have always been pawns to men's politics. It is our fate.'

'The politics are against it. You said King Abu agreed this would be disastrous for Mishkhat. It's – it's abnegation of responsibility. The king has become . . .' I had to bite my tongue because what I had been about to say was treasonous.

'What has my brother become, Samuel?' she asked me severely.

'More and more detached from affairs of state,' I said sullenly.

'No more than he was when Salim was wazir.'

My anger was mounting again. I could not control it. 'With respect, Lady Janifa, the state was in safe hands when Salim was wazir.'

She grunted and picked a sugared nut from a bowl nestling among the cushions, twiddling it between her fingers while she brooded. Eventually she put it back. She looked at me searchingly, then seemed to make a decision. She beckoned me to move closer to her on the carpet, and when she spoke it was almost in a whisper. Clearly, she was about to say something that even deaf and dumb Mary was not meant to hear.

'You don't know my brother. You see the amiable lover of women and wine, the eccentric who builds palaces and mosques. You cannot comprehend how ruthless he can be. The throne was never his by right, you know. My elder brother, Yahya, Salim's father, was the chosen heir. Our father, the king, saw in Yahya the likeness of himself, a man of blood. You have probably heard that my father was a great conqueror. He was also a monster – and Yahya was like him. Sadists, both of them, to their subjects and also to their families. I hated them.'

She paused to observe my reaction. 'My other brother I loved. He was the opposite of Yahya. Abu was a thinker rather than a soldier. He enjoyed life. He liked poetry and songs. He was always a devout Mussulman, but he got to know the Christians and the Jews and began to appreciate their different virtues. He made many friends among them and – yes, yes – he dallied with their women. In time he developed a great love for Mishkhat and its people, of every colour and creed. It pained him that they were being taxed so heavily to pay for my father's wars, and coerced into the army where many perished. Our father never cared about his subjects' livelihoods.

'Abu kept his thoughts to himself. He was always wily and used his charm to make friends of potential enemies. In that way he avoided suspicion. One evening he came to my rooms. It was just after my father came down with the illness that killed him. He asked me what I thought Yahya would be like as king. "He will be like our father," I told him.'

'"He has inherited the brutality," he replied, "but not his intelligence. He will continue to wage costly wars against our neighbours, but one day he will be defeated, because he is no strategist and never listens to wise counsel. We will be invaded, and what do you think will happen to Mishkhat and its people then?"'

Again she paused, her eyes searching mine. 'You see, Samuel, what I am trying to show you is that Abu has never been motivated by personal ambition. He has always had a deep sense of the responsibility and obligation he owes his subjects. That was why I joined his conspiracy and supported him. I knew his concern was only for the good of our country. He probably loved his brother – Abu is an affectionate man – but he loved the people of Mishkhat more, and it was for their sake that he decided to remove him. I will spare you the details. Suffice to say that, shortly after my father's death, the day before Yahya was to ascend the throne, he died in a hunting accident, impaled on his own spear after an unlucky fall from his horse. So claimed the only two witnesses. Abu was one. The other was Salim.'

'Salim?' I gasped. 'You're saying that Salim helped assassinate his own father?'

Her eyes did not waver. 'Yes. He pinioned Yahya's arms while Abu stabbed him. Poor Salim, it must have been hard for him. He was then not much older than you. He was rather like you, too. A scholar who lived for his books. Yahya despised him and treated him abominably, but it was not hatred that made him a parricide. It was love of Mishkhat, which he shared with his uncle. He did it out of duty, Samuel, duty. To save our country from harm.'

'Well, you know the rest. Abu became king and Salim his wazir, and together they brought peace and prosperity to our beloved kingdom. Mishkhat Mussulmans, Christians and Jews lived in harmony on equal terms, and such has been the case until recently. Everybody benefited – except the two men who made it possible, for they had to live with their guilt. Why do you think Salim worked himself to an early death? I am convinced it was his way of expiating his crime. Why is Abu so obsessed with Paladon's mosque in the cave? It's because he thinks his homage to Allah may save his soul from damnation. That's men for you. As a woman I see things more clearly. I haven't the slightest worry about damnation because I know Allah will forgive us. That murder achieved only good. It was the right thing for Mishkhat and for our people, and – do you know? – despite his fears for his soul, I think Abu would do it again. You still believe he is abnegating responsibility, after what I've just told you? Do you really think, after the sacrifices both he and Salim have made for Mishkhat, that

Abu's not despairing about what is happening in his kingdom today?'

'But he publicly approved all Aziz's actions. The day after the massacre of the Christians, King Abu attended the thanksgiving service in the mosque.' I had not been impressed by her self-serving account of the grubby murder that had brought Abu to power and I was appalled that my revered benefactor, Salim, had had a part in it.

'Events moved too fast for him to stop them,' said Janifa. 'When Aziz released the mob into the Christian Quarter there was no going back. The chief faqi praised Aziz in the pulpit, and the majority of our people supported his action, Abu had to give it his blessing. Even kings must bow to reality, Samuel. It was politic to bide his time until the mood of our people changed. Anyway, he no longer had the power to remove Aziz. The state of emergency tied his hands and the only few generals and councillors he could rely on were packed off to insignificant postings out of harm's way. One by one Abu's old advisers were retired. Now Aziz's men hold every seat in the king's council. He's isolated. Oh, clever is not the word for that viper, that reptile.' She spat into her spittoon.

'Aziz?'

'No, Ephraim. He may deal with finance but he is also head of the secret police. He's the evil intelligence behind it, dripping his poison into my great-nephew's ears and playing on his weaknesses. You cannot believe that Aziz plotted such villainy by himself, can you? He's vain and ambitious, sometimes spiteful and terribly misguided, and he has a desperate desire to prove himself – but at heart he's well intentioned. I'm sure he sincerely believes he's acting for the good of Mishkhat.' She snorted. 'It was always Salim's hope that you would be his influence. Poor Salim. His son ended up with the wrong Jew.'

'I'm sorry.' I was aghast at the way this royal family, thrown into a situation they could not control, were trying to excuse and protect each other and their selfish interests.

'Nobody blames you, Samuel. In fact, my brother hopes one day you will guide Aziz again. Abu has a high regard for his Joseph, as he insists on calling you. He still wants Salim's son to succeed him, and believes Aziz will mend his ways. As a woman, I'm less sentimental than he is. I'm worried for Aziz. Power is a drug that may inure one to evil. It warps the soul. Should the day come when you become his guardian angel again, you will find it a hard task. But that's immaterial now. At the moment, we are powerless to do anything but wait for Ephraim to overreach himself.'

'Why wait? Why doesn't the king speak out now?' I was near despair. Janifa, in whom I had put my hopes, was justifying inaction. 'Even I could give him the evidence he needs to impeach Ephraim. Every day I hear him wheedling Aziz into asking for a new loan. Examine the books in his bank and you'll find he owns half the kingdom. Why can't the king reveal that to the people?'

'For the same reason that you said nothing when Aziz asked you what you thought of this proposed marriage. Like you, he knows it wouldn't do any good if he did. Abu's waiting his opportunity. Maybe he sees it in this summons from King Yusuf. Ask yourself why he is sending Aziz to this conference of kings and not going himself? Aziz is not the diplomat his father was. Abu hopes he will disgrace himself. Then Abu will have a chance to go to the Umma and gain their support. Perhaps he wants, too, to open his great-nephew's eyes to his own limitations. That's the way to prick vanity, you know. If Aziz is humbled, he'll come back asking questions: who gave him ill advice? The finger will point to Ephraim. My brother is playing a long game.'

'A long game in which King Abu will allow Aziz to prostitute his sister. It is the cruellest, most cynical and evil thing I have ever heard. And what if the blinkers remain over Aziz's eyes? What happens if his mission is seen by the people as a success? Ephraim is clever enough to play it so, whatever the truth of it. It's a gambler's throw, and you're content for Ayesha to be the innocent stake.'

She started back in shock. 'That's unjust, Samuel. I'm terrified for poor Ayesha. You know how sympathetic I am to her. Why else would I have arranged that meeting for her with Paladon yesterday?'

I leaned forward. 'Then what are you prepared to do about it now?'

'What can I do? My brother has agreed to the marriage. I can't disobey the king.'

'With respect, Lady Janifa, why not? You told me just now you murdered your other brother because you sensed Mishkhat was in danger. I applaud you for your courage. You were acting, as you said, for the greater good of Mishkhat. Well, Mishkhat is in danger again. This time, to save it, you do not have to commit a crime in the eyes of men or God. Rather, I am asking you to perform an act of virtue. Maybe your brother's hands are tied, as you explained, but yours are not.'

'Are you trying to bully me, Samuel? I don't like your tone.'

'No, Lady Janifa. I am pleading with you to do what's right.'

'But the king . . .'

'The king has lost his way. You know it as well as I do. He's old and scared. He doesn't know what to do any more. We can no longer rely on his judgement.'

I was committing sedition and disloyalty, even treason, but I no longer cared. Suddenly everything had become very simple. It would take Aziz five days to muster his army. Then he would leave, with Ayesha, guarded by soldiers, in his train. I believed I could prevent it, but to do so I needed this woman's help. I would say anything, do anything, to get it.

'I – I told you, he—'

'I heard everything you said, Lady Janifa. But you've told me, too, that you are a woman and therefore can see more clearly than men. So look into your heart, Lady Janifa, and tell me that by doing nothing you are not condoning cruelty and evil as your brother is. Otherwise, shame on you. Shame on both of you.'

I thought then that I had gone too far. Her face was twisting and her body was shaking, but it was not with anger at my temerity. She was weeping.

'I do want to help the sweet girl – but I don't see how I can,' she moaned. 'I don't see how I can.'

'There's always a way,' I said.

'Nothing can be done now. Nothing.'

'What if she were married already?' I asked softly.

Her sobbing stopped as quickly as it had started, and she stared at me open-jawed, the folds of her chin wobbling. She looked like a bewildered turkey.

'Are you mad?' she whispered.

'No, Lady Janifa, I am not. I have a plan.'

'You can't marry Ayesha to Paladon, if that's what you're thinking. Her father stipulated that Aziz should agree.'

'I think Salim would waive that condition. Aziz has disqualified himself.'

'But Paladon's a Christian. The chief faqi has issued a ban on his conversion.'

'I know a faqi who would be prepared to defy that ban. Well, he's not a practising faqi, but before he came to Mishkhat, he was an imam in the theological school in Cairo. As a foreigner he owes no allegiance to the chief faqi of Mishkhat. He has the authority to bring Paladon into the Mussulman faith. He can also officiate at a marriage. He knows the sincerity of Paladon's wish to convert. Besides, he was a great friend of Ayesha's father and understands what Salim desired for his daughter's happiness.'

'You're not talking about that fat ibn Sa'id? He's a heathen, like you are, his mind full of celestial spheres.'

'He's not a heathen, Lady Janifa, and neither am I. He is perhaps an unorthodox Mussulman, but he really is a faqi. If he were to bless Paladon and Ayesha's marriage, it would be sanctioned by Allah. No man – not King Abu, not the chief faqi, not Aziz – could annul it. The only thing they could do is widow Ayesha, but I don't think your brother would want his architect murdered. This time he would act, and in our favour, for the selfish reasons that drive him.'

'You are very hard on us, Samuel,' she murmured. 'You're like the stern prophet after whom you're named – he had no fear of criticising a king.'

'Actually I was named after a wazir,' I said. 'A good one, like Salim. I think we should consider his wishes now. If he were still alive, we would not be in this predicament.'

'We would have to act very secretly.'

'Can you think of another way?'

'Oh, this is foolhardy, Samuel.'

'It solves Mishkhat's problem – and it would be the right thing to do, Lady Janifa.'

'You trouble me, Samuel. Yes, if Ayesha were already married, Aziz could no longer offer her to Yusuf. I see that. And, yes, to unite Ayesha with Paladon, according to her father's wishes, would in itself be a virtuous act. But the risks . . . Let me think.' She was silent for several minutes. Then she nodded and gave me a shy smile. '*If* I agreed to help you in this madness, I would want to meet Paladon first.'

I breathed a sigh of relief. 'You'll like him, Aunty.' She had been urging me to use this familiar appellation for some time. I had always been too shy to address her so before, but now I felt we were truly co-conspirators and friends, and it expressed the thanks in my heart.

I looked up and noticed Mary. I had forgotten her in the intensity of our conversation but she had been fanning her mistress all the while. Now she gave me the warmest grin.

Janifa provided me with directions to a hidden doorway into the palace. She told me that most palaces have bolt-holes for it is the nature of every king to fear the turns of Fortune's wheel, which might one day make him a fugitive. Abu was no exception. Its location was known only to the royal family and Toscanus, who had built it and taken the secret to his grave; he had never even revealed it to his son.

After midnight, Paladon and I climbed up the goat path among the crags. Janifa herself was waiting for us at the concealed entrance with a candle. She led us into a tunnel. Halfway along it a metal door opened into a sumptuously furnished room, a hideaway designed for toppled kings to wait for their chance to escape. Inside Ayesha was sitting on the edge of a sofa. She started when Janifa entered, and gasped with astonishment when she saw me. When the great height of Paladon darkened the doorway, she put her hand to her mouth and burst into tears. He strode forward and folded her into his arms, covering her cheeks and then her lips with kisses. Janifa glanced at me, and the roll of her eyes indicated we should leave.

'Is this appropriate, Aunty?' I asked her, when we were in the corridor. My heart was thumping, partly with joy, partly with fear, partly with surprise.

'Well,' she said, the candlelight illuminating her plump face, which was wrinkled with a smile, 'perhaps not, but if we had stayed a moment longer, I would have been weeping even more than Ayesha.' She giggled. 'You told me to be a woman, didn't you? You should be content. I *am* being one. By God, I am. Anyway, what's the difference? Ibn Sa'id will make it legal tomorrow.' She peered at me with a wicked grin. 'How are you going to get such a mountain of lard up that goat path, by the way?'

'Probably with a great deal of ingenuity and much effort,' I said. I gazed at her admiringly. 'That was a short interview you gave Paladon. I thought you planned to interrogate him.'

'I did. It took three seconds – first, when I saw how handsome he is, second, when I saw the honesty in his eyes, third, when I saw the joy on Ayesha's face when she beheld him. What else need I know about him?' She clapped her hands and gave an undignified whoop that echoed in the rocky tunnel. 'Ah, I feel young again. I haven't enjoyed myself so much for years.'

I shall never forget that night. A carpet was leaning conveniently against the wall, and I understood that she had planned it all. She made me unroll it and lay it over the damp stone floor, then lowered herself on to it, wrapping herself in the blanket that had been folded inside. She produced a pack of cards. We played Tarok in the chill, flickering candlelight, occasionally pausing to smile at each other when we heard a moan or a cry from behind the iron door.

'You know what we both are?' she murmured, as she trumped my Fool with her Empress. 'A couple of pimps. Imagine what dear Abu would say if he could see us now.'

'I think Salim might be smiling,' I answered.

'Oh, I hope so. How I hope so,' she replied, serious for the first time that evening.

I accompanied Paladon down the goat track in the dawn light. His face was radiant, and it was hard to keep up with him. He was skipping from rock to rock like a frisky ram. He did not say much, but occasionally he would stop and turn towards me, once on the narrowest ledge, to crush me in his arms. 'My truest friend. My one and only friend,' he would exclaim. 'How can I ever thank you?' And I would answer with a request to give me back my footing because the height made me giddy and I was terrified of falling off the rock. Perhaps it was not only the height, though, that made me giddy and unsteady on that beautiful morning. As we watched the first rays of sunlight bursting over the mountain peaks, its rays turning the rivers and streams in the valley into pathways of molten gold, I realised that I, too, was drunk with joy.

Fortunately we had sobered by the time we reached the bottom. Conscious that we had returned to a world of martial law and ubiquitous spying, we hid for a while in the thickets to make sure we were unobserved. Paladon left first, waiting until a troop of cavalry and a carter had clattered past. I crept out later, and made my way to Salim's house, where I slept until noon. Then I roused ibn Sa'id from his third nap of the day and, for the rest of the afternoon, we went over and over the details of the ceremony until his nicety was satisfied.

'Are you sure he's learned his responses?' he asked, peering at me solemnly.

'He spent months being groomed by the chief faqi. He knows the Qur'ān by heart,' I said, for the tenth time.

'We must do this properly, Samuel. A conversion is no small thing, not to be taken lightly. It has to be witnessed too, by a congregation of the faithful.'

'There'll be Janifa and Ayesha,' I said, 'And me, I suppose.'

'You're not a Mussulman, Samuel, and the others are women. It's not ideal. Not ideal at all.'

'I'm sure you can find some sort of dispensation.'

'Oh, yes. There have been cases of people recognised by the Umma as Mussulmans who were converted to the True Faith when they were alone in the desert. It is, after all, the depth of devotion manifested to Allah that is important – not the temporal and, if I may say so, rather venal wishes of a chief faqi or a young wazir.' He blinked at me myopically. 'We are not discussing the rules for a debating club, you know. Candidates cannot be voted out simply because other members don't like them. What matters is Paladon's personal relationship with God. His sincerity. Well, I can be the judge of that. I will have to consult the Hadiths one last time, though, to check the procedures for witnesses who are women. So that everything's done properly, you understand.'

And so, interminably, it went on. It only occurred to me afterwards that his fussiness might have been his way of disguising his nerves, for he, too, knew the risks we were taking in organising a clandestine meeting in a police state.

* * *

It was a nightmare getting him through the streets to the goat path, for he was the least equipped man in the world to flit through shadows. In fact, his panting and my efforts to support him probably gave us our cover, because the patrols passing us laughed, assuming we were a couple of drunks. Only a little late, we arrived at the thicket where Paladon was waiting impatiently for us – and then it became easier, for Paladon, without a word, heaved his old teacher on to his back and, surefooted as ever despite the weight, carried him up the mountain. Perhaps it was love of and desire for Ayesha that gave him the strength. Certainly no other man I knew could have done it.

Again, Janifa was waiting for us by the door. She led us into the same room, which was now an empty space, last night's furniture stacked against the wall. It was dominated by a huge blue carpet, in the centre of which Ayesha was standing, draped from head to foot in a white robe, her face covered with a veil. She was holding a bunch of lilies in her clasped hands. Paladon took a step towards her, then paused, suddenly as shy as she was. Janifa was beaming with happiness. And I was doing my best to pull up ibn Sa'id from the doorstep where he had collapsed.

'Everything is prepared as I instructed?' ibn Sa'id wheezed, when he was on his feet again. He peered round the room. 'Excellent. Excellent. This will do very nicely. The lamp on the eastern wall. Perfect, Princess Janifa, perfect. An emblem of Mecca. And the ablution bowls all in place. This is as good as a mosque. Oh,' his eyes gleamed as he saw the feast laid out on the side table, 'what sumptuousness you have prepared for the celebrations to follow. That is so considerate of you, Princess. I can hardly wait, but – ahem – you may wish to hide that flagon of wine, I'm afraid, during the conversion. Not that I will be averse to a little, just a little, afterwards, perhaps.'

'Of course we can't have wine in here. I know that,' said Janifa, tartly. Her first impressions of ibn Sa'id had clearly not been encouraging. She sniffed. 'It's nectarine juice, seasoned with a little lemon.'

'Nectarine juice?' The fat features crumpled in momentary disappointment. 'Oh, how appropriate, and delightful.' He beamed at us. 'Shall we begin? Shoes off. And, ladies, perhaps I can ask you to hold the jug and the bowl for Paladon's ablutions. You should be men, of course, but Allah is compassionate and merciful, and I'm sure will understand.'

Janifa glared at him, but when she took her place by Ayesha, who was already holding the goblet of water, her features softened and a tear of pleasure gleamed in her eye.

I had never witnessed a religious conversion ceremony before. After ibn Sa'id's ruminations during the afternoon, I had expected something elaborate and liturgical, but in the event I was struck by the simplicity. Ibn Sa'id's transformation into an imam was nothing as dramatic as we had seen when, before our eyes, he had turned into a stern philosopher debating with al-Gazali. He remained his amiable self, gently steering Paladon into the right responses with the patience and tolerance he had shown us as our teacher. It was Ayesha and Janifa who did the rest. Behind Ayesha's veil and above Janifa's maternal smile, two pairs of eyes shone with welcoming joy. I was reminded of births I had assisted at with Dr Isa. The two women were like midwives, quietly showing their encouragement and hardly concealing their delight as a new life came into the world.

And I was moved by Paladon's dignity and humility. He wore a simple white jellaba, and knelt like a penitent before Ayesha. His gaze was sure, his lips firm. Confidently he pronounced the word to begin the ceremony. '*Bismillah*.' He stretched out his arms and deliberately, right to left, left to right, washed his hands and forearms in the clear stream that Ayesha was pouring into the bowl, smiling tenderly at him as she did so. Paladon rinsed his face, his mouth, his nostrils, the back of his neck, and finally his feet and shins. In a strong voice he recited the closing prayer: 'I stand as a witness that Allah alone is the absolute Supreme Lord, the absolute Remover of difficulties and there is none who shares His absolute authority . . .' He ended by sprinkling a handful of water on the front of his jellaba then settled back on his haunches, waiting for ibn Sa'id to question him, which he did in an easy tone, as if they were engaged in conversation.

'Now, Paladon, you've performed the Wazu and recited the Kalimah correctly, the eight gates of Paradise should be open to you. Have you read and studied the Qur'ān, and inwardly understood it?'

'As much as any ordinary mortal can understand the Word of God,' said Paladon, softly.

'Do you believe that the Qur'ān *is* the Word of God, Paladon?'

'Yes, as communicated to his Prophet.'

'And supersedes and surpasses all previous scriptures ever written, including the Christian Bible?'

'I do believe that.'

'You know the Suras and can quote from them if I ask you to? Have you read the Hadiths? And do you accept them as a sure guide to a way of life in Allah?' To all these questions, Paladon assented.

'Then we have come to the moment of Shahada in which you make your formal testimony. I now ask you to make a declaration of your sincerity and your faith, Paladon.'

In a ringing voice of absolute conviction, Paladon declared the words that would make him a Mussulman. '*La illah illa Allah, Muhammad rasoolu Allah*. There is no God but God and Muhammad is His Prophet.'

Janifa and Ayesha sighed, and ibn Sa'id smiled kindly. 'Well done, my boy,' he whispered. 'I now formally declare you to be a Mussulman. That's all it takes, you know. A single statement of what's in your heart.' He spoke in a louder voice. 'The honour falls on me to choose a name for you that you will bear henceforth as a sign you are of the True Faith.' From his gown, he drew out a dog-eared copy of the Qur'ān, and randomly pressed a plump finger among the flipping pages. 'Ah,' he said. 'It couldn't be better. My finger has stopped on the Sura of Yasin. The Awakener. The Bringer of Joy.' His eyes twinkled at Ayesha. 'I hope you approve, my dear. That's the name by which I shall marry him to you.'

'I will sometimes still think of him as Paladon because he is dear to me by the name I first knew him, Teacher,' she murmured, her voice trembling, and then her eyes blazed, and even behind her veil I could see the flash of her white teeth as her lips parted in a radiant smile. 'But he is also Yasin. Oh, yes, yes. He has been my Yasin since the first day I met him, because from that day forth he has brought me joy.'

'I'm glad you're pleased, Ayesha. So am I. Praise be to Allah, the Merciful and Compassionate. I ask you all now to join me in the first prayers that Yasin, as we will henceforth call him, will make as a member of the Umma.'

I watched from the corner of the room as all but ibn Sa'id prostrated themselves on the carpet towards the lamp that represented the direction of Mecca. Perhaps for the first time since my boyhood I felt lonely because I no longer held myself to be a member of a formal religious community. I had put my Jewishness behind me long ago when I adopted the more universal faith in the Prime Mover. I said a humble little prayer of my own in thanks that, for once, events had worked in harmony with the spheres that bring, when they are in their proper order, consolation to mankind. And, like Janifa, I had a tear in my eye when I saw Paladon, hand to head, bowing right and then left, following ibn Sa'id's lead, and repeating those beautiful words in Arabic, 'God! There is no god but He, the Living, the Merciful!' and the message was echoed in Ayesha's soft tones by his side.

There was a little break afterwards during which everybody hugged each other, and Janifa gave us each a glass of her nectarine juice. Paladon and Ayesha had eyes only for each other. Her beautiful white hand nestled in the crook of his arm, and she was murmuring, 'Yasin, my Yasin,' and he was replying, 'Yasin and Ayesha. Even the sound of it's lovely. And it'll be for ever. Do you realise that, Ayesha? It'll soon be for ever.'

Janifa, laughing, clapped her hands. 'I think it is time, if we can ever get our dear faqi away from the table, for a wedding!'

'I'm coming. I'm coming,' he called, stuffing a last date into his mouth.

After the solemnity of the conversion, we approached the wedding as if it were a festival. I am sure there was no alcohol in Janifa's nectarine, but we did not need it, for we were intoxicated with the pleasure of seeing our hopes fulfilled. Soon ibn Sa'id was busily telling us where we should stand. Paladon and Ayesha were already there, in the middle of the big blue carpet. 'Hurry, Samuel,' he chivvied me. 'Your religion doesn't matter for this. You're the witness for Paladon – I should say Yasin – so you must stand beside him. That's perfect. And, Princess, you stay where you are, beside Ayesha, because you are for the purposes of this ceremony her *wakeel*, or guardian. Excellent.'

We stood in a line facing him, as he positioned himself in front of the lamp on the wall.

'I shall make this very simple,' he announced, his red face beaming behind his henna beard, 'because *nikah*, marriage in the sight of God, should be simple. After all, why are we here if not to witness the most natural gift granted to mankind at the beginning of creation, the union of two young people who love each other and who together provide the means that God who fashioned the universe has ordained to generate life?' He looked fondly at the couple we flanked. 'As it was for Adam and Eve, so will it be for Yasin and Ayesha. There were no interfering clerics making speeches in the Garden of Eden and you need few words from me, though Samuel has spent all afternoon trying to make me write a sermon. My role, as *ma'zoon*, or officiator, is to listen to both of you make your vows, then lead you in prayer as we plead for Allah's blessing. It is your own vows, bound in sacred oath to Allah, that will marry you – no words of any other – and if you are sincere, I have no doubt that Allah will bestow the mercy of His blessing upon you, and then no man will have the power to break you asunder. There are a few formalities. A presentation of *mahr*, the marriage gift. The Prophet set great store by that because it betokens the husband's future responsibility for his wife. In sickness and health, all of that. Ah, you have a gold ring, Yasin. Excellent. Money, sheep and such things can come later. And there will be an official marriage contract you will need to sign and at some point file in the mosque. I have one prepared. Now, are you both clear on the procedures?'

They nodded.

'Good. I will begin with a prayer, because *nikah* is also a solemn act of worship in which we praise Allah, in thanks for His mercy that brought you together. The fourth Sura may be appropriate because it is about women.' And he began to intone: 'O men! Fear your Lord, Who has created you of one man, and from him created his wife, and from these twain spread abroad so many men and women. And fear ye God, in whose name ye ask mutual favours – and reverence the wombs that bare you. Verily is God watching over you!' The others repeated after each verse, 'In the name of Allah, the most Compassionate and Merciful,' and after a while I too joined in the response.

And then there was silence. Ibn Sa'id looked solemn. Paladon turned to Ayesha and in the doe-like eyes behind the veil I saw tears of pure happiness.

'Yasin the Mussulman, once Paladon, son of Toscanus,' said ibn Sa'id, sternly, 'do you, before God, wish to take this woman, Ayesha, to be your wife?'

'Before God, I do,' said Paladon, in the same ringing tones that he had used when he announced his change in faith. He reached into his pocket for the ring and slipped it on her finger.

'And Ayesha, daughter of Salim—'

I felt a sudden gust of chill air on my back at the same time as I heard the clang of metal against stone. I turned in shock and saw, framed in the doorway, Aziz. He was dressed in chain mail, with a sword in his hand. He stepped forward and Ephraim, with a sly smile, emerged from the shadows behind him. He had his hand firmly on the shoulder of an old woman, whom he was propelling into the light. Her features were crumpled in terror. It was Mary, Janifa's handmaid.

Aziz's voice squeaked in his rage and excitement: 'What is going on? It smells of treason to me. Aunt Janifa, what is the meaning of this secret gathering?'

In the silence that followed, ibn Sa'id cleared his throat, and in that moment he resembled a glowering prophet. 'Prince Aziz,' he rumbled, in a voice that resonated with authority, 'you are interrupting the worship of God. You are stepping into a room that is temporarily consecrated to Allah. You may join our congregation in prayer, and your friends too, but you will have to put away that sword and take off your boots. Otherwise you will be committing sacrilege.'

Aziz's face paled with astonishment to be addressed so. Then he screamed, 'Hold your tongue, fool.'

Ibn Sa'id remained rock-like. 'Have a care for your soul, Aziz. Don't add another sin to the many on your conscience. As I said, you are interrupting holy worship. This petulance and foolishness is unworthy of you. Now, Princess Ayesha, daughter of Salim, do you accept this man, Yasin, son of—'

Ibn Sa'id's words were drowned in an inhuman bellow of frustration and rage. Aziz had raised his sword arm and was about to rush forward to strike him, when he was stopped in his tracks by the tall, broad figure of Paladon towering in front of him. 'Go away, Aziz,' he said evenly. 'You're not wanted here.'

Many things happened at once. Janifa let out a wail and collapsed on the carpet. Mary bit Ephraim's hand, releasing herself from his grip. He howled with pain and she threw herself at her mistress's feet, crying, 'Forgive me. They forced me.'

I heard Ayesha's piercing voice, 'I do. I do,' and then, a scream of anguish, 'Paladon!' for Aziz was slashing with his sword at his former friend, who was nimbly dodging away. I grabbed Ayesha, pulling her towards the side of the room away from harm, and for the next few seconds I was oblivious of anything but her scratching fingers tearing at my cheek and her furious attempts to struggle out of my grasp, all the time screaming, 'Paladon! Paladon!'

I was vaguely aware of ibn Sa'id's rumbling voice behind the clamour. 'Therefore I trust you both to the mercy and compassion of Allah and declare you both, before God and man, to be husband . . .' And there he stopped, and the whole room was suddenly silent because, aghast, we saw that Paladon was trapped. Aziz had backed him against the piled-up furniture so that he had no room to retreat, pressed into the gap between an up-ended sofa and a table.

Aziz stepped back, his sword point poised at Paladon's chest. Paladon stared with calm scorn at the man who was about to despatch him. Aziz, sweat pouring down his cheeks, was panting heavily, but his eyes gleamed with excitement and his lips twisted into a sneer of triumph. 'Oh, how I have longed for this moment,' he whispered. His elbow crooked elegantly upwards as he lightly withdrew the sword point so it was ready to stab.

'. . . and wife,' said ibn Sa'id, equitably, as he smashed the great silver flagon of nectarine juice on Aziz's head. The sword slipped from his grasp and rattled on the stone paving. Nectarine juice mingled with blood from his head wound poured down Aziz's face. His eyes rolled, and then he slid slowly down the up-ended sofa to lie spreadeagled on his back on the floor. Ibn Sa'id lowered his enormous bulk on top of him, settling himself comfortably as if on his favourite cushion in his study. 'I hope, Samuel, you observed that simple demonstration of the effect of mass over motion,' he said calmly. 'And I doubt there'll be any motion from my former student for a while. He rarely had time for the weight of knowledge at my disposal in the past, but I'm sure he feels it now.' Unconcernedly, he pulled a handkerchief from his sleeve to wipe away a spot of juice. 'Ayesha and Yasin, you are married. The ceremony was unconventional and more abbreviated than I intended, but I assure you—'

Again, he was interrupted, this time by a scream from Janifa. Ephraim had been cowering against the wall by the door. Suddenly he had leaned forward and snatched Ayesha, who had been tottering past him, her arms outstretched to Paladon. In a quick movement, he hugged her as a shield, one arm pinioning her head back, the other pressing a knife to her throat.

'Please,' he was whimpering. 'Please.' His mouth was opening and shutting in his plausible, wheedling smile. The neat tuft of his beard and the blue ribbons on his ringlets shook as he trembled. 'I never meant any harm . . . You must understand . . . I had no part in this. I am a peaceful man, only a merchant, a humble adviser of finance . . . If you just let me go, I would be happy to provide guarantees . . . Please, Samuel, I've always been your friend. You know the reliability of my bonds . . . I'm sure we can find a way to—'

Paladon had picked up Aziz's sword close to the end of the blade, and its jewelled hilt was dangling by his side. He strode slowly but grimly towards Ephraim. He paused in front of him, contemplating the cringing face with the same concentration I had seen him peer at a block of stone he intended to carve into an angel. He seemed oblivious of Ayesha, looking only at Ephraim, who was scrabbling back against the wall, screaming 'Get away from me! Get away from me!'

After a moment Paladon took a step back. 'Take your filthy hands off my wife,' he said softly.

Ephraim was gibbering. 'I'm warning you – I don't want to hurt her but if you threaten me, I'll have no choice—'

Paladon struck with the decisiveness and accuracy of sculptor making a first cut into marble with his chisel was the strength of the blow that the point of the sword rammed into Ephraim's left eye, out through the back of his skull and became fixed in a crack in the stone wall behind him. In the same movement, he caught Ayesha as she fell and pulled her to safety. He hugged her, and held her moaning against his chest. The body he had discarded shook like a fish caught on a hook, then slumped lifeless and remained hanging on the wall. One of the blue ribbons, sliced off its ringlet by Paladon's great thrust, fluttered down and settled on the pool of blood that was now seeping over the slabs and soaking into the carpet.

Frozen into silence, we stared in horror at the impaled body, then in amazement at Paladon, who was calmly murmuring words of encouragement to Ayesha. Paladon looked down and noticed Janifa and Mary. 'I'm sorry I had to kill him, Lady Janifa, but from what Samuel told me, you and the king will not be grieved by his loss. Neither will Mishkhat. But it was an abuse of your hospitality and kindness, which I regret.'

He turned to ibn Sa'id, who was goggling at him, lost for words. 'How is Aziz? Does he live? Good. Let us hope that the king can bring him back to his senses now that his adviser is gone. Thank you for saving my life and for . . . everything. I fear I am no credit to you as a new Mussulman. Murder is not the best way to start a life of religion. Or marriage.'

'My dear fellow, you were rescuing your wife,' ibn Sa'id answered softly. 'And possibly we can say you were serving the state. I must consult the Hadiths. In the meantime may I suggest that you and Ayesha be gone, and quickly. I hope you have somewhere safe to hide until this situation is resolved.'

Paladon turned to the old maidservant, who was wiping Janifa's brow as she gaped open-mouthed at the corpse. 'Did Aziz and Ephraim tell anyone else they were coming here?'

'Just – just before we entered, Ephraim ordered his secre-
▓▓back into the palace with instructions to bring troops.'

▓▓ha and I had better hurry,' said Paladon. 'You should
as well, Lady Janifa. I suggest you take Aziz straight to King
Abu and tell him what has happened before anybody else does.
▓▓uel, can you help her? I'm sorry to leave you – but I will
be a fugitive after this until the king pardons me. Better I take
Ayesha to safety. Nobody will see us on the mountain. I've
surveyed almost every inch of it and know many paths. I'll
send word to you.' With the arm that was not holding Ayesha,
he embraced me, pressing his cheek against mine. 'My true
friend,' he whispered. 'Words cannot express the gratitude I
owe you. May God go with you.'

'And with you, Paladon,' I managed, despite my emotion.

'I'm Yasin now.' He grinned.

Pausing only to pick up his cloak to drape over Ayesha, and
to pull Aziz's sword from the wall – Ephraim's body fell with
an ugly thump on to the stone floor – he gave us one last look,
and then, supporting Ayesha, who was still numb with shock,
he disappeared out of the door.

Ibn Sa'id pulled a document from his robe. 'Oh, cat's
whiskers, I forgot to ask them to sign the marriage contract.'

And that was when we heard the shouts and the clash of
steel outside, and I knew that all was lost.

A captain of the guard entered first, pulling Ayesha behind him.
He threw her unceremoniously on to the carpet beside Janifa.
With a jangling of mail, the room filled with soldiers. I was
pressed against the piled-up furniture with three spears pricking
my chest. Ibn Sa'id was pulling his bulk to his feet. 'Captain,
there is no need for violence. If you're looking for the wazir,
you'll find him here. Don't worry, he's not—' A mailed fist
smashed into his face and he collapsed, bleeding, on to the floor.
Then they began to kick him, and afterwards me.

* * *

Ibn Sa'id and I awoke in the palace dungeons, manacled to the wall among Christians who had been accused of treason.

It was many months before I discovered what had happened to the others. Before the king had even heard about it ~~she~~ was removed to Salim's house, where she was imprisoned ~~in~~ Ayesha's old rooms. Mary was allowed to attend her. ~~That was~~ Aziz's only gesture of kindness.

Ayesha was kept in seclusion in a room next to her brother's office. She was under constant guard to ensure that she made no attempt on her life. When Aziz set off on his mission to King Yusuf, he took her with him, blackmailing her into continued silence by threatening her with the instant decapitation of ibn Sa'id, Janifa and me if she said an untoward word to her future groom. That was the only reason we were left alive.

Of course, no marriage had taken place. The king was told that Janifa and Ayesha had lured Aziz and Ephraim to the cell under the palace to murder them. Paladon and I were paid accomplices. Abu found no difficulty in believing it. After all, his sister had once conspired to kill a prince, as he had, and Ayesha was the daughter of his fellow assassin. Parricide and fratricide ran in the family. Anyway, there was nothing he could do about it. He was more powerless than ever.

And Paladon, whom I'd thought was dead? He disappeared. He killed two soldiers before he escaped through the concealed door on to the goat track. They followed him. He threw another soldier off the cliff before he got away. There was a hunt for him throughout the city but he could not be found. One of his workmen informed the troops that he had seen Paladon rushing into the mosque on the rock, still dressed in the white jellaba in which he had been married, stained, the man said, with blood. The troops searched thoroughly but since the rest of the caves had been sealed off there was no other way in or out except by the main door, and the workman was adamant that Paladon had never emerged.

He simply disappeared.

Andalucía, 1938

3

The Parley

Well, it had been a nice idea, he thought, as he closed the book and put it back in his pocket. Samuel's story had concentrated his mind, but it had not provided him with any answers.

Pinzon had found the parallels depressing. Samuel's and Paladon's idealism when they had embarked on their great enterprise in the cave had been little different from his own and Lorca's when they had set off confidently into the countryside to build a new Spain. The mosque, which had enshrined tolerance, had, like their beloved Republic, attracted the same unthinking hatred. Mishkhat's slide into factional hatred followed by mob violence was different only in degree from what had taken place in cities throughout the country at the beginning of the war. There had been the same fatal combination of good intentions, incompetence, malevolence and ambition. The military response had been equivalent. In each case María's father's 'men of blood' had risen to the top of the dung-heap. Freedom had shrivelled and died – and the best and noblest of hearts had been sacrificed then as now. Raúl had died in Barcelona; Paladon had disappeared; the Ogarrios and Elderics had triumphed.

It was a damning indictment of mankind. More immediately, it was a chilling prognosis for their future.

And he was still no nearer to coming up with a plan.

From the darkness behind him came small stirrings, occasional sighs and snores. He envied the sleeping hostages, who had succumbed so naturally to the animal needs of their bodies. By God, he was tired too, even more so after his labour of translation, but sleep was the last thing of which he was capable. He felt agitation in every part of his spirit. His blood was pounding in his veins. He craved relief in violent exercise. He wished he could burst out of the claustrophobic space and run in the freedom and chill of the night air. As a government minister, working into the early hours, he had more than once eased his tension by pounding through the silent, palm-shadowed avenues of the Jardines de Monforte in the cool of dawn. His bodyguards had had to sprint after him as best they could. They had been thirty years younger than he was but he could outpace them. There was no question of such release now.

But he was desperate to do something – anything. He glanced at Felipe slumped against his pillar. Why not? he thought. He had to sound Felipe out some time. Wrapping his blanket around his shoulders like a poncho, he crouched beside the sleeping guard and shook his shoulder. 'Felipe,' he whispered. 'Wake up.'

The young man's eyes opened, and for a second Pinzon saw inarticulate terror, replaced by bewilderment as he made a frantic grab for his rifle, rocking with it like a frightened child with his favourite toy.

'What's the matter, lad? Were you having a nightmare?'

'I was dreaming about the bombs,' he muttered. 'The aeroplanes. When we were in the trenches at Teruel.'

'Was it the Condor Legion?' asked Pinzon, softly. 'I've heard they could be very frightening.'

Felipe froze. Sweat trickled from the base of his cap as he recited, trance-like, verses he must have learned by rote. '"Heinkel five-one C, drop your rifle and flee. Heinkel double-one-one, no time to run. Savoia-Marchetti – you're mince and

spaghetti. Dornier one-seven will blow you to heaven . . .'"
After each mnemonic, he whistled and hummed. With a chill,
Pinzon realised he was mimicking aircraft engines.

'It was going round and round in my head, Señor. I got the
numbers right this time, though.' Briefly he looked triumphant,
then his cheek muscles twitched. 'In my dream I kept muddling
them. I was scared I wouldn't be able to get to cover in time.
You see, we have to know the sounds because that tells us how
long it is before the bombs . . .' His words petered out and he
looked miserably at the floor.

'You were bombed often, Felipe?'

He slipped back down against the pillar. 'Every day,' he whispered. 'Sometimes all day. It was worse than the snow and the
cold that killed us too.'

'Would you like to tell me about it?'

Felipe was silent. He shook his head violently from side to
side.

'I think I can imagine. I had a son of about your age, a few
years older perhaps. He told me a little about what it was like.'

Felipe looked up curiously. 'He was at Teruel?'

'No, other battles. He said that when the aeroplanes came, it
didn't matter how many other men were in the trench with
him, he felt completely alone. And that every time he was
bombed it was like the first time all over again. He could never
get used to it.'

'That's true,' said Felipe, his eyes widening. 'It was like . . .
I don't know . . . When the bombs came, there'd be a whine
like a kettle hissing, and then . . . silence – only for a second
and then you knew it was right on top of you . . . and before
you could even pray there'd be noise everywhere . . . It seemed
right inside your head and you were all alone and nobody could
help you. Nobody. It was just you with . . . mountains of earth
and – and volcanoes of fire . . . And legs and heads flying around
you . . . Bits of people. Bits of people . . . You had to rub your
face against the flint or the soil until it hurt because that was

the only way of knowing you were still alive . . . And sometimes, like when they were softening us up for an attack, and
the waves and waves of bombers kept coming, it didn't stop,
it didn't stop . . . Then – then you didn't want to live any more
. . . You wanted it over with . . .' He closed his eyes tightly as
if he was trying to expel the memory.

Pinzon hardly dared breathe, willing him not to stop, to get
it off his chest.

'I had a friend, Professor, called Anselmo Delgado. He was
an old soldier, but he liked me, treated me like a son, looked
after me. He'd been everywhere . . . Madrid, Brunete, Belchite
. . . Everybody said he was brave as a lion. Well, in one of the
raids, he just put his rifle into his mouth and pulled the trigger
. . . Right next to me. Ogarrio threw a· blanket over him and
our *teniente* never mentioned what really happened in his report
. . . We all understood, you see . . . It could have been any of
us. Some of us maybe wished it *had* been them next time the
bombers came.'

'Did you lose many friends, Felipe?'

'All of them . . . all the ones who volunteered from the same
village . . . Some got sick, others died in the attacks. That didn't
seem so bad . . . It was like a fight back home, somebody wins,
somebody loses, you could understand it . . . You see, I can
handle the fighting. I'm even good at it. I'm big and strong and
I shoot well – that's why I was picked for this mission. But the
bombing's not the same, Professor. It's got nothing to do with
what we're fighting for . . . the – the people, and the Party, and
discipline and all of that . . . because it's . . . I don't know . . .
madness, and there are no rules any more. Nothing makes any
sense . . . nothing . . .'

Pinzon's heart was quickening with excitement.

'There was one day . . . I was up with the *teniente* on the
lookout. There'd been four days of fog and we'd lost three men
to frostbite but there'd been no bombing 'cos the planes couldn't
fly, so when we woke up and it was one of those bright, starry

dawns, we all felt bad because it meant clear skies. It didn't seem like a war day, though, not at first . . . There was this eagle circling over the ruins of Teruel, which we could see on the hilltop – we'd taken it and then they took it and we'd taken it back and now the Fascists had it again, but that day it was peaceful and calm, like – like a white Christmas morning. I heard the drone first, and pointed out to the *teniente* the glint of silver in the sky. I knew already it was Savoias. Two flights of Pipistrellos, eighty-ones, with the whining Piaggio engine that screams at you when it comes near. I wanted to get back into the trench and take cover, but the *teniente* had to count them for his report, so he trained his field glasses on the shadowy blue crosses that were slowly moving up the snow slopes. Right towards us. Then he shouted, "Sixteen." That's how many there were, and we both jumped down the steps back into the trench. "Down, down, down!" he's screaming, but the roar's already over our heads and the bombs are whistling, and I'm already flattening myself against the muddy wall because I've heard the silence and know I've only got three seconds to live.'

'And then?' prompted Pinzon softtly. 'What was special about this raid?'

'Nothing,' he whispered. 'It went on and on for ever, like all of them, and I got buried in a snowdrift when one of the bombs landed inside our trench close to me, and I couldn't hear properly for a day after that, but . . . but it was the Hernandez brothers, you see. The elder twins and Luís, who was the younger brother and my best friend because we were the same age and grew up together. The four of us were the last remaining of those who'd come out of Old Castile. Anyway, I found they'd been huddling together when the bomb hit and . . . we couldn't tell them apart any more. It took hours to find what pieces were left and we couldn't tell if they belonged to Luís or Rafael or Juan . . . Suddenly they didn't exist. Later the *sargento* said their widowed mother was lucky because she'd be honoured for providing three martyrs in the struggle against Fascism and her food ration would triple. One of his jokes. He's good at jokes, knows how to cheer us up. We all laughed at the time. I did too, but afterwards I – I wondered if they'd ever been real, my friends, because there was nothing there any more, nothing that remained. Nothing. There wasn't even the smell of death. It's real with a bayonet or a bullet. You see the body, but with a bomb there's nothing left of you. You're . . . gone.'

'And that disturbs you?'

Felipe's eyes were pleading. 'I told you, there's no sense any more. And how can you believe anything after that? Communism and . . . history. It's pointless. Everything's pointless . . .'

'But you're a loyal Communist,' said Pinzon. 'You believe in the Party. Its orders are correct by definition. They have to be, because otherwise there wouldn't be any meaning in anything. And you trust Ogarrio because he represents the Party.'

'He *is* a good man. The best. I'd die for him. That's what I told myself. That's why I agreed to come with him on this mission, but . . . but . . .'

'But now he wants to blow us up in a big explosion, and if that happens we'll be like your friends, the Hernandez brothers, who don't exist any more?'

'Yes,' he whispered, after a long pause. 'I couldn't bear that. I couldn't.'

'But if the Party wants you to follow orders. If Ogarrio feels there is a purpose in such a death . . .' Pinzon hated himself for pushing the boy, but he had to be sure.

Felipe's mouth opened and closed. Tears were pouring down his cheeks. He was shaking in his agitation.

'It's all right,' whispered Pinzon, reaching an arm around his shoulders. 'I understand. I really understand.'

'And how can he kill these women and children? Tomás? Little Tomás? How will that help the Party – or our struggle – or anything?'

'It's all right,' said Pinzon.

'That's why – that's why last night I asked you . . .'

'You know, Felipe,' said Pinzon, 'that if I come up with anything, it may not be what Ogarrio will like.'

'No, Professor, killing women and children is wrong. And blowing them up! Professor, you must let me be part of your plan. Please. I swear I'll help you. I'll do anything. Anything.'

'And Ogarrio? Your loyalty to him? And the Party? You surely don't wish to betray your comrades or your beliefs.'

Felipe hugged his knees, shaking. He was blinking rapidly. Sweat was again trickling down his brow. Eventually he turned a loose-lipped, pathetic face to Pinzon. 'I don't know what I believe in any more,' he said, and dropped his head into his hands.

'We'll work something out, Felipe. I promise,' said Pinzon. His instincts had been right. He had another ally.

But his heart churned. The truth was he still had no plan, only one more victim of Fate who had put his trust in him.

'Professor! Professor!' A rough hand was shaking his shoulder, only seconds, it seemed, after he had finally started to doze.

He heard María's voice murmuring, 'What is it?'

'They're unbarring the door,' Felipe was whispering urgently. 'I think it's Ogarrio. What do you want me to do?'

'Your job, Felipe,' said Pinzon, curtly. 'You're our guard. For God's sake, act like one.'

'Privato Muro, is everything all right?' It was Ogarrio's cheerful voice from the back of the nave.

Felipe stamped to attention, his rifle butt thudding against the tiles.

Pinzon heard the echo of boots on the stone floor. Ogarrio was marching down the aisle towards them, followed by two of his soldiers. He ignored the scared looks of villagers who had been woken by his sudden entry.

He stopped in front of Pinzon. 'Señor Pinzon, I trust you're well rested. Actually, I don't give a fuck if you are or not. You are to come with me. And I also need a woman.' He surveyed María. 'Is this your *puta*, Professor? Well, well, and I thought you were some crusty old philosopher. I'm impressed. Voluptuousness in a nun's habit. It's a pity we're not in Valencia. It could have been a new revolutionary style. Very decadent, quite in keeping with a bourgeois Republic on its last corrupt legs. *Mis cumplidos, Señorita.*'

'*Y mis maldiciones a usted*,' María retorted, her lip curled in contempt.

'I like her. She has spirit,' said Ogarrio.

'She has decency, which you do not, Ogarrio.' Instinctively, Pinzon's hands had clenched into fists. He felt a flush in his cheeks.

Ogarrio was watching him with amusement. 'What a bull you've become. Be careful, Professor, remember your age. Don't want you having a stroke on me.' His voice hardened. 'Whoever she is, *puta* or saint, she'll do. Put on your coif, or your wimple, or whatever you call it. You're to look like a real nun, not some fantasy from a bordello.'

'And if I refuse?'

'You won't, because if you do, somebody will get hurt. And it won't be you so you'll feel bad about it. Now, hurry. You too, Professor.'

'I'm not going anywhere without my grandson. I won't leave him.'

'He'll be all right. You won't be gone long.' He leaned forward. 'It's good news,' he murmured. 'They've come back with an answer. The negotiation's on.' He grinned. 'You see? It's working out as I'd planned.'

The courtyard outside was washed in moonlight. Over the black silhouettes of the battlements the snow peaks glistened palely on the horizon. The sky was filled with stars. Ogarrio led them forward at a fast pace.

'It still won't work,' said Pinzon. 'If they've occupied the town they'll discover the bodies in the corn exchange and know you're lying.'

'Do you think I'm an idiot?' muttered Ogarrio. 'We spent the evening cleaning up that bastard Levi's mess. Sure, they'll find the bodies eventually, but we'll be long gone by the time they do.'

'And when they discover their nuns and priests are townsfolk?'

'They won't. We take them with us. There's a bridge over a gorge in the Seguras mountains. We cross it, send the hostages back to their side, then blow it so they can't follow us. When they find out we've double-crossed them it'll be too late.'

'You have everything worked out, don't you?' said Pinzon. 'And me?'

'Ah, well, there I'm sorry. You don't come with us. As I told you, they're interested in you. You get handed over first. I'll tell everybody about your noble sacrifice when we get back to Valencia. Look on it as the fortunes of war.'

'And my grandson? What happens to him?'

'That rather depends on you. If you co-operate he can come with us. Muro's taken a shine to him. Maybe he'll find his relatives for him if he has any. Or the Republic will look after him. Honour him as the son of a martyr. Give him a fucking stipend and the nation's gratitude. If you don't co-operate he gets handed over with you to the Fascists. Perhaps they'll turn him into a nice little Roman Catholic. More likely they'll shoot him with you. Your choice.'

They reached the battlement steps. At the top Pinzon could see the silhouette of Becerra holding up a white flag above the crenellations. Martínez was beside him with the generator they had taken to the crypt, shining one of the lamps into the courtyard beyond.

Ogarrio scrutinised María. He adjusted her coif so that the black hood hung lower over her forehead. 'You'd better co-operate too,' he said. 'The nice Fascist officer is going to ask you who you are. You tell him you're Sister Catherina, twenty-eight years old, originally Consuela Lopez from Málaga. He may ask you about some of the others. Expect tricks. He will give you the names of nuns or monks who weren't even here. I have a manifest I got from the prison. If I tap you on the left arm you say they're fine. If I tap your right arm, you look confused and say you don't know them. *Entiendes?*'

She looked at him scornfully. 'You don't need to touch me anywhere, you murdering bastard,' she said. 'I used to visit them in the prison. I knew all of them. Some were my friends. I can answer the questions more accurately than you.'

Ogarrio laughed. 'That's even better then, isn't it? Remember, though, I'll be listening behind you. If you make one false answer, you'll get a bullet in the head straight off and you'll condemn all the other hostages along with you. Now.' He gave a mock bow. 'If you'll kindly take your positions, Señor and Señorita, we'll get on with the show.'

They mounted the steps. Ogarrio pushed them forward so they were leaning over the parapets. Below them, on the sloping flagstones, there was a circle of light from Martínez's lamp. Inside it were three men. A young Fascist officer in a neat tunic and peaked cap stood a little in front of the others. His leather straps and boots gleamed in the lamplight. He sported a dandy moustache and was smoking nonchalantly. Behind him, stiffly at attention, were two dark-faced soldiers, one wearing a German-style steel helmet, the other a Moroccan fez. Each had a chequered prayer cloth wrapped round his neck. With a chill, Pinzon recognised them as two of the dreaded *moros*, the Moors of the fables, Berber mercenaries in Franco's élite North African Legion, whom every Republican soldier feared because they gave no quarter and had a reputation for raping and looting after their victories on a scale of horror that terrorised every town and village in Spain.

'Capitán Maranda,' Ogarrio shouted. 'We have your hostages.'

The young officer shielded his eyes with a gloved hand against the glare. 'Be so good as to shine the light on the politician first,' he called, in a pure Castilian accent.

Martínez swung the arc lamp away from Maranda so it now illuminated Pinzon. For a moment he was blinded. When he could see again, he noticed that the Fascist *capitán* was examining with his own torch what looked like a piece of newspaper that contained a photograph.

'Thank you,' he called. 'I am satisfied. Now for the other. Have you brought a sister or a brother?'

'I have a fucking nun, if that's what you mean,' said Ogarrio, propelling María so she half hung over the parapet. The harsh light of the lamp was now on her, accentuating every freckle. Pinzon was amazed by her calm.

'Good evening, Sister. May I ask your name?' The *capitán*'s torch was now shining on what looked like a telegram.

'It is Catherina. That is the name I took when I was honoured to be received as a bride of Christ. My family name is Lopez, I was christened Consuela.'

'Ah, yes.' The *capitán* was peering closely at the flimsy. 'From Cartagena, yes?'

'From Málaga, Señor,' said María.

The officer grinned. 'Oh, yes, how stupid of me. It's this bad light. Málaga, to be sure. And how are you being treated, Sister? Have any of you been harmed?'

'No, Señor, but we are locked in the cathedral under guard, and we are frightened.'

'My sympathies to all of you,' called the *capitán*, 'and I also bear those of our general, who urges you to be patient and calm.'

'We are so, Señor, because we are confident that the Lord Jesus and the Holy Mother are with us.'

'Quite so,' said Maranda. 'You also have our prayers and those of every true patriot in Spain. By the way.' He was again peering at the telegram. 'Your cousin? He is ill, I believe. Is he being well-treated?'

'I have no male cousin, Señor,' she said, with a touch of confusion in her voice. Pinzon sensed Ogarrio stiffening behind him. Roughly he slapped María's right arm. She ignored him. 'If you mean my uncle's daughter, Sister Beatriz, she was ill two years ago, at the beginning of the war. By God's grace, the doctors here diagnosed a hernia and she recovered fully after an operation. She is in good health now. She is praying inside the cathedral with the others.'

Ogarrio's brow was perspiring with tension. His fingers were playing with his revolver holster.

'I'm pleased to hear it, Sister,' called the officer. 'Will you please pass her father's wishes to her? Tell her he is safe in Málaga.'

'That cannot be, Señor. My uncle, Don Ignacio, passed away three years ago in Seville. Beatriz and I received permission from the convent to go to stay with his grieving family in their home there during his funeral.'

'Of course,' said Capitán Maranda. 'Sargento Ogarrio,' he cried, in a louder voice. 'I am satisfied. I take the sister's word that your hostages are who you say they are and unharmed. You must understand. Some of the townsfolk we interrogated told us it was their own people you have taken. Perhaps they were lying to us.'

'We have a few of them too,' Ogarrio shouted. 'You can have them as part of the bargain. Now you are satisfied, we should discuss terms.'

'I am sorry, Sargento.' Martínez had swung the lamp back towards the courtyard again, and the *capitán* was shielding his eyes again. 'These things take time. I must report to my general and he will no doubt wish to consult his superiors in Seville. You have a truce now, but no deal. I will return soon after dawn to give you our answer.'

'If I have not heard from you by eight o'clock, I will begin to shoot the hostages, one every hour.'

'You may do as you like. If you harm a hair on any of their

heads, though, I guarantee all bargains are off.' Maranda looked as composed as ever. He gave a snappy salute. 'My compliments,' he called, and stepped smartly out of the pool of light, followed by his Moors.

'Coño,' muttered Ogarrio.

'You still believe they will negotiate?' asked Pinzon. 'You don't think they're just buying time while they deploy?'

'For your sakes, you'd better hope they do negotiate. Becerra, put down that damned flag. We don't need it any more. Take these two to the cathedral.' As she passed him, he put a hand on María's arm. 'You,' he said. 'You did well. What's your name?'

She looked him coolly in the eyes. 'It's "vengeance", as far as you're concerned, you pig. One day, I'll stamp on your bleeding body, and all of you Communists who have destroyed our revolution.' She spat on his boots.

Ogarrio laughed. 'And to think that just a moment ago you were acting a sweet-voiced nun. Becerra, you'd better watch out for this one. She might scratch. I'll see more of you later, perhaps, little tigress. I like your style.'

He marched off down the parapet, shouting orders. Becerra and the two soldiers who had brought them pushed them towards the steps and kept their rifles trained on them all the way back to the cathedral.

The townspeople were waiting for them.

'Good news, Professor?' came the harsh voice of Grandmother Juanita.

He saw the expectant eyes around her – the mothers and children, the old men and women. 'Yes,' he said. 'The Fascists have accepted Sargento Ogarrio's story. They believe you're all nuns and priests. They're going to give us their answer in the morning,'

There was a ragged cheer. Hector García stood on a pew and waved his hands like a conductor. Delighted faces lit up as the hostages joined him in the stirring Anarchist anthem, 'A Las Barricadas'.

'Negras tormentas agitan los aires
nubes oscuras nos impiden ver . . .

Black storms shake the sky
Dark clouds won't allow us to see
Although pain and death await us
Against the enemy we must go . . .'

María caught his eye. She was pale and her lips were set in an expression of disgust. He shook his head, feeling sick at heart. He could guess what she was thinking. He felt the same. They were celebrating a victory – when in fact the trap was closing further.

He remembered a bright summer's day in Madrid, when every street and boulevard in the city had rung with this anthem. The day before, the Fascist attack had been thrown back from the suburbs. Everybody had been mad with joy because the *madrileños* had done the impossible. All political factions had united and saved their city. Pinzon had watched the processions from his apartment. Hearing the thousands of voices singing this hymn of defiance, the exhausted soldiers of the International Brigade had quickened their step, looking up in amazement at the flowers being thrown at them from every balcony, at the boiler-suited girls who broke through the ranks to kiss their grimy cheeks, and at the red flags waving from every window . . .

'The most precious good
Is liberty
And we must defend it
With courage and faith . . .'

He had felt sick at heart then, too, because even as the over-joyed *madrileños* had been celebrating their triumph and the bitter siege was already being turned into legend, he had had in his pocket secret orders from President Azaña, instructing him and all other members of the government to join him at midnight in a convoy of limousines that would take them to Valencia, abandoning the miraculously saved capital like rats from a sinking ship. They had known, as the people had not, that this victory was only a respite.

The song ended on a note of elation. Hector's deep baritone could be heard above the others:

> 'Raise high the Revolutionary flag
> That brings emancipation to the pueblos . . .
>
> . . . A las Barricadas! A las Barricadas!
> Por el triunfo
> De la Confederación!'

María took a long inhalation of the cigarette she had just lit with her Zippo, then pressed the end carefully on a flagstone, returning the half-smoked stub to the packet. 'I must preserve these,' she said. 'I'm running out.'

'You were magnificent,' he said.

She turned a blank face towards him. He sensed her anger. 'No, I was just whoring again,' she said bitterly. 'First for Paco, now for Ogarrio. That's what it was, you know. Pretending to be that poor nun. I felt dirty inside. Lying to save our hides. Knowing that Catherina's dead body is down a well somewhere or in a woodpile, or wherever those bastards hid her. She really was a friend, you know. Now I feel I've betrayed her.' She shivered, then suddenly she brightened and her face was transformed with an affectionate smile.

Tomás was running down the aisle towards them. 'Aunt María! Grandfather, you're safe!' María scooped him into her arms and covered his cheeks with kisses.

Hector's impromptu choir had broken into another song, equally inappropriate. It was the famous '¡No pasarán!', another hymn to victory. Hector again led the verses:

'*The Moors brought by Franco*
Want to come to Madrid
As long as there's a militiaman left
The Moors will not pass . . .'

And the others repeated the chorus, '¡No *pasarán!* ¡No
pasarán!' at the top of their voices.

Pinzon was about to follow María and Tomás back to their
pew by the altar when he felt a bony hand grip his arm.
Grandmother Juanita's coal-black eyes were looking up at him.
'What's the real news, Professor?' she asked, in a low voice.

'That we have until eight o'clock tomorrow morning to think
of a way out of here.'

She nodded, taking this in. 'And are you nearer coming to
a plan? Or are we still watching and waiting?'

'I've talked to Felipe,' he said. 'He's with us.'

'Him!' she said scathingly. 'That doesn't take us much further.
What can he do? A fool is useless to man and beast.'

Pinzon felt very weary. 'Perhaps when the fighting starts, we
may see an opportunity to do something.'

She peered into his eyes. 'You must not feel that you should
take all the responsibility on your shoulders. You are only one
man. We peasants know we cannot always avoid what Fate has
written for us. We are already grateful for what you have done
for us. Listen to them singing. You put that fire into their hearts.
Whatever happens we will not die like dogs. That is something.' She brushed his cheek with her hand.

'I won't give up, Doña Juanita,' he whispered. 'I can't.'

Her mouth widened into a grin. 'No, I believe you are not
the sort of man who knows how to rest. Well, this is a church.
Look around you for inspiration. Those superstitious religious
who built it believed in miracles. Perhaps you'll find one yet.'
Her old eyes followed the pillars up into the shadowy traceries
above. 'I believe in no God and I hate the Catholics for their
oppression of our people, but I can admire their works. I am

also old enough to know that little happens in this world that is purely chance. You said the architect of this cathedral was the man in your book. It is possible he hid secrets within it, as he did in the mosque you were reading about earlier. You found that strange book underneath the church, didn't you?' She shrugged. 'Perhaps it was a sign.'

Pinzon sighed. First Tomas's 'magic'. Now Grandmother Juanita's 'sign'. As far as he was concerned, Samuel's book had already served its purpose. If he had had time he would have liked to know the outcome of the tale, but this might well be his last night on earth and he had no intention of spending it in the company of a medieval philosopher. And certainly not to satisfy the superstitious fantasies of those around him. 'Alas, I read enough last night, Doña Juanita,' he said, 'to know that it contains nothing of practical value. Anyway, the architect was driven away from the city before the end of the book so I doubt there'll be any more secrets to discover. Paladon disappeared. Those were the last words I read.'

'Disappeared? That sounds miraculous enough.'

'I don't think it involved any magic. He just escaped those who were seeking to kill him.'

'Isn't that what we, too, are trying to do, Professor?' Again, she touched his cheek. 'Good night, Señor. If you can't find a miracle, at least seek some peace.'

He watched her make her way back to her pew. She had to pass Paco to reach her place. He stood up surlily to let her pass, staring resentfully at Pinzon, who felt his eyes on the back of his head as he walked away.

A miracle? he thought. They had reached a grim pass if that was all they could rely on – but what else was there? What else?

An hour later, Pinzon was still awake. He realised, to his shame, that he was thinking as much about María as Tomás. He recalled with admiration how she had confronted Ogarrio.

What an example of courage she had been! What a woman! My name is 'vengeance'. How proud he had been of her. He tried to persuade himself that he was thinking of her as a younger friend in the classic Platonic relationship of teacher and brilliant student: mutually intrigued, she by his wisdom, he by the fresh ideas of her youthful mind, each benefiting from the other's experience. Or even as the daughter he had never had, on whom he could bestow affection as well as guidance. How well she would have got on with Raúl and Julia. They would have seen what he saw in her, admiring her free spirit and even her waywardness. From wherever they were now, they would welcome this friendship, knowing that, in his declining years, he had companionship and Tomás a surrogate mother.

But he knew he was deceiving himself. He was not thinking of her as a daughter or a friend. She was a woman who attracted him as a man. He could not forget the touch of her lips on his cheek, the perspiration on her hot hand when he had put his palm on hers, the swell of her breast against his chest when, briefly and accidentally, they had embraced, her smell— Oh, God, even her smell . . . Then he told himself he was being a fool. A pathetic one. She had given him no indication that she felt anything for him, except as a comforting companion in a terrible situation.

And it was that terrible situation he should be thinking about, not – not goatish desires! He looked down at Tomás's thin, serious face asleep on the pew next to him. That was where his responsibility lay, and each minute that went by emphasised how much he was failing him. He twisted and turned on the hard pew, trying to see a way out, any way out . . . but, like iron filings to a magnet, his thoughts kept returning to María. This time he envisaged her as a muse, whose indomitable example might inspire him to some brainwave. It was as pathetic a self-deception as before. He wanted her body in his arms, not her mind.

'Enrique?'

It was barely a whisper, but he sat bolt upright. She was standing in front of him wrapped in her blanket.

'I didn't think you were sleeping,' she said. 'I couldn't. I felt lonely lying on the other side of the church. I missed both of you. Would you mind if we sat together for a while?'

With a sinuous movement, she twisted herself into his pew. Before settling gently against him, she leaned over and brushed Tomás's hair from his eyes. The boy moaned a little and turned over. Pinzon felt a sudden pang. He had seen Julia make exactly the same gesture as she tended her sleeping son.

'María.' In his mind he tried to form the words.

She touched her finger to his lips. 'No, don't say anything. Let's just sit close together. We can . . . we can pretend, can't we, for a while, that that – that everything's all right?'

'Of course,' he said. She stretched up and pressed her lips to his. It was only a touch. Her finger had lingered longer, but afterwards she sighed and snuggled against him. Again he felt the roundness of her breast. 'I'm so glad you're here,' she whispered, and it turned into a yawn. She murmured something else. It might have been 'family'. Then he heard her regular breathing. She had fallen asleep.

He sat for a long time with his arm around her shoulders. Her hair tickled his cheek. He smelled the musk of her skin. He remembered Manuela, how on the long train journeys south she had also nestled against him, while Raúl lay in his basket on the seat opposite. After a while, he began to feel the same contentment. Just holding her was enough. He could not expect more.

Gradually, his mind wandered into the past. He remembered his house in Madrid, the long summer holidays, the time he and Manuela had taken Raúl to the beach in Málaga, and how he and the boy had made sandcastles while Manuela, swathed in silks and sitting under her parasol, had watched them, her plump cheeks shining like apples.

Paladon had disappeared . . . Suddenly the implications electrified him. The watchman had seen him go into a locked cave. There had been only one entrance in and no other way out – but he had not emerged. Could it be possible? Grandmother Juanita had told him she did not believe in mere chance. *You said the architect of the cathedral was the man in your book. It is possible he hid secrets within it* . . .

Miracles? His mind was racing. There were many kinds of miracle, and almost all were explicable when scrutinised by science. Paladon was a master craftsman. He had achieved his wonders in stone. Whatever else corrupted, stone did not. He had carved his own image in stone and left it, an everlasting sentinel over whatever secrets he had fashioned below.

He felt the hard edge of the book in his pocket, remembering as he did so the inscription on Paladon's sarcophagus. The enigmatic biblical quotation. *Ask, and it shall be given you; seek, and ye shall find; knock, and it shall be opened unto you.*

Gently he lifted María and settled her on the pew next to Tomás.

He looked around. Everybody was sleeping, or seemed to be. Felipe was again leaning against his pillar. The rifle lay on the paving and he was snoring.

There were still three more chapters, thought Pinzon. It was only just past one in the morning. Three chapters. Three hours. Dawn came at about six. There would be time . . .

He felt a buzz of excitement – the same as he had felt as a young man when he had tried to seek historical truth in unreliable medieval chronicles and suddenly saw patterns unfolding among the words. It was a matter of following the clues.

And Grandmother Juanita had given him a clue . . .

He knew what he was looking for.

Al-Andaluz 1086–91

Codex VI

The Crusaders

(I) In which I tell how a philosopher is offered a pot of nitre and a physician heals himself

'Did you ever hear the story of al-Razi and the fat woman?' ibn Sa'id's voice creaked out of the darkness.

It was so weak after more than a year of imprisonment that I had to strain to hear it. With an effort I drew my attention away from the spider that was crawling up my thigh. I hadn't the energy to shake it off. 'I think so.' In our state of hunger, speech was an effort. 'But tell me again,' I added, because I did not wish to offend my old teacher. And there was another reason to keep conversation going, however banal: only by talking could we tell if the other was alive.

Still chained to the wall, we were slowly wasting away. So much so that the gaolers had changed ibn Sa'id's irons three times to accommodate the shrinking of his wrists and ankles. The last time they had come, they found that one of his hands had fallen out of its manacle. The gaolers had glanced at each other. The older of them had lifted the arm and, without even a blow or a curse, slipped it back through the metal ring.

'A man and his wife went to al-Razi's surgery,' he said slowly, carefully articulating each word. 'They wanted to consult him because the woman was barren.' He paused, getting his breath back or his thoughts together. Our conversations were usually punctuated by long intervals of silence.

My mind wandered back to the spider. I wondered if it was

poisonous. I decided I didn't care. Our naked bodies were already so covered with pus, sores and half-healed scars from old beatings that another insect bite would hardly make a difference.

'He examined the woman, then asked for her birth sign so he could consult the astrological charts.' There was another long pause. 'As is the right and proper procedure, I believe.'

'Yes,' I said. 'You would definitely check the patient's horoscope.' I found myself blissfully recalling happier days with Dr Isa in the hospital. That was another good thing about conversation. It helped you remember who you once were.

My reverie was interrupted by a piercing scream from another cell. Ibn Sa'id sighed. 'Poor soul. We're very fortunate, you and I, Samuel.'

'Yes.' The rack was a refinement of punishment that he and I had been spared. I doubted that Aziz wished the gaolers to hear what we might reveal under duress. 'Who do you think it might be? There can't be many Christians left.'

'Let us be hopeful, Samuel. Perhaps the brutes are turning on themselves. That sometimes happens in revolutions and *coups d'état*. Recall the account of the revolt in Corcyra written by . . . written by . . .'

'Thucydides,' I said.

'Dear, dear, my memory . . .' His voice petered out. We waited in the deep silence, but the scream was not repeated. Soon the insects became emboldened again and there was the familiar patter and splash as rats scuttled over the wet stone floor. Life had returned to normal.

Ibn Sa'id continued his story: 'When al-Razi had completed her horoscope, he told the woman that he could probably make her fertile, but there was little point because the astrological charts stated quite clearly she'd be dead in four weeks. Saturn ascendant in the dark quadrant of Venus. The woman was a Libra born under the influence of Cancer.'

'You can't argue with the stars,' I grunted.

'That was what al-Razi told his distressed patient before he asked for his fees.'

I faded in and out of the anecdote. The worst aspect of hunger is not the constant throbbing pain in the intestines but the lassitude that literally unhinges the rational capacities of the mind. What amazed me was ibn Sa'id's absolute refusal to succumb to reality, treating our dank dungeon as if it was a literary salon, maintaining civilised conversation even as our minds and bodies were dying. I did not like to look at him any more when the guards brought in lamps to change the straw or give us our bread and water. When I did, I was always saddened. A straggling white beard hung over an emaciated rack of ribs on which hung, like rags, folds of dry, loose skin that had once been his belly. His cheeks had sunk inwards. My old teacher had become a living skeleton, his head a skull. I preferred the darkness when his voice, weak as it was, could still make me imagine that the gargantuan ibn Sa'id of old was beside me.

'Samuel, are you listening to me? I was telling you that the fourth week was approaching. Desperate with fear, the poor woman waited at home for death – she couldn't eat, she couldn't sleep. But death didn't come. Five weeks passed, six, and she was still living. Husband and wife were understandably furious. They stormed back to al-Razi, enraged at the misery he had caused them . . .'

I began to giggle uncontrollably. Oscillations of mood from despair to unwarranted elation are often symptoms of the later stages of malnutrition, the next being madness. 'Ha-ha,' I chortled. 'They wanted their money back. Ha-ha – al-Razi had read the horoscope wrong.'

'Yes, he had – but deliberately so,' said ibn-Sa'id. 'Al-Razi admitted the error, then told the man, "But observe your wife. Think of all the pounds of fat she's lost."' He, too, began to giggle softly. Our feeble convulsions of nearly silent laughter set the chains rattling gently like a bell brushed by the breeze.

'He said . . . He said . . . al-Razi said, "Examine her vagina and you'll find the fatty folds that were blocking it are no longer there. The way is clear. Go to it tonight, my man, and you'll find she'll bring forth a healthy child."'

Like a couple of bats in a cave, we hung on our chains and squeaked with mirth.

'Perhaps I should be grateful to Aziz,' giggled ibn Sa'id. 'Like that woman, I'd never, ever have dieted unless a good physician had forced me to. I feel . . . I feel . . .' He mumbled something I did not catch. I heard the slump of chains. He had fainted. I waited, recalling the spider. I could not feel it now, but there was a new pain in my groin. It must have bitten me and gone.

Chains rattled. Ibn Sa'id was awake again. 'How rude of me. I'm sorry, Samuel, I wanted to tell you how I feel after my treatment.'

'How do you feel?'

'Svelte – positively svelte.'

'That was . . . that was . . .' My head was swirling. I guessed I had been weakened by our laughing fit.

'I didn't hear you, Samuel.'

'. . . generous of Aziz,' I said. 'Maybe he should have been your doctor and not me.'

'Keep your spirits up, Samuel. Think of al-Razi. He knew the power of . . . of the mind. I am . . . astonishingly . . .'

'Astonishingly what, Teacher?'

'Astonishingly encouraged, when I think about it. It makes me – optimistic. You can explore the whole universe, but our own minds remain the ultimate mystery . . . I am sure if God dwells anywhere it is in the human brain. You – you and Isa with your investigations into madness are on the edge of a mighty ocean of discovery, Samuel. I envy you.' He groaned and began to wheeze in short, rapid breaths.

I was suddenly alarmed. 'Teacher?' I cried. 'Are you all right?'

'Oh, yes. A little tired, that's all. I . . .' The wheezing transformed into something like a chuckle. 'I was thinking of a brimming glass of hot mulled wine. That's what I usually take before one of my afternoon naps. Dear Samuel, would you consider it rude if I . . . absented myself for a spell? I thought . . . it might be pleasant . . . if I took . . . a little doze.'

'You rest. That was . . . a good story you told.'

'Thank you, my boy,' he murmured. 'You are . . . a fine companion to have in . . . adversity.'

I was relieved when, a few minutes later, I heard his breathing compose itself into a regular pattern. I was glad for him, because the discomfort of our contorted positions made sleep difficult. Mercifully, exhaustion bestowed its balm on us from time to time, and we would wake stronger. I suppose it was the sound of those soft snores that lulled me, too, into a deep sleep.

I dreamed of the three of us sitting at ibn Sa'id's feet in the old days. In my dream, ibn Sa'id ignored Paladon and Aziz, concentrating only on me. 'Keep to your philosophy, my boy,' he told me. 'You are the best of my pupils and I rely on you to keep this pot filled.' In the dream he was holding the flagon that he had smashed on Aziz's head during the wedding ceremony. He poured its contents over my hands. What came out was not nectarine juice but pure red wine. Its rivulets trickled over my skin and glistened in the kaleidoscopic reflections of the sun's rays coming over the mountains and irradiating the king's terrace with light. 'This is celestial nitre,' he said, 'the spirit of wisdom. The more you pour, the more remains, but you must keep hold of the pot, Samuel. Hold on to the pot. Then you will have justified my pride in you. Here.' He passed the silver flagon to me, while Paladon and Aziz clapped. I looked up to thank him, but he had gone, leaving only a rumpled impression on the cushions, and a scatter of crumbs on the grass.

When I woke again into the darkness of the dungeon, I could no longer hear breathing beside me, or the tinkle of chains.

Eventually the gaolers came with their torches, and I was able to confirm that my old teacher had died in his sleep. I like to think that mysterious dream was his last message to me.

I was not lonely after his death because he returned soon afterwards, fully restored to his former shape, hennaed beard, turban and all. On his visits he brought ample supplies of food. He laid his surprises on the carpet in front of me, then toppled back on to his cushions, chuckling at my delight. He and I shared chicken legs and quails' eggs for breakfast, great shanks of lamb for lunch and dinner, and at all hours of the day bowls of seasonal fruits and the choicest assortments of confectionery that Hassan himself had made for him as once he had for Harun al-Rashid in his famous emporium in Baghdad. I rarely felt hungry now. The gaolers had to force-feed me their dry crusts and stagnant water. At first I resisted. What need had I of bread and water when a banquet was ready for me whenever I desired? Ibn Sa'id advised me to go along with them. 'Take it as medicine, my boy, and I'll give you a carafe of sherbet and fresh figs afterwards to banish the taste.'

We had tremendous discussions about all aspects of natural philosophy. He would read to me the latest extracts from the great compendium he had finally found time to complete in his new home. He said his task had been made much easier because whenever he had a question he could consult al-Razi or ibn Sina in person. Sometimes he would bring them to join our debates, as well as Ptolemy, Aristotle, Dioscorides, Galen and others. Hermes Trismegistus came one day and set up his alchemical equipment to demonstrate to me an easier method of creating the philosopher's stone.

Often my cell was so crowded that I wondered how the gaolers managed to jostle their way through the crowds of chattering sages.

I was embarrassed once when, unexpectedly, my father and Elijah came to visit me just as Ptolemy was finishing a debate with al-Farghani about the rotational velocity of the celestial spheres. He did not agree with some of the theories of the Arab astronomers and the two scholars were busily scratching star charts all over the dungeon walls. Elijah thought such studies to be heretical and was soon fiddling menacingly with his staff. Inevitably an argument resulted and it took all of ibn Sa'id's and my diplomacy to make peace between them. Just before he left, my father looked tenderly at me, stroked my legs and murmured, 'I'm so proud of you, Samuel. So very proud. You are everything I ever wanted you to be.'

I was relieved to hear it because I had felt guilty about abandoning him in his declining years. I was also grateful when ibn Sa'id brought Salim along to tell me that I had fulfilled his expectations and done well by his son in difficult circumstances. 'I knew I could rely on you to do the right thing, Samuel,' he said. 'Aziz will appreciate it, too, in time, and come back to you.'

My days and nights passed happily in illustrious company. I don't think I had ever been as intellectually satisfied in all my life. It was occasionally frustrating because, being manacled to a wall, I was not able to make notes or to write down the new theories and inventions that my own stimulated powers of reason were daily generating. At least I was no longer troubled by physical discomfort, for by now I was living entirely in my mind.

The first day ibn Sa'id failed to appear, I was bored and the itching, torn muscles and insect bites manifested themselves again. On the second day I was alarmed. The bread and water I was fed tasted foul because there was no sherbet to follow it. The third day I began to yell and rattle my chains in the darkness.

'I'm afraid you've only me for company now,' said an apologetic voice.

'Isa?' I looked up and saw him standing in front of me. He was modestly dressed in a black doctor's gown. His careworn face observed me with a shy smile. 'How can you be here? I thought you were treating soldiers.'

'I was.' He sighed. 'I went with Prince Aziz to the wars. They decided they had no need for doctors, or not Christian ones. I became an infantryman. I wasn't very good at it, I'm afraid. I couldn't forget my Hippocratic oath. There was a big battle. In front of a castle.' He shrugged. 'And here I am.'

'You're dead too?'

He did not answer me directly. He approached where I was hanging, examined me and said gently, 'Those are terrible sores, Samuel. You must be in great pain. I wish I had the means to relieve your discomfort, but sadly I have no remit to do so.'

'Remit?'

'Yes.' His gentle eyes surveyed me. 'I'm only allowed to treat your insanity, I'm afraid.'

'I'm not insane.' I was outraged at the idea.

'No. Perhaps not entirely,' he said softly. 'You called me here. That's a very encouraging sign.'

'I did no such thing,' I said. 'If this is ibn Sa'id's idea of a practical joke, you can go back and tell him it's in poor taste.'

'I can't do that. Not unless you conjure him here, and I don't think you want to do that any more.'

'What are you saying? That ibn Sa'id's a figment of my imagination?'

'What do you think, Samuel?'

'I know that patient tone of yours, Isa. It's the one you use on madmen.'

'Is that what you think you are?'

'Very well,' I said. 'If you wish to play games, let's bring a little logic into this, and scientific observation.'

'By all means.'

'Well, look at that wall over there. Below the astronomical charts. Who do you think drew those mathematical equations? The gaolers? It's ibn Sa'id's handwriting. He did those calculations only four days ago. Now tell me he's not real.'

'I'm afraid I can't see anything on the walls, Samuel. I can't even see the walls. It's pitch dark in here. I don't think you can see anything either.'

'I can see you,' I said.

'What do you think I'm illuminated by? The physical eye perceives objects reflected to the pupil by an outside source of light – but we are in a dungeon, deep in the bowels of a mountain, and there is no light. Granted you see me, because otherwise we would not be having this conversation, but is it not more logical that I am a creation of your inner eye, the eye of the imagination that perceives objects in dreams? In which case, would you not deduce that I and ibn Sa'id, if he were here, are phantasms created by the workings of your own brain?'

'And why would I wish to conjure phantasms? I am a philosopher and scientist trained to observe only what is real.'

'May I remind you of something you told me once when you argued with me that madness can be a form of rationalism in certain circumstances? If reality became intolerable or unbearable, would it not be rational for the mind to protect itself by escaping into another reality?'

'Then I have you,' I said. 'There is a flaw in your argument. Granted, life in prison is intolerable. A rational man might want to escape into a delusional state. Granted, too, that that may be what I have done. In which case, since my circumstances have not changed, why should I then conjure you to bring me back to a life that is intolerable? It would not serve my self-interest, would it? I would be better off remaining mad.'

'I am merely here at your pleasure, Samuel. You could easily wish me away again. Would you like me to go?'

I felt a longing to see ibn Sa'id. I had an aching hunger for his reassuring company, not to mention Hassan's confectionery. I wanted to be rid of Dr Isa, who disturbed me. As I thought harder about ibn Sa'id I saw a glimmer at the other end of the cell. His round figure was taking shape, a carpet rolled under one arm, a covered wicker basket of food hanging from the other. As he became more substantial, so Dr Isa began to fade and soon all that was left of him were his sad eyes and his sympathetic smile.

Another figure was forming behind ibn Sa'id, a portly man, with an unkempt beard and dressed in a loose Greek toga. With a thrill of pleasure I realised that this must be Socrates, who had never visited me before despite my repeated pleas to my teacher to introduce him to me.

'There, Samuel, you have congenial company again,' said Dr Isa's voice. 'If you greet them you will be happy for the rest of your life. I cannot offer you such happiness. I can only bring you back to the world as it is, not what it should be. Make your choice quickly, though, because if I go now, you will never again be able to recall me.'

And suddenly I was shaking in a state of terror. 'No,' I muttered. 'Stay. Please stay.'

Socrates vanished. Ibn Sa'id began to fade. Before he disappeared he gave me a nod and his most benevolent smile, as he had done when I was a boy and had answered a question correctly in his class.

Pitch covered my eyes again. I heard the scratching of rats. I smelled the cesspit stink of the gaol. My stomach gnawed with hunger and my arm stung with a new insect bite. I slumped on my chains and wept.

'Was that so very hard, Samuel?' I heard Dr Isa's voice inside my head.

'Yes,' I sobbed. 'Yes.'

'Do you think it was the right choice?'

'Yes,' I said, 'though I will miss him.'

And that was how I began to cure myself of the madness brought on by the loss of my companion and teacher. It was a long, slow process, with many relapses, but Dr Isa, or the part of my mind that manifested itself as him, was always patient with me, and helped me through.

He departed as modestly as he had first arrived. 'It's better I go, Samuel,' he said, after several months had passed. 'Your mind is strong again. You have demonstrated an extraordinary will to survive. That is why you're still alive. There's nothing more I can do for you. You should face the world without me now.'

'If I conjure you, will you come to help me again?'

'A sane man doesn't conjure ghosts, Samuel.'

'You said you were only a figment of my imagination, not a ghost,' I said.

He gave me his sad, enigmatic smile. With a wave of his hand, he was gone.

I never saw him again. I never saw the real Dr Isa either. I found out afterwards that he had been slain in the siege of Aledo, just as he had described and at exactly the time when his phantasm first appeared to me in my prison. That is something I have never been able to explain.

Neither did I understand why, only a few hours after my imaginary doctor had judged me sane again, I heard the murmur of many voices in the corridor outside. The doors of my cell opened with a clang, and when my eyes had become adjusted to the glare of the torches, I recognised Janifa, who had come, with King Abu's permission, to release me.

The timing seemed more than coincidental. No philosophy that I have ever studied could explain it.

(II) In which I tell of a prince's dilemma and a king's festivity

Wrapped in a blanket, I was fed a chicken gruel, and when I was strong enough to hobble, I was taken to the harem where Janifa had ordered the great pool to be made steaming hot for me. Her girls wept in shock at my emaciated state. I probably disgusted them. There were no giggles this time when I shared a bath with them. Yet because of their old affection for me they washed me tenderly, and when they judged that every living maggot or tick had been parboiled and the filthy water was draining away, two of them shaved off my beard, and every other hair on my body, while three others bound my wounds, smeared ointment on my sores and talcumed me from head to foot. When they had given me new clothes Janifa, having put on her cloak and veil, led me to the king's chamber, where Abu was waiting for me.

'My poor dear Joseph,' he exclaimed, as he waddled over to embrace me. I noticed he had aged and both his legs were bandaged. Clearly nobody had been bleeding him for his gout. 'How I have missed you. You can't imagine how many doctors have been through my palace since you left, but none was as good as you. None. I'm so glad you're back.'

'I was never far away,' I said, pointing at the gleaming blue and white tiles on the floor that covered the dungeons far below.

'No.' His eyes widened and his fat lips trembled with alarm. 'It was a terrible misunderstanding. Terrible. When I think of what we owe you . . .' His words ended in a mumble of embarrassment.

'I have told the king everything, Samuel, and he is very grateful to you,' said Janifa. 'Even Aziz now understands that what we tried to do was for the good of the kingdom.'

'Aziz?' I asked in incredulity. I had assumed that if I had been released then Aziz must have been removed. 'He's still wazir?'

'Very much so. He is our saviour,' said Janifa. 'Aziz came back last week from the wars. He used his troops to replace the so-called government that was ruling in his absence. He executed the vilest and imprisoned the rest. Ephraim was not the worst, as we discovered to our cost. The creatures that serpent made Aziz install in high positions were more terrible than their paymaster. His death and Aziz's absence freed them to pillage the state as they pleased. Don't be hard on my brother. Those villainous clerks made the king a prisoner in his palace and forced him to sign his name to laws that were wicked and cruel. While you were in your dungeon, the rest of us were living under a reign of terror. I was confined like you, but I heard of things that were unspeakable. Extortion, rapine, not just of Christians, but also Jews and Mussulmans. They imprisoned the chief faqi when he protested. Respectable women were kidnapped and subjected to monstrous indignities unless their husbands paid ransom, while the taxes imposed on the common people made it hard for them even to find enough food. And there was nothing anybody could do about it because the secret police that Ephraim had appointed looted the streets they were meant to patrol, and committed murders as they pleased. Oh, Samuel, you cannot imagine what went on.'

I stared at her. Should I be grateful that my two years chained to a wall had somehow spared me this?

'Anyway, Aziz changed that,' she went on cheerfully. 'He rid us of our scourges, then made a public announcement from the qadi's office, declaring an amnesty for all the Christians and anybody else those brutes had persecuted. And – and, Samuel, there is hope again in Mishkhat. Old wounds are healing. Aziz has allowed any Christian to leave unmolested if they wish to – of course, it was they who suffered most and many are still bitter but some have agreed to remain, a sign that Mishkhat may return to what it once was. Aren't you pleased, Samuel? It means that we have achieved what we struggled for.'

'It is convenient for Aziz to have scapegoats to blame for the misery his ineptitude created in the first place,' I said.

'Oh, come, Joseph,' said the king. 'I know you have suffered but be a little forgiving. My great-nephew was young, inexperienced and very badly advised. He's a different man now, and he has made up for his mistakes. After all, this amnesty . . .'

'With respect, Your Majesty, your great-nephew's amnesty won't bring ibn Sa'id back or any other of his victims.' I did not care that I was standing in front of the king. I was too angry. I might have been restored to sanity, but I was not composed enough suddenly to let bygones be bygones. 'And, Lady Janifa, you may remember that one of the things we were struggling to do was to save your great-niece from an unspeakable marriage. Does the reformed wazir's amnesty stretch to the benighted seraglio in Marrakesh or wherever Ayesha is wasting what remains of her life?'

At the mention of Ayesha, the king and his sister exchanged a look in which I saw panic, grief, fear and, above all, guilt. I suddenly had a terrible intuition. 'Where is Ayesha?' I demanded.

'Oh, Samuel,' moaned Janifa, while the king looked away. I felt a chill colder than the prison cell I had just left.

'She took her own life,' I said, feeling the energy drain out of my body.

Janifa began to weep. It confirmed what their look had told me. Ayesha was dead.

'The marriage to that desert mongrel never took place,' muttered the king. 'At least she was spared that abomination.'

I turned my back. I had nothing to say to them. All the joy I had briefly felt on my release had vanished. Slowly and stiffly – I was still very weak – I made my way, step by step, to the door.

'Joseph, where are you going? You can't just leave an audience without permission. I'm the king – and I need you as my physician.'

I turned. 'My name is Samuel, Majesty. It always has been. And I am going to where my services are really needed, to the only innocents left in Mishkhat – the madmen in the hospital whom I doubt anybody has treated since your great-nephew took their doctor away from them. Another crime not covered by any amnesty. Excuse me.'

'Samuel,' wailed Janifa, 'at least talk to Aziz. He can explain everything to you. He's waiting to see you. He wants your forgiveness.'

'He is the wazir. If he wants me, let him send his soldiers to the hospital to arrest me.'

I left.

Falteringly, I made my way down the mountain. I had to stop and rest several times before I reached my mother's house. It was boarded up. I collapsed on the step. A neighbour took pity on me. She took me to her home, fed me, and put me to bed. Next morning she told me my mother was dead. Tabitha, she said, had spent many months trying to find out what had happened to me. She heard eventually from a cousin of one of my gaolers that I was incarcerated in the palace. She tried to bring me food, but was turned away. She tried again, and was beaten. She continued to go to the palace every day with her basket of food, bowing to every official who passed through the gates. She became a figure of fun. Sometimes she would be kicked; sometimes she would be thrown a coin. She continued to plead to see me. One winter morning she was found frozen to death under the snow-covered branches of a thorn tree. A Jew was in the party assigned to take her body to the rubbish dump outside the walls, where dead beggars and vagrants were usually thrown to be eaten by dogs. He recognised her and told Rabbi Moshe, who arranged a proper burial for her. Now she lay next to my father in the Jewish cemetery.

Once I had discovered who held the keys to the house, I spent many days sitting in my mother's kitchen or in my father's library or on the steps to the pig pen in the cellar, looking at the dusty and cobwebbed alchemical equipment. Then I was angry with Dr Isa. I wanted my parents to come to me so I could fall down on my face in front of them and beg their forgiveness – but they never did.

My kind neighbour continued to feed me until I was strong enough to go to the hospital. The doctors were wary of me. They knew I had high connections in the palace, and the costly clothes that Janifa had given me awed them. I did not have to say anything. I waited patiently while they argued themselves into giving me my old job back.

Aziz did not bring soldiers. He came alone.

I had just changed night shifts and was making my way from the insanity ward to the refectory. Moonlight was washing through the arches and deserted corridors, leaving pools of silver on the tiles. As I passed the outpatients' hall, I noticed a solitary figure sitting on a bench. I stopped in my tracks. Although he was wrapped in a heavy cloak and a hood covered half of his face, I knew instinctively who he was.

He stood up. His hood fell back. I expected the familiar features to be the same as when I had brooded over them in my cell, sometimes with anger, sometimes with hatred – always, to my shame, with longing – but they had changed. The smooth forehead was creased with worry lines. There were deep clefts at the sides of his mouth, and the once brilliant black hair was flecked with white. Even the short beard he now wore was grizzled. The eyes no longer gleamed. They were tired and preoccupied. Aziz was no more than twenty-eight, my own age, but he looked forty.

I should have seen justice in the fact that suffering and remorse had lined his face to become a mirror of my own, for any beauty I had ever possessed had been scoured away in the dungeon he had put me in. Yet so irrational is love that, despite the bitterness that raged inside me at the man whom I blamed for the deaths of my mother, Ayesha and ibn Sa'id, I felt sorry for him. I wanted to embrace and comfort him. I had to stop myself running forward to clasp his hands.

'Is there somewhere we can talk?'

It was a matter-of-fact question but his voice was still as musical as I remembered, and it moved me as it always had. Disgusted with the weakness of my will, I indicated the empty courtyard behind him.

'Yes, this is private enough. Will you walk with me, Samuel?'

I wanted to say the words I had rehearsed: 'Apologise if you feel guilty and be done with it. Leave me to my work. I am finished for ever with palaces and princes.' Instead I answered, 'If you wish.'

We circuited the square in silence. The eaves and chimneys made dark stripes across the moonlit sand. Aziz's head was bowed in thought. His first question surprised me. 'Do you believe in redemption of sins?'

'The scriptures promise it,' I said. 'If a sinner repents, Allah is expected to be compassionate and merciful, as is Jehovah. I'm not sure that man is always prepared to be.'

He glanced at me nervously. 'I'm not asking for your forgiveness, Samuel. I don't deserve it, and I would never expect it. I – I wasn't thinking of myself. Do you – do you remember the Cid? How he was convinced that God was with him when he fought? You – you once said he might be touched by divine madness.'

Again I was surprised by the course of the conversation. 'If the Cid came to me today as a patient, I would diagnose him as a madman with a fractured soul that manifested in multiple personalities. I would suspect a pathological fear of death for which he compensated with a delusion of immortality. Why do you ask?'

'I've spent the last two years with armies who believed the same thing – that God was with them – and, Samuel, they weren't insane. They were humourless, single-minded and terrifyingly in control of themselves. The Normans we captured after the battle of Sagrajas went to their executions with satisfaction on their faces, like those monks I burned. Just by fighting in what they considered a holy war, they believed they would go straight to heaven, with free remission of their sins.'

'What are you saying? That your burnings of those pathetic monks were justified because you later met fanatical crusaders?'

'No.' A look of pain crossed his features. 'I regret what I did here. I would have done better to listen to you. I should have locked up Jaime and the others as madmen. My hastiness and ill-considered decisions will always be on my conscience, but – I wanted to say that the Mussulmans who defeated those Normans, and later beheaded them, were no different from them. They worshipped another God, but they had the same fanaticism, the same desire to make holy war, the same belief that if they lost their lives fighting the infidel they would become mujahideen, guaranteed a place in heaven. And they were equally sane, Samuel. Joylessly, tediously sane.'

'You're talking about the Almoravids? Your own side?'

'Yes. I fought two campaigns with them. They were deadly in battle. I've never seen anybody like them. When we surprised Alfonso at Sagrajas, boys rode on donkeys beside them, setting the pace with the deep beat of their drums. The Almoravids marched steadily towards the enemy in their blue burnouses and turbans – no armour. They were in neat ranks, chanting prayers, levelling their long spears at the enemy. Their discipline was extraordinary. They swept everything before them. I think they really believed there was a divine force that made them unstoppable. Their front ranks were scythed by Christian archers and crossbowmen. Those behind just picked up the long spears and stepped over the bodies of their slain comrades without a glance at them, without a pause in the beat of the drums or a break in the chant. The Christian knights attacked them again and again. They calmly skewered the horses, leaving the knights to be despatched by the javelin men behind. It was nothing like the Cid's glorious, irresponsible charge. They were implacable. They killed quickly and efficiently and slowly marched on. They hardly seemed human.'

'I'm still not sure what you're trying to tell me. It sounds as if you had a strong ally. You beat the Christians. Wasn't that good for your *jihad*? For Andaluz?'

Aziz's features twisted in perplexity. 'I – I don't know, Samuel. Yes, of course we were allies and shared what we believed was a common goal – to throw back Alfonso who is a threat to

Islam. But King Yusuf didn't do that. He slaughtered the Christians on the battlefield and let the rest of them go. He could have annihilated Alfonso and his whole army. We had the combined forces of Seville, Granada, Badajoz, Mishkhat – probably a bigger army than al-Mansur wielded in his day. Yusuf refused even to use us. I thought he was keeping our cavalry in reserve so we could pursue the enemy once his Almoravids had broken them – but instead, when the Christians were streaming off the field and we were ready to charge, Yusuf's messengers told us to dismount and join him in a prayer meeting to thank Allah for his victory. Our men, who hadn't lifted a sword all day, had no option but to go down and join the Africans, prostrating themselves where they could find a space among the corpses.'

'What are you saying? None of the Andaluzi armies took part?'

'No, Samuel. It was as if he was putting on a demonstration of the Almoravids' strength. He seemed more interested in cowing us than the Christians.' He shook his head, disturbed by the memory. 'Al-Mu'tamid of Seville was having none of it. He disobeyed orders and charged off with his two thousand horsemen. He harried the fleeing Christians all the way to the river, but Alfonso had recovered by then and formed a strong rearguard. If all of us had been pursuing we'd have smashed it and gone on to Toledo, but al-Mu'tamid didn't have the strength on his own. When he returned to camp, he showed his disgust by piling the Christian heads he had gathered outside Yusuf's tent. He left with all his men the next day and returned to Seville. He was the first of us to be disillusioned. Yusuf responded by ordering another prayer meeting of the whole army, in which he called down Allah's wrath on al-Mu'tamid's head for cowardice and impiety.'

'For somebody who was not allowed to fight, you managed to lose a lot of men.' The futility of what he had described had wakened in me a more recent anger. When I had arrived at the hospital I had found a ward full of wounded soldiers whom Aziz had brought back with him, every one maimed in hideous ways. It was like a charnel house. Yet, from what they told me, they were the lucky ones. Two-thirds of the army that had set out two years before had never returned.

'You know how to wound me, Samuel,' said Aziz, quietly. 'I feel the loss of every Mishkhatid as an empty space in my soul. Yusuf did not want to share the glory of his pitched battles, but he was content to let Andaluzis die when it suited him. In the following campaign we attempted to take Aledo, on Alfonso's southern border. He'd fortified it, knowing it would block our advance to Toledo. Yusuf's desert warriors didn't know much about siege works, or they found the business of sapping, mining, building towers and operating mangonels and trebuchets demeaning. It did not suit their idea of holy war. The skill involves planning, staff work and patient grind, while Yusuf prefers to ride on the breath of God. So he left this aspect of modern warfare to the Mishkhatids and the Granadans. That was how I came to lose half of my men. Ignominiously, wastefully slaughtered before the walls of that damned Castilian castle we'd spent a year trying to invest.'

His eyes were blank and inward-looking. He seemed to be talking more to himself than to me.

'You've never been in a siege. You'd find it hideous. Mud, boredom, disease. So close to the enemy you can't avoid their arrows and molten lead. Inching forward with your trenches and tunnels. Vicious little battles under the earth because the enemy are digging their counter-mines against you. It might have been different if Yusuf had supported us – but he didn't. He held court in an airy camp on a nearby hill, daily sending his sons to report to us Allah's displeasure that we were making no progress. Well, eventually my Mishkhatids mined one of the walls. We sapped a great pit underneath it, and when we burned the wooden supports, a furlong's stretch collapsed in a pile of masonry and dust. The way was open. All we needed were the Almoravids to storm through our breach – but Yusuf decided not to attack. God told him that the signs were inauspicious that morning and he kept his army in its tents, fasting and praying. My brave men were massacred by a sally in force, and by noon the Christians had refilled the breach. We had to start all over again.'

He stood silently, clenching his fists. I could sense his seething anger in the deep breaths he was taking. 'Six months afterwards, Yusuf ended the siege. God had told him that the impiety of the Andaluzi kings made further campaigning pointless. Next day we were ordered to march south. That was when I became disillusioned, too, and with what men I had left, I returned home. Yusuf, as far as I know, has gone back to Africa, but he's left his army behind him under the command of his sons. They're in Algeciras, which they've taken as their fief, watching the border with Seville. I think they consider al-Mu'tamid to be a greater enemy than the Christians. See what it's all come to.'

I wondered why he had chosen me as his confessor. I felt I was being used and spoke savagely: 'So you never became friends with Yusuf, or indispensable to the Almoravids?'

He stared at me. 'What do you mean? Oh, yes. I remember. You were there, weren't you, when Ephraim was advising me to take advantage of my opportunity, as he called it? Well, you've a right to throw that in my face. I was naïve. Then so were all of us – al-Mu'tamid, abd Allah, the other kings who thought we'd found a champion to protect Andaluz.' He turned towards me, his eyes like ash. 'The Almoravids are not like us, Samuel. They're alien. Yes, they're Mussulmans, good ones, I suppose. They're always quoting the Qur'ān. The chief faqi would love them. Rolling out prayer mats is almost part of their weapons drill. It's – it's their God who seems different. We share the same rituals and He has the same name, but He's not the merciful, compassionate Lord I've worshipped all my life. He's certainly nothing like your Prime Mover. Their Allah is hard, implacable, unforgiving, a terrible God of war, a jealous, intolerant God, demanding self-denial, submission, sacrifice.

'Another thing. We spent two years with them without our soldiers even fraternising. You can't talk to them. All you can see are their eyes behind their face cloths, and they're hard and appraising, like those of moneylenders calculating what you're worth. They despise us, hate us, and they don't disguise it. Yusuf treats even our kings like dirt. It's not just because we drink wine, or appreciate poetry and music. They think we're weak and one day will be their prey. For the last two years I've had the uncomfortable feeling of a mouse paying audience to a cat, watching its claws.'

'Perhaps King Alfonso feels the same way about the crusaders and churchmen he's enrolled to help him. People like Elderic.'

'I don't think so. He's just using them. He's cleverer than we are or more powerful in his local domain. I find in a strange way that Alfonso's like one of us. Andaluzi. Part of our world. I've even come to respect him. He's our enemy but he knows us, thinks like us. I've heard he treats the Mussulmans in Toledo well. Allows them to worship in their mosques. Uses Mudejar designs in his churches. He's even set up academies so his people can share our learning. The Almoravids are completely different. They have no culture, only a relentless fanaticism. They scare me. Yusuf's playing a game with us – and I don't know what it is. I'm worried, Samuel, worried for Mishkhat.'

There was a long silence. Eventually I said it. How could I keep it back? It was foremost in my mind: 'And this was the man for whom you sacrificed Ayesha. Damn you, Aziz, damn you to hell.'

Aziz's face hardened. He strode forward three paces and, with his back to me, muttered, 'I told you I'm not here to ask for your forgiveness. My crimes are my own to expiate. I don't want to talk about Ayesha.'

'What about ibn Sa'id and Paladon?' I was weeping. 'You threw them away too.'

He turned and spoke coldly. 'Paladon is not dead, though he might as well be to us. I don't know how he escaped, but he did and has resurfaced in the court of Duke Sancho. Remember the boy who came on the Christian embassy? After his father died at Sagrajas, he persuaded Alfonso to give him a fief in southern Toledo so he could take the war forward against the Mussulmans. Paladon's with him now, on the borders of Mishkhat, plotting his revenge. Curse me for ibn Sa'id. Curse me for Ayesha, if you like, but don't blame me for Paladon. He's an apostate Mussulman. He's worse. He's a crusader. He's joined Sancho's other Frankish mercenaries – and he's one of my most pressing problems because my spies tell me Sancho leans on him as a counsellor.' He punched his hand, in a gesture extraordinarily like Paladon used to make when he was distressed. 'And I will never forgive him, Samuel. Never. He's a mortal enemy. Do you know what he did? I don't know how or when – she refused to tell me – but he debauched my sister. Oh, I was the laughing stock of Andaluz when I offered her to Yusuf because he sent his old women to inspect the prospective bride. At the banquet next day, in front of all the other Andaluzi kings, Yusuf, with exquisite politeness, made me drink a toast with him in the disgusting camel's milk that's all they consume. He thanked me for my generous offer. Then he rejected it, saying it was the custom in Africa for kings to marry only virgins. You can imagine the response to that round the carpets and tables. And when, humiliated, I returned to our tents and confronted Ayesha, she laughed at me, too, and told me she'd been Paladon's lover, behind my back, for years.'

Oh, Ayesha, I thought, while he shuddered and passed a hand over his eyes, had you so little desire to live? In horror I realised that my earlier intuition had been wrong. She had not taken her own life – or not directly. She had deliberately taunted her brother until he had exercised his right under Mussulman law to avenge his shame. I remembered what Janifa had once told me: fratricide ran in the family. I sank to my knees. 'Oh, you monster, how could you? How could you have . . .?'

He stared at me. He seemed about to say something but held back, only whispering: 'I told you I do not want to talk about her. What's done is done.' He began to pace again. Suddenly he fell to one knee beside me and looked urgently into my face. 'Samuel, I know we can never again be friends, and I demand nothing of you, but consider coming back to the palace. The king misses his Joseph. Janifa loves you and your absence hurts her. And I – I need your counsel. You are the only honest man I know and – and if you hate me, that's all the better, because I'll know you won't be flattering me.' He leaned forward quickly and kissed me, then hurried away, fumbling with his hood.

I was left in a pool of moonlight, longing for shadow to blanket my grief.

In time I succumbed – I could not bear to be apart from Aziz.

It was not honourable. I despised myself for giving in to my weakness. I had not forgiven him. I never would – but neither could I prevent myself loving him and, cruel as his deeds had been, he was all that remained to remind me of the Brotherhood of the Craft and the happy paradise in which I had grown up.

I was torn for a while by the thought of leaving the mental patients, but I knew that with Dr Ali, once Dr Isa's bright assistant, now mine, they were in competent hands. Anyway, I would visit regularly and continue Ali's training. Also, I was unwelcome in the hospital. For all Aziz's amnesty and the new propaganda of reconciliation, many doctors remembered I had been Dr Isa's friend, and because they had harmed him, they now hated me. I knew that they would be relieved to see me go.

Three weeks later I found myself toiling up the steep path to the palace, a slave following with a small box of my belongings. The king received me warily but soon warmed when he understood that I had not come to extort compensation. Then he became generous, offering me this diamond, that piece of land, a beautiful German boy, a sinecure as keeper of the royal aviary. I refused his presents, saying I would be happy with the same salary I had had before. Only then did he relax and embrace me as his old physician. Pathetically grateful, he led me to his chamber where, to his immense satisfaction, I bled him till the bowl overflowed. I did not massage him. That was beyond me now. I had lost the strength in my arms and there was a residual numbness in my fingers, known only to those who have hung in manacles for a long period. The king seemed happy enough to submit to Dr Ali's sensitive hands, as long as I was there to supervise. He was careful not to call me Joseph, but he never did remember my real name. I didn't care. For me he was just a patient I despised.

I was welcomed by Janifa and the girls in the harem, and soon my life, as far as its external details went, differed little from what it had been before, but I felt miserable within, remembering those I had loved and who were gone. Also, although the ghostly Dr Isa had pronounced me cured, there were times when I continued to doubt my sanity. From time to time I still heard voices. I never saw or heard from ibn Sa'id or Dr Isa again, let alone the symposium of philosophers who had been my companions in prison: it was Ayesha who haunted me now.

Sometimes I would be tending one of the concubines and I would hear her lute and her soft voice singing a lullaby or a love song. I would turn towards the alcove in the harem where she used to sit but, of course, it was another who turned her perplexed face to me. Sometimes the music was so clear that I asked whoever I was treating, could they not hear it? Their faces would pale and they would stop in the middle of whatever story they were telling me. Eventually Zubayda and two other girls told me I must cease my joking because I was frightening them. So I never mentioned it again. But I continued to hear the music and the singing, and once I heard the wail of an infant. Then I knew I was imagining things. There were no children in Abu's harem. How could there be? He was physically incapable of producing them.

When I was ready, I went to see Aziz in the wazir's office. Gone were the flocks of acolytes who used to hang around the vestibule. There was only a grey-bearded secretary who ushered me in. Aziz, dressed in a simple jellaba, sat at a table piled with papers. When he saw me, he threw down his pen and embraced me. 'Thank you,' he said. 'Thank you. You have mended a small part of my broken heart by coming to me.'

He led me to the carpet, settled beside me and began immediately to speak about matters that concerned him. King Yusuf's sons had annexed Granada, sending King abd Allah under guard to Marrakesh. They had declared formal war on Seville and King al-Mu'tamid was rumoured to have despatched an embassy to King Alfonso in Toledo, proposing an alliance against a common enemy.

I stopped him and asked why he was telling me these things. I was only a physician and could not advise him on affairs of state.

'I know that, Samuel. I have my own advisers, experienced ones – King Abu's generals whom I have recalled, some of his old councillors whom I retired. All I want from you is a moral check. Is what I am doing right or wrong, wise or foolish? I don't want to make mistakes again. I trust your honesty and your instincts. I have written to King Yusuf condemning al-Mu'tamid. As you know, my sympathies are with al-Mu'tamid, but Yusuf is the greater threat to Mishkhat. It seems I have to dissemble. Am I wrong?'

'No, Aziz. You are being a statesman, like your father.'

'Thank you,' he said. 'That's all I wanted to know.'

He picked up another document. 'Now, the matter of Sancho's crusaders on my border. They have taken to raiding our territory. Our fortresses and garrisons are strong enough to throw them back, but we'll need money and men if we are to repel a full-scale invasion. Our army and our treasury are depleted. I will be forced to put up taxes, and perhaps reimpose a draft. That will be unpopular, but I see no help for it. What is your view?'

And so on. We would meet two or three times a week, and he would explain his problems and ask my opinion of his decisions. I don't think I once opposed him or offered an alternative suggestion, but he appeared satisfied. I was no more than he had said he wanted: a moral sounding board. At first I was touched by his trust in me, and later moved when I saw how much he had changed. It occurred to me one day that Salim would at last have been proud of his thoughtful and hard-working son. He might also be pleased that he was consulting me as that had always been his wish. And then I was saddened the more. This had come so late and at such cost.

One morning, about seven months after I arrived in the palace, I went to Aziz's office and found him trying on a new coat of chain mail. The silver frills he had once affected were gone. It was a ringed hauberk that any man of arms might wear. He was practising lifting his sword arm, and the armourer was adjusting the tightness of the rings around his shoulders to ensure he had enough movement.

'Samuel,' he said, 'we must limit our talk today. We've had word that Sancho is massing troops on the border. I will be leaving shortly with the army. There'll be no fanfare. I don't want to panic the city. Almería – yes, our old enemy – is coming in on our side, and we should outnumber the Castilians. I've put Generals Haza and Kabir in command. They're my father's men and both are reliable and experienced. I'm counting on bringing Sancho's Normans to battle. If we can entice their army into the open we should beat them. I hope to be back in three or four weeks, if all goes well. Will you wish me good fortune, Samuel?'

I wondered what I could possibly say to encourage him. I was in a state of shock. My first thought was that Aziz and Paladon would be on opposite sides in battle, and would certainly attempt to kill each other if they met. I knew also that this was the one area where, as a moral sounding board, I was useless, for Aziz's hatred was too deep, and I suspected Paladon felt the same. 'Look after yourself,' was all I said.

Aziz's white teeth flashed in his old smile. 'I intend to risk neither myself nor my army. And, if it's of any consolation, I shall not seek out old enemies. This is no time for private feuds.'

'Thank you, Aziz,' I said.

'Dear Samuel,' he said, 'my oldest, truest friend.' The very words that Paladon had last said to me struck a hollow in my heart. 'I'll be relying on you in my absence. I want you to look after the ladies and the king. A calm court will make a calm city. I don't want to hear of any lurid scandals while I'm gone.'

He was affectionate, teasing and in the highest spirits.

The next morning I got up at dawn and watched the dark shadows of the horsemen file down the rock. There were no trumpets, no drums. A ground mist absorbed them before they reached the bottom. One by one I watched their hazy figures disappear.

The Christians ambushed our army in one of the mountain passes. It was well within our own border. By any reasonable logic, no enemy should have considered the long ravine to be a weakness in our defences. It should not even have been accessible. High precipices rose up on either side. There were strong castles at each end of it. Yet somehow they had discovered a goat track that avoided them, and were waiting, concealed on ledges and behind rocks, when our unsuspecting army approached.

Aziz might have taken precautions had he recalled a summer

excursion during our boyhood when Paladon, he and I had roamed those same mountains. Paladon had stumbled upon a goat path and raced us to the top of the peak. Aziz did not remember. Paladon had – and had told Sancho about it.

Our men had no chance to retaliate. The Christian archers were hidden in the rocks high above and slaughtered Aziz's men in a rain of arrows. Later the Norman knights swept through with their cavalry. By then most of our horses were maimed. There was little resistance.

I heard about it when I was in the hospital helping Dr Ali with a new patient, a man who refused to eat because he believed the end of world was coming and did not want any impurities inside him when he was called on Judgment Day. I heard a tap on the door and, irritated, opened it, intending to tell whoever it was to come back later. I was amazed to see an old man in a workman's smock. I recognised him. He had been one of Paladon's stonemasons on the mosque, and was a member of the small group who had been ordered to keep the great enterprise going. Starved of funds and direction, they had not achieved much. The half-finished dome had barely progressed.

'I'm sorry to disturb you, Master Samuel. I have a message for you. Rather mysterious, how it got here. The mosque is mostly locked now, since the building work stopped. No one can get in or out and I'm the only one with a set of keys. I keep 'em in this pouch on my belt, and I can swear no one's tampered with them. King's property. Value it like my life. But when I went in this morning for my daily check, there, just by the mihrab, on the fancy floor tiles, was this piece of sealed parchment with a ring of white stones all round it. Lord knows how it got there. I thought I was imagining things. Fairies or sprites. Nothing was there yesterday. Anyway, I saw writing on it. I've been taught letters, so I was able to make out your name with a message saying it was urgent and had to be delivered to you immediately.' He lowered his voice almost to a whisper. 'And I recognised the hand, sir. It's Master Paladon's – I've seen it on his drawings a thousand times. Well, I thought I'd better be careful, him being a traitor. Maybe I ought to take it straight to the qadi's office. Then I remembered how Master Paladon had always been kind to us, and . . . and so had you, sir, that time there was the rock fall and you set all those bones . . . Anyway, I hope I've done the right thing bringing it to you.'

From behind me I heard the madman calling, 'Doom! Doom! Lo, the messenger of doom approaches.'

'Thank you,' I said, and gave the stonemason three dirhams from my pouch. 'Keep silent about it.'

'Thank *you*, sir,' he said, his eyes glowing.

My heart beating with excitement, I excused myself to Dr Ali, and when I was alone in the dispensary, I tore open the seal. There were only a few lines.

Samuel, may God go with you.

If you haven't heard already, you will soon. There's been a battle and Aziz was defeated. We couldn't find his body among the slain, so perhaps he survived. If you see him, tell him I will find him, for we have an account to settle.

But never mind that now. We are a half-day's march from Mishkhat. I've ridden ahead. I must go back before my absence is noted. In future, when things calm down, we can communicate in the old way with messages under the first milestone, but now you are in danger. The sack will be terrible. These Normans are brutes.

Get out of the city. Take Janifa, ibn Sa'id, Dr Isa or whoever is dear to you, but leave now, for we will be upon you shortly. Sancho has no love for you. He remembers your alchemical experiment and will try to burn you as a sorcerer.

Leave now, my dearest friend. Go with God.

Paladon – or Yasin, in memory of Ayesha, and so you know this is genuine

I left the hospital immediately. The city was still quiet, but just before I reached the marketplace, I was jostled aside by a troop of horsemen. Their mounts were lathered, and the hauberks of many were bloody. The arms of some were in slings; others had bandages round their heads. 'All is lost,' one was yelling. 'Our wazir is slain. Flee if you can.'

The result was predictable. Panic. Women screamed for their children. Men hauled goats and sheep from their stalls. Overloaded carts blocked the way to the city gates. Fights started between crazed, frightened citizens and others began to loot the shops that had been deserted, taking all that they could carry. The sack of the city began even before Sancho's Normans arrived.

When I reached the road that led to the palace I had to push against a jostling procession of slaves and servants, who had also heard the news and were fleeing for their lives. A knot of guardsmen tried to stop them. They were overwhelmed by the sheer numbers and hurled off the cliff. I slipped past. When I reached the palace there were no guards at the gates. The halls inside were deserted, except for the occasional corpse, and in the throne room, three drunken grooms were making free with the king's wine. Outside Aziz's office, his grey-bearded secretary was quietly sifting papers at his table, burning some in braziers and leaving others in neat piles. He nodded politely to me as I passed.

In the gardens that separated the main palace from the harem, even the peacocks seemed to have fled. I entered the carved alabaster doorway. Here there were guards, three enormous Nubians, leaning on executioners' scimitars. One grinned and beckoned me to pass with a gesture of his thumb.

King Abu was seated in a chair in the bright hall that once I had used as a sick ward. He was stark naked, as were Zubayda and some of his other favourites. Zubayda was sitting on his plump knee, her beautiful face a mask. Her pupils were dilated, as if she had been drugged. With one chubby hand Abu was fondling her thigh; with the other he was holding a tall silver goblet from which he was abstractedly sipping wine. His other concubines, all one hundred and ten of them, were sitting cross-legged in silent rows on the huge Persian carpet. When they sensed my presence, their long necks and dark eyes twisted nervously in my direction like those of startled antelopes. Some were shaking with fear.

'Joseph,' I heard Abu's slurred voice. 'Damned if I can remember your real name, but welcome. We're having a last party. Join us. Look, all the girls have glasses in front of them. Get one for yourself. We'll be drinking each other's health soon, before we say farewell.'

I noticed then that a small cup of wine had been placed before each concubine. Traces of white powder on the carpet and the faint smell of almond told me what they had been laced with. I glanced towards my dispensary next to the pool room. The door chain had been hacked apart.

I pleaded with him: 'There's no need for this, Your Majesty. There's time to escape. You have a secret way out. We could all go together.'

'What? My chickens clambering up rocky paths? It would be a diverting sight.' He rolled back his head and laughed. 'But no, Joseph, I'm too old and they're too pretty.' He leaned back in his chair and contemplated his women fondly. 'Those brutish crusaders would round you up, wouldn't they, my doves, my darlings? Better to leave on a happy note, remembering the taste of good wine, beauty, a song or two, a last bout of love-making. Don't you think, Joseph? We shall die as we've lived. For the glory of Mishkhat.'

I looked wildly around the room. If there were only two guards, there might be a way to overpower them. Then I heard a whimper from the direction of Janifa's room. Through the curtains I could make out limbs on the bed, heavy black ones over a slim white body. More Nubians were there. As my eyes adjusted to the dim light I saw the scimitars of those waiting their turn.

Abu had followed my glance. He laughed again. 'Tips to

faithful servants, Joseph. One or two of the girls volunteered to show them what Paradise has in store for them. They deserve a reward, the poor fellows, since it will be their hard task in a little while to help everybody take their drink. They won't be coming with us. They've sworn to die in the way they prefer, defending our tomb.' He gave me a sympathetic smile. 'I know what you're thinking, but don't spoil things by making a scene. It'll only end with your head on the carpet and everybody upset. Leave us a little dignity. The girls have agreed. They know what'll be in store for them otherwise. Zubayda, my rose, tell him.'

The royal favourite raised her chin proudly. I could see the faint scar on her cheek where I had operated on her carbuncle. 'I am a lowly concubine, slave of our good lord the king, but he has made me feel like a queen.' She had started hesitantly, but now her voice rang with passion. 'That is how I have lived. I will not die the plaything of an infidel and barbarian. I fear death – oh, how I fear it – but I fear shame more. My lord has promised that it will be quick and painless, like taking a sleeping draught. You will know, dear Samuel. You have always been our good doctor. Is that so?'

I lowered my eyes in assent.

'Then I am joyful. Do not grieve for us. It is better this way.'

Sick at heart, I saw several of the others nod. One or two began to weep, and their companions reached out, pressing their hands to give them courage. Abu was looking at Zubayda tenderly. 'Thank you, my dear,' he said. He pressed his lips to her breast. She shivered a little. Her expression remained no less solemn, but her brilliant green eyes smiled at him. She raised a languid arm, tinkling with bangles of amber, and gently stroked his bald crown.

I saw there was nothing I could do. I told the king I had a message for Lady Janifa and asked where I could find her.

The king waved his goblet. 'Oh, she's probably hiding down that secret passage you're not meant to know about. She and her wards.' He chuckled. 'You didn't know about them, did you, Joseph? Another secret. We have so many.' He sighed. 'I would have liked to see my mosque completed. It's the only thing I regret. I blame you, Joseph. I'm sure you were well intentioned, but you interfered in matters that didn't concern you. I was angry with you for some time. That was why I kept you locked in the dungeons, even though my gout was killing me. Anyway, it's all in the past now. Be off with you. Save your life if you can. And if you see my great-nephew, tell him I died like a king.'

I found the secret door behind the hanging. I hurtled down the stone stairs, crashing and falling, chafing my knees. I came to the door of the room in which Paladon and Ayesha had been married. It was locked. I banged with my fists on the heavy iron, the echoes clanging down the tunnel. I screamed, 'Janifa! Janifa! It's Samuel!' There was only a ringing silence. I slumped against the stone wall, exhausted and in despair. If Janifa had left already, I would never find her.

There was a loud click and the door creaked open. A heavy figure was silhouetted against the light. I felt the prick of steel against my throat. As the door swung further, candlelight revealed the features of the man with the sword. I recognized the short grey beard and the leathery cheeks of General Haza. 'Wazir,' he called, 'it is the Jew.'

Aziz's voice answered. It sounded unnaturally weak. 'Bring him.'

My collar was twisted by a mailed fist and I was thrown bodily inside the room. The door banged behind me and there was again the rattle of the lock. I found myself on my hands and knees on the same carpet where last I had stood at a wedding. I looked up as Janifa slumped on her knees in front of me. 'Oh, Samuel, you found us.' I saw alarm in her eyes.

I looked beyond her. Aziz was lying on a sofa. His hauberk was crumpled on the floor. His naked upper torso was wrapped in bloodstained bandages. The shaft of a broken-off arrow protruded from his shoulder. A veiled woman was dabbing his forehead with cloths she had dipped in a silver bowl of water.

Aziz chuckled. 'You're remarkable, Samuel. We were just saying we needed to find a doctor and here you are.'

'You're alive,' I whispered. 'They were shouting in the marketplace that you had been killed.'

'Not yet,' he said. He was smiling, but I saw in his eyes the concern, or perhaps embarrassment, I had just noticed in Janifa's.

The veiled woman turned. As she did so, a tiny boy with blond hair peeped out from under the sofa where he had been hiding.

I thought I had gone insane again.

For when the veil dropped, it was to reveal the wide smile, the mole on the vellum-like skin and the brown-speckled eyes of Ayesha.

Codex VII

The Cave

(I) In which I tell how two Jews met a naiad and a ghost and how one was offered a job by a cardinal

Everybody knows the legend of the fall of Mishkhat: how the lustful Norman and Frankish knights, hot with killing, went hallooing through the echoing marble of the palace in search of its fabled harem; how they followed the lure of perfume and found in a silent hall the sleeping king and all his ladies seated in precedence of rank in their richest clothes, golden goblets clutched in their dead hands, pride and triumph on their wax faces, hauteur in their empty eyes. Minstrels sing of how the Christian knights, the blood of the Nubians still dripping from their swords, froze, awed and frightened before the silent majesty of death; how, one by one, abashed and troubled, they turned away, chastened by the power of Allah.

I am told that poets recite the tale in courts as far away as Baghdad and Cairo. It would not surprise me. As castles, towns and territories fall daily to the crusaders – in Sicily, in Asia Minor, in Syria, in Palestine – it must be tempting for Mussulmans to seize on King Abu's last act of selfish hedonism as a stirring example of how moral victory can be snatched from defeat.

Personally I doubt that the murderous Christian knights were remotely affected. More likely, they set to with those bloody swords, hacking at pretty necks to get at the emerald and topaz chains, or chopping fingers the more easily to snatch diamond rings.

We saw the extent of the sack after nightfall as we made our way cautiously down the goat path from the hidden door. The Mussulman and Jewish parts of the city were burning. Great billows of fire were erupting from the dome of the town mosque. It collapsed as we watched. Welling up through the blazing night, the shrill screams of women pierced the thunder and crackle of the inferno, echoed by the drunken laughter and the coarse jeers of the conquerors. We could also hear thinly, from the churches in the Christian Quarter, the Latin chants of monks.

The road leading up to the palace was a procession of wagons, loaded with gold, silver, silks, furniture and all the other booty the Christians had collected before they consigned the houses to the flames. On one cart, suddenly silhouetted by sparks rising from the burning mosque, I saw the seven branches of a menorah looted from one of the synagogues. The veteran soldier whom General Haza had assigned to help me along the path – he was a Jew – had tears running down his cheeks.

We moved silently. Haza had ordered his men to bundle their hauberks so they would not jangle and give us away. The women, the child and I were carried on strong men's backs. The general did not want to risk our clumsy footing setting off a rock fall. Behind us, four soldiers were skilfully steering over the boulders and ledges the stretcher to which the unconscious Aziz had been bound. It was dangerous to move a patient in his condition, but we had had no choice. It would have been certain death if we had remained.

I had had the presence of mind to bring my medical bag and I had operated successfully on him, removing the arrow and cauterising the wound with one of my potions made from the universal Elixir. I was reasonably optimistic. Aziz's fever was low and there was no sign yet of serious infection. Janifa had wanted him to rest in the safe room until he showed signs of recovery, but I whispered to Haza that Paladon was with the enemy: he knew the secret of the path and the hidden door.

The general understood the threat and ordered our immediate evacuation. I took the extra precaution of drugging Aziz with poppy juice, in case he awoke and let out a cry of pain that might alert our foes. As I did so, I noticed that Ayesha was watching me strangely, almost hungrily, but there was no time to wonder about that now, or at the greater mystery of how she happened to be alive, or why the charming, mischievous smile remained on her face even in our perilous situation. The only imperative was to escape.

We would not have done so had it not been for the bravery of General Haza.

At the bottom of the hill a company of his soldiers were waiting with horses. Frowning anxiously, they pointed through the thickets at the road, and I despaired. Our way out was blocked. Six armed knights were sitting on their horses in a circle. They were drinking wine from looted silver flagons and laughing as one of their number had his way with a young Arab girl in the mud, next to a dead man, perhaps her husband, his throat slit. The others were ironically imitating his grunts and the girl's sobs and cries. As we watched, the crusader on the ground finished with her. Another dismounted, throwing him his wine flagon, and took his place between the spread-eagled legs.

Haza's face was grim with anger. 'She is of good family,' he muttered to Janifa, 'you can tell by the quality of her clothes, and I knew the dead man. His name was Achmed bin Talif and I have yet to pay him for a breeding stallion he recently obtained for my stables. The time has come to honour my debt.' He gestured for his captain, and whispered his orders.

Moving quietly, his men readied the horses, stroking their heads to keep them quiet. Janifa, Ayesha and I were given mounts. The Jewish soldier who had been helping me down the hill held the child in front of him. Aziz's limp body hung across the captain's saddle. The men who had come down the mountain donned their hauberks, while the others continued to pacify the horses.

When Haza had briefly prostrated himself in full armour and helmet in the direction of Mecca, he drew his sword and inspected our little troop. 'Ride east. Ride as fast as you can to the hills. If Allah wills, I will meet you on the ridge near the village of Green Waters.' He put his foot into his stirrup and mounted in a single fast movement. Pausing only to adjust his shield, he levelled his sword and charged, yelling, '*Allah Akhbar!*' The rump of his horse disappeared through the thicket. Immediately there was the ringing of steel, the crash and neigh of a tumbling beast, alarmed shouts and the grate of more steel on steel.

By then we were moving fast, the thorns scratching our legs, and suddenly we were in the open, hunched in our saddles as we made our wild escape at full gallop. I caught a glimpse of Haza swinging his sword and a knight falling. Soon, the cries and the noise of combat faded and we were riding away from the glare of the burning city, hearing only the thundering hoofs beneath us.

A day later we were still waiting anxiously at the top of the path that had led us up to the small village that was our rendezvous high in the hills. Paladon, Aziz and I had hunted deer there one summer and I knew the area quite well. Armed only with slings, we had failed spectacularly to kill any animal but had enjoyed a swim in the clear spring that had given the village its name. We had lounged naked in the hot sun afterwards, no doubt offending the devout villagers but not, apparently, one shepherd girl, with whom Paladon had spent a pleasant hour in a nearby olive grove.

I had little time to consider such bucolic memories because I was fully occupied with Aziz. The strain of the ride had increased his temperature: he was feverish, and a little delirious. Ayesha helped me change his bandages while her son played hide and seek with the Jewish soldier among the olive trees. She still wore the same inane smile. I found out why when she whispered confidentially to me, her eyes radiant and imploring, 'Samuel, dearest friend, have you a little of the poppy juice you gave Aziz?'

I grasped the truth: Aziz had not been merciful. He had found another way to punish her for the shame she had caused him. He had told me only half of it. King Yusuf's old women had not just discovered the lack of a hymen. The mare Aziz had offered was in foal. That was the humiliating fact with which King Yusuf had taunted him at the camel-milk banquet, embarrassing him in front of the Andaluzi kings. Mussulman law would not permit Aziz to slay a pregnant woman because the life inside her was innocent so he had devised a worse hell for her. He had made her a drug addict. He had kept her with him all this time, isolated, indulging her habit. No wonder Janifa and the harem women had preserved the secret from me even when, on occasions, I had heard her singing. Such scandal in a royal family could be revealed to no outsider.

I had Aziz's half-conscious body in front of me. I hated him then. My whole soul cried out to avenge this innocent girl. I had the means to do so. My medicines were in my bag. Everyone would have thought he had died of his wound. I was tempted, oh, so tempted, but I stayed my hand. What would be the point of another murder? I remembered the look of affection between brother and sister when she was bathing his head in the safe room only a few hours earlier. Who was I to take God's role and dispense death? I also recalled what Aziz had said to me in the hospital: 'My crimes are my own to expiate. I don't want to talk about Ayesha.'

Then I understood why remorse had lined his forehead. His regret and his subsequent kindness to her had come too late. I saw what my task had to be. I was a doctor. I had two patients I loved. I could mend wounds. I could reduce cravings. I could even cure the insane. I swore – kneeling in that stony field among the burned husks of the last harvest – that I would do so, not for Aziz but for Ayesha and her son, whose name I did not yet know, and for his father, Paladon. And perhaps also for me.

For the moment I could only indulge her habit. 'Yes, Ayesha,' I said. 'Of course I have poppy juice for you.'

'Oh, sweet Samuel,' she murmured, her greedy eyes on the vial I extracted from my satchel.

Later, when Aziz was asleep and Ayesha was dozing, lost in her dream state, I asked her, 'Do you ever think of Paladon now, Ayesha?'

Her eyes blazed. 'Don't mention him, Samuel. If you love me, don't ever say that name again. I hate him – hate him. My brother told me he's become an apostate and our enemy, and – and he is married again, to a fat Christian whore. Aziz told me. A fat, ugly, horrible Frankish whore. Whore!'

I nodded sadly. 'Calm yourself, Ayesha. I won't speak of him. I was really thinking of your son – how beautiful he is.'

Her eyes gleamed and the radiant smile returned. 'Oh, isn't he?' she murmured drowsily. 'Isn't he adorable? My sweet little boy. My treasure. My Yasin.'

As she spoke the name, I knew at last why Dr Isa had come to me, and why I had returned to the world. It was because I had a duty to perform that only I could accomplish. I swore another oath, calling as my witness the divine fire of the Prime Mover that illuminated the rolling clouds, glittered on the high mountain peaks and burned yet in the pale orb of the autumn sun. I swore that one day I would restore this family, and our brotherhood, whatever alchemy it took.

At that moment, a shout erupted from the lookouts on the rocks. 'He's coming. He's coming. He's alive!'

I ran to them and saw two riders moving slowly across the plain far below us. The tall, erect figure on the Arab pony was General Haza. In one hand he held a lance from the tip of which fluttered the pennant of Mishkhat. With the other he was leading a Norman charger. A woman was slumped in the high saddle, her head resting forward against the mane. She was wrapped in the general's long cloak. We cheered until they disappeared under the steep slopes and crags that hid the mountain path they had to climb.

When they rode into our makeshift camp, the soldiers mobbed them, running by General Haza's horse, touching his feet and stirrups in their admiration and obeisance.

He came to a stop and observed the ring around him. He smiled. 'I am glad that you are safe. I was worried about you.' He saw me. 'Doctor,' he asked, 'how is the prince?'

'He is doing as well as can be expected. I think he will recover.'

'Praise be to Allah.' He indicated the woman. 'I have another patient for you. Her name is Khalisa. She is in shock. Treat her well, for she is of honourable birth. The insult committed on her body is one for which she cannot be blamed. She remains pure.' He turned a fierce face to his men. 'Let all of you remember that. God has given me the honour of avenging and expiating her shame. I have also repaid the debt I owe her husband.' He raised a small leather pouch. 'And here is the coinage.'

He up-ended the bag, and what at first I took to be chickens' giblets fell to the ground. Then I recognised them to be the genitals of six men. Without dismounting from his horse, he spat on the bloody parts, and waited. One by one his men mounted their horses, and as they passed, spat too. Finally the woman, Khalisa, waking from her trance, her eyes glinting with hatred, moved her horse to them and, with a quick movement, tugged the reins. The charger reared and its front hoofs stamped the bloody remnants into the earth. Her piercing ululation chilled my blood.

'So will we avenge them all,' cried Haza. 'From now on there can be nothing in our hearts but *jihad*. First, we move to the high passes. There we will restore our strength. When more men join us, we will return to Mishkhat. *Allah Akhbar!*' he cried, drawing his sword.

'*Allah Akhbar!*' The hillside rang with the cry. It startled a flock of pigeons, which flew towards the distant mountains of the south.

The wind in the passes blew bitter gales all winter and the snow drifted sometimes to the height of a man. In the shepherd's lodge that General Haza gave us, Aziz, Ayesha, Yasin, Janifa and I huddled together, like a peasant family, for warmth. There was always an icy draught hissing through the cracks in the planks but, relatively, we could be thankful. At least we had a roof. That made our humble dwelling palatial compared to the ruins and sheep pens in which the soldiers were billeted.

Since Haza kept most of the men out on patrol, we had no servants, only David, the Jewish soldier, whom the general, before he left, appointed Aziz's bodyguard. The brunt of the work therefore fell on Janifa. She adapted to it extraordinarily well, enjoying the novelty, and perhaps because it appealed to something that had lain dormant in her throughout her pampered life: a craving for simplicity. She would cheerfully carry water from the spring, cook, sew and clean. Wrapped in her shawls and stirring the cauldron bubbling on the fire, she did not resemble a royal princess. She relished the work. Her cheeks coarsened, like the skin of cider apples, and her hands were red, like crabs. David offered himself as her manservant, and became very quickly her inseparable friend. I would smile as I watched them happily set off down the white pastures to collect logs and kindling, he with an axe over his shoulder, she with a basket, chattering like a fishwife.

I would have helped if Aziz had not taken so much of my time – his wound festered and he eventually developed pneumonia. It needed all my skill – medical, alchemical and astrological – to save him. In his delirium he would rave about his lost kingdom, blaming himself. 'Mishkhat, my throne . . .

What have I done?' His eyes would open wide as plates and he would raise himself on his elbows, his body shaking. Ayesha would patiently wipe the sweat from his brow and soothe him to sleep again.

With Janifa's agreement, I was also attempting a withdrawal treatment on Ayesha. Over the first two months I gradually reduced the dosage of the poppy juice, and then I stopped it altogether. That was a terrible fortnight. We had to send young Yasin with David to sleep in his shack. When we tied Ayesha to the sturdy bed we had made for her, she screamed, vomited and cursed with such foul oaths that Janifa believed there was a devil inside her. She tied round Ayesha's neck a peasant's talisman, a locket full of herbs and crumpled paper on which was written the Buduh, a magic square consisting of potent numbers and mystical letters drawn from the Qur'ān. She told me it would ward off the evil eye. I had no objection. In our way we were conducting a sort of exorcism, not just of the addiction: there were deeper laid devils inside all of us that we exhumed over those short winter days and long nights.

By the spring, Aziz was up and moving about, and Ayesha, now cured, was herself again, though silent and withdrawn. Her body was healed but it would take time for her to come to terms with what she had been. I had expected her to be angry with her brother when she remembered what he had done to her. Ironically, because of the recent illnesses they had shared, she had grown closer to him. She would spend hours with him, the two sitting together by the fire, blankets round their shoulders, watching Yasin playing with Janifa and David. Their mental wounds were too raw for them to talk about the past, and certainly there was no mention of Paladon. That would come, I thought, in due time, when they were ready. Then perhaps I could help. I still had Paladon's letter, with its instructions on how to contact him. For now there was reconciliation of sorts. I clung to my hopes. I persuaded myself that this nadir of our fortunes had a benign purpose, and nightly sought confirmation in the stars.

We had seen little of General Haza, who had set up his camp in an abandoned village on the mountain slope opposite ours. It had originally been in worse condition than our poor cottage – the buildings there, unlike ours, were roofless shells. That was why we never complained. The conditions in which they passed the winter must have been intolerable, and it is to Haza's credit that he lost no men to frostbite or disease. He lived there with Khalisa, the woman he had rescued.

The gossip in the camp was that they were lovers because they shared a tent, although I am sceptical that this was so. I suspected that the general, whose world had collapsed around him like everybody else's, saw in this strong woman a new light to guide his life. Her hatred for those who had violated her had woken inside her an insatiable desire for revenge, which she had sublimated into a frenzy of *jihad*. Haza probably venerated her as a saint or martyr, who embodied the call to faith that proved so intoxicating for men who had lost all, who blamed the sins of their kings and princes for their predicament and sought to vindicate themselves in holy war. Whatever motivated her – whether she was Haza's lover or not – she was a malign influence, and it did not bode well for Aziz.

David, who sometimes rode there, told me she ruled the camp like a queen. News had spread across the Mishkhat plain of a centre for resistance in the mountains. Refugees came, men, women and children, and also many soldiers. One day we heard that the chief faqi had arrived, as well as three former ministers. Soon General Haza, in Aziz's name, was presiding over a government in exile, as well as a small but expanding army. When the snows cleared, he began to make raids into the plain. Sometimes they would bring back Normans or Franks as captives. Haza would interrogate them before handing them over to Khalisa and the other women. On those nights we heard the screams echoing across the distance that separated our camps.

David did not like going there any more. As a Jew, he felt an outsider. 'My comrades have changed, Samuel,' he muttered once to me, when I was helping him gather firewood.

'What do you mean?'

'In the old days, religion didn't matter. We were soldiers of Mishkhat and proud of it. Now my Mussulman comrades shun me. Conversations stop when I pass. Even my old friends, men I've fought with side by side in battle, avert their eyes. I avoid conversation. I go to the storehouse and tell them what I need, then return here.'

Angrily, he snatched up some kindling and viciously hacked off the dead leaves with his knife. 'They remind me of the Zealots in our histories. They call themselves mujahideen and have taken to wearing green scarves wrapped round their mouths. The chief faqi has persuaded them to build a small mosque, but they don't need it. Wherever I look, at any time of day, there's a prayer mat out and somebody prostrated on it. The other day I thought I'd bring back a barrel of wine for the prince – they captured cartloads of it on their last raid. Well, there wasn't any left in the store. I found out General Haza and the chief faqi had held some ceremony and poured it out onto the ground. They said alcohol was evil, their religion banned it – and the whole camp cheered. Samuel, these are soldiers and Mishkhatids – and they no longer drink wine.'

I felt a chill in the pit of my stomach. I remembered what Aziz had told me about the Almoravids. But I did not wish to tell David of my foreboding. I tried to change the subject. 'Aziz is not the prince any more,' I said. 'He's the king.'

I understood why David had forgotten it. Since nothing in our circumstances had changed and Aziz was living with us in such intimacy, we had taken time to get used to the idea. There was no joy in his elevation because of the tragedy that underlay it. When the first refugees had brought rumours of Abu's death,

Aziz had refused to believe them, but the torture of Christian knights had confirmed it. One day Haza and the chief faqi had ridden over to collect Aziz and Janifa. They had held a coronation in a cowshed in front of the army, and afterwards Aziz had formally appointed Haza as his wazir. Ayesha, David and I had not been invited. When they returned Aziz and Janifa were morose, clearly disturbed, but neither had wanted to talk about whatever was troubling them. Since then Haza, accompanied by a squad of cavalry, had called on our little homestead once each week. Aziz and he would wrap themselves in cloaks and walk in the meadow. Aziz would always come back depressed. For a day after he would sit at Ayesha's side in moody silence. No one dared disturb him.

'Well, perhaps he should behave like a king,' growled David, 'assert his authority. He's well enough now, isn't he? If he doesn't, we'll be ruled by puritans and fanatics.'

'I'll speak to him, David,' I said. 'But watch your tongue.'

A gust rippled the undergrowth, and I shivered, not with cold but with fear.

As it happened Aziz wanted to talk to me. He was waiting for me by the woodpile when David and I returned to the camp. 'Walk with me, Samuel.' I knew by his tone that it was a command.

'Haza has just been here,' he said, when we were in the meadow. 'He wants you to go to Mishkhat with a secret message.'

I laughed because I thought he was joking. Then I saw the serious set of his brow. 'To Mishkhat? Is he mad? Why me? And what message? For whom?'

'Paladon,' he said. 'You are to bear a message to Paladon.'

I stared at him.

'Haza's spies tell me he's working on the mosque – only it won't be a mosque any more. Duke Sancho has ordered him to erect a cathedral on top of it. Haza thinks that if you can find a way to reach him he will listen to you because of your past friendship. He might then give the message you will be carrying to Sancho.'

'What message?' I asked.

'That Haza intends to make a raid on the castle the Christians are building near Green Springs. That it will be a larger raid than usual, involving our full force. You will tell him the day we intend to attack, and the place where we will be gathering. You will describe it in such a way that Sancho will realise it is an ideal place for an ambush. You will be very convincing. You will even have stolen a map, with details of Haza's strategy, numbers of our men, how they will be deployed, everything. Once he's seen that, Sancho will not be able to resist the opportunity to march out against us with his whole army, so that he can destroy us once and for all.'

'And why would I be so stupid as to walk into Mishkhat when I know that Duke Sancho has put a price on my head, and what on earth would impel me to betray my country anyway?'

'This is a ruse, Samuel.'

'Of course it is,' I said. 'Unfortunately it's so transparent that anybody would see through it and know immediately that Haza wants to bring the Normans and Franks out into the open so he can spring a trap of his own. Isn't that what it's about?'

Aziz looked at me with surprise. 'Yes – our men are fewer than theirs but well armed and trained. Haza believes that if we can bring them to battle in a place of our choosing we can defeat them and drive them out of Mishkhat.'

'Our force can only number a few hundred men and the Christians have two thousand, but putting aside inconvenient military reality, why would Paladon believe me? Or Sancho, for that matter. They're not fools.'

'Sancho will believe it if Paladon tells him the information came from a Jew, and you in particular,' said Aziz. 'Jews are treacherous by nature, and you are a sorcerer, in league with the devil. You'll betray anybody if it's to your advantage, and you have motive because I imprisoned you. You want your revenge. You've only fled with me because you think Sancho has a vendetta against you, but you'll be expecting your treason to earn you a pardon and a fat reward. Don't look at me like that, Samuel. I'm only telling you what Haza told me to say. He's my wazir and commander of my army. I'm as good as powerless. He, the chief faqi and that evil, bloodthirsty woman of his are a . . . triumvirate. Fanatics running a theocratic state in my name.' He was stamping on the grass in his agitation. 'I'm sorry, Samuel, I couldn't bring myself to tell you what Janifa and I saw when we went over for my coronation. If I hadn't known they were Mishkhatids, I'd have believed I was among Almoravids again. My own people transformed into . . . I don't know what. *Jihadis*? Fundamentalists? And Haza has them under his thumb. They swore loyalty to me, but as long as I'm exiled on this Godforsaken hillside they see Haza as their leader. I'm a puppet, and effectively a prisoner. How could I tell Janifa and you? If Ayesha knew . . .'

I nodded. 'I suspected it.'

He clenched his fists. 'When I'm back in Mishkhat, I'll be able to reassert my authority – but for now I need Haza to get me there. I must go along with him.'

'So you approve of his mad scheme?'

His eyes were almost pleading. 'Haza is confident, Samuel. Why would he suggest it otherwise?'

'It's convenient, then, that he has a treacherous Jew to hand who can convince Sancho. To persuade Paladon that his oldest friend has turned into such a stock character may be more difficult. Did General Haza have any wisdom on how I might do so?'

Aziz looked embarrassed. 'Haza believes Paladon can be bought, Samuel.'

I laughed out loud. 'Paladon? He's the most honourable man I know.'

Aziz's face darkened. 'He betrayed Mishkhat.'

'Out of revenge,' I said. 'Because he believes you sold his wife to King Yusuf.'

Aziz frowned. 'Let us not quarrel. As you know, I do not recognise that a marriage took place. His conversion was questionable and I interrupted the wedding. That he debauched Ayesha beforehand makes them both guilty of sin punishable by death.' He held up his hand to stop my protest. 'But over these last few months with Ayesha, I've been . . . reconsidering. That you saved her from her addiction and brought her back to me, and that she seems to have forgiven me, has . . . moved me. I – I will put all my objections aside. I will forgive them both and give my blessing to their union if Paladon performs the service Haza requires.'

'So that is how you intend to buy him? Was it Haza's idea? No, it was yours, wasn't it?' He looked away. 'Oh, Aziz, you disappoint me. Once again you are planning to use your sister as a political tool. Have you asked her if she wishes to be with Paladon again? The last time she spoke to me she said she hated him – because of the lies you told her about his marrying a Christian. Or is your change of heart another lie?'

'I will tell her the truth, Samuel. I swear it. He is the father of her child. She will agree.' His eyes were again imploring me. 'By God, Samuel, I am a changed man. You must see that, surely.'

'Perhaps.' Now I was pacing the grass, thinking furiously. 'Very well, I will go to Mishkhat and deliver Haza's message, but I have conditions. First, I will tell Paladon of the deception that Haza is planning. He will guess we are conceiving a trap, so it would be pointless not to. If he then goes to Sancho and reveals our true plans . . . That is a risk you will have to take.'

'Knowing the trust between you, I expected you to approach him in no other way,' he said. 'And if they do not take the bait, we have lost nothing.'

'Second, I want a safe conduct for him in the event that we are victorious over Sancho, signed by you and also by General Haza. And if Sancho discovers that Paladon has betrayed him, I want Haza to offer what protection he can. And he must write a guarantee to that effect.'

'Agreed. I will persuade Haza.'

'Third, I shall tell Paladon every detail of what has happened to Ayesha since he last saw her. He will learn from me of your cruelty, Aziz, the evil you have inflicted on her and others, including ibn Sa'id. I will also express my opinion that your repentance is genuine. I want to believe it, but it may not be enough for him to trust or forgive you. So you will write to him swearing by Allah that you will deliver to him Ayesha and his child as soon as you have returned to Mishkhat and that you will henceforth treat him as an honoured brother-in-law, or if he wishes to leave Mishkhat with Ayesha and Yasin, you will allow him to do so.'

'Janifa told me that you once browbeat my great-uncle. You are hard on your kings, Samuel. But I deserve your chastisement. I agree.'

'I haven't finished. I want your letter witnessed by the chief faqi, who must also formally recognise that ibn Sa'id truly converted Paladon and married them before Allah.'

His eyes widened in surprise. 'That may be difficult.'

'If Haza wants his battle, then he had better find a way to persuade his fellow triumvir. Otherwise I will not run his errand. I have one last condition.'

Aziz took a deep breath. 'Tell me,' he said.

'I want Ayesha to write to Paladon. I, and only I, will be present when she writes her letter, and I will take it when it is sealed and show it to no other man but Paladon. She may write what she likes, of her love or her loathing for him, whatever she truly feels. I do not think she is capable of dissembling. You may speak to her before she writes it, but the words will be hers – and on them will depend the success or failure of my mission. That is another risk you will have to take.'

'You should have been a lawyer, Samuel.'

'No, Aziz, if I can be a physician that is enough for me. All I seek is to heal those I love, and this may be a way.'

A day later, David and I set off for Mishkhat. We travelled by night and hid by day. On the third evening, after dark, we dismounted at the first milestone outside the city. I placed my message in the hollow behind it. We had to wait three more days, hidden in the hayloft of a barn in the looted ruins of a rich Arab's country estate before we received a reply. Every few hours one of us would creep to the road to check the milestone, crouching behind bushes when the Norman patrols passed by. Just before dawn of the fourth day, David brought back a letter.

Samuel, I thank God you are alive. Your letter was the answer to my prayers.

I long to see you – and soon – but there is nowhere in the city we can safely meet. You are still wanted by Sancho. I am hated by every surviving Mishkhatid for what they see as my treason. Nowadays every dark alley has eyes and ears. Even the beggars would knife me if they could get me alone. That is why I am always under the protection of three knights, who never leave me. The only time I am ever undisturbed is when I work in the mosque in the cave, very often through the night. Then my bodyguards stand outside the closed doors allowing no one to enter, or me to leave unobserved.

But I can and I do. As soon as I am in our temple – that is how I think of it, be it mosque or cathedral, it is the shrine to our brotherhood – I have the power to vanish and reappear at will. You are not the only sorcerer, Samuel! And you never did fully understand the extent of my Masonic powers.

Tonight, between the third and fourth watch, be at the Gully of Two Djinns. You remember that magnificent gorge I took you to deep in the Sierra, where we fished for trout in the fast stream?

Look for the pinnacle of rock called the Maiden. It leans into the waterfall like a girl washing her hair. You will recall that I showed it to you and told you that I loved it because it reminded me of Ayesha. You will see me materialise on the ledge that lies within the crook of her arm.

I understand that you can only travel after dark. Ride hard, my friend. It is five miles as the crow flies from the city, but it is a fifteen-mile journey through the hills. The moonlight and my anticipation will guide your horse's steps. I will be waiting for you.

And take care. Besides Ayesha, who has long been lost to me, yours is the only life I tender dear.

Your friend and brother
Paladon/Yasin

I read the letter to David, who raised his eyebrows. 'So, we are to ride to some desolate waterfall and meet a man who says he can vanish in one place and reappear somewhere else.' He shrugged. 'Why not? It makes more sense than two Jews walking into an occupied city to persuade a Christian duke to send his army into a trap. But you be the one to talk to him, Samuel. Whether he's wizard or sprite, I'll have my arrow on him. Or if he looks harmless I'll go fishing and we can have trout for breakfast.' He cast his melancholy eyes over the loft and the pile of bones that was all that remained of the rat he had caught for our dinner. 'I'm so hungry that if the Lord God Jehovah sent a pig into this barn, I'd cook it without conscience.'

We had to lead our horses over the stony track that skirted the riverbank. On either side, black-forested precipices blotted out the night sky. We were in a dark world of rushing water that rattled and roared over invisible rocks in the phosphorescent stream beside us or drenched us as it trickled down the crags. The constant murmur was occasionally broken by the louder rustles of woodland birds or animals, the eerie calls of wolves or the moan of a nightjar. David, making his way in front of me, would startle and freeze when he heard the sounds, and mutter into his beard before he went on. Once I caught his expression in a pool of moonlight that had broken through the covering of firs. From his look of terror, I realised he had half believed we were on our way to meet a sorcerer.

'Give me a Norman charging at me with an axe,' he muttered, 'and I'll stand my ground – but this place is evil, Samuel. And I still cannot understand how your friend is expected to get here from Mishkhat if he is locked in a cave.'

'Paladon is no sorcerer,' I told him. 'There'll be an explanation, I promise.' I had already worked out the riddle in his letter. It was not, after all, the first time he had vanished or reappeared in the mosque. 'Keep up your spirits. It's not far now.' I had perceived that the roar of the river was louder, which meant we were nearing the waterfall.

We broke out of the forest into a moonlit glade. The stream had widened into a dark pool, and when we skirted the last rock on the path we saw, rising before us, a high, flat cliff curtained by the wide sheet of the cataract and next to it the giant Maiden that Paladon had described. Her body, twenty feet high, curved gracefully towards the bubbling cascade. The shadows on the smooth stone rippled like a diaphanous dress over firm limbs. Her head was a smaller rock crowned with weeds that rippled like long, dark hair in the white tumble of the water. The cracks in her face revealed a shy smile and an eye that seemed to watch us wherever we moved. She trembled in the shimmering moonlight, a naiad, half startled, half amused to have been observed by mortals at her ablutions.

The vision unnerved David. He paced back and forth over the wet turf. 'So we're here. What do we do now?'

'Wait for Paladon to appear,' I said.

About an hour later he did. At one second the hollow between the two strands of rock that formed what Paladon had described as the crook of the Maiden's arm was empty. At the next a tall figure in a long dark gown was standing there in the moonlight, his arms crossed, looking down on us. David, his face white with fear, had already primed his bow, certain that this this must be a ghost, but I gently put my hand on his arm.

'You've aged since I last saw you, Samuel,' came the familiar tones.

'You haven't, Paladon,' I replied, my heart thumping with excitement. 'Except maybe to seem bigger.'

'I've aged inside, my old friend,' he said softly. The natural amphitheatre of the glade amplified his voice so it echoed. 'Here.' He reached out and pressed a recess in the rock. There was the creak of a pulley, and a rope ladder slowly descended. In a minute he had climbed down, and I felt myself in his huge embrace while David looked on suspiciously, fiddling with his bow and arrow.

'Simple mechanics?' I smiled. 'No flying? Or vanishing and reappearing? My friend David must be disappointed. He was expecting a magician.'

Paladon grinned. 'No, David, you can put away your weapon. I'm just an ordinary mason. I have no magic. I came here on my own two feet as you did, though forgive me if I don't tell you exactly how. That's a secret between Samuel and me, and I need to preserve it.'

'Are you satisfied he's flesh and blood, David?' I asked. 'Do you think you might fish for a while and let me talk to my old friend?'

'Try the rock pool where it narrows. You'll find trout feed there at night. Sometimes carp,' said Paladon.

David nodded sullenly and moved out of earshot, but he did not relinquish his bow.

'So, you discovered a long tunnel from a cave and followed it to its exit, Paladon?'

Paladon laughed. 'I expected you to have guessed.' He sighed. 'There was a time, after Ayesha was taken to the palace, in which I did little during the long nights but explore the tunnels.

I penetrated further down some of those we went potholing in as boys. I probably hoped I'd fall into one of the damned clefts and end my misery – but I didn't. Instead I found out that ibn Sa'id had been right. The cave *was* made by molten lava. One of the boreholes stretched five miles into the bowels of the Mishkhat rock, continuing under the plain, emerging here. Over the year I opened up some of the narrower passages, set up ladders at the steeper bits and covered the more dangerous fissures. I brought you to this gorge once, intending to tell you the secret, but those were dangerous times, when Aziz and his creature, Ephraim, were at their worst, so I kept it to myself, suspecting that one day it might have a purpose – if I could get Ayesha away from the harem, for example, in which case I wouldn't have wanted to compromise you.' He looked up sadly. 'Later I ended up escaping through it alone – again as you probably surmised.'

'I assumed something of that nature when your first letter to me was discovered inside the mosque.'

'Twist the lamp in the Niche of Light in the mihrab and it operates a door,' said Paladon. 'I made it long ago, before I knew about the tunnel. I was going to surprise you one day, show you that the mosque had not superseded the darker more ancient mysteries – you know, the temple of Apollo, the shrine to Cybele and the cave paintings. I thought you'd be pleased that they'd still be accessible behind it. More symbolism.' He added bitterly, 'Not that it matters now. The brotherhood's dissolved. Aziz saw to that.'

'I heard you're turning the mosque into a cathedral.'

He looked at me uncomfortably. 'I told Sancho I'd come up with a plan, and I've done a few drawings, but my heart's not in it. Not since I saw what the Christians did when they sacked Mishkhat. Sancho promised me he wouldn't put it to the torch. He lied. Or, rather, Elderic did. He urged the Norman and Frankish mercenaries on. "No mercy," he screeched, on the battlefield. That was why I rode out to warn you to get away.'

'Elderic's here too?'

'He's become the Pope's plenipotentiary. He wants to incite a holy war. Bastard.'

'You haven't returned to the Catholic fold, then?'

Paladon turned, and I saw for the first time the creases on his broad, honest forehead and the grim furrows on his cheeks, but his flowing hair was still the brilliant corn yellow of his youth. 'Samuel,' he said, 'I'm damned by every religion. The blood on my hands can't be washed off in a mosque or a church. Innocent women, children . . . friends I'd known in the market since my youth had their skulls split open by Norman broadswords, wielded by men I helped to bring in. My concubine Theodosia – you remember her? I found her body eventually. She'd been violated, as every woman was, but afterwards the foot soldiers who enjoyed her ordered her to sing to them. She was mute. She couldn't sing to them. So they impaled her on a spear through her loins.' Tears were running down his cheeks and his fist was punching his hand. 'That is what comes of hatred and a mad desire for revenge. It's not even as if killing Aziz, which was all I wanted to do, would have brought Ayesha back to me. I can't even bring myself to hate him any more after what's happened here. I've done as much evil as he has.'

'I come with a message from him, Paladon. He wishes to make amends.'

He stared at me blankly, then lowered himself on to a fallen log and slumped forward with his head in his hands. 'It's too damned late for that,' he said. 'Let him deal with his own conscience. I'm busy enough with mine.'

'I have a message from Ayesha too,' I said.

His brow tautened with anger. 'You're my friend, Samuel, the only one I have left. I've trusted in your honesty. That's why I'm here. I know you've probably come with some proposition, not that I'm interested, and because it's you I'll listen – but don't mock me with Ayesha's name. Please. Don't you lie to me too. She's lost to all of us. There can be no messages from . . . Marrakesh.'

I reached into my satchel and withdrew her letter. I handed it to him without a word and walked away. I gazed at the waterfall, its spray streaming down my cheeks like tears. The Maiden looked back at me with her fixed, amused stare.

Later, when he called me back, I told him the whole sorry tale. He said nothing. Only when I told him of my imprisonment with ibn Sa'id and his death did he utter a groan. Otherwise he sat on the log in the moonlight, head bowed. He barely glanced at the letters from Aziz and General Haza, and showed no interest in the forged map.

After I had finished, he stood up and began to pace.

Twenty minutes must have passed before he muttered, 'It's late. I should get back to the mosque in case my bodyguards come looking for me.' His pale blue eyes showed his confusion. 'Forgive me, Samuel. This is not the reunion I'd planned. I'll – I'll meet you tomorrow at the same time. If you like you can hide inside the entrance to the tunnel – there's food there and a flued alcove where you can make a fire. I'll show you how to pull up the ladder. Even if someone finds your horses they won't discover you.'

'You'll consider Aziz's proposal?'

'Yes – but I want twenty-four hours to think it through.'

I breathed a silent sigh of relief. I couldn't resist adding, because the question was burning in my mind, 'Ayesha's letter . . . I didn't read it . . . did she . . .?'

'She says she hates me, Samuel.' His tone was flat. 'She doesn't consider her child to be mine.'

It was the risk we had taken, but I was stunned all the same. I had hoped that after Aziz had talked to her her feelings might have changed. 'Then why do you . . .?'

'Because, old friend, it confirms you were telling the truth.' He gave me a weak smile. 'I once told you I would never give up. Do you remember? By the fountain in Salim's house? This isn't perfect – but she is alive and I can hope again. Call your man. Tell him to bring his fish if he's caught any.'

We waited all through the long day in the little cavern above the rope ladder. Around midnight we made out the faint glimmer of an approaching torch and, shortly afterwards, the giant shadow of Paladon. He had a basket of provisions, which he gave to David, and a safe-conduct for me, stamped with Duke Sancho's seal. While David was cooking what remained of the trout he had caught the previous night, Paladon spoke softly to me. 'I saw Sancho and Elderic and showed them the map. I spun them a yarn about how I had got it. You were disguised as a beggar and jostled me in the market. It was in a leather pouch you thrust into my hands while my bodyguards were distracted, along with a letter from you, telling me how to make contact with you. It was a passable forgery. I still remember your handwriting. You're very greedy by the way – you demanded ten thousand dirhams and a pardon as a reward. I think they were convinced. Sancho couldn't contain his excitement – but Elderic was more cautious. He wants to hear it from your own lips.'

I felt a chill in the pit of my stomach, but I nodded. I had expected as much. I quickly read the safe-conduct. 'I see I'm to eschew sorcery and convert to Christianity. Elderic's requirement, I presume?'

'If you're to live on in Mishkhat once Aziz and Haza have been defeated. Yes, Elderic's insisting on it. After the battle, of course. If they find your information's false you'll be burned as a warlock.'

'A pleasant prospect. How did I acquire the safe-conduct? They can't know we're meeting here.'

'You haven't got it yet. I'm just showing it to you. You'll find it tomorrow behind a loose brick in the arch of the bathhouse. You won't miss it. I'll mark it with the *pi* sign. You'll read my letter accompanying it, then go to Salim's house and give yourself up. You'll probably be followed but they won't arrest you.'

'Why Salim's house?'

'Elderic and his monks live there. They're cataloguing the library before taking it back to Toledo. It was one of the few houses in the Mussulman Quarter they didn't burn. They're going to keep you there until we go off to battle. No doubt you'll have to put up with a degree of religious instruction, but I may be able to visit you from time to time.'

'You'll come back here and tell David the plan's worked – assuming I convince them – so he can ride back and tell Aziz?'

'Of course.' Paladon paused. 'Samuel, you don't need to do this. You could go back with David now, tell Aziz you've passed on the message and I've delivered it.'

'You will be compromised if I don't appear. And we'll be unable to ensure they've taken the bait.' I made my bravest attempt to smile. 'Where's your old sense of adventure? It's worth the risk, isn't it, if we can restore the brotherhood and reunite you with Ayesha and your son? He's a dear little boy, Paladon. He has your colouring, and your impetuosity.'

'If anything goes wrong, Elderic really will try to burn you at the stake, Samuel.'

I put my hand on his. 'We have to do this. What sort of life would any of us have if we didn't try? This is our chance, Paladon, our chance to make amends for everything.'

He clenched my hand in his. He was about to say something when David called, from the mouth of the cave, 'Fish is ready. Crisp and brown.'

I stood up and pulled his sleeve. 'Come on, Paladon. Let's not think about it. You've brought wine and cheese so we'll enjoy it. We're together again, and we have a great task ahead. Let's use what precious moments we have left and celebrate the happiness to come.'

But it was a sombre gathering for all our attempts at merriness. I was uneasy. Paladon was preoccupied, and David made no attempt to hide his scepticism. I was relieved when Paladon said it was time for us to take the long walk up the tunnel. I embraced David and followed the flickering torchlight that led me into the bowels of the earth.

Paladon's secret door was as simple as it was ingenious. He had made two Niches of Light, one contained inside the mihrab in the mosque, the other, identical, facing the back of the cave. By twisting the base of the lamp, twice to the right, once to the left and right again, a catch was released that allowed a double-faced door to swing on a pivot. I watched him demonstrate how it was done. He applied the mechanism, and when the marble plinth on which the alabaster niche rested swung round, he slipped through the gap as it swivelled to its new position, and I was left alone in the cavern, staring at the niche that a moment before had been inside the mosque. A few seconds later, it swung the other way and he reappeared.

'You see? It's quite easy,' he said. 'If the mosque was in use, you'd have to light the lamp in the niche first because it's meant to have a perpetual flame.' He pointed at several barrels of oil that he had lined against the cave wall. 'But all you have to do is practise twisting the catch and slipping through.'

I released it a couple of times. 'It's easy, as you said.'

He took my hands and stared intently into my eyes. 'Samuel, I say this again – you need not do this.'

I embraced him. 'No more words, Paladon. I'll follow fifteen minutes after I hear the doors of the mosque close behind you.'

He hugged me, kissed my cheeks and moved towards the niche. He was about to twist the lamp when he turned. 'You have the spare key? Remember to lock the doors after you. And be careful when you make your way down the hill. There are patrols everywhere.'

'Don't worry,' I said. 'We've been through it over and over again. I'll be in the market at noon.'

'God go with you, my friend.'

'And you,' I whispered, as he disappeared.

I scarcely recognised the city I had grown up in. Passing under the great gate that led to the Mussulman Quarter I entered a wasteland. Everywhere was rubble and the blackened husks of houses. A few haunted figures would occasionally emerge from a shanty dwelling. If a troop of soldiers passed, they would scurry away like scared rats. I was lost several times before I found the marketplace, which at first seemed as lively as it had ever been. Then I saw that it was not Mishkhatids behind the stalls but foreign soldiers bartering booty they had stolen. A crowd of men at arms were ogling the slave pounds where several half-naked girls were being inspected and prodded like animals, as many Jews as Arabs, including a few I recognised.

The bathhouse had once been hidden behind tall houses. Now it stood alone among the rubble. Another crowd was gathered at the main door. An old woman was proffering a young girl dressed scantily in veils to lounging Frankish soldiers who were hooting and laughing at her. I knew the crone. Her name was Alia Bibi. She had once been a respectable matron, a friend of my mother's, whose job it had been to collect money from clients before their baths. She was now a brothel madam. The girl she was offering was her granddaughter.

No one seemed to notice the bowed beggar who sidled against the door and removed a letter from behind a brick. The disguise Paladon had given me was perfect. In a city of beggars another was invisible.

Only when I had left the market and was trying to get my bearings to Salim's house did I hear the heavy metal footsteps behind me that stopped when I stopped and sounded again when I moved. I clutched my safe-conduct and hurried on.

I was pushed through the familiar courtyard into what had been Salim's divan. It no longer bore any resemblance to the tasteful room I had once known. The fine tiles were invisible under rushes and straw. Paladon's carvings on the alabaster walls were covered with purple drapes, and in front of a huge crucifix stood a chestnut table at which sat three men. In the middle, wearing the red robes of a cardinal, was Elderic; on his right was Duke Sancho (the surly boy had grown into a podgy but still surly young man) and on his left Paladon was doing his best to avoid looking at me.

'Sit down, Jew,' murmured Elderic, indicating a stool that a monk placed in front of the table. 'The last time we met you were conjuring devils. Today you sneak into the city proposing to betray your pagan masters, demanding money and more for your treason. You are no savoury character, are you?' He glanced at the paper in front of him. 'Alchemy, astrology, sodomy – is there anything repulsive or evil you have not done? Even your wazir once imprisoned you for disloyalty – or was it necromancy? It seems that Prince Aziz has the same distaste for your evil practices as I do. Yet he had the foolishness to release you, on the orders of your even more foolish and disgusting king, who apparently required your medical services. Or were you his catamite too?' He shook his head. 'The degeneracy of these credulous Mussulmans never ceases to astonish me. Be that as it may, we are apparently to believe that the information you have brought us is genuine. Is that credible? Your history does not inspire confidence.'

I pretended to whine. I thought it would be in character. 'I have been maligned, my lord. I am none of the things you call me. I'm a scientist and a doctor – a good one. Otherwise I wouldn't have been King Abu's physician. I wasn't imprisoned for disloyalty. I was punished for my patriotism, because I criticised Prince Aziz's persecution of the Christians and the disorder it brought. He imprisoned me out of spite and fear that I would talk to the king, who loved me. It was unjust, unfair.'

'Spare me your self-righteousness. As if any of us would

believe that a Christ-murdering Jew might speak up on behalf of Christians. Remember that the duke and I saw you practise your diabolic arts with our own eyes, and the duke even suffered under one of your spells. If I had my way I would burn you in the marketplace this very afternoon. But . . .' he sighed and raised his palms upwards '. . . we must be pragmatic. If the information you have brought us is true, then you may have performed a useful service to Christendom. We are aware that God sometimes uses the most unlikely agents to achieve His Divine Will. But is the news you bring us true, Samuel? That is what I wonder.'

The duke spoke: 'How came you by this map, Jew?'

'I am a physician, Highness, and therefore have free entry to royal quarters. I overheard the king – Aziz, Your Holiness – and General Haza discussing this plan. I am a doctor and I hate bloodshed. I have taken the Hippocratic oath, my lord, and I thought that if I could prevent further killing it would be an honourable act. I promise you, I have the interests of Mishkhat at heart, whoever rules. All I seek is a quick end to war. Peace and prosperity again.'

Elderic was observing me with disgust. 'Listen to him, my lord duke, his hypocrisy, his lies.' He pointed a long finger at me. 'Admit the truth, Jew. You are betraying your king, the renegade Aziz, out of ignoble revenge, because he once spurned you as a lover and later imprisoned you. Also, you see profit in this for yourself. You want your thirty pieces of silver, don't you, Samuel? Paladon, I am surprised that you ever befriended such a worm.'

'That is in the past, Eminence. It was he who betrayed me to Aziz with a story that I planned to elope with his sister. He was always jealous of me, he and his fellow Jew, Ephraim. I killed Ephraim but this one escaped me. For all that, I believe the information he brings is genuine. Why would he lie? If Haza's army is not in the place he says it will be, my lord duke will burn him as a sorcerer. He knows that, yet he came here of his own volition.'

'Yes, there's no denying the logic,' murmured Elderic, 'though it sticks in my craw.'

Sancho thumped the table. 'I say we put it to the test. Ride out and find them. We have nothing to lose and all to gain. As for this creature, hang him – burn him. We have the map. We don't need him.'

I threw myself on the rushes, waving my safe conduct. 'Please, lords, mercy. You swore no harm would come to me. You swore on your Christ, who, yes, I will embrace. I see the error of my ways.' I began to scrabble under the table in an attempt to kiss their feet. Sancho's iron boot kicked me and I was dragged back to my seat by three monks.

Sancho had pulled his sword half out of its scabbard but Elderic put a restraining hand gently on his arm. 'I'm afraid, my lord duke, that the Jew has a point. You did swear when you signed that piece of paper that no harm would come to him.'

'Oaths don't apply to Jews and devil-worshippers.'

'They do to Almighty God, my son. I have no love for this Jew but I have concern for your immortal soul. Sheathe your sword. We will put the information he has brought to the test. We will also try the traitor's sincerity in his stated wish to convert. Who knows? Perhaps one day he may be useful in other ways.'

He contemplated me severely. 'Samuel, do you understand what I'm saying? If what you have told us is true, we will give you the benefit of the doubt, and on the defeat of the infidels, we will give you the thirty pieces of silver – but it is dependent on your repenting your sins and acknowledging Jesus. If I perceive sincerity in you, I may be more generous. With God's blessing, I may even, one day, ordain you as a monk. Until now your skills and scholarship have been employed in evil purposes. I will allow you to use them for the glory of God. When I take the library of your former patron back to Toledo, I have a mind that you will accompany it. You will translate this so-called philosophy for the benefit of Christians. What say you to that? Together we will try a truer alchemy than any performed in a state of ignorance. By God's grace, we will discover within the dross of heathen literature pure nuggets of truth that may be acceptable within the teachings of His church. We will use the calumny of lies with which the devil beguiled the pagans and turn them on our enemies. See the opportunities that are open to you. Thank Jesus for His mercy. Thank also the good lord duke for his charity. Ponder on what I have said while you repent your sins. Now take him away.'

The monks pushed me down the corridor and locked me in a cell. Ironically it was the same room that Aziz and I had once shared. The walls had been plastered and whitewashed. The only furniture was a trestle bed, a stool on which rested a basin and a small table on which stood a cross.

Here I spent the three most tedious weeks of my life: every day I had to study the Bible, learn catechisms and prayers and attend religious services, morning, afternoon, evening and several times in the middle of the night. After ten days, I found myself dreaming in plainsong.

It was a relief when Paladon, dressed in chain mail and accompanied by three knights – presumably the bodyguard that he had told me about – came to collect me. I was his prisoner, he told me coldly. We would ride together in the baggage train. If there was any sign of treachery on my part, he would have the pleasure of executing me himself. Then he turned on his heels and left, while his men bound my hands.

An hour later, for the second time in my life, I was riding through the city gates among armoured men who were setting off to war.

That night we camped by the stream where General Abu Bakhr had fallen off his horse. Paladon passed me. I was tied to the wheel of a wagon, shivering in the drizzle. He looked to right and left. No one was about. He unclasped his cloak and draped it over my shoulders. He pressed a piece of cold mutton pie into my hand, and whispered into my ear, 'Be of good heart, Samuel. It won't be long now till the brotherhood is together again.'

'With Ayesha,' I whispered.

'So I pray.'

'To which God?' I asked.

He grinned. 'All of them.' He winked and was gone.

Next day the Christian army left the road and we made our way up obscure tracks penetrating deep into the mountains. The knights had done their reconnaissance well. We moved invisibly and silently. I had no idea how Haza could ambush us in these conditions, or even discover where we were. We camped in a forest in the hills somewhere beyond Green Springs, which we had skirted by devious paths.

Tied again to my wheel, I listened to the raucous laughter of the Normans and Franks round their campfires. They expected to do battle within the next two or three days. They were sure of victory. Word had got round that the enemy would be caught unawares. They were already debating how they would parcel out the booty and the women. I thought despondently of Ayesha and Janifa, and what would happen to them if Haza's plan failed.

Andalucía, 1938

4

The Witch's Cauldron

Pinzon closed the book and stood up trying to contain his excitement. Energy coursed through every muscle and vein in his body. His surroundings, which had been so dark and grim only hours before, were luminescent with mystery. Everything around him seemed animate and alive. As he watched, the Christ hanging over the altar appeared to lift itself off the great gold cross and float towards him. The icon of the Virgin in the chancel turned her gentle face and smiled.

He looked down at his sleeping grandson. *Out of the mouths of babes and sucklings.* A lock of hair had fallen over María's forehead. She looked as cherubic as Tomás, who lay in her arms. Perhaps it was a matter of opening one's heart, he thought.

He glanced at his fob watch. Ten minutes past two in the morning, four hours to dawn. Ogarrio had given an ultimatum for eight o'clock. He had so little time. He wanted to shout the news of his discovery and had to remind himself that trusting in new-found hope was as dangerous as giving way to despair. He remembered the intellectual discipline to which he had always adhered in his academic researches. Nothing was proved until it had been authenticated.

There were still many imponderables. He was basing his plan on a book that had been written eight hundred years ago.

He had to be certain that nothing had changed in the inter-vening centuries.

Still reeling from the sheer improbability that an ancient manuscript, penned by a Jewish alchemist and written in archaic Arabic, could contain a message that might save them, he walked towards the sleeping Felipe. Gently he prised the elec-tric torch out of his belt, carefully so as not to wake him. Then he made his way down the nave towards the western transept.

Fighting an urge to run, he could not but marvel at how the past had been calling to him ever since he had entered the cathedral. He recalled the vision of old Andaluz that had impressed him in one of the stained-glass windows, the moving statue in the vault, the words of Paladon's inscription: *Ask, and it shall be given you; seek, and ye shall find; knock, and it shall be opened unto you.* Samuel's mad old father had told his son to look for the hidden white letters in the Torah that spelled the name of God. What he had just discovered between the pages of the memoir had been no less remarkable.

As he made his way down the steps, past the sleeping knight, he had the strange feeling that he was being pulled onwards by some inexorable destiny. He was unable to dismiss it as mere chance. It made more sense to imagine that some beneficent force of the universe – ibn Sa'id's numen or Samuel's celestial nitre – had come throbbing out of the mysterious cavern to their aid. It was as if the curtains of reality had parted to give him an intimation of the divine, as they had for the initiates of Cybele who had come to this same cave to experience the mysteries, or the shepherd boy who had seen the vision of Mary, or the Muslims who had been saved by the faqi's holy light.

Moving as silently as he could through the darkness, he remembered a long-gone Christmas when, as a little boy no older than Tomás, he had left his shoe outside his door on the eve of Epiphany in the excited certainty that magic would bring the Three Kings before dawn to fill it with gifts. He had looked up at the stars burning brightly in the night sky and imagined they were angels. The heavens were alive and there was order and purpose in the universe. He found he was experiencing just such feelings of wonder and immanence today. While he had been reading Samuel's book, the centuries had telescoped and he was back in a cosmography where angels and spirits affected the lives of men.

His step was steady. He passed through the gallery of bones without thinking about them. It was as if the spiritual emanations in the stone were leading him forward. He hardly glanced at the statue of Paladon. He bent forward into the sarcophagus and grasped with firm hands the wooden ladder that Ogarrio's men had put there instead of the pulley. A minute later he stood on the paving of the mosque.

Ahead of him, caught in the torch beam, was the mihrab, exactly as Samuel had described it. Paladon's instructions were seared into his memory. *Twist the lamp in the Niche of Light in the mihrab and it operates a door.* He mounted the plinth. There in front of him rested the lamp in its alabaster niche. He placed the torch on a ledge to the side so that its beam illuminated the marble base beneath it. Trembling a little, he reached out both hands. The stone was cold and clammy to his palms. He braced himself.

Turn twice to the right, once to the left and right again.

The numen was burning inside him. He felt sublimely confident as if he had superhuman force at his command.

He twisted the lamp.

And nothing happened.

He heaved, he sweated, he strained.

It did not move a millimetre.

He slumped to the ground. The numen left him. He was drained and panting with despair. The cold air from the vaults that entered his lungs seemed like a touch of death. His heart was palpitating. He had failed.

He had wasted hours of valuable time, exhausted himself

for nothing. He would have been better off sleeping. At least then he might have woken with a clearer mind. Angrily he pulled the manuscript from his pocket. In his vexation he wanted to tear the pages. It was a book of lies and he had been a fool. A complete and utter fool.

Unless he had misread or missed something.

Feverishly, he shuffled through the pages to find Paladon's instructions. The words were inexorable and clear. He had indeed followed Samuel's description of how Paladon had opened the door from inside the cave, and it hadn't worked. Unless . . . He realised his mistake.

Samuel had described how the door opened from inside the cave – but Pinzon was standing in the mosque, on the other side, where the instructions would be reversed. If he turned the base to the left initially, not the right, and in reverse order . . .

The spiritual energy was back inside him, burning as brightly as ever. He leaped to his feet and bounded back to the plinth. His hands grasped the stone again. He had hardly applied any pressure before he heard the click. With a shout of triumph he turned it the other way. The stone moved as smoothly in its grooves as if it had only recently been oiled. Now, two more turns to the left . . . His heart in his mouth, he twisted . . .

There was a grinding, rumbling sound and the face of the niche began to turn. He slipped through the gap and was standing in the cave. Swinging the torch over the great empty space, he saw a table and a chair covered with dust and cobwebs. He made out a pile of vellum and an inkpot, a small knife and, unmistakably, the feathery remains of a quill pen. Samuel's pen.

Quietly, he slipped back into the cathedral, and searched the rows of pews, where his fellow prisoners stirred restlessly in their sleep. Somehow he knew that the man he wanted would be awake. He knelt beside him and whispered, 'Please, come with me. I need your help.'

Paco frowned, but he stood up and followed him. 'Why in God's name would I help you?'

'Because I've found an escape route, a way out. But I've yet to prove it'll work. You can help me do that. You're young, brave, intelligent and a leader of the community. We may be able to save everyone.'

Paco laughed harshly. 'Do you ever give up, politician? Still hoping you can pull the wool over my eyes like you've done with the others?'

Pinzon looked at him steadily. 'All right,' he said. 'Let me give you proof.' He reached in his pocket for the knife he had found on the table in the cave. 'Have a look at this,' he said, holding it up for him to see.

Paco examined it warily. 'It's a knife. So what?'

'Look at the handle, Paco. It's silver, solid silver, blackened with age. See the carvings on it? They're Arabic characters. And the blade is oxidised and chipped. That means it's hundreds of years old. A museum would pay thousands of pesetas for something like this. Maybe tens of thousands.'

With satisfaction, he saw Paco's eyes light up. He proffered it to him. 'Here, take it. Keep it, if you like. When we get out of here, you can sell it and become a rich man.'

Paco folded his arms. 'You think I want to get myself shot for hiding a weapon on me?' But his eyes had narrowed calculatingly.

Pinzon waited, trusting in his greed.

'All right,' Paco said. 'So you found an old knife when you were helping them put bombs in the mosque. How will that help us?'

'Because I didn't find it in the mosque. It was in a cave. There's an entry to it from the mosque. I got inside it only a few minutes ago. And there's a way out of it. A tunnel.'

Paco's face had paled. 'You're lying,' he said.

Pinzon shrugged and made as if to put the knife back into his pocket. 'All right, Paco, I'm lying.'

'Let me have another look.'

Pinzon passed it to him. Paco ran his hand over the handle. He looked up suspiciously. 'How did you find out about the cave you said this came from?'

Pinzon pointed at the book. 'From that,' he said. 'My fairy stories.'

Paco's eyes widened. 'In truth?'

'In truth,' said Pinzon. 'Listen.' He read: '"Be at the Gully of Two Djinns . . . Look for the pinnacle of rock called the Maiden. It leans into the waterfall like a girl washing her hair."' He looked at Paco. 'Well, does that mean anything to you?'

Paco grunted dismissively. 'La Caldera de la Bruja. It's about eight kilometres north of here as the crow flies. We all know it. I used to take my sheep through there to the pass for the summer grazing on the *meseta*. There's a dam there now, with a power station and a small reservoir.'

Pinzon wanted to be sure. 'And what about the pinnacle of rock that looks like a woman? Is that still there?'

'Yes, on the side of the dam.' He spat. 'What's the point of this?'

'The point is that the Cauldron of the Witch, as you call it, is where the tunnel leads to from the cave.'

'*¡Hijo de puta!*' Paco punched his fist into his hand. 'Then we're saved!'

'If I can get us there, would you be able to lead us through the mountains, away from the Fascists?' asked Pinzon.

'Easily. It's all forest. Nobody could track us. We could—' He stopped. His expression was suspicious again. 'Why did you say if?'

'Because someone has to go down that tunnel to check it out first,' said Pinzon. 'Remember, this book was written eight hundred years ago.'

'Then why don't you go yourself? Or send that whore?'

'Because we might be missed. Ogarrio knows both of us but he doesn't know *you*.'

'The guard knows me.'

'I've dealt with him. Felipe's with us.'

Paco rubbed his stubble. '¡*Joder!*' He seemed still to be in two minds. 'And you want me to go down there all alone? What if there are rock falls? It sounds dangerous.'

Pinzon observed him calmly. 'More dangerous than fighting our way out of the church? Or waiting to be blown up? And, as a member of the revolutionary council, don't you have a duty to your people?'

Paco glanced at him savagely. 'You'd better show me.'

Pinzon nodded. 'Follow me.' He turned in the direction of the western transept noticing that Paco had slipped Samuel's knife into his pocket.

'Politician?'

He halted, and looked over his shoulder. Paco was grinning maliciously. 'How do you know you can trust me? If I get out, what makes you think I'll come back?'

Pinzon sighed. 'Paco, we cannot waste time. It will be dawn soon.'

He eased back into the pew beside María and Tomás, who were still sleeping. After the momentous events of the last hour, it was eerie that nothing in their enclosed world had changed.

He took stock. It would take Paco about four hours to make the two-way journey. By then the hostages would be up and about. He was reasonably confident that Paco's absence would not be noted. But so many things could still go wrong – Paco getting killed or lost, or simply deciding to abandon them to their fate. He wondered whether he had been right to trust him.

And that put him into another quandary. If Paco did not return, should he still take the villagers down the tunnel? Staying in the cathedral would probably mean certain death, but to be trapped underground if the tunnel was blocked, especially in

view of Ogarrio's plans to destroy the cave behind them . . .
He didn't want to think about it. Not until he had to.

Shifting in his seat, he felt Samuel's book and remembered
that he had not finished the last chapter, only skimmed it. He
had at least an hour to kill. And he needed to blot out his
ominous thoughts. He settled back and began to read.

Al-Andaluz, 1091

Codex VIII

The Brotherhood

(I) In which I tell of our last adventure

Just before dawn Paladon came to me again, slipping through the shadows. 'Samuel, wake up,' I heard him whisper. 'Something's wrong.'

'What?' I asked, my teeth chattering despite Paladon's coat.

'Sancho's scouts have come back. They've found Haza's army within two hours' march of here – but it's camped exactly where the map should have them be. So what's happened to the deception? Numbers. Deployment. Everything matches. Sancho's drawing his battle plan as we speak. He's elated. Our numbers are twice theirs, and they're on the plain. In one charge we can probably smash them as the Cid did the Almerians. They can't even run. There's a precipice behind them. It'll be a slaughter.'

'That can't be right. They were planning an ambush. You told David to pass the message to Aziz, didn't you?'

'Of course I did. I saw him ride off with a letter I'd written to Aziz explaining everything, including the route we were going to take. To be honest, I expected we'd be attacked today in the defiles.'

'Perhaps he didn't get there,' I said glumly. 'Perhaps he was discovered by a Christian patrol.'

'I doubt it. They'd have found my letter and the two of us would have been arrested. But I don't like it. I'm worried about

Ayesha. If the Christians win and the Normans find her in the baggage train, you know what they'll do to her.'

'She won't be with the army. She'll be in the camp in the mountains.' I was trying to convince myself as much as Paladon. It was what I wanted to believe.

'Let's hope so. Anyway, be ready. If it looks as though the battle is going Sancho's way, you and I will have to move fast. We must find her before his soldiers do.'

He froze as we heard jangling mail and the approaching steps of soldiers. 'I'm sorry, Samuel,' he whispered, and kicked me. 'You dirty Jewish dog,' he shouted, and kicked me again. 'The duke may have pardoned you but I haven't. You wait till after the battle and then you'll learn the true wages of treachery.' I felt his spittle on my brow, and I heard the harsh laughter of men at arms, which turned into a cheer when the early-morning stillness was broken by the bray of a trumpet, which was the signal to march.

The Mishkhat army was taken completely by surprise. There was no opportunity for them to untether and mount their horses. They barely had time to organise the infantry into formation. General Haza did his best. From the small hillock on which Paladon, his bodyguards and I were observing, I saw him, followed by Aziz, running from rank to untidy rank, chivvying them into what order they could and marshalling their long spears into the porcupine formation that was the only defence against cavalry.

They were still shuffling into their final positions when Sancho gave the order to sound the trumpets. Elderic, who had been saying mass, interrupted his blessing and, followed by the other monks, ran for his horse. Those bloodthirsty churchmen were as eager as the knights to take part in a massacre of pagans. Chain mail glinted as they tore off their habits, then raised their maces and swords.

Sancho, on his caparisoned charger, rode slowly forward.

Trumpets blared again. The crusader banner, carried by the knight beside him, unfurled, and a blood red cross cracked in the morning breeze. Two thousand armoured horsemen yelled, '*Deus lo volt!*' and, in an even line, began to trot down the gentle incline of the meadow.

Haza and Aziz turned and walked slowly, with enormous dignity, to take their places just behind their front ranks. Their bodyguards gathered around them. The simple green flag with Allah's name in gold letters swirled open in front of them. We heard above the stamping hoofs a distant cry carried on the wind: '*Allah Akhbar!*'

The knights had increased their pace to a canter, their spears levelled. I glanced at Paladon's stony face. He caught my look and his lips twisted hopelessly. My heart ached as I thought of Aziz. Four hundred men on foot – that was all there were – had no chance against this horde.

The Mishkhatids released a volley of arrows. It looked as innocuous as a small cloud of midges as it rose and fell in the clear air. One or two horses fell. It had no effect against the mass of cavalry bearing down on them. By now the crusaders were charging at full gallop. The line had become ragged as each knight rode at his own pace – I knew that, indisciplined or not, nothing could withstand their momentum. Their sheer weight would crush Aziz's flimsy defences. And it would happen imminently. I felt I was counting out Aziz's life in yards. There were fewer than five hundred to go.

Beside us, Paladon's three bodyguards were standing in their stirrups, waving and hallooing like excited huntsmen at the end of a chase. Their yells were echoed by the cheers of the cooks, the muleteers, the carters and all the other villeins in the baggage train, many of whom were waving their felt caps in the air.

Suddenly we heard the terrible crash of metal. Horsemen and defenders disappeared in a cloud of dust, through which we could only make out shadowy shapes of stamping horses and stumbling men.

'Time to move, Samuel,' Paladon muttered. He kicked his horse with his spurs. It reared. There was a ringing sound as he drew his sword from its scabbard. The Norman knight beside him grinned happily, thinking he shared his elation. Paladon edged his mount closer to him, and raised his sword high above his head. The pupils in his eyes had shrunk to tiny dots as he prepared to strike.

'No, Paladon,' I yelled, and galloped between them.

'Samuel, you fool, what are you doing?' I heard Paladon's angry voice, as he tried to control his rearing mount.

'Just look!' I screamed, and pointed.

Patting his horse's neck, he turned. His face paled. Behind him his three knights were sitting like statues in their saddles, their cheers frozen on their lips. Like everybody on our ridge they were staring at the battleground in amazement. After a moment I, too, became hypnotised by what I was seeing.

The flat empty plain had sprouted men. Thousands of them. As we gazed, more and more were materialising from the grass. Some were still throwing off the turf matting that had covered them. A fat friar who had pushed himself in front of my mount to see what was happening crossed himself. Chilled, I thought of the crude paintings that Rabbi Moshe had once shown us of Judgment Day. Here before us the dead were rising from their tombs, and devils were pouring out of the open gates of hell.

Across the plain, green and gold flags fluttered in the breeze, long spears rose in the air and levelled in deadly precision. We heard the hollow boom of hundreds of drums.

With immaculate precision, the scattered soldiers spaced themselves into companies, then into divisions, each one becoming indistinguishable from another as the mass of men coalesced into a host. Within moments a thick blue crescent of ten thousand infantrymen marched forward. The corners of the great half-moon curved, its points stretching to enclose the mêlée before them. The ranks moved with the fluidity and speed of a rushing river. It seemed more like a force of nature than an army of men.

From an outcrop on the plain, we saw the flash of silver. Columns of cavalrymen, half on camels, half on horses, were pouring like foam on a tide through their infantrymen's ranks. We were deafened by the roar of their battle cry, '*Allah Akhbar!*' It was repeated even more thunderously by the soldiers in the crescent, and then, more faintly but triumphantly, by the beleaguered army of Mishkhat.

'Who are they, Samuel?' Paladon was shouting.

Already, panicked Christian knights were tumbling out of the battle, their horses rearing and colliding in their attempts to escape. The blue crescent moved inexorably forward. The drums boomed faster and the march quickened to a run.

'Almoravids,' I said, my heart breaking for Aziz. 'General Haza has double-crossed us all. He's given Mishkhat to King Yusuf.'

As I spoke the Almoravid cavalry hit the confused Christian knights. The infantry reached them a moment afterwards. The trap had closed.

For a few moments Paladon trotted his horse in a circle. 'This changes everything, Samuel. We have to go – now!' He jerked his horse's head in the direction of the hills we had come from.

Before he kicked his spurs into the beast's flanks, I shouted at him. He turned and I jutted my chin in the direction of his three knights, who were still slumped in shocked paralysis on their saddles.

The blue eyes flared. 'What about them? They're no threat any more.'

'Sides don't matter now. Not after this. And five swords are better than two.'

Paladon swung his eyes in the direction of the battle. A troop of Almoravid cavalry had separated from the mêlée and were riding fast towards our ridge. 'Damn you, Samuel.' He cursed me but he had seen my point. Violently he turned his horse's head again and pulled up in front of his bodyguards. 'Tancred, Jocelyn, Lotho!' he shouted. 'Are you with me? You're dead men if you stay here.'

They blinked blearily at him. One saw me and his face twisted into a mask of hatred. 'Stinking, betraying Jew!' He raised his mace. Paladon's sword came down and knocked it out of his hand.

'Samuel's one of us,' he said, 'and my friend. Are you with me or not?'

We could already hear the thunder of the Almoravids' hoofs. One by one the three knights nodded.

'Good. Then follow me.'

We galloped towards the mountains, leaving the noise of carnage behind.

I guided them into the high passes, to our little shepherd's lodge and then to Haza's larger encampment. Both were deserted. I was not surprised. Haza had known that, with the Almoravids' help, victory was certain. Why leave anybody behind?

Paladon gave his knights a choice. They could return with him to Mishkhat or try to make their way over the mountains to Toledo. They asked what reward they could expect if they stayed with him. 'What I can give,' he said. 'We will be rescuing a king and a princess, and where there's royalty there's money.'

Two of them – Tancred, a short, muscular, flat-featured Basque from just across the Pyrenees, and Lotho, a crop-headed Burgundian, the younger son of an impoverished nobleman in Orange – agreed to stay. Both were experienced soldiers of fortune, men of few words, who had sold their services in wars throughout Europe. The third, the Norman Jocelyn, was a devout crusader. He had been the one to try to mace me and had been bitter since in the company he had reluctantly found himself. He said he would seek King Alfonso's army. Paladon let him go.

In due course we made our way back to the Maiden's pool. A journey we could have covered in three days took ten because we could only travel safely at night, and even so there were several skirmishes with Almoravid patrols. We were lucky to have Tancred and Lotho with us. They were stout fighters and served us well.

Feeling more secure in our secluded valley, we spared a day to fish and hunt, and another to salt the fish and venison. We anticipated that we would need provisions to last us some time. Then we headed up the tunnel into the cave. To our amazement, Paladon found signs that someone had been there in our absence. An unfamiliar cloak lay over a chair, fish bones littered the table, and there were the remains of a fire. I was inclined to despair, thinking that the Almoravids had discovered our secret and all was lost, but Paladon kept his head. 'No, if they'd come, it would have been in companies. I see signs of only one man. Whoever it is may still be here.' He and the two knights went off down the side tunnels to explore, leaving me on guard in the main chamber. It was not long before I heard a shout and the rasp of steel. I yelled for the others and ran down the tunnel that Lotho had taken and found him kneeling on the chest of the man he had overpowered. The Burgundian grinned at me and murmured, in his aristocratic drawl, 'It appears you need a cat, Master Samuel. The rats in your cave have claws. Shall I put this one out of its misery? If only because it stinks.'

'No,' I said. My heart was pounding with relief. 'He's one of ours.' I had recognised, behind the pallid cheeks and the ragged beard, the features of my friend David.

He had not eaten for three days. We fed him and then he told us what he knew.

He had been at the battle. Afterwards he had marched with the victorious troops back to Mishkhat. He confirmed that few Christians had escaped. Sancho had fought bravely until the last few men around him were overpowered. Surrounded by the silent Almoravid horde, he had flailed with his sword, wanting to fight to the end. King Yusuf ordered a donkey to be brought. Sancho was stripped naked and tied to it backwards. He was beaten out of the camp by the desert warriors, who slashed at him with their camel sticks as the donkey passed between their ranks. 'Let him take the news of Allah's invincibility to Alfonso,' Yusuf told the men. 'We want no infidel princelings among us when we prostrate ourselves before Almighty God in thanks for our victory.'

The few knights and soldiers found alive were auctioned as slaves. Monks were summarily decapitated – except Elderic, who had been found hiding under a pile of corpses. He had pleaded with his captors, showing his papal ring of office. 'I am a prince of the Church. You must ransom me. For the mercy of God. For the mercy of Allah. Ransom me.' The Almoravid who had found him peered at the ruby with interest, then pulled out his knife and cut off the finger that bore it, stone and all. He tucked it into his belt and took the Pope's plenipotentiary, bleeding, to King Yusuf, who ordered him to be despatched like the other churchmen. As Elderic wailed that he would convert to the Mussulman faith, General Haza leaned forward and begged a boon, to which Yusuf agreed. So it was that Elderic was handed over to Khalisa. His screams lasted through the night, ending only at dawn when the king sent a messenger with an executioner's sword and a polite request that there might be silence in the camp for the morning prayers.

'You haven't mentioned Aziz and Ayesha,' said Paladon, in the silence that followed.

David looked stricken. It took him a moment to find the words. 'Aziz had no idea of Haza's plans before the battle. The negotiations with Yusuf had taken place in secret. He was as stupefied as we were when the Christians attacked us because we had been told we would ambush them. He fought – magnificently. I was by his side. He was a true king, determined to die with his people. I was still beside him when the Almoravids appeared. He was thunderstruck, knowing only then that he had been betrayed. Bloody and exhausted, he turned on Haza, there in the mêlée, and called him a traitor to Mishkhat. Haza's men surrounded and disarmed him. Now he's a prisoner in his father's house. Yusuf intends to send him into exile in North Africa, as he has the other Andaluzi kings he's deposed.'

'And Ayesha?' Paladon was frighteningly calm.

'She's . . .' David gulped.

'Out with it, man!' shouted Paladon.

'The women were brought before Yusuf. He was in his tent with his sons and his great-nephew, Karim, whom he's appointed as viceroy of Mishkhat. Yusuf was interviewing the royal prisoners and I was allowed in as Aziz's attendant. I saw it all.

'The African king asked for Ayesha's veil to be lifted. He wanted to see the fallen woman who had once been offered to him as a wife. There was much laughter at Aziz and Ayesha's expense – but she stood there, so beautiful, so dignified, so like a queen. Our new viceroy seemed fascinated by her. He drew the veil completely off her head, and stroked her hair and cheek. Then he turned to the king. "Uncle, I grew up in the desert and there we slake our thirst at any well, whoever may have used it. I have a mind to wed this princess of Mishkhat. I desire to sire on her a beautiful son whom her Christian bastard can serve."

'Aziz was so angry he had to be restrained, but Ayesha was icy and composed. She said, "You have the advantage of me, my lord. You have seen my face but I have not seen yours." There was renewed laughter at her audacity and Karim lowered the fold of the turban that wrapped his mouth, revealing the tribal scars on his cheeks, his thick lips and short beard. As quick as a cobra, Ayesha spat in his eye and, as he recoiled, she scratched his cheek so the blood ran down his brown skin. "Now slay me," she said, "for I have insulted you in front of your king. I would prefer to be wedded to death than to you. In the eyes of Allah and in my heart I am married to another, a better man than any of you. My son is no bastard."'

'She said that?' whispered Paladon.

'I gave her the letter you wrote to her. She wept a long while after reading it.'

Paladon closed his eyes. 'And did he slay her?'

'No. I think after she attacked him, he was attracted to her the more. There was a deathly silence, but Karim, wiping the spittle from his face with the fold of his turban, simply laughed. "She is a lioness, Uncle, who will be a mother of lions. Sell her to me. I will pay you a fifth of my share of the spoils from this battle, all in horses."

'King Yusuf smiled. "You may keep your horses and I will give you a fifth of my greater share of the spoils as her dowry. She is yours. As she is a captive and a slave, you are free to do with her as you will. There may even be wisdom in raising her to the status of a princess again. Our new subjects will be pleased. Except, Nephew, in future I will be cautious about drinking water from any wells that you have been near." Oh, Paladon, they were jesting even as they decided her fate.'

'That she's alive is all that matters,' said Paladon. 'Where is she now? Did the wedding take place?'

'I think not. I doubt Karim's back in Mishkhat yet. He left with half of the army shortly after we arrived to negotiate surrender terms with some of the outlying Christian garrisons. Ayesha and the Lady Janifa were taken to the palace.'

'You have brought excellent news, David. Thank you. All that remains to be asked is why you are here. Should you not still be with Aziz?'

'He asked me to escape, Paladon, and find you and Samuel. It was easy enough to slip away because they allowed me to go out and buy fruit where I could find it for Prince Aziz. I stole a horse and rode to the Maiden's pool, then found my way up through the tunnel, thinking you might come here if you were still alive. After a week I was beginning to despair. And this place frightens me.'

'And why did he ask you to find us?'

'He said something about a brotherhood and that you and

Samuel were his only true friends. He wants you to rescue him before he is sent to Africa. And Ayesha, of course, if you can.'

Paladon and I exchanged a glance.

'We have noted his priorities,' said Paladon, coldly.

David's face began to twitch. I, too, was glaring at him, feeling the familiar sense of disappointment at Aziz's selfishness. 'I did not explain myself well. It's Ayesha he's most concerned about.'

Paladon's steely expression showed his disbelief.

In his anxiety, David's words tumbled out. 'You must believe me, Paladon – he's terrified of what she might do to herself if she's forced into a marriage with Karim. He wants to be there with you when you rescue her. He knows the only reason you would come here would be to save your wife. He accepts that. In his heart, I believe, he's resigned to his own fate. But he thinks he can help you. Ayesha and the Lady Janifa may be more difficult to find than you think. They're locked up, but we don't know exactly where and in what condition. King Aziz has been trying to find out more from his captors. And – and there were other things he said that I didn't understand. He talked of seeking your forgiveness, Paladon, and proving himself to you. And to Samuel. And to somebody called ibn Sa'id. His manner was – penitent. Humble. He was not behaving as a king. Or not the one I'd known. But that's why I'm sure he's sincere. He wants to help you.'

Paladon looked at me questioningly. I shrugged. What was I to say? I wanted to believe David, but I was not convinced of Aziz's sudden change of heart towards Paladon. Certainly I wanted to rescue him – the thought of him living out his days in Africa appalled me – but Paladon was our general. It was his decision.

His brow knitted. He rose from his stool and began to pace. Then he surprised us by laughing. 'He mentioned the brotherhood, did he? And he wants to prove himself? Then we'd better give him the chance to do so.'

'Do you mean that, Paladon? You always said we would rescue Ayesha and Yasin first and consider whether we could do anything about Aziz afterwards.'

'No, Samuel, David's right. We have no idea how to get into the harem, assuming that's where they're being kept, and if Aziz thinks he can help us find a way, well, we shouldn't pass up the chance. Anyway,' he slapped the table, 'he's our friend.'

I stared at him in wonder.

'Is he not?'

'Yes,' I breathed. 'He is.'

'We're agreed, then.'

'You have a plan, I suppose?' I asked.

'Not yet.' He grinned. He was suddenly as full of life and energy as he had been when he was a boy. 'But remember, I'm a steeplejack. I know how to get on to the roof of Salim's house without being seen. I worked it out long ago. Not that I ever tried it. There was no point because I lived there. Maybe now is the time.'

As I watched him, stamping around checking weapons, throwing ideas over his shoulder as he drew a map of Salim's house with a charred stick on the stone floor, cajoling Tancred and Lotho until they were infected with his enthusiasm, I felt I was suddenly back in our old academy as we fired ourselves up for a new adventure. I sensed the celestial salt and nitre of the cave coursing through my veins and I believed that the mad task we had set ourselves might succeed.

One by one we climbed the rope ladder that Paladon had lowered. We had to be careful not to break any tiles when we scrambled over the parapet that lined the roof above the kitchens. We were prepared to silence armed guards, but none of us had any wish to murder cooks.

When we were crouching on the baked-mud roof, Paladon drew up the ladder, and pointed at the next level of roof we had to ascend. It was much higher and topped with crenellations.

Behind it – a dark shadow against the moonless sky – rose the harem quarters that were our destination. Candlelight shone through lattice windows. If David was correct, Aziz was in one of those rooms.

He had told us that Aziz was confined in a pavilion that could be reached by a staircase from the courtyard. He thought it must once have been part of Salim's harem, but it was effectively a separate wing, distanced from the rest by two chambers and a patio. The larger, more luxurious quarters that had been occupied by Salim's concubines had been taken by General Haza and his consort Khalisa, whom King Yusuf had appointed Aziz's gaolers. Aziz was therefore under constant surveillance, by Haza on the same floor and from the courtyard by Almoravid soldiers, who had been given the downstairs rooms of Salim's house as a barracks.

It was clear to Paladon and me that he was describing Ayesha's old quarters, and we saw our chance. We knew the layout intimately. Also, since Ayesha's pavilion was apart from the rest, we would not have to enter the main harem, with its complex passageways and corridors. We could approach it at roof level, unnoticed. With luck we could enter Aziz's window and escape with him the way we had come.

We had buried our hauberks and the Almoravid cloaks we had been using as our disguise in the rubble of nearby ruins. We had darkened our faces and limbs with mud, and dispensed with shoes and all our clothing except our jellabas, which we had blackened with ash. Paladon and his knights had kept their sword belts and I had my little shoulder satchel, which contained my knife and sling. David carried his bow and a quiver of arrows.

At Paladon's signal, we moved cautiously along the roof to the higher wall, while David remained behind, covering with an arrow the crenellated parapet above us in case a guard appeared. Only when we were all in place did he follow.

From where we huddled we had a view into the orchard and the courtyard. Paladon crawled over to the tiled parapet. Then he motioned me to join him, putting his finger to his lips. The courtyard was a red blaze of light, as it had often been when Salim gave his banquets. The great fire was crackling where lambs and calves had been roasted for his guests – but tonight the crackle was of burning parchment and vellum, and the black ash was that of paper. An Almoravid approached from the library with a pile of books and threw them on to the fire. He was followed by other soldiers bearing similar loads. I recognised the leather and gold bindings of Ptolemy's great *Cosmographica*, the green boards that bound the wisdom of ibn Sina's *Compendium*, and the calfskin box that contained the original manuscript of al-Khuwarizmi's *Algebra*. With a heave, two desert tribesmen hurled this into the flames and went back to collect more. I realised, my heart breaking, that the puritanical Almoravids, probably at King Yusuf's orders, were destroying Salim's library. For the first time in my life, I was conscious of an urge to kill.

Paladon's hand touched my arm and I saw the sympathy in his eyes. Of course he was right. Aziz and Ayesha and our love for each other were all that mattered now. My anger turned cold and, with renewed determination, I turned away from the funeral pyre of so much that I had once held dear and followed him back to where the others were crouching.

Tancred had been tying a noose at one end of a coil of rope Paladon had foraged from the building-site storeroom outside the cave mouth. He inspected it and, satisfied, looped it expertly over one of the crenellations. He tugged it tight, testing its strength, then nodded at Lotho who, a knife between his teeth, scurried up and rolled over the top. We waited what seemed an interminable time. Once we heard a grunt and the scrape of metal. Finally we saw his cropped head and his thumb gesturing upwards. Paladon threw the rope ladder to him, and he secured it for us to follow.

On the parapet lay the bodies of two Mishkhat men in armour. Their throats had been slit. I felt nothing.

There was no need for ropes now. Ayesha's wall was covered with thick ivy and a vine. During our evenings with her, Paladon had climbed down it a hundred times to pick sweet grapes. He scrambled up it now and peered through the lattice. He beckoned Lotho and me to follow. Tancred, who had picked up a bow from one of the dead guards, stayed with David, who was keeping watch below.

When I reached the top I could hear voices. I peeped through the lattice and saw Aziz, red-faced with fury and dressed only in a loincloth, pacing back and forth. Behind him on the carpet sat two men. One was General Haza in hauberk and helmet, the other a turbaned, veiled Almoravid. I could not see clearly who was standing to the side, draped in a black cloak.

Aziz shouted, 'I have told you a thousand times! I have no hidden treasure, neither in my palace nor on my person. You have already humiliated me by strip-searching me before a woman and torn the linings of all my clothes. What jewels did you find? None.'

'If you'd been co-operative, we wouldn't have had to search you, my lord,' said General Haza. 'None of us finds this pleasant, but yesterday you abdicated in favour of our viceroy and you must give him his due. Every royal asset belongs to him now – or, rather, to our holy cause, for my lord Karim will surely use it to finance further *jihad*. Is that not so, my lord?'

The Almoravid on the carpet grunted.

Aziz turned on him. 'Is it *jihad*, my lord, when you steal the kingdom of another Mussulman king? Is it *jihad* when you turn your lustful eyes on my sister whom you intend to dishonour? No, my lords, this greedy camel man with pretence to royalty, has plundered everything I had and now looks for my supposed wealth because he wants further dowry for his bigamous marriage. That is what it will be, Karim. You will damn yourself if you marry her. Ayesha's husband is Paladon and they were united in the sight of Allah. Neither you nor Yusuf – nor anybody – has the power to divorce them.'

When I heard this I gasped and looked at Paladon. His face was impassive, but as he lifted a finger to his lips to silence me, I thought I saw a gleam in his eyes. The Almoravid, however, who was presumably the new viceroy, only laughed.

It was the figure in the dark cloak who stepped forward, close enough to Aziz for her spittle to flick his face when she screamed, 'You are the damned one, Aziz! Lover of Christian violaters and treacherous Jews, protector of sorcerers and heretics, wine-drinking heathen! You brought ruin on our kingdom with your blasphemies and licentiousness. Oh, if I had you alone for an hour.' She slapped his face. 'As for your Paladon, he is dead – or will be as soon as Lord Karim finds him. He will perish from memory, he and all his blasphemous works. Did not the king – praise be to Allah – give orders that his evil mosque be destroyed so we can restore the rock to the holy shrine it once was?'

General Haza had stood up and put an arm round her. 'Gently, Khalisa, gently. Let Lord Karim handle things his way. You have done a great service that both he and King Yusuf appreciate. You are a handmaiden of the Prophet through whom holy truth speaks. Everybody knows this – but leave this matter to us.' He waited, smiling at her fondly, while with bad grace she returned to her former position. 'Now, Aziz, we have been very patient but Lord Karim does not have all night. Tell us, please. Where have you hidden the treasures of Mishkhat?'

Paladon leaned towards Lotho and, in a barely audible whisper, said, 'Go down. Tell David to come up here. I need a bowman. And you return with him. I need a swordsman, too.'

Lotho nodded and disappeared.

When the two of them were beside him, Paladon whispered, 'David. Through the lattice. Aim for Haza's throat. Samuel, you support him. Lotho, be ready.'

I had to wrap my legs round the tendrils of the vine, and even so I nearly lost my balance when I felt the weight of David's body as he leaned backwards. He sighted carefully. I heard the thrum and hiss as the shaft was released, and Paladon's urgent 'Now.' Then there was the crack of wood as the frail lattice broke and first Lotho, then Paladon tumbled into the room. David swung to the side. I scrambled upwards.

Through the window, I saw Aziz pressing his naked back against the wall and staring in bewilderment. Paladon was standing above Karim pressing a sword to his throat. Haza was crumpled in a heap of chain mail with an arrow in his eye. Lotho was on his back, both hands clutching the wrist of Khalisa, who was lying on top of him, panting as she pressed a curved butcher's knife towards his heart. I rolled over the lintel and snatched up Lotho's sword, which had caught in the broken lattice. Three steps and I pulled back Khalisa's head by the hair. I knew exactly where to cut. I felt no regret. She had been wronged but she had become a monster. When her body had stopped shaking, I let it go.

Paladon was speaking in a whisper: 'I'll take it that you yield, Karim. I am the Paladon whose wife you wish to marry. I have more than enough reason to kill you, and I will if you make a single sound.' Still keeping his sword at Karim's throat, he turned. 'Well done, Samuel. The best physic I've ever seen you perform. Lotho, gag this man and bind him. We will take him with us. David, that was a good shot. Go down now and bring up the rope ladder. I—'

He did not say more because Aziz had put his arms round him and embraced him. Paladon was at first confused. Then he lowered his sword carefully so that it did not clang on the tiles. He swung his arms round Aziz's back and hugged him with all his strength.

'Can you forgive me – can you?' Aziz's head was pressed against Paladon's chest. His nose was running. He was shivering with tension. His eyes were imploring. He looked like a frightened deer. I had not seen such genuine emotion or regret on his face since he was a boy. I felt a pang of sorrow thinking of all the wasted years . . .

'It's all past, Aziz,' said Paladon, who also appeared moved: his firm tone wavered. 'We're together again. That's all that matters.'

Aziz was sobbing. 'I can't forgive myself for what I did to you and Ayesha.'

Paladon kissed his forehead. 'We're a brotherhood, reunited, and that's a cause for joy. For too long we've had to make do on our own, but now we're three again. Aren't we, Samuel? Where are you?'

I dropped the sword on Khalisa's body and stumbled forward. Paladon's arm took me into his huge embrace. I curled my fingers round Aziz's waist. It was the first time I had touched his naked flesh in twelve years, but it was not passion I felt. It was a sense of oneness mixed with peace, calm, relief and, yes, as Paladon had said, joy, overriding, overwhelming joy. Silently we rocked together, and the years fell away. It seemed then that the natural order of the universe had been restored, and everything that had separated us was in harmony again. We were once more what we should always have remained: a selfless, undemanding brotherhood of friends.

'Come,' said Paladon. He was the first to break the spell and spoke what was in all our hearts. 'It's not over yet. We've another adventure to undertake before we're done, because there's still one missing from our circle. Anyway, Aziz, you should put some clothes on.'

Yet we remained hugging each other for a few seconds more, loath to let each other go.

When we did, I saw Paladon's prisoner, Karim, his arms pinioned behind him by Lotho, a rag bound tightly over his mouth. He was contemplating us thoughtfully.

With Tancred's knife at his back, Karim crouched when ordered to do so and crawled as silently as we did over the flat roofs. I was above him when we descended the rope ladder by the kitchens, and he suddenly looked up at me. The eyes above the gag that had replaced the blue cloth over his mouth showed no fear. They were amused.

When we reached the ruin, a merchant's house that had been burned to the ground, we donned our hauberks – Tancred had stripped the dead guards so there was armour for Aziz and me, as well as weapons. Karim sat cross-legged on the rubble, observing us coolly. Paladon squatted beside him and, with his knife, cut the gag.

'Thank you,' said Karim, after he had taken two great gulps of fresh air. 'My congratulations to my captors. That was as neat a military operation as I have ever seen.'

'It was bloodier than I'd intended,' said Paladon.

Karim shrugged. 'Haza and his devil woman are no loss. They were too riddled with hatred to be considered true Mussulmans. My uncle or I would have had to deal with them in time. You saved us the trouble.'

'You are very composed about your situation,' said Paladon.

'Have I reason to fear? I have been observing you, Paladon. I have perceived in you several virtues. You are loyal to your abdicated king and a good leader of men. You seem to be of a courtly and generous disposition. You had fair reason to kill me because of the woman, but you restrained yourself. I can only presume that you consider I am more valuable to you alive than dead. So I am curious to find out what you intend to do next. You and your . . .' his eyebrows rose humorously '. . . formidable little army.'

'Don't count on my mercy, Karim. If you wish to see the dawn, you had better convince me that you can be of use to me. I want Ayesha, my son and Princess Janifa alive and away from here.'

'Alas, my friend, if you expect my great-uncle to barter my life for a woman, you will be disappointed. You do not know him. He has many great-nephews, all of ability. One more, one less, he will accept what Allah dispenses. He certainly will not negotiate with rebels. He would find it demeaning. You had better save yourself the trouble and slay me now. I am quite ready. Death is but a momentary discomfort before an eternity of joy in the courts of Allah.'

I saw momentary confusion on Paladon's face and suspected that an exchange of hostages was exactly what he had had in mind.

He sheathed his sword. 'Gag him again, Tancred. We'll decide how to dispose of him later.'

'Before you do, perhaps you will consider a humble sugges-tion,' said the Almoravid. I was struck by his imperturbability. He spoke in as light a tone as you might hear over a convivial dinner.

'Be brief, then,' said Paladon. 'We have little time to spare.'

'I understand. You must complete your enterprise tonight because tomorrow morning Haza's body and Aziz's absence, not to mention mine, will be discovered and you will be hunted. I have told you I do not fear death, but life is sweet while it lasts. What would you say if I proposed a ransom of my own? Ayesha and the others delivered to you in exchange for my life?'

'You said King Yusuf didn't bargain.'

'He doesn't. I would be offering my help. This is a matter entirely between us.'

'Paladon, don't trust him,' said Aziz. 'He's a snake, as are all Almoravids.'

'I'll hear him out, Aziz. If I don't like what he has to say, you can do with him as you please. Karim, you have a minute to convince me. If you fail, Aziz will probably kill you.'

Karim, still smiling, nodded in courteous acquiescence. 'You are not madmen, so obviously you have a safe means to enter the palace. I guess by some secret door. My uncle suspects one exists – most palaces have them – but he has not found it yet. Suppose that you do break in and reach the harem. What then? Do you know where Ayesha, her son and Janifa are impris-oned within it? I will tell you. My uncle has built an iron cage for them, comfortably furnished and curtained to ensure their modesty. It is locked, however, and you do not have the key. It is also guarded by many more men than you have at your disposal, archers who will slay you before you get near. And do not think you can use me as a shield. Almoravids tend to be literal when it comes to obeying orders. They will fire their arrows regardless and I will be rewarded with many virgins in heaven, but that will not help you.'

'So what do you propose?'

'That you release me, allow me to return to the palace and fetch the ladies myself.'

'You're wasting our time,' said Paladon. 'Aziz, he's yours.'

Karim laughed. 'I am not expecting you to trust me. I am your enemy, and once I am absolved of my obligations to you as my honourable captors, I will hunt you down and take back the woman I desire. I am confident I will do so, and regrettably I will have to kill you, if only to do away with the slur of bigamy – but that is for tomorrow if Allah wills. Tonight, because you have treated me with honour and I respect you, I am prepared to help you. To ensure no duplicity on my part, I suggest that you send with me the Jew. He can walk beside me with his knife concealed against whichever part of my body he chooses. His skill with a blade suggests he is either a butcher or a surgeon. In either case he will know how to silence me instantaneously. Of course, if he kills me, he would be cut down himself afterwards and therefore the risk may not be to his liking. If he were an Almoravid he would face the prospect of such a death, having done his duty, with equanimity.'

'We are not Almoravids,' said Aziz.

'No, you are a heretical Mussulman and the others are infidels, and you have no place in this land we are restoring to Allah. There can never be peace between us – but there need not be hatred. We Almoravids do not hate. Why should we? We are soldiers of Allah, the Compassionate, the Merciful. And our word is our bond. I am offering you a temporary truce because Paladon spared my life. His mercy impressed me and I would like to thank him – but if you choose to reject my offer of help, I will not waste your time any further. Do with me as you will.'

'Gag him and guard him, Tancred,' said Paladon. He beckoned Aziz and me to a further part of the ruin where we could converse unheard.

'What do you think?' he asked.

'Kill him,' said Aziz. 'Or use him as a hostage. I don't believe his people would sacrifice him, even if they are fanatics.'

'Samuel? Would you trust him?'

'No, but if only half of what he told us is true – about the cage and the guard – we have little chance of success. Paladon, you knew this enterprise might be suicidal. None of us said it, but we were all prepared to die in the endeavour. On the other hand, if he can bring Ayesha, Yasin and Janifa to us . . . We wouldn't lose anything by trying it. He won't know how we plan to get into the palace. He won't have a chance to warn anybody that a raid is being made. If he opens his mouth, he'll be dead within a few seconds. So will I, but that doesn't matter. Aziz can still guide you to the harem where you would be taking the same chances as you would if we hadn't found Karim. It would probably be the death of you all anyway, so what's the difference? As I see it, Fortune has suddenly given us a windfall and we'd be mad not to take it. And I'm impressed by the man. He comes across as honourable.'

'I think so too,' said Paladon. 'Samuel, you're prepared to do this? I'm sorry that I can't volunteer because of my resemblance to a Frank.'

'I will be the one to accompany Karim,' interrupted Aziz. 'Let me do this. I am Arab. My skin is paler than theirs but dark enough to pass unnoticed. I also have a reason for hating this man so he will have no doubt I will kill him, and he should therefore be all the more co-operative. Also, you have risked so much for me after I have so grievously offended you that my conscience insists. I see it as my chance to atone for all the hurt I've caused the brotherhood. Grant me this.'

'Samuel?'

My first instinct was, as always, to be protective of Aziz, but I saw the imploring look in his eyes and understood how much he wanted to prove himself. 'I have no objection,' I said. 'I can tell him where to put the point of his knife against Karim's body.'

'I'll leave you two to make your farewells then,' said Paladon, 'while I explain what's happening to Tancred and Lotho. Don't forget to put your blue burnous over your armour, Samuel. Remember, we're Almoravids until we get to the goat path. Aziz, bring Karim and the women to the secret room in the tunnel. There, we'll do the exchange. You and Karim will leave here first in five or ten minutes. The rest of us will follow fifteen minutes after.'

Five minutes. That was all we had. There was so much to say that we said nothing. I spent most of the precious time rehearsing Aziz on how to hold his knife against the carotid artery and, like my scolding mother, muttering useless injunctions to 'be careful' mixed with a pompous little lecture about blood circulation to the heart and the seconds it would take for a man to die. The black wells of Aziz's eyes watched me fondly as I fussed, and his lips were curved in an affectionate smile.

Whether by art or design he eventually dropped the knife. I leaned forward to pick it up, and he put his hands on either side of my head and pulled me towards him. In the next moment his mouth had covered mine. His hand moved down my back to lift my jellaba. I felt the cool touch of his fingers on my thigh, on my belly, then across my chest until his palm rested on my heart. I clutched him closer. Gently he broke the kiss. His lips touched the tip of my nose, my eyes, and pressed into my forehead. 'Thank you for giving me permission to take your place,' he whispered. 'It's the first time you've ever trusted me, I think.'

'I've always trusted you.'

'No, you haven't – and you were right not to because I'm . . . not very capable. To tell you the truth, I could never understand what you saw in me. You frightened me a little, Samuel. I couldn't live up to you. I . . .'

I ran my fingers through his hair. It was still soft and curly. 'Don't say it. There'll be time for all of that later.'

His shoulders quivered. 'I meant what I said about expiating my crimes. I won't leave you ever again, you know.' He attempted a smile. 'In fact, if somehow we survive this, you'll have to keep me away, even if you're not interested in me any more because I look old and grey and—'

'You just get through this, Aziz,' I cut him off. 'Come back. Safely . . .' I heard the shuffle of stones and a cough and saw Lotho's eyes above the wall, staring phlegmatically over our heads.

'It's time,' said Aziz, stiffening.

I pulled him to me violently and kissed his lips, then thrust him away. 'Watch him like a snake, Aziz. He's clever, and dangerous. Just keep that knife to his neck. I won't forgive you if anything goes wrong.'

'Samuel,' he murmured. 'My dear, dear Samuel.'

After he had left I sat with my head against a broken pillar, staring into an unknown future that, after a decade of sorrow, suddenly mattered again. Thinking of Aziz going off alone, I felt a sense of heavy foreboding.

Then I smiled. I was proud of him. I was certain, too, deep inside, that everything would be all right. Aziz and I were together again. Fortune was on our side.

It was as if we were invisible. As we passed through the town we came across several Almoravid patrols, but they only muttered, '*Salaam aleikum*,' and went their way. We slipped easily into the bushes and climbed, unnoticed, up the goat path. There were no guards outside the walls. We reached the little door and unlocked it with the key Aziz had told us we would find under a brick. Soon we had gathered in the secret room.

It was as we had left it the night we had fled with General Haza. The bloody bandages I had taken off Aziz's shoulder were still lying on the mildewed carpet. I sat on one of the damp couches, my heart heavy now. I thought of how this room had been the scene of both joy and tragedy in our previous lives. It was as if Fate was steering us back to our beginnings, although whether for good or ill I could not tell.

Paladon positioned his men in the corridor and joined me. He saw my glum expression and punched my shoulder. 'All's well, Samuel. We will succeed, I promise.'

'There are so many imponderables,' I said. 'I'm terrified for Aziz. If – if something goes wrong up there . . .'

He sat down beside me. 'It won't,' he said gently.

I saw his strength and confidence. 'Yes, we must believe so,' I said.

We sat silently side by side, taking comfort from each other's presence.

'Paladon,' I said, 'have you thought what we shall do afterwards?'

'Leave Mishkhat.' He grinned. 'With my wife and son.'

'No, I mean after we leave Mishkhat. The Andaluz we love is no more.'

'Some territories still hold out. King Mu'tamin still rules in Saragossa. We could go there. He would welcome Aziz.'

'For a time, but we have seen the future. The war between the Christians and the Almoravids will continue, and everything that is dear to us is already being ground down by their hatred. The Christians will continue to pour in. Europe is full of men like Elderic. Crusaders and fanatics. The Almoravids are strong and may push back the tide for a while, but Yusuf is old – and the society he wants to create is barren and joyless. It will wither and become corrupt. I despair, Paladon. Mussulman ignorance and hatred. Christian ignorance and hatred. What sort of world will it be? There is no place for our brotherhood.'

'I'll be happy wherever I am, as long as I'm with Ayesha and Yasin, but for what it's worth, I think you're wrong.'

'Paladon, this very evening we watched books burning.'

'Oh, Samuel, don't you understand? It doesn't matter. We can survive without them. We have the ideas here.' He tapped his head. 'And here.' He tapped his heart. 'That's where God is. It was you who taught me that, although I've probably only realised it recently, when I saw what horrors Christians and Mussulmans are doing in His name. Then I remembered what you always said. The world is rational and creative. It's a wonderful mystery for our minds to discover and celebrate. God's everywhere and we're all different. That's the beauty of it – the sheer diversity. What a tapestry to enjoy.' He chuckled. 'Do you remember that old fanatic al-Gazali? And the Cid? You were always saying how similar they were and I never understood what you were talking about – but I think I do now. Life's for living, and they drank it to the lees. They were aberrations – one was a mystic and the other was a homicidal maniac – but they were healthier than the crusaders and Almoravids. I pity them. Going through the small print of their Bibles and Qur'āns every day, like lawyers, seeking justification for their atrocities. It's a sapless world they're making, like a dying tree. But we don't have to live in that world, Samuel. As long as we breathe, as long as we see that God is life and joy, as long as we cultivate the best in us, not the worst, we're free. You and ibn Sa'id created a beautiful system of philosophy, which I never totally comprehended but I loved the symbols. Prime Mover. Celestial nitre. All of that. That's what the brotherhood was about. The mosque we built together was beautiful. As long as we have that, we're untouched inside.'

'We don't have it any more. Tonight we heard that Yusuf's going to destroy it.'

'It doesn't matter. The idea remains. I'll rebuild the mosque some day, if I can. Stone is the only way I can express myself properly. Who knows? Maybe I'll even come back to Mishkhat if the tides turn again and Sancho or Alfonso is victorious. Who cares if the outward form is a mosque or a cathedral? I told you, for me it's the temple of what we believe. And if I don't get the chance to restore it, it's no loss, because as long as we three live, or any one of us lives, the idea of the building we created remains. Andaluz lives, Samuel, or the idea of it. Tolerance, generosity, harmony, everything we've loved. And if we die, today or another day, it'll still be alive, in the heavens, in the earth, wherever there is love.'

He looked embarrassed. 'Sorry – looks like I was giving you my version of a holy war to counter theirs. But, come to think of it, we are mujahideen of sorts, though for a better cause than crusaders or Almoravids. We're doing something worth dying for in our small way.'

'You're right. It all comes down to love.'

'Exactly. And isn't it a brave adventure? However it ends. I'm optimistic, Samuel, and I'm as happy as I've been since . . . since we found you up a fig tree and the whole thing began.'

'It may end badly,' I said.

Paladon clasped my shoulders, and his blue eyes gazed into mine. 'We may fail,' he said softly, 'but it won't be a defeat. Not now. Isn't it a comfort that we'll all die together, our brotherhood restored? That's a victory of sorts, isn't it? Though only we know it.'

He leaped to his feet, suddenly alerted to a noise outside, which I had heard, too – a clang, and a confusion of footsteps. Grimly he unsheathed his sword and took two steps towards the door. Before he reached it, it opened.

Ayesha rushed in, with a shy Yasin behind her, and threw herself into Paladon's arms. They were followed by Aziz and Janifa, whose red face was beaming, and behind them came David, grinning at Janifa, and finally Karim, guarded by Lotho. But Paladon had eyes only for Ayesha and she for him. There were no tears, no hesitations. It was as if they had never been apart. Paladon smiled, and she smiled in return. They kissed and then she laid her cheek against his chest. For a while they rested quietly in each other's arms. From their actions, they might have been an old couple greeting each other after one had returned from market, taking tender pleasure in their closeness. Yet none of the rest of us was unmoved, for the strength of their love appeared more powerful in its restraint and confidence. They appeared to grow in stature. Their skin glowed. I felt again the holiness I had witnessed once before. There was a feeling of a natural order being restored, like the co-alignment of two planets, or the emergence of day after an at first imperceptible dawn.

Ayesha knelt down, smiling, and gestured for Yasin to come from his hiding place among the folds of Janifa's skirt. The little boy was staring in wonder and some fear at the tall figure of his father, whom he was seeing for the first time. She leaned forward and, after kissing his brow, took his hand and presented him to Paladon, who also knelt – somewhat clumsily – to offer his own big hand. Then he stroked his son's cheek, his eyes misting with tears.

'He has your looks,' he murmured.

'His hair and colouring are yours,' she replied.

Those were the only words they spoke. It did not seem strange. There was no longer a need for urgency. They were reunited. Their universe was whole again and eternity lay ahead of them.

Karim had his arms folded. He was watching the reunion contemplatively.

I approached Aziz and embraced him. 'My Gazelle, you triumphed.'

'I'm not so sure, Samuel,' he whispered, and pulled me out of earshot of the others. I noticed how sombre he looked. 'It was too easy,' he continued, glancing at our captive. 'We walked through the palace like ghosts. There was nobody about. And when we entered the harem, the soldiers bowed to Karim without a word spoken and stepped aside. We unlocked the metal cage – it was exactly as he described it – then left with the women and Yasin. Ayesha and Janifa were confused, of course, and my sister was reluctant to go anywhere with Karim until I showed her the knife pressed against his back – but nobody followed us. It was as if it had been planned.'

I felt a chill go down my spine, and glanced at Paladon, who was still kneeling in front of his son. Ayesha was laughing because Paladon had just reached into his pocket and given his boy a carved wooden horse, certainly fashioned by his own hands, perhaps long ago, waiting for this day. A tear ran down his cheek as Yasin's eyes opened wide with delight. Then Paladon seemed to become aware of the rest of us and that we were waiting for him. He rose to his feet, turned and went to Karim. He took his hand and shook it. I heard him say something about 'honour among enemies'. By then I was already outside, Aziz behind me, running up the tunnel.

Lotho had handed Karim to David to guard and had returned to his position by the door that led to the upper floors of the palace. Had he heard any sound? I asked him. He shook his head. I went down the passage and asked the same of Tancred, who was guarding the outer door. 'Nothing,' he said. I told him to open the door a fraction and peered outside. I saw only bushes waving in the slight breeze and the dim lights of the city below. 'Stay on guard. Have your bow primed.'

'There's nobody there,' he said.

'No one we can see,' I answered. 'Keep your ears open and warn us if you sense anything is wrong.'

'You think it may be a trap?' whispered Aziz.

'I don't know,' I said. As we reached the door to the room, I pulled my knife from my sheath. I was right behind Karim, and pressed the point against his throat. 'Kneel,' I said. 'Slowly.'

Paladon was staring at me, aghast. 'What are you doing, Samuel? This man's kept his promise.'

'To deliver the princesses,' I said. 'He hasn't told us what he intends to do afterwards. Paladon, we must leave now. I think we've been fooled all along.'

I ripped the cloth from Karim's face. He looked up at me scornfully.

'Where are your men going to attack us? Do they know about the path?'

He said nothing.

'Paladon, get the women and child out of here.' He nodded. I was in command. 'David, join Tancred with your bow. Aziz, put your knife where mine is. Press in half an inch and he's dead.' I looked into Karim's unperturbed face. 'So, you're an Almoravid, my lord, and don't fear death. Virgins await you in Paradise. I shall ask you again. Where will you spring your trap?'

He began to mutter a Mussulman prayer. '*La illah illa Allah, Muhammad rasoolu Allah.*'

'There's no need to prepare yourself for death, my lord,' I said. 'I, like Paladon, am merciful – but I'm a surgeon and I enjoy practising my skills. If you don't answer my question I will make sure that you'll never service another woman in your lifetime and you can be assured that when you eventually reach Paradise the virgins will laugh at you because you will be of no use to them.' As I spoke I cut the cloth of his burnous to the hem. 'I ask you again. Where will you ambush us, Karim?'

And this extraordinary man smiled. He still spoke in conversational tones, even with a knife at his throat and another at his groin. 'I am impressed, Samuel. When I saw you kill Khalisa, I knew you were the formidable one in this party. When I discovered your name I realised you were the Jew who walked bravely into the Christian camp with false information. A very dangerous man, I said to myself. That is why I wanted to take you to the palace where I could dispose of you.'

'You would have been dead if you'd tried.' The two halves of his burnous dropped to the floor.

'It was a risk, but my hidden archers would have been as quick and as accurate with their arrows as you are with your knife. I did take precautions, in case we didn't capture your party in Haza's house.' He lowered his eyelids gracefully. 'I must acknowledge that there your little expedition surprised me. My congratulations to Paladon were sincere. It was neglectful of us, but we had not expected a quiet assault from the roofs.'

'Do tell us how you knew we were coming. Did you hear word from the patrols we fought in the hills on the way here? Is that why you let David escape so easily so that he could find us and tell us where Aziz and Ayesha were?' As I spoke I began to cut at his loincloth.

'It was a combination of many things,' he said. 'When my uncle found the secret door in the palace, we suspected there might be a loyalist attempt to rescue the royal prisoners. We have been trained to hunt in the desert. It is large and empty. If you can lure your game to come to you, it saves effort.' He frowned. 'You do not sincerely propose to go through with your . . . surgery?'

'You have not answered my question.' My knife cut through and his loincloth, fell away. 'Where are your men waiting for us?'

He sighed. 'Very well. It is vanity but I prefer to keep my manhood intact. I will tell you, not that it will do you much good. My soldiers wait halfway down the goat path by the rock-hang where you must go in single file.'

I saw the shock in Aziz's eyes and watched his knife waver. Before I could react, Karim moved – as quickly as an uncoiling serpent. He twisted the knife out of Aziz's hand and hurled him aside. Then he was jabbing the point at me. I shouted a warning as I backed away and immediately tripped. That fall saved me because the knife slashed the air above my chest – but Karim leaped nimbly forward and I saw the triumph in his eyes as the knife plunged down. I felt a thump on my upper body and then a great weight on my chest. I saw Aziz's imploring eyes above me, a thin trickle of blood forming in the corner of his mouth. Then I understood that the knife was buried in his back.

At first I could not take it in. There was the clatter of feet, a roar of rage and Paladon, his right hand wielding his sword, shoved Karim against the wall. He was about to bring the sword down on his head. Somehow I still had the presence of mind to call out to him: 'No, Paladon, we need him as a hostage. They're outside.'

I heard Paladon groan. He dropped his sword and banged Karim's head against the stone. The unconscious Almoravid slipped to the ground, on almost the very spot where Paladon had killed Ephraim. Paladon turned his stricken face towards us. I could hear Ayesha moaning as she was restrained by Janifa. I became aware that Tancred and David were moving Aziz from on top of me, laying him on his side.

'Leave him,' I screamed. 'Don't you see he's hurt? None of you touch him. He's mine – mine.' I probably yelled other imprecations too. Tancred and David rose, sadness in their eyes.

'Keep awake, Aziz,' I pleaded. 'Breathe slowly. I need to remove this knife, and then I can cure you . . .'

With an effort he smiled. 'Samuel . . . loyal, loving Samuel . . .'

'Don't talk. There, it's not too deep a cut. All I need to do is bind it up and apply a potion. Where's my medical bag?' I yelled. 'Somebody, fetch me my bag.'

His eyes clenched shut in a spasm of pain. When he opened them he was smiling again. 'I'll be waiting for you,' he said. 'I told you . . . I shall not let you leave me ever again . . .' His limbs began to shake and his eyes widened. 'Forgive me,' he whispered. He sighed, as if he was falling asleep, and his eyes half closed.

Paladon had to carry me away from him.

*　　*　　*

Of course Karim had lied again, as he had when he told us Yusuf did not know about the secret door. His men were not halfway down the path. They were all around us. When Paladon opened the door a crack and stepped outside with the Almoravid in front of him, we heard the hiss and thump of arrows. Several hit the door, and more than one thudded against flesh. Paladon jumped back inside, unhurt but without Karim. 'The wretch was right. Yusuf's great-nephews are expendable.'

Paladon ordered Tancred and Lotho to bring the table from the room. He was a monument of calm and cheerfulness, ruffling his son's hair and whispering encouraging words to Ayesha and Janifa. I think he was already a little mad. 'We only have to get into the bushes up and to the left,' he kept saying. 'They won't be able to catch us because I know the paths and they don't. We'll move slowly leftwards keeping our heads behind the table so the arrows won't hit us. We have only to get to the cave, and then, my darlings, we're away.'

It sounded lunatic but we did as we were told. None of us had a better idea, and somehow Paladon's desperate energy made the impossible happen again.

It was like a hailstorm outside, the arrows rattling and thumping on the walnut planks of the table and pattering on the ground around us. Amazingly, we must have travelled crab-wise fifteen feet, and were almost near the bushes, when an arrow caught Tancred in the leg. He stumbled, and the table dropped. I took his place. I saw him crawling towards a rock and stringing his bow. He winked at me as he leaned his back against the stone, pulling a shaft to his chin. I will never forget that wink.

That was just before I was hit, in the flesh just above the ankle. It burned and I stumbled, but I kept on.

At the edge of the bushes we stopped, and rested the table. David and Janifa were on the far left. David put his arm round the old princess's shoulders and the two dived for cover, disappearing into the bushes. So might we all have done, if Ayesha had not lost sight of Yasin, who had been clutching her skirt in his terror. In fact, Paladon had picked him up but she had not seen him do so.

In her panic she stood up and an arrow went through her throat.

That's another impression that will never leave me – the angelic, mischievous face I loved, closing her eyes as if in vexation at the blood pouring from her mouth. Her beautiful hand fluttered as if to wipe it away and, as elegantly, fell when her legs gave way.

Paladon dropped to his knees and caught her. I managed to grasp Yasin and cradle him, covering his eyes as he screamed, 'Mama, Mama.' Paladon had entered some realm of unearthly calm. I had never seen a more tender expression on his face as he hugged Ayesha's body to his chest, bending his head over hers, whispering into her unhearing ears and smiling at the answers he imagined from her still lips.

'I understand . . . You must rest, my love. We'll move when you're ready. We've plenty of time . . . It's not far. Not really. I've prepared a place for us to live, yes, a little cottage looking over the river at Toledo. All those towers. So beautiful at sunset. There's a studio for me, a nursery for Yasin, and for you . . . Yes, I've made it just like your old pavilion. Your lute's there and waiting for you . . . We'll be happy, so happy . . .'

Lotho caught my eye. The flights of arrows had ceased. We could hear the crunch of stones and the rattle of metal. He pointed at Paladon and jerked his head at the bushes. Suddenly he grinned. '*Deus lo vult*, eh?' Then he leaped over the table. I heard shouts and the clash of steel.

I crawled towards Paladon, pushing Yasin in front of me. 'You have to leave Ayesha now, Paladon.' I spoke firmly, as to a child. 'I'll look after her. You take your son. Remember, you have a temple to build. You can teach him the craft. He can help you.'

He raised his face towards me. His eyes were uncomprehending, a little irritated perhaps that I had disturbed him. 'Your son. Save your son,' I said.

He uttered a terrible cry. It sounded as if his soul was being wrenched from his body. I hear it to this day. I knew what it meant too. It was the cry of a man who wakes from madness into a world that is intolerable. Every time I close my eyes in the darkness I hear those reverberating echoes, and sometimes they are his voice and sometimes my own.

He glared wildly about him, picked up his boy and ran. As he did so, the string tying his satchel to his belt must have loosened, because it thumped down on the grass.

I leaned my head against the table, listening to the sound of Lotho's last battle. It seemed to be going on for a very long time. I learned from admiring Almoravids afterwards that on Lotho's body they found eighteen wounds. He had killed six men and Tancred another five.

I was relieved when there was silence again. I could concentrate on the task I had set myself. It was suddenly very important to me that I made Ayesha presentable. I did not want the Almoravids to see her in this state. I closed her eyes, wiped the blood from her mouth and chin, and straightened her dishevelled clothing. I sensed the presence of people around me but nobody disturbed me and for that I was grateful.

After a while, the handkerchief I was using to wash Ayesha's face became soaked with blood. I thought of the bag Paladon had dropped. I found some spare clothes in it, with which I finished my job. I also found a tiny oaken carving. It was masterfully done, varnished and polished. The detail was immaculate. It was an eagle, its wings opening to soar. Its base consisted of two hearts clutched in the bird's talons. As he had given a wooden horse to his boy, I assumed this was to be his gift to Ayesha on the occasion of their reunion. Well, I thought, sadly, I had been a go-between and passed messages before.

There was a small ring on the eagle's crown, and through

this I threaded a thin chain of gold that I had worn since my father died, unclipping first the charm my mother had given me. I secured the necklace round her neck, tucking Paladon's carving into her dress, as close to her heart as I could. Then I lifted her in my arms. I don't know how I managed to do it with an arrow through my tendon, but I did. Of course, she was very light. Sometimes bodies are when the spirit leaves them.

The soldiers, who had been watching me curiously, were Almoravids, with cloths over their mouths, but their eyes did not seem unsympathetic. Only one officious fellow irritated me a little by demanding over and over again that I should surrender.

'No, you don't understand,' I told him patiently, speaking slowly and clearly so he would comprehend. 'The Lady Ayesha is a princess. We must take her to the palace where she will be more comfortable and so she can be close to her royal brother, the king.'

I had to repeat myself several times. Eventually it was his own people who told him to desist. One said that I was touched by Allah. I wasn't sure what he meant at the time but, again, I was grateful.

I tottered on. The ranks of soldiers parted for me. The solemnity of their expressions behind their face cloths showed appropriate respect. Some even had tears in their eyes.

But I didn't get far along the track. The pain from my wound, and sheer exhaustion, caused me to pass out long before I reached the door into the palace.

Andalucía, 1938

5

The Niche of Light

Dawn had already paled the stained-glass windows, and shadowy saints were taking form. Pinzon, wet-eyed, felt a little ashamed, thinking that at heart he was no different from the peasants who had been his earlier audience or children who only craved a happy ending. There were a few more pages, but he did not have the stomach for more tragedy.

Behind him, he heard the rustle of waking bodies and the murmur of voices. He sighed. He had still to work out what to say to the hostages, especially in the event that the news Paco brought back was bad, or if he did not come at all.

He slipped the book into his pocket, and as he did so, he recalled Samuel's last conversation with Paladon while they waited in the secret room. They, like him, he thought, had been prepared to stake all on a gamble. Paladon and Samuel had sent Aziz into the palace on a suicide mission to rescue Ayesha. Pinzon was relying on the untrustworthy Paco to verify his tunnel. The chances of success in either situation were slender – but there was no going back. What intrigued him was how, in this moment of uncertainty, Paladon and Samuel had accepted, with courage and fortitude, whatever the outcome would be. 'We may fail,' Paladon had said, 'but it won't be a defeat . . . Isn't it a comfort that we'll all die together, our brotherhood restored? That's a victory of sorts . . . though only we know it.'

Pinzon was amazed that the preservation of Samuel's 'Idea' had been as much in their minds as the rescue of their beloved Ayesha. At the time of their greatest peril they were thinking of something beyond themselves.

Pinzon's task was to save those he loved – his grandson, the strange woman who had mysteriously come into his life, and the other hostages, who had put their trust in him – but as he sat there he had the unsettling feeling that he was missing something crucial. Fate had brought him here, the manuscript had revealed a means of salvation, and last night, hallucinating in his exhaustion, he had experienced something akin to a spiritual awakening, when the very stones in the walls seemed to be throbbing with unearthly power. He had for a while believed that a divine force was leading him on. Was it purely so he could uncover a tunnel through which he and his companions could crawl to safety leaving death and destruction behind them? In the grander scheme of things, it seemed petty, almost selfish. Or was there another purpose which he had not yet grasped?

The Idea. The Idea. He kept coming back to the Idea.

Looking around him at the cathedral, which was slowly emerging in all its glory, he marvelled at the exquisite traceries and perfect lines, remembering Paladon's prayer to the Master Builder, the Prime Mover of the Celestial Spheres, the Lord of the Line and Circle, the True Form and the All-seeing Eye. He wished he had the time to explore every corner and compare it with the equally breathtaking mosque below.

He was horrified that such beauty could be sacrificed to mindless destruction. He and his grandson might escape, but the cathedral and mosque, secret symbols of tolerance and harmony, would be consumed by hatred, leaving Samuel's great 'Idea' another fractured dream. Already the little men were triumphing . . .

As he looked into the future, Pinzon could foresee only the triumph of evil. Petty squabbles between empty ideologies had already destroyed his ideal of a republic: anticlericalism against the Church, left against right, unions against the landed classes, republicanism against monarchy, all subsumed into the brutal struggle between Fascism and Communism. Such a polarisation of forces might soon conflagrate into a general European war. The new tyrannies would never tolerate the humanistic dream, carved by Paladon in stone – though the message was as relevant now as it had been eight centuries ago. These were darker times than Samuel's. Science had been conscripted into the ranks of man-made gods and new materialistic ideologies fought fanatically for primacy in a world that had banished wonder, condemning mankind to a mind-numbing conformity of thought.

And now Ogarrio with his modern explosives was about to consign one of the last shining messages of hope into darkness.

He stared sadly at Tomás, wondering what the future held for him. Then he gazed longingly at María. He tried to imagine what the philosophical Samuel would say to him in this situation. He would probably murmur kindly, 'These are only constructs of stone and mortar. Truth exists in the mind and heart, not in the symbols we make of it. Your duty is to those whom you love and whom you can save.' And it was true, but looking into his own soul, he was conscious only of anger and revulsion.

What life was worth preserving, he wondered, when every human value had been corrupted? What separated men from beasts but the ideas that, through millennia, had created civilisation? Destroy those and humanity would enter a new dark age of barbarism. Was that the world he wished on his grandson?

Something had to remain.

He straightened his back and sat erect on his pew. He felt a new spurt of energy. He knew what he had to do. It was not really a question of choice. It was simply a matter of accepting responsibility and doing the right thing. There was no point in thinking of what might have been, although, looking at the sleeping faces of his grandson and the woman with whom he might have shared a life, he felt a pang of bitter regret. Fate had placed him here at this time and had given him a job to accomplish. It was as if the elements that had made up his existence had distilled to this point, revealing its purpose.

It would not be easy – nothing worthwhile ever was – but everything was in motion. All he had to do was adjust his plan a little.

And that made him think of Paco.

Where was he? He pulled out his watch. He should have returned by now. Paladon had said it took two hours each way between the cave and the pool. What had happened to him? He remembered again that sly smile and feared the worst.

He made another decision. If Paco had not returned in an hour, he would take the hostages down to the cave anyway. It was certain death otherwise. At least the tunnel offered a chance of survival . . .

A ray of sun streamed on to his face through a stained-glass window. It was a depiction of Jesus being apprehended in the Garden of Gethsemane. The reds and greens and blues shone like rubies, emeralds and sapphires and he was dazzled by their brilliance. He looked into the face of the Christ and saw in the expression only kindness, forgiveness and calm. He also recognised an extraordinary resemblance to his son, Raúl.

María stirred, opened her eyes and smiled. Gently she lifted Tomás off her knees, and laid him on the flagstones, using her blanket as a pillow. 'Better let him sleep on while he can,' she said. 'The poor little thing.'

He wondered at her brightness and beauty in the growing light of the morning.

She sat down on the pew beside him and kissed his cheek. 'And you?' she said. 'Did you sleep?'

'No, I finished the book.'

She raised an eyebrow. 'Please tell me it had a happy ending.'

'Sadly Aziz died,' he said. 'So did Ayesha, but Paladon escaped with his son, and Samuel survived. It ended on a note of hope.'

She laughed. 'But not for the woman. That's not very encouraging.' She nudged him. 'Don't look so miserable. I'm teasing you.' She frowned. 'No magical answer, though. Tomás will be disappointed. You think there's any hope left for us at all?'

'We must believe so,' he said. He felt a pang of guilt, but it was too early to tell her about the tunnel. He wanted to raise no false hopes until he was sure.

She yawned. He felt her arm lightly brush his shoulder. 'The world doesn't change, does it? Funny how all those characters seemed so real to me when you were reading. As if I knew them.' She sighed. 'I'm sorry Ayesha died. I saw Paladon's and her love affair as a sort of symbol. All those ghastly trials and tribulations they had to face. Maybe if they'd managed somehow to get through, we would have too. Is there any news from Ogarrio?'

'Not yet,' he said. He wanted to change the subject. He pointed at Felipe who was still asleep against the pillar, his head crooked at a grotesque angle as he snored softly. 'We'd better wake him in case Ogarrio comes in suddenly and finds his guard in dereliction of duty.'

It was Felipe's panicked shout of alarm when he jerked into wakefulness, glaring around him in terror and clutching his rifle, that woke Tomás.

The little boy yawned and stretched. Then he saw Samuel's book lying on the pew. His eyes lit up with hope. 'Did you finish it, Grandfather? Did Samuel tell you a way out?'

Pinzon glanced towards María, who was busy folding the blankets. He leaned towards Tómas and squeezed his hand, at the same time putting a finger to his lips. 'Yes, he did, Tomás,' he whispered. 'He did.' He tapped his head. 'And I've got the secret inside here. But I can't tell it to anybody yet, not even you or María. Not until the right time – or the magic won't work. Do you understand?'

Tomás nodded solemnly. 'It's like making a wish when you break a chicken's wishbone, isn't it? If you tell anyone what it is, it'll never happen. That's what Lupita said.'

'That's right, Tomás. You must never reveal this secret to anybody, even afterwards. We must protect Samuel, too, if he's helping us, mustn't we? No one must know about the magic book and what we discover below. Will you promise your old grandfather?'

Tomás frowned. 'Like a bandits' code of silence?'

'Exactly.'

María passed by, her arms full of blankets, and gave them a smile. 'What are you two whispering about?'

'It's a secret,' said Tomás, proudly. 'I can't tell you.'

María raised her eyebrows at Pinzon, who shrugged. 'Men's talk, I suppose,' she said.

'Yes, Aunt María,' said Tomás, importantly.

'Oh – well, I'd better get out of earshot then, hadn't I?' Laughing, she moved over to the other side of the chancel where, Hector had placed the buckets for the hostages to use as a lavatory.

'Do you like María, Tomás?' asked Pinzon.

'Yes, Grandfather, and I think she likes us too.'

'Would you be happy if she looked after you, as – as Lupita did?' He found the words catching in his throat.

The boy's mouth opened wide with excitement. 'Would she come and live with us, Grandfather?'

'Well, we'll see what the magic brings,' said Pinzon. 'I'd be very happy if you and she were together.'

'And you, Grandfather. The three of us – it'll be such fun!'

He braved a smile and ruffled Tomás's hair. 'Go on, off with you,' he croaked. 'Felipe will probably be looking for you.'

The little boy ran to find his friend. Pinzon watched him,

his heart pounding with love. He thought of the decision he had just made. This might be more difficult than he had anticipated.

Later, Grandmother Juanita and some of the other women made a fire in the side chapel, using the lectern stool as fuel. In a while, she called that stew was to be served. The hostages dutifully lined up for their meal. Then came the realisation that there were no plates or bowls. Ogarrio had provided food – meat, cheese and bread – but few utensils, apart from a cauldron his men had purloined from one of the houses in the town. Hector remembered that the church plate was still stored in the vestry. Some of the men broke down the door, went inside and came out loaded with gold platters and silver chalices.

The novelty, not to mention the sacrilege, had the effect of releasing the tension that had been building throughout the night. Grandmother Juanita, in buoyant mood, mimicked a priest at holy communion, making the sign of the cross as she ladled the stew, and the hostages, in their rumpled cassocks and nuns' habits, genuflected accordingly.

To Pinzon, the merriment was bizarre. The playacting of the villagers in their religious garb, sipping from ruby-encrusted cups, or prancing after Hector who had put a bishop's mitre on his venerable head and was leading a procession holding a crucifix, had all the elements of a *danse macabre*. All it needed was somebody costumed as a skeleton.

He felt María's hand on his. 'It's all right,' she said. 'Grandmother Juanita knows her people. She's giving them a carnival.'

He was struck by the bitterness in her tone. 'A carnival?'

'Better that than turning on one another, isn't it? Yes, you and Grandmother Juanita have done a good job persuading them the hostage exchange has a chance, but deep inside they must know the odds are slim. Haven't you felt the violence and

451

terror building up behind us through the night? Do you think these peasants are any different from the murderous soldiers outside? Or anybody else in Spain, for that matter? Sometimes I think this whole war has been one big carnival. A great *corrida* where we consummate our national love affair with death.' Her voice had become shriller. Tomás was staring at her, his eyes wide. 'Perhaps the Fascists are right,' she said. 'We need the Roman Catholic Church with its hell and damnation and *auto da fés* to control us. For centuries we've relied on their damned rituals to check our morbidity and fear.'

'You don't believe that. Last night you were telling me about your father and Anarchism and the ideal society you believed in.'

She tossed her head, then picked up Tomás and hugged him fiercely. It seemed to calm her. 'I'm sorry,' she said. 'I'm only raging at this absurd position we find ourselves in. Maybe it's because I'm out of cigarettes. I'll get over it. Come, little one,' she said, attempting a bright smile. 'Let's get your grandfather some stew.'

A little later they were dipping bread into mutton broth in a silver bowl. The frenzied exuberance of the hostages had not lasted long. Most had returned to their pews and were finishing their meal silently.

Grandmother Juanita came up to Tomás. She looked tired, as if she had performed a great physical feat. She stroked his hair then whispered softly to Pinzon, 'Peace be with you, Señor. I have come to tell you that you have my support and that of the townspeople when you need it. They have forgotten their fear. They will do as you tell them when the time comes.'

'I don't understand,' said Pinzon.

She smiled enigmatically and turned to María. 'He is a good man, Señora. And you are a good woman to give him comfort. This child needs a mother. You have my blessing.'

Now they were both staring at her. She laughed and tapped her head. 'Grandmother Juanita is old but she has not lost her wits yet. I see what I see and hear what I hear.' Her leathery cheeks shook with amusement. 'Do not worry, Señor. I know also when to keep my lips sealed. Maybe we will drink soup again together soon from another, safer, witch's cauldron after Paco returns.' She cackled and left them abruptly.

Pinzon watched her go, aghast. Of course – she had told him she never slept. She must have overheard his conversation with Paco during the night. So much for his secret.

María looked at him thoughtfully. 'What is it you're not telling me?' Her eyes lit with hope. 'Oh, God, is it true? Do you have a plan?'

He did not have time to answer. There was the whine of a shell, faintly audible through the stone walls, a colossal crash, followed by silence, then the tinkle of glass as part of a window fell to the cathedral floor. Pinzon and María groped desperately for Tomás, and ended up with the boy between them and their arms around each other.

They huddled in the pew, bracing themselves for a repeat, but it did not come. A cloud of wispy grey smoke floated in through the broken panes. The doors banged open and they heard the cracking of boots on the stone paving: Privatos Becerra and Martínez were stamping down the aisle.

'You and the woman are to come with us. Ogarrio wants you on the battlements.'

The Fascist *capitán* was standing alone in the courtyard, this time without his Moorish guards. A white flag of truce flapped nonchalantly over his shoulder in the morning breeze. In the pale light, Pinzon could make out his features more clearly than he had been able to the night before. He saw the black rings under the man's eyes and the shadow on his cheeks. He looked older – a man in his thirties rather than his twenties. What had not changed was his expression of supercilious calm.

Behind and below him fog was lifting. Mingled with it, black pyres of smoke coiled from several burning buildings. The town hall, some of the banks and other municipal buildings had been demolished, presumably to clear lines of fire. In the square, Pinzon noticed the glint of metal. He had been right. The enemy had used the hours of darkness to prepare. They had brought their tanks and field guns into position.

He thought of the townspeople below. Concern for their lives seemed to play as little part in the Fascists' plans as it did in the Communists'.

Ogarrio, his eyes red and puffy with lack of sleep, was stamping with impatience. 'All right,' he shouted over the wall to Maranda. 'I've brought you Pinzon and Sister Catherina, as you requested. Why did you fire on us, you son of a whore?'

'Just a formality,' called back the *capitán*, cheerfully. 'To tell you we've come to a decision.'

'It'd better be the right one,' bellowed Ogarrio. 'My terms, if you remember, were that if you deceived us in any way, I'd start shooting the hostages, starting with Sister Catherina.'

'And I told you last night, Sargento, you may do as you like, but I would have thought it unnecessary in the case of the woman pretending to be Sister Catherina. My compliments to her, by the way. She's a fine actress. Last night she nearly had me fooled. It's a pity she's so tall and good-looking and, as I see in this better light, that she has white skin and freckles. This morning I received a telegram from Seville confirming the real Sister Catherina is short and swarthy with a black mole on her lip.' His voice became harder. 'Sargento Ogarrio, my general is not pleased that you have been playing games with us. Here are our terms. You release all the nuns and priests, as well as the villagers you are holding captive, within the next half-hour or we attack, with no quarter given. As a sign of good faith, you hand over to me the traitor Pinzon and this woman, whoever she is, right now.'

'You get no hostages unless we have a safe-conduct,' shouted Ogarrio.

'That is out of the question. Our terms are unconditional

surrender, but if you hand over your hostages, we may – just may – treat you as ordinary prisoners of war, rather than the bandits you are. You will be given the privilege of a fair trial. There may even be the possibility of mercy.'

With an elaborate gesture of his arm, he looked at his watch. 'Make up your mind quickly. You have a minute to pass Pinzon and the girl into my custody.'

'And if I refuse?'

'Then God help you, Sargento.'

Ogarrio let out a roar of rage. He pulled out his pistol, pinioned María to his chest and pressed the muzzle to her temple. 'You give us a safe-conduct or I blow out this *puta*'s brains.'

Pinzon threw himself at him, but Becerra and Martínez caught his arms and pressed him to his knees. 'Ogarrio, don't do this,' he pleaded. 'Don't take out your anger on María. Shoot me, not this innocent.'

Ogarrio gave him an irritated glance, then turned back to the square. 'I mean it, Capitán. I will kill her,' he yelled, 'and all the others.'

'Ogarrio, I beg you. You're a decent man. We both know that. Release her. Take out your frustration on me.'

'What an edifying spectacle,' came Capitán Maranda's sardonic voice from below. 'You are a bandit after all, Ogarrio, certainly no gentleman. You have ten seconds left, by the way.'

The pistol was trembling in the *sargento*'s hand. Sweat was forming on his brow. In contrast María, whose neck had been twisted so that she was staring directly into her executioner's face, showed cold, derisory calm.

'Please,' whispered Pinzon. 'You're not a murderer. Don't do this. It's not necessary, and it won't help.'

'Sixty seconds,' he heard over the battlements. 'Gentlemen, the truce is over.'

Ogarrio pushed the girl violently aside and pressed both

hands, including the one holding the pistol, on to the masonry so he could lean further outwards. 'Capitán,' he yelled.

The soldiers released their grip. María stumbled into Pinzon's arms. For a moment he clasped her to him. Meanwhile Capitán Maranda had been retreating at a fast pace and had nearly reached the steps that led down to the city. At the sound of Ogarrio's cry, he paused and turned, shielding his eyes against the glare of the sun that had just crested the citadel walls. 'What is it? I've already told you. Negotiations are over.'

'Just this, you little shit,' said Ogarrio, and fired three shots into the square. The first must have glanced off Maranda's shoulder. He staggered and clutched his arm. The flagpole clattered to the pavings and he dropped to his knees. The second ricocheted off the stone. By then Maranda was rolling towards the steps. The third shot sparked on the pavings and, with a yelp of pain, the Fascist *capitán* disappeared.

Becerra and Martínez laughed.

There was an angry shout from below the steps. 'You'll regret that, you scum. I was holding a flag of truce.'

'Fuck you,' shouted Ogarrio, his good humour restored. 'I'll see you in hell.'

A volley of shots came from the enemy's concealed positions around the square. As they ducked behind the battlements, bullets cracked through the air over their heads. Pinzon, cradling María, could hardly believe his eyes. Ogarrio, Becerra and Martínez were sitting with their backs to the parapet, nudging each other and laughing. 'You're mad,' he shouted. 'Your plan's in ruins. You're condemning innocent people to death and you're laughing.'

Ogarrio smiled at him. 'Fortunes of war, Señor, fortunes of war. How's my little tigress, eh?' María spat at him. 'You two had better get back to the cathedral before it gets really hot out here. Say a few prayers for us, eh?'

'I thought you didn't believe in prayers.'

'I'll believe in anything that brings a division of Fascists on top of my pile of explosive. I'm going to turn this citadel into an ants' nest. The longer we can hold out, the more of them we'll draw in. We'll have them crawling behind every rock and stone. So, yes, if I were you, I would pray. Pray for a long siege. Remember, you'll live only as long as we can keep fighting. When I blow the hilltop, we'll all go together.' He nudged the soldier beside him. 'Won't we, Becerra?'

The *privato*'s wolfish features had stiffened with resolve. 'It'll be a soldier's death,' he said quietly. 'A good death.'

'Indeed it will,' said Ogarrio.

Suddenly Pinzon saw the horrifying truth. On his way out of the cathedral, he had been toying with the idea of telling Ogarrio that there might be an escape route for all of them. It would be a way of preventing bloodshed, and even save Ogarrio the necessity of destroying the mosque and cathedral, preserving a unique architectural site for posterity. But now he knew he had been dreaming. Ogarrio would never agree. He would even prevent the hostages using the tunnel if he knew about it – for the man he saw smiling in front of him showed every indication of a death wish.

He remembered what Ogarrio had said to him about making a legend of their deaths. It was clear that since he had found the cave, the die had been cast: the *sargento* was no longer interested in escape – for anybody.

'You made up your mind when you saw the underground mosque,' he said softly. 'That was when you realised how much damage you could do to the enemy. All this negotiation since then has been a charade, hasn't it?'

Ogarrio shrugged. 'So what? Plans change. You yourself kept telling me that they wouldn't give me a safe-conduct. *Demonios!* Even I knew it was a chance in a million, but I couldn't think of a better idea. Yes, when I saw that big, natural vault, I knew it was a gift from the devil himself. We don't need to leave. If we can take a division with us, our deaths here will be more useful than if we waste them on the Ebro.'

'Then why do you need to keep us as hostages? You can blow the hill without us. Why didn't you release us just now when you had the chance?'

'And risk one of you telling them about the surprise I've planned for them? Come on, Señor, you're a politician. You know the importance of deception. You think the Fascists will make an all-out attack if they suspect I'm drawing them into a trap? That's why I went through with the phoney negotiations. They have to believe we locked ourselves into this death hole because we thought we could bargain our way out. Señor, your role as sacrifice is more useful to me than ever.'

'You won't last the day with only thirty men.'

'Then we'll meet Marx sooner rather than later, won't we? Console yourself. We're doing a great thing for the Republic, and you and the hostages have a noble part to play. As I told you yesterday in the crypt, the value of anybody's life is only its usefulness. Martínez, take them away.'

As they left, he was blowing his whistle. They saw soldiers running from the castle to mount the battlements. Bullets hissed through the air, and one of the turrets ballooned into flame.

'Are you all right?' he asked María, when the door slammed behind them.

'Hold me.' She pressed her face to his shoulder and began to sob.

He grasped her tightly, his cheek sticky against her sweating forehead, her breath blowing hot against his skin. He willed her calm, murmuring the soothing words he had so often used with Tomás on the nights the little boy had woken screaming for his parents. It seemed fragile protection against the barrage of guns and mortars pounding the citadel, the endless firecracker volleys of rifles and the explosions of grenades as the battle intensified outside.

'Just tell me you have a plan.' She raised her tear-streaked face. 'Even if you haven't, and that old woman is mad, tell me you do.'

'But I have, my dearest. There's a secret door leading to a tunnel. If it's not blocked, we can all get away to the mountains.'

She smiled. 'And live happily ever afterwards.' She nestled closer to him. Gradually her shaking stilled. 'Thank you,' she whispered, and closed her eyes. 'That is the sweetest of lies . . .'

He was startled by a scornful grunt behind him. A statue of a priest in a cassock seemed to have separated from the masonry. For a moment he wondered if he was imagining things again, then saw it was a living human being, covered from head to foot with clay and dust. Red-rimmed eyes surveyed him sardonically as the lips curved into a sneer. 'True love, Professor? How touching.'

'Paco?' he gasped. 'Thank God, you made it. You found the way out?'

'Yes, I found it. Here, I have a present you can give to your *puta*.' He thrust something soft and moist into his hands.

It was a sheaf of fern fronds, still sticky with sap where they had been cut. Pinzon breathed a prayer of wordless thanks.

'What is it?' María whispered anxiously. 'It looks like maidenhair.'

'It is, María,' he said, a tear forming in his eye. 'But not just any maiden's hair. It comes from the head of the Maiden in Samuel's story.'

'Hair of the witch, more like. I had to climb to the top of the dam to get it. That's the point from which the path leads to the pass. You should be pleased, Professor. The tunnel opened exactly where your old sorcerer said it would.'

María's eyes were shining stars. 'A tunnel? Oh, Enrique, you weren't humouring me after all. Tomás was right. There *was* magic in Samuel's book.'

'Magic?' Paco's voice was caustic. 'That's one way of

describing an endless black borehole full of crevices that damn near swallowed me at every step.'

Pinzon only saw the light in Mariá's eyes. 'Forgive me, I didn't want to raise anybody's hopes until Paco had confirmed it—'

She didn't allow him to finish. She kissed his lips.

Paco snorted. 'Don't I get one too, María? It was me who waded through the bat shit down that hole. Your hero of a professor wouldn't risk his own life, would he?'

'I'm sorry, Paco,' he said. 'Thank you. I'll tell everybody how brave you were. I must talk to them immediately. There's no time to lose. As you can hear from the firing outside, the truce is over. We must get everybody, including Felipe . . .'

Paco twisted something off his shoulder. Pinzon had been vaguely aware that there was a leather strap round his chest. He saw with amazement that it was connected to a rifle, which had now swung into Paco's hands. 'No need to concern yourself about our guard, Señor. I've saved you the trouble. We haven't been wasting time while you and your bitch were having fun with your friends outside.'

Pinzon saw the hard smile. He felt ice in his spine. 'What have you done?'

'What have I done?' Suddenly Paco cocked the rifle. He kept it at belly height but aimed it in their direction. 'You'd better wonder what I'm going to do. Hands in the air where I can see them, and move really slowly towards the nave.'

They had no choice but to obey. They could see the venom in his eyes. As he prodded them forward, his voice trailed behind them. 'It's over. For you and this woman. Oh, yes, you might have fooled some of us for a while. They were all so scared they went along with you, wanted to believe you, but not any more, not after I explained a few new facts to them. We've worked out your game, Professor, and we see you now – both of you, you and your whore – for the spies and traitors that you are. And don't think you can hide behind the skirts of the old woman you thought was such a great friend of yours. Juanita's come round to my way of thinking, along with everyone else.'

'And what are these new facts?' asked Pinzon, in a level voice.

'The tunnel itself for a start. When I was crawling through that hell-hole you sent me down, I confess I was puzzled at first. How come you were helping us all of a sudden? Well, one thing about stumbling around in darkness is there's not much else to do but think, and suddenly it made sense to me. Oh, you were very convincing with that Arab fairy tale of yours, but life doesn't work that way, does it? You don't suddenly come across long-lost tunnels in books just when you need them. No, but you were in the government, weren't you, with access to all sorts of secret military files? I bet you knew about this escape route all along. Maybe not exactly where it was, but that it existed. That was why Ogarrio brought you with him, planting you among us as a hostage, so you could dig around at your leisure. You already had one accomplice – this spy you'd already planted in our village. Got me to do your dirty work too, didn't you, so you and your soldier friends can conveniently slip off after blowing up the citadel and the enemy behind you? And don't tell me you were going to take us with you. We're to be left behind – convenient victims of a Fascist atrocity. That'd be good for your propaganda, wouldn't it? You see, I understand how you Stalinists think.'

'You know that's nonsense,' said Pinzon, still trying to keep his voice calm.

He was silenced by what he saw when they stepped out of the vestibule into the main expanse of the cathedral. The hostages were all gathered in the chancel, staring sullenly at something by their feet. Pinzon's spirits sank as he recognised the gangly body. The forage cap had fallen off Felipe's head and his untidy straw hair flopped over one eye. The other was staring in foolish surprise at the Baroque painting on the ceiling. Buried in his neck was the silver handle of a knife – Samuel's pen sharpener, which Pinzon had given Paco. Blood from the ragged wound was still dripping down the altar steps.

'Grandfather! Aunt María!' Tomás's terrified voice screeched above the noise of gunfire outside. He broke out of the grasp of the woman who was holding him and ran towards them. María scooped him into her arms, her face pale with shock.

Pinzon looked down at his grandson's soldier friend, feeling helpless sorrow. 'Why, Paco?' he asked bitterly. 'I talked to him. He would have come voluntarily.'

'With you and your friend Ogarrio? I'm sure he would. After he'd made sure the rest of us were dead meat.' He called to Grandmother Juanita, who was kneeling by Felipe's body, looking down on the corpse with stony repugnance. 'Grandmother, I've brought them. What do you want me to do with them?'

'Hector?' Grandmother Juanita gestured at the former *alcalde*.

'If Paco is right,' said the old man, 'and they're *extranjeros* we can't trust, we – we deal with them.'

A few hostages muttered agreement. Grandmother Juanita nodded slowly. 'And the little boy, what about him?'

Hector looked horrified. 'We don't have to kill him, Juanita. He's a child. An innocent.'

'Who's innocent these days?' she asked coldly. 'And why should we spare him? Isn't he an *extranjero*, too? Are you becoming sentimental in your old age, Hector? Are your balls as shrivelled as your brain? Do you not have what it takes any more?'

There was a whine of a shell and a crash outside the walls. Everybody ducked. It took the chandeliers above the chancel a moment to stop swinging. Only Grandmother Juanita had remained rigidly still. Now, slowly, she rose to her feet, her hard eyes moving round the circle of townspeople. 'Never mind, Hector, it's no longer our decision. We have a new leader. No question about *his* manhood. We all saw how bravely he despatched the guard. The donkey didn't even see you coming, did he, Pacito? He was playing hopscotch with the professor's child, trying to take his mind off the fighting outside. And you crept up on him like a fox stalking one of your innocent lambs. Bravo, Pacito, bravo.'

Paco was scowling. 'I did what I had to do. It isn't right for you to mock me, Grandmother. I thought we were going to conduct a proper trial.'

'Mock you?' She hobbled past Pinzon and María without acknowledging them, and looked up at Paco with her hands on her hips. 'Who would dare to mock you after the great thing you have done?' She smiled at him, running a wrinkled hand down his cheek. Her fingers rested on the stock of his rifle. 'Here, show me. Is it with this firearm you propose to mete out justice?'

'Grandmother Juanita, we have very little time.'

'Come on, give it to me,' she said.

He sighed, exasperated, and shook the strap off his shoulder. 'Be careful. It's heavy.'

But Grandmother Juanita held it with steady hands. 'Ah, yes, a Mannlicher. I thought I recognised it. It's the same as my son used.' There was a dreamy look in her eyes. 'He was a gentle boy, my Julio. He hated killing, even animals, but he put on the uniform of the Republic and gave up his life for it, defending our freedom, our decency and our honour.'

Paco was fidgeting with impatience. 'Grandmother, there is no time for this.'

'No time for honour and decency, Paco?' With a quick and expert movement, she pulled back the bolt and cocked the rifle. 'Why do you look so troubled? You're our saviour. You have just killed one enemy and found three more to get rid of.'

She was pointing the barrel directly at Pinzon. 'Not very fearsome ones, though, are they? What's their crime again? The professor, I think you said, is working for our enemy. Shows how stupid I am. I thought he was a kind-hearted fellow trying to find a way to save his grandson and the rest of us. Was I dreaming, then, last night, Paco, when I heard him telling you how to find the tunnel? If I'd been you, I might have been grateful to someone who showed us a way to escape.' Her eyes hardened again. 'But I've no reason to be jealous like you have, have I? Because the woman you once tricked into sleeping with you treats him more kindly than you.'

Paco bunched his fists.

She chuckled and swung the rifle towards María, who flinched and covered Tomás's eyes. 'And what about her? Well, we're not used to free spirits, are we, in our little town? They make us uncomfortable – but all through last night I could have sworn she was looking after the professor's child as gently and compassionately as if she were his mother. You'd almost believe there was good in her. Upset, are you, Paco, that she called you an adulterer? Think she revealed the blackness of her soul by telling everyone how you stole goods from the commune?'

Keeping the rifle aimed at María, she turned to look at the former *alcalde*. 'Who are we to believe, Hector? Pacito because he's one of us and they're *extranjeros*? Or the evidence of our eyes and ears?'

'Grandmother Juanita.' Paco's tone was furious. 'Give me back my rifle.' He strode forward and proffered his palm.

She ignored him. 'Are we afraid of him? Is that it?' She was addressing the silent hostages, who were staring at her with a mixture of incomprehension and fear. 'After all, we know it was Pacito who really ran the council, not that fool Ramón Zuluaga. It took María, whom he abused and now wants to kill, to speak openly about his corruption. None of us dared, although we suspected it. It makes you wonder, doesn't it?'

She paused, allowing her words to sink in. Then she raised her voice: 'You tell me what to do, comrades and citizens. I'm not afraid of vendettas or vengeance. I'm too old. Give the word and with this rifle I'll do Pacito's work for him, and shoot these people, if that's what you want – though in my heart I will be sorry because they have done nothing but try to help us.'

Her words were greeted with silence. One or two of the townspeople who were standing next to Paco edged away.

'Don't listen to the stupid old crone,' he yelled. 'She's mad.'

'The trial is over, Paco Cuellar,' said Grandmother Juanita, 'and it is you who are found guilty.'

Paco bellowed with anger and bounded towards her. In his hand was Felipe's torch, which he was now brandishing above his head as a club.

Almost casually, she swung the barrel and fired. The force of the recoil knocked her back on to the chancel steps. The explosion echoed among the stones and pillars. Paco's eyes widened with astonishment. For a second, his fingers tried to staunch the blood swelling from his chest. With a groan, he fell backwards and sprawled lifeless on the paving.

She did not even look at his corpse. She staggered to her feet and slowly appraised the townspeople. 'We deal justice to our own,' she said. 'That has always been our way. Hector, is it not so?'

The old man bowed his head.

'I did not hear you, Hector.'

'Yes, Juanita, that is our tradition.'

'So be it. If any of us have the good fortune to survive this and meet his widow, we will tell her that Paco was killed in the fighting. There is no need for his family to know the shame he has brought on our town. He died bravely. Is that clear?'

One by one, the hostages nodded, even the small children.

'Good.' Leaning on the rifle, she looked at Pinzon. 'Pacito was right about one thing,' she said. 'We need to hurry. Take us to the tunnel – we will follow you.'

Deep below ground, the noise of battle had been snuffed out. They had descended into another space or time. The column moved slowly through the alleys of the mortuary. In religious robes, holding the candles they had taken from the church, they resembled a medieval procession. Only the occasional whimper from a child, or a gasp from one of the women who had inadvertently brushed a skeletal arm, or the swish of robes along the stone floor broke the deep silence and the eerie illusion that these were clerics of the past who had come to inter one of their dead.

Pinzon took the lead, holding Felipe's torch, followed by María, grasping Tomás's hand, and the other mothers clutching their children. Hector García, rifle hanging on his shoulder, volunteered to be the last. They had to wait some time for him after they reached Paladon's tomb because the old man was supporting Grandmother Juanita, who could only hobble. Like the early Christians who had sought refuge in the catacombs, they were listening for the clatter of boots and the jangle of weapons, which would signify that they had been discovered by their persecutors.

'This is an evil place,' Grandmother Juanita spat, after Pinzon and Hector had lowered her on to a seat in the hall colonnade and she had regained her breath. She pointed at the rows of skeletons. 'It depresses me to see what we will become.'

'You'll outlive all of us, Juanita,' said Hector. She ignored him and looked up at Pinzon with narrowed eyes. 'So? What now?'

He indicated Paladon's sarcophagus. 'Inside, a hole leads to the cavern below. There is a ladder, but it will require some agility to climb down it. My apologies, Doña Juanita, I've discussed it with the others and we've decided to use a coil of rope the soldiers left behind to lower the children and also some of the frailer among us.'

'Meaning me?' She laughed bitterly. 'Well, I've just killed a man for the first time in my life. I probably deserve hanging. Why not be trussed like a pig and dangle in the air? You'd better lower me first in case we find the rope's weak. It won't matter if my old bones break.'

'The rope is perfectly strong,' said Pinzon. 'María will go down first with the torch. She will need your help when the children begin to descend.'

It took more than an hour for everybody to reach the bottom. Grandmother Juanita and the children were lowered safely. Pinzon felt a pang of love for his grandson when he saw the boy's face, lit by the faint torchlight that María was directing from below. As Tomás disappeared into the gloom, he had piped up cheerfully. 'Don't worry, Grandfather, I'll be there ready to catch you when it's your turn.'

It was easier once the ladder was secured back in place and the other women began to climb down, their squeals of fright, when they sometimes missed a step, echoing in the vaults, followed by calls of encouragement from María and rougher exhortations from Grandmother Juanita.

But it was taking far longer than Pinzon had anticipated. Each second that passed made the chance of discovery more likely. All it needed was one of Ogarrio's men to look into the cathedral, or the *sargento* to decide to use the cathedral as a makeshift hospital for his wounded.

There was another concern too. The thin altar candles they had managed to find in their hurry to leave the cathedral would not last much longer. Many were already mere stubs of wax when they had gathered them up because they had been burning through the night. One electric torch between them would not be enough to guide thirty men, women and children down a dangerous tunnel pitted with crevices and potholes. Already its beam appeared to have dimmed a little since they had begun their evacuation.

What they needed, he realised, were lanterns or flambeaux such as Paladon and Samuel had used in medieval times. Presumably all it would take was to fashion a holder and wrap some flammable material round it. María had her Zippo lighter. They would have to find something to burn.

'Señor García,' he asked, 'do you think these old cassocks

and winding sheets wrapped round the skeletons would burn well?'

'Very,' said the old man. 'I was a bit anxious when Juanita and I were walking past with our open candles.'

'Do you think we could use them as fuel for torches? How long do you think they would last?'

He saw comprehension flicker in the old man's face. 'Not very long, I'm afraid. Better if the material was dipped in pitch or tar first to make it burn slower, but oil might do,' he said. 'Do you want me to go up again to the vestry? We'll see what we can do with holy oil.'

'No, we haven't the time. Let me go down first to see what I can find below. It's a long shot but what we need may be in the cave already.' He thought of the barrels of oil that Paladon had lined against the walls. They had still been there, as Samuel had described. He hadn't looked inside because he had assumed they would be empty after so many centuries.

'You want me and the others to gather the clothes from the corpses?'

'Yes, as many as you can, then throw them down below. And thigh bones to wrap the cloth round.'

'Miguel, Juan, Pedro, follow me,' García was shouting, but Pinzon already had his feet on the first rung of the ladder.

María held the torch steady while he mounted the plinth. She gasped when the door began to turn. 'Quickly, through the gap,' he said. 'I'll be right behind you.'

When he reached her she was standing by Samuel's table, the torchbeam illuminating the pile of parchment and the pen. 'Enrique, is this . . .?'

'Yes, this is where Samuel wrote his book. I'll show you later, but now could you shine your light on that wall? Yes, on those barrels.'

The first was empty. So was the second, and the third, but in the fourth he saw the bulb of the torch mirrored in liquid.

Trying to contain his excitement, he reached inside. There were at least six inches of precious oil. He hurried along the line of barrels, lifting the lids in turn. There was more oil – one barrel was almost half full – but there was no pitch, which was what he had been hoping to find.

'Enrique, can you tell me what you're looking for?'

He explained. She listened to the end. 'You're going to wrap bits of cloth from dead bodies around thigh bones?' she asked, deadpan.

'Have you a better idea?'

She flashed her torch into an alcove in the cave wall. 'Would those not do?' she asked.

In a jumble on the floor there was a pile of metal objects. She reached down and picked one up. It was a flattened pot-like container, blackened with age, and had a thin spout at one end. 'Well, what is it?' he asked irritably.

'You really don't know? And you such a great expert on the ancient Moors? Tomás would recognise it immediately.' She was grinning mischievously. 'Have you never read a children's version of the *Arabian Nights*? It's an Aladdin's lamp. And there must be fifty of them. It's as if Samuel or Paladon knew we were coming.'

They still found a use for the skeletons' robes. María had shown the hostages how the dry cloth could be fashioned into new wicks to replace the original ones that had rotted away. Under Grandmother Juanita's brisk supervision, the women set up an impromptu production line, sorting through the wispy material, cutting and rolling it into strips. These were handed to two of the younger women, who inserted them through the spout of a lamp for inspection by Grandmother Juanita. She sat in state on Samuel's old chair, which she had had the men move near the barrels. When she was satisfied, she passed each lamp to Tomás, who had elected to help her. It was his job to pour oil into them. Using an earthenware cup, he filled each to the brim. Then he gave it back to Grandmother Juanita, to whom María had entrusted her Zippo lighter. At this point everybody stopped what they were doing to watch as Grandmother Juanita flicked the Zippo. If the protruding wick failed to light or only smoked, there would be a groan and the lamp would be passed back down the line. When it burst into a bright flame there would be a cheer, and the women shouted the number. 'One . . . two . . . three . . . twelve . . . thirteen . . .' They were already on number twenty-four.

The light in the cavern grew, and as each new lamp burned on the table, the huge shadows of those working on the cave floor became sharper on the walls and the distant ceiling. They seemed to be surrounded by toiling black giants. Hector and the other men, crouching on the flat stone near the tunnel mouth, had blown out their candles and were working faster in the clearer illumination. Hector, worried about potholes in the tunnel, had decided they would be safer if they were all tied together. Miguel, the last man to descend into the mosque, had brought the rope with him down the ladder. They had also dragged in a large sheet of canvas that had been covering some of the explosive and cut it into long strips. They were now busily braiding them into strong loops that could be attached to the rope as harnesses, one for each hostage.

Pinzon and María, with nothing else to do, were standing by the Niche of Light, admiring the alabaster of the alcove and the marble facings that were now revealed in all their bright colour. It had taken some experiment but, using oil and cloth, María had managed to light the lamp inside it. The pink sapphires that had been studded into the tracery of flowers and birds suddenly caught and reflected the flame. In the warm, rosy glow, the delicate flowers seemed to wave in a breeze and the birds to flutter around them.

'It's so beautiful,' whispered María. 'To think it hasn't been lit for nearly a thousand years.'

'Paladon was certainly an artist,' said Pinzon, forcing a smile to disguise his heavy thoughts, 'and a craftsman. You've noticed how this niche is mirrored in exact detail on the other side of this wall?'

'Only there the lamp is unlit,' she said, 'and it will never shine again. That beautiful mosque . . . I walked around it, among the pillars, with a candle. I couldn't see much but, though I'm not religious, it seemed to me the holiest place I have ever been.'

'Its designers weren't religious, María. Not really. We'd call them theists now. They believed in a Prime Mover, a force for good that animates everything that grows or moves or breathes. Even the stones in the ground and the stars in the sky. That was what Samuel and Paladon were celebrating when they built this. This is their monument . . . Well, not just theirs. It's a monument to humanity and knowledge and love of all that is noble and what humankind aspires to be.' He felt incipient tears and had to force himself to go on. He did not want her to notice his anguish. 'Perhaps it was a religion of sorts, but a strange one, of acceptance, tolerance. Ultimately love. That was what gave Samuel and Paladon their strength in the end. I think that was what they meant by the "Idea" that would outlast their terrible times.'

'A monument to love,' she repeated. 'And we've filled it with explosive, and are going to destroy it.'

'Not us,' he said. 'Ogarrio. The soldiers.'

'You think we're any different? We're not part of it?' She began to pace back and forth. 'What did Grandmother Juanita say when Paco was going to kill us? "Who's innocent these days?" Nobody is neutral in this war, Enrique. Nobody. Paco wasn't really a bad man, nor is Ogarrio or Becerra or any of them, really – but the war's corrupted them, destroyed them, and us as well. We've all become people of blood, like those crusaders and *jihadis* in Samuel's story. Half-people, brain dead, fighting for this stupid ideology or that one or, if we're not fighting, dragooned into supporting one side or the other, like – I don't know – some fucking football team. God, I wish I had a cigarette. Sometimes I just want to scream. I feel powerless, impotent. If only I could stand up and say, "This isn't how the world is meant to be." Samuel did, didn't he? And Paladon. They built a whole great mosque out there, then a cathedral on top of it.' Her lips were trembling and her cheeks were streaked with tears. 'And they're not going to be there tomorrow. They'll be gone. In an explosion that will kill thousands of people. What sort of perversion is it when a monument to love is turned into a temple of human sacrifice?'

He hugged her. He wanted to tell her he loved her. That they had found each other. That good things lived on. That miracles existed . . . But he knew it would be wrong to do so. Instead he told her to remain hopeful. At least they were saved, he said. Tomás had been spared. He now had the chance to grow up in a better world.

She turned a tragic face towards him. 'I hope so.' She broke away and began to pace again. 'But I've little confidence any more. Whichever monstrous side wins this damned war, we'll be fugitives and refugees in our own country because it won't be our country any more. It'll be run by Fascists or Communists, and beautiful things like this cathedral won't be allowed to exist. My father was an atheist, but I think he'd have died rather than let them blow up that lovely mosque. His ideals and Samuel's idea weren't that different as far as I can see. Not much chance of either surviving now, is there?'

Pinzon felt his heart was breaking. 'But you and Tomás will remain,' he said. 'I hope you can continue to look after him, María.'

María stopped pacing. She had her back to him. The lamplight reflected the gold tint in her hair. She turned her face to him. Her lips were red in the lamplight that also brought out the hazel in her eyes. 'Of course I will, Enrique. For as long as you need me, or he needs me. Better be careful, though. You might find I won't ever let him go. I'm getting mighty fond of him, you know. Like finding a son again, I suppose.'

'If you think of him as your son, then my mind and heart will be at peace,' he said, in as light a tone as he could manage.

She laughed, tossing her hair. 'Oh, I wouldn't be expecting too much peace from me. If you want me to stay with you, you can expect the whole neurotic package.'

'Tomás will only benefit from that,' he said, 'for I would call it courage, honesty of conviction, intellect, kindness and . . . well, a remarkable person being herself.' He knew he was failing. Tears were pricking his eyes again.

She stared at him curiously. 'It's . . . odd how close we've all become in such a short time. Like we're a family already.'

'In these situations friendships can form very quickly,' he said. 'One sees the best in people.'

Her shoulders shook and she hugged herself. 'But we are friends, aren't we? Real ones.' Her voice softened as her eyes widened and looked into his. 'There've been one or two moments when I thought we could become . . . more than friends.'

He wanted to clasp her in his arms, hug and kiss her, and tell her that he loved her. It took all his effort to say the cold words he had to in reply. 'Of course we're more than friends. You're as dear to me as my daughter-in-law, María. If you were my own daughter I would be no less proud of you than I am.'

She blushed and reached automatically into her pockets for her cigarettes and Zippo, then folded her arms and laughed. 'Well, I've certainly put my foot in it again,' she said. 'That's me, though. Too forward for my own good. Will you forgive me?'

He hated himself. He could see the hurt in her eyes. 'There's nothing to forgive,' he whispered. 'Nothing. I hope one day you might forgive me.'

She looked at him thoughtfully and gently ran her palm down his cheek, straightening his collar and brushing away a loose strand of his hair. 'You're a good man, Enrique. Really you are. I'll always respect you, and be grateful to you. Wherever you and Tomás are. Wherever I am. I'll always remember what you did for us. I'm – I'm happy with just friends. We are that, aren't we?'

'For always,' he said.

There was a triumphant shout from the women. 'Thirty-five!' They clustered excitedly round Grandmother Juanita who had risen to her feet, grinning as she brandished the flaming oil lamp in her hand.

'That's the last,' said María. She gave him the brightest of smiles. 'I'd better find Tomás. Will you be with us at the front like last time?'

'No,' he said. 'Hector is more experienced in rocky terrain than I am. He'll be a surer guide through the difficult stretches. I'll be more useful at the rear in case anybody has an accident or needs a hand.'

'All right. See you at the Witch's Cauldron, then.' She gave him a brisk peck on the cheek. 'Don't worry about Tomás. He'll be fine with me.'

'I have no doubt of that,' he said, his voice catching in his throat. 'None at all. I pledge him to you from the bottom of my heart. Give him my love and . . . God go with both of you.'

She glanced over her shoulder. For a moment she looked puzzled, then she chuckled, evidently thinking he had been joking. 'We'll only be a few feet in front of you,' she said. 'Anyway, don't you mean the Prime Mover?'

'I suppose I do.' He managed to retain his smile as he watched her grab her lamp from the top of the table, scoop up Tomás, who was hiding underneath it, and, holding his hand firmly, stand in line to wait for Hector to rope them to the growing chain. Tomás, looking back, saw his grandfather and jumped up and down waving wildly. María was kneeling beside him and pointing. Pinzon pulled his handkerchief out of his pocket and waved back. Only when Tomás returned his attention to

Hector, who was attaching his harness to the rope, did he return the handkerchief to his pocket.

Suddenly he felt a crumbling of his resolve. A voice screamed in his head that it was not too late. No one would blame him. Nothing was irrevocable. All he had to do was walk over to where María was standing, her arms raised above her head, while Hector tightened the harness around her chest. He would smile and crack another little joke. She would laugh and make space for him. Perhaps she would give him another peck on the cheek. She might take his hand, though she'd be a little wary of him – had he not just rejected her? But with patience and time . . . He knew he was fooling himself. It was not to be – it couldn't be – and she would see that for herself one day. With any luck she might come round to respecting him as she had respected her father and be proud of him. She would understand what impelled him. The Idea, as Samuel had said, was a sort of love. One day she might explain it to Tomás. Yes, he thought sadly, she would know what to say. And the boy was courageous. As his father had been.

He felt the welling of a tear. Tomás. That was the hard part. He closed his eyes, trying to blot out the image of his trusting little face. He could not afford to think about him now. Not if he was to do what he had to do.

Three heavy steps took him over to where the old lady had sat down again on her chair, waiting her turn to be roped into the column.

'May I have a word with you, Doña Juanita?' he asked quietly.

He waited until the last glimmer of lamplight had faded down the tunnel. There had been no goodbyes, only a cheery wave over their shoulders when they entered the black gloom. Tomás's eyes were shining with excitement at this new adventure and María looked preoccupied.

It pained him to think that he had deceived them, but it was for the best. They would be taking comfort from believing that he was close behind them, and it would give them courage as they went through the dangerous passages. If all went well, they would suspect nothing until they reached the Maiden's pool.

At least in spirit he would be with them.

For a second the finality of what he had just done stunned him, but then he felt a growing sense of elation, and liberation. Like a great ship cut away from its moorings, its engine rumbling to full power inside, nothing now held him back. He wondered if this was the berserker state that Samuel had described of a knight going into battle. He smiled wryly. A touch of madness might be useful now. It was a desperate enterprise he was contemplating and there was no guarantee that he would succeed.

He lingered for a few seconds in front of the mihrab, watching the play of the birds and flowers. In front of it, only minutes ago, María had promised him happiness. He remembered her when they had first met – the boyish face and the freckles, the glint of green and gold in her eyes, flicking her Zippo and grinning through the smoke. How young she had looked, and how attracted he had been, even then . . .

He really was a foolish fellow, he thought, as he put his hand on the plinth. A madman indeed. He smiled grimly. As the proverb said, 'Let a bear robbed of her whelps meet a man, rather than a fool in his folly!' Ogarrio had better beware. Confidently, he turned the lamp back and forth until it clicked. The alcove swivelled, and, following it, he stepped into the mosque.

It was no longer the pitch dark cavern he had left. The lamp in the Niche of Light cast a pink glow on the first two lines of pillars, and he imagined the forests of them stretching back towards the mouth of the cave in lines of seven, representing the planetary gods. He felt their power around him. Above him he imagined the turning spheres and Samuel's celestial energy coursing through the lines and circles . . .

But the neat symmetry was interrupted by the ugly heaps

of explosive. He wanted to kick them away. They made a sacrilege of this holy shrine. He remembered what María had said: *What sort of perversion is it when a monument to love is turned into a temple of human sacrifice?*

With extreme caution, he lowered the flaming lamp in his hand. He had little idea of how to disarm the explosive, but he assumed that if he cut the wires connecting the various piles of charges, that would be a start. Before the column had set off along the tunnel, Grandmother Juanita had given him the knife that Juan, one of the male hostages, had removed from Felipe's body. He took it out of his pocket. Carefully placing the lamp on the tiles away from it, he twisted the wire over the blade and cut it. Then he saw another line of wires and another and another. It seemed as though the entire floor of the mosque was covered with serpents.

There had to be a better way than this. He noticed that the wires all led in a similar direction. He followed them and, sure enough, nestled among the central pillars, he found a small black box with a handle. He cursed his stupidity. He should have thought of the plunger earlier. All he had to do was to disconnect it. He cut the wires and, for good measure, carried the box back to the mihrab and into the cave, where he left it, then returned to the mosque.

He had a disturbing thought. Was this enough? What if Ogarrio threw hand grenades down the hole from Paladon's sarcophagus? Might the blast and flame ignite the explosive anyway?

He nearly despaired. Then he set to work, heaving one sack after another away from the area around the ladder to the other end of the mosque.

After an hour he was sweating, exhausted, slumped on the mountain of explosive he had piled up. He was reasonably confident that the heavy sacks he had dragged, one after the other, more than fifty metres along the tiled floor would be out of range of any explosion.

There was only one thing more to do here. His muscles aching, he staggered back down the line of pillars to find the box that Rincon had discarded in disgust when he found no treasure inside it. He withdrew Samuel's book from his pocket and laid it inside. Then he replaced it below the urn of Paladon's ashes in the niche where it had been discovered.

He glanced at the soft light in the mihrab. He had been intending to blow out the lamp before he left in case anybody discovered it. He chuckled quietly. He really was going a little mad. The whole point of what he was doing was to ensure that nobody would ever come down here again. And it was appropriate that he left it burning. It restored Paladon's creation to its original sanctity. The mason had designed the mihrab specifically so that a perpetual fire could shine in the Niche of Light. It was what gave the mosque its soul.

For a while he watched its glow. He doubted that he would live for as long as it would take the wick to burn out, and that meant, at least for him, it really would be a perpetual flame. The idea fortified him. From now until he finished what he had to do, he would take comfort from imagining its light in the darkness, and with it the shades of Paladon and Samuel, helping him in his task.

With renewed energy, he climbed the ladder. The large plank he had picked up from one of the discarded explosives boxes was heavy and unbalanced him, and it took time and one or two precarious tumbles before he reached the top. Only after several attempts did he succeed in pushing it through the hole. He wedged it against the inside wall of the sarcophagus so it would not slide down again. Then, when he was satisfied it was safely secured, he climbed down the ladder to retrieve the lamp he had left on the floor below.

Back at the top, he knelt in the enclosed sarcophagus, using his last reserves of strength to pick up the ladder and dislodge it from its base. Then he pushed. It moved a fraction. His muscles screaming with agony, he lifted it, pushed again, and repeated the toing and froing until the top posts of the ladder had slipped under the edge. It still took three final heaves before the ladder loosened and clattered to the tiles of the mosque far below.

He felt as much melancholy as triumph. Even if he wanted to, he could not get back into the cave. He thought of the hostages making their way through the tunnel. He had burned his bridges. Then he relaxed. He had made his choice. Now it was irrevocable. That made things easier.

There was little more to be done but he wondered where he would find the energy to go on. He lay, still gasping a little, on the cold stone floor beside the sarcophagus for a full five minutes before he could move again. He had to summon all his willpower to push himself to his feet.

The plank he had brought up was a little too short, but that was better than being too long. Once he had shuffled and wedged it in place with stones from the floor, he was satisfied that nobody would think it covered a hole.

And that left him just one last task to perform before he could rest.

Lamp in front of him, he tottered through the arch of the amphitheatre into one of the alleys of bones. He selected a monk at random, a tall prelate with a moss of overgrown hair, blond like Paladon's. Not that it mattered. One mouldered corpse was like another. He did not even feel revulsion.

He carried the skeleton to the sarcophagus and laid it inside. He had to make two more journeys to pick up the bones that had fallen on the way. Fastidiously he laid them in place.

There was nothing he could do about the hole in the side of the sarcophagus except to fill the gap as tightly as he could with the fragments of obsidian that the soldiers had dislodged with their pickaxes. The final result was not perfect, but neither did it look as though the vandalism had been recent. People would presume that the sarcophagus had been broken into centuries ago. There had always been grave robbers. He doubted that anybody would give it a second glance.

He sat down, leaned against the amphitheatre wall and viewed his handiwork. For the moment, his job was done.

There was still Ogarrio to deal with, of course. In time he would come, but he was ready for him. He had the means, something even better than Samuel's little knife, which had already been sullied in one evil deed today: he did not wish to use it for another. While working on the sarcophagus, he had tripped over a pickaxe that a soldier had left behind. He was now holding it.

There was nothing more to do but wait. He blew out the lamp – and with the pitch darkness, the temperature seemed to drop. He was glad of his overcoat, which he had taken off below when he was pulling the bags of explosive. He had only remembered it at the last minute and brought it up with him when he retrieved the lamp. Even so his sweat-dampened shirt hugged his body like ice. He had no idea of the time: his watch was not luminous. He hoped he would not catch cold. He wouldn't want to give himself away with an ill-timed sneeze. For some reason the idea struck him as amusing. His laughter echoed eerily round the cavernous vaults of the morgue.

He wondered where María and Tomás were now. They would be in darkness too. Or perhaps not. At least two hours had passed. Perhaps they were coming to the end of the tunnel. The grey stone walls might be faintly visible. In a moment they would be dazzled by light . . .

And when they saw it they would cheer, and hug themselves with joy. He smiled, thinking of the relief they must be feeling. Then a tear came into his eye as he imagined Tomás turning his head to look for his grandfather to share the moment of triumph, and María looking back expectantly.

He felt a thump of pain in his heart. Yes, that would be the moment.

She would frown at first when she did not see him. She

would peer in puzzlement from side to side. Then she would remember the words he had said to her. She was too intelligent not to be able to grasp immediately what he had done. Instinctively she would clutch Tomás's hand.

Grandmother Juanita would have been observing them, as she had promised him. She and Hector García would come up beside them, and from their faces María would know for sure, and hold Tomás tightly, while he, sensing something was wrong, would pale.

But he would not cry. Pinzon was sure of that. He was Raúl's boy. And Julia's. He had inherited his father and mother's courage. He had also become used to tragedy at an early age. His grandson knew in his guts already, even though he was too young to articulate it, that you don't get anything in this world without paying a price. He would probably say, very quietly, 'Grandfather's not coming with us, is he? He's gone to join Mamá and Papá, Lupita and Felipe. That was the cost of the magic that saved us, wasn't it?'

And probably when he said that, tears would run down old Grandmother Juanita and Hector's cheeks.

And María would clutch to her breast – he hoped with pride as well as sorrow – her adopted son . . .

He had been lucky, he told himself. Lucky. He had found the right person to look after his grandson. A woman to mother him. It was Fate. It was Providence. Everything had worked out for the best. The best . . .

After he had repeated and repeated this to himself, the thought eventually comforted him enough to make up a little for his aching sense of loss.

At least he could rely on Doña Juanita. She had agreed to everything. During their escape and afterwards, she had promised both María and Tomás her personal protection. No one would persecute María as they had before. As far as the world was concerned, she would be a respectable widow and Tomás's mother. If Republican soldiers, Guardia Civil or anybody else ever stopped them, that was what every inhabitant of Ciudadela del Santo would swear. In time the relationship would be made legal. The old woman had wrapped in her handkerchief the ration cards and passports that would act as proof of Pinzon and Tomás's identities, as well as the other papers he had given her, with the money he had had left in his pockets. Everything was now enclosed in the leather pouch that hung inside her shirt. The letters were only hurried scribbles on Samuel's parchment, but his lawyer in Madrid would be able to decipher and act on them. It was a simple enough will, counter-signed by Grandmother Juanita. Tomás would inherit his estate on the death of María, whom he had adopted as his daughter with rights to everything he owned, including access to a Swiss bank account where he had deposited, like most of the other government ministers, all his savings. It was no fortune but it would pay for the two of them to smuggle their way out of Spain, to France or England or wherever they could find safety. His lawyer, a loyal and resourceful friend, would see to it.

That took care of business. The short letter for Tomás was personal. Grandmother Juanita would give it to María when they reached the Maiden's pool. He had not written separately to her. There had been no time and, anyway, everything he had to say to her could be read between the lines he had written to Tomás. And she would understand. He was sure of it. What had she said about her father? That he would rather die than allow something so lovely to be destroyed.

He felt no regret for his decision, only a little sadness that he would not see Tomás grow up, or ever know if, one day, the boy would forgive him. But María would explain, he comforted himself. She would convince him.

He could afford to be content. He had handled his affairs as well as could be expected. He had even honoured his debt to Samuel and Paladon. Juanita had sworn a solemn oath to the memory of the great Anarchist leader, Durruti – he was as near a saint as the old atheistic woman had – that the townspeople would keep the secret of the cave. He knew that the peasant code of *silencio* would hold.

He smiled wryly, his mind wandering to his wife – his plump, good-hearted Manuela – who had died in the most ludicrous fashion, walking in front of a tram. Now her husband, the great politician, would die obscurely in the crypt of a church. What he was doing was equally ridiculous on the surface. Why should a man give up his life for a pile of stones?

But she, like María, would have understood. She had known him better than anyone else. For many years she had been his conscience. Now he had found his own. At the end of the day what was any man but his commitment to an idea? Ideas not only underlay civilisation. They were the spark of the divine, separating order from chaos, evoking a wonderful vision of eternal harmony and hope. It was simple, really. By preserving these stones, Pinzon, like Paladon and Samuel, would be ensuring that a small flame continued to shine in the enveloping darkness. Even if nobody else knew about it or what he had done to preserve it, the idea would remain a while longer, waiting to be discovered in better times. It was like the lamp in the alcove, burning perpetually below.

He chuckled silently. Tomás might be proud of his grandfather after all. At least there was life in the old boy yet. Real life. Everlasting life. Whoever said it wasn't worth the candle?

He closed his eyes. He suddenly felt very tired. Soon he was fast asleep.

He was woken by distant gunfire. At first he thought he was still dreaming. Surely it was impossible for the noise of battle to come down into the crypt.

But it continued, mixed with shouts and muffled explosions.

His mind cleared and he realised that, if he could hear it, the fighting had progressed to the cathedral. Ogarrio and his men must have been forced to retreat to their last line of defence.

Instantly alert, he grabbed the handle of the pickaxe. If they were in the cathedral, Ogarrio would be with him soon.

He had just hidden behind a pillar when there was a colossal explosion. He heard a rustle as a row of skeletons behind him toppled to the floor.

There was a long silence, then a volley of rifle fire. During intervals in the fusillade, he made out the soft whirring of a motor – and voices moving closer. 'Steady does it. Push when I pull.' It was Ogarrio. 'Rincon, damn you, push those fucking skeletons out of the way.'

A pale pool of light was shining on the granite wall. It increased in intensity as the grunts and oaths grew louder.

The statue of Paladon was now floating clearly out of the darkness.

'Not far to go. Becerra, can you manage?'

'I'll be fine, Sargento.' It was a wheezing croak.

'Good man.'

Pinzon watched as the three came into view. Rincon was first, holding the arc lamp. He was limping, dragging a leg. The torn trousers were soggy with blood. Ogarrio came next, bent almost double as he pulled the trolley on which rested the generator. Becerra was behind him. His head was wrapped in a bandage that covered one eye. As he straightened Pinzon saw that an arm hung limp and the whole of his side was crimson. Clearly he had been shot in the chest or shoulder.

'All right, that's it,' said Ogarrio. 'I can manage from here. You two, get back to the stairs and hold them off for as long as you can. I'll relieve you as soon as I'm done.'

Becerra laughed. From the gurgle in his voice and the bubbles coming out of his mouth Pinzon imagined that the bullet had penetrated his lung. 'Strange . . . fucking . . . relief,' he said. 'Blowing us . . . sky high.'

'Taking a whole division of the enemy with us, my friend,' said Ogarrio. 'That won't look bad on the company report. Here, you bastard.' He embraced him tenderly, careful of the wounds, and kissed him on both cheeks. 'You're a bloody good man, Becerra. Wouldn't choose to die with anybody else.' He hugged Rincon. 'And you, you slacker. Good soldiers the lot of you. I'm proud as hell. Now, fuck off, and keep the enemy off my back.'

Ogarrio watched them go. He rubbed his forehead and picked up the lamp.

It was only when he reached the sarcophagus that he noticed something was wrong. 'What the hell . . . ?' he muttered, picking up one of the obsidian rocks that blocked the entrance. Pinzon stepped over the balustrade and took a silent step towards him.

Some instinct made the *sargento* turn. He dropped the rock and reached for his pistol. It was in his hand before Pinzon had taken three paces. 'You!' Ogarrio gasped and fired.

Pinzon felt a thump in his chest, which rocked him, but his arms were already descending and the point of the pickaxe entered the *sargento*'s body in the centre of his ribcage just above his solar plexus. He felt a moment of almost childish pride that his blow had been accurate, before the chamber began to turn around him, his knees crumpled and he lost consciousness.

He could still hear sporadic rifle fire from a distance away, but he was confused by the clunking sound closer to him. He tried to rise, but the burning pain in his chest prevented him. After a few attempts, however, he found he could move his head and turned it in the direction of the strange sound.

A slither of blood led to Paladon's sarcophagus. Ogarrio was lying beneath it on his back. With immense concentration he was raising his arms above his head and shaking a rock out of position. When he had it in his hands, he hurled it aside and reached for another.

'Are you badly hurt?' asked Pinzon.

Ogarrio paused with a rock in both hands above his head. 'You again. Aren't you dead?' He threw the rock aside. 'Of course I'm bloody hurt. What do you think? You've broken my spine, you fucker. I can't use my legs.'

'I'm sorry. I only wanted to stop you blowing up the mosque.'

'Well, you haven't. I've nearly cleared the entrance. I can still pull myself down that ladder.'

Pinzon began to laugh but a spasm of pain spread from his chest to every limb. It passed, but it took him some time to regain his breath. He remembered what he was going to say. 'You're . . . you're welcome to try – if you can find the ladder.'

'I'll find it,' said Ogarrio. There was another clunk as a stone hit the pavings. 'What is it with you anyway? All right, somehow you and the hostages managed to escape. I don't hold it against you. Anybody's entitled to save their own skins if they can. Killed one of my men in the process. I'll forgive that too.' He dislodged another stone. 'But,' he panted, 'why did you stay behind with a fucking pickaxe to prevent me hurting the enemy? Do you know what I have out there now? A whole division of Fascists, maybe more. Just where I can destroy them. They're your enemy too. You used to be in the damned war cabinet.' He paused as he struggled with the weight of the last stone. 'I just don't get it.'

'I thought the price was too high,' said Pinzon.

'What? The lives of me and my men?' He hurled the rock away. 'You saw Becerra just now. He's happy to die this way. So am I. We all are. It's for – I don't know – the cause. It makes everything worthwhile. It'll help bring victory for the working man. Everything we believe in. It means something.'

'It means nothing if in doing so you throw away your humanity.'

'What's a shitty mosque got to do with humanity?' He was dragging himself upwards painfully by his elbows.

'Nothing,' he whispered. 'And everything. Something a fanatic like you will never understand.'

'Well, fuck you, Professor Pinzon. It doesn't matter because

I can still get down there and blow you and me and everybody else to hell.'

There were two loud bangs of exploding grenades, a yell, a volley of shots and then the sound of boots.

'Shit,' muttered Ogarrio, and heaved himself round so that his body tumbled into the sarcophagus. There was a roar of anger, outrage, horror and perhaps fear, and immediately he slid out again. The blond-haired skull rolled after him. 'It's a corpse. A fucking corpse!' he cried.

'Perhaps Paladon has come back to protect his cathedral,' said Pinzon, quietly.

He heard a shout in a language he couldn't understand. Turning his head, he saw four Moorish soldiers advance with their rifles aimed ahead of them. Ogarrio was grunting and swearing. Turning his head again, Pinzon saw that the pistol was raised in his hand. All four rifles fired, and Ogarrio slumped backwards, his head inside the sarcophagus.

He heard shorter, brisker footsteps behind him. Rolling his head back, he recognised Capitán Maranda. The officer moved elegantly in his battledress despite the sling binding one arm. He poked Ogarrio's body with his boot. 'Well done, soldiers,' he said. 'This was their leader. I think he's the last.' He peered up at Paladon's statue. 'What the hell was he doing here?'

'I think he was trying to hide in the grave of a dead man, Effendi,' said one of the Moroccans.

The others laughed.

'Pull him out of there. You,' the capitán ordered one of the men, 'stay behind and fill up that hole. Put the monk's head back in first. Reverently. This is a sacred place and there's been desecration enough. I want this monument sealed.'

Pinzon sighed with gratitude and release. He had fulfilled his task. The cave below would be preserved.

The footsteps moved closer to where he was lying. Maranda knelt beside him. 'Minister Pinzon, I'm glad to see that you are still alive. I hope you will be well enough to attend the trial my general has prepared for you.'

Pinzon tried to answer, but red mists were swirling behind his eyes.

'Oh, Christ, he's badly wounded. Quick. Get stretcher-bearers.'

He heard the urgent shouts of the *capitán* as if through a tunnel.

'And bring the doctor. Hurry!'

What a fuss, thought Pinzon. He wished they would leave him alone. He was content now, and wanted to go into a deep sleep. He had a sudden vision of the lamp burning in the Niche of Light and birds flying among the leaves.

They strapped him to a chair in the public square with a placard round his neck saying, 'Enrique Pinzon – Heretic and Traitor'. Next to him squirmed the fat figure of Zuluaga, the *alcalde* turned chairman of the Revolutionary Council. His sign read 'Ramón Zuluaga – Anarchist and Traitor'. The poor man had been squealing so much in his terror that they had had to gag him.

It was all done hurriedly. The usual chaos after the sacking of a town prevailed.

It had taken Capitán Maranda ages to find his general on the field telephone to explain that the former minister of the Republic was dying and not expected to last another hour. The general had therefore abandoned his plans for a public trial in Seville but he demanded that Pinzon must be executed and be seen to have been executed – and that meant he had still to be alive when he was shot. It had taken all of the doctor's skill, and a blood transfusion to ensure that Pinzon's heart kept beating long enough. That he was unconscious was judged immaterial.

There had been another delay because the cinematographer who was to record the scene could not at first be found.

Eventually he had been spotted on the battlements filming the bodies scattered over the parapets of the citadel. He was still panting from running down the hill with his heavy equipment.

There was no crowd to witness the event, only a few townspeople who had been rounded up to make a burial party and a disinterested line of Moorish soldiers, who were waiting outside the offices of a trading company that had hastily been turned into a brothel. Since few of the remaining female inhabitants of Ciudadela del Santo were still capable of performing such a service after the ravages of the previous night, the queue was rather a long one.

There was therefore little fanfare. Maranda read a prepared speech. The firing detail emptied their bullets into the bodies of the two condemned men and, relieved of further duties, joined the queue outside the brothel. Some of the few male townsfolk who had not been shot or gaoled lifted the bodies into a truck to take them to the pit in an olive grove outside the town where, in due course, the bodies of Ogarrio and his company were also brought to be buried.

The next evening Capitán Maranda played the film to the general at his headquarters in a requisitioned farmhouse three miles away.

'It seems satisfactory enough,' he murmured at the end, as he chewed a fat cigar.

'Thank you, General,' said Capitán Maranda. 'You are very kind.'

'I thought you said Pinzon was already in a coma.'

'Well, he was. The doctor was afraid he would die any minute.'

'Yet just before he was shot he seemed to be gazing up and smiling.'

'Yes, General, that was a little surprising. Perhaps the expression on his face was not exactly what our propaganda department wanted but, you must admit, it proves he was still alive.'

'What was he grinning at?'

'I beg your pardon, General?'

'What was he looking at that made him smile?'

'I'm not sure,' said Maranda. 'From where he was sitting, if he raised his eyes, he'd have been able to see the cathedral. It's quite visible from the square. Its spire had just caught the first light of dawn, actually. I admired the effect when I moved over to inspect the bodies. Perhaps such beauty inspired him, General.'

'A beautiful dawn inspired him?'

'It was a particularly lovely dawn, General, and, as you have said many times, it is a magnificent cathedral.'

'Perhaps he wasn't such an atheist after all, then.'

'Excuse me, General?'

'It was a joke, Capitán.'

'Oh, I see. Yes. Most amusing, General.' Dutifully, he attempted to laugh.

Al-Andaluz, 1097

Postscriptum

There is little more to tell. I woke up in the hospital in the town to find myself being treated by Dr Ali, who had, like the hospital itself, somehow survived everything that had happened since the Christians came. My old patients in the mad ward had never noticed a disturbance. An Almoravid guard sat on a stool near my bed, but he spent most of the time dozing. Nobody really expected me to escape.

When I could walk I was taken back to the palace. As I passed through the great halls I could see a myriad stonemasons chipping out the metals and marbles from the walls. King Yusuf had decided that he would not allow such a symbol of decadence to remain. That did not mean he did not appreciate the value of precious stones. I may already have mentioned that his devotion to Allah went hand in hand with his greed.

He had pitched his own simple tent in King Abu's gardens. I expected that I would receive notice of my execution, but instead I was offered a job. Royal physician again, but for considerably less payment. It appeared that King Yusuf had heard of my role in tricking the Christians to come out and fight, and Karim, who had somehow survived his arrow wounds, had spoken in my favour. Like Paladon, I had impressed him so I was rewarded rather than punished.

Karim became viceroy when Yusuf left, ruling from Salim's

old house. I was his doctor and companion, and sometimes his lover, although it hardly gave me satisfaction. My heart had died with Aziz.

Mishkhat, which had once been glorious and colourful, became a town of mud hovels, dominated by nondescript mosques. The Almoravids told me proudly that it was like any God-fearing city you might find in Africa. As Karim had once said, they were literal people. They liked to re-create what they were used to at home.

There were few atrocities once the executions of those who had 'collaborated' with the Christians had taken place. These were largely their victims – women who had been raped, then forced to become concubines of their conquerors, and those shopkeepers who had faced starvation if they had not provided provender to the Christians. Alia Bibi, the bathhouse brothel-keeper, was hanged and the granddaughter she had prostituted was sold as a slave. Many Jewish merchants were hanged, too; in most cases a charge of treason was an excuse for Almoravid soldiers to confiscate their wealth.

After a while the city settled into dull monotony. Inevitably I was pressured to convert to the Mussulman faith. It was just another symbol as far as I was concerned. I believed in a universal God, so to me it hardly mattered if, on the surface, I was Mussulman, Jew or Christian – but in this case I balked. It was the last straw. For five years I had served the Almoravids. I found them tedious and their form of religion odious.

I had thought often of ibn Sa'id. He had urged me to study in Khairawan or Cairo. On a whim I pressed a letter into the hands of a trader who was setting off for Egypt. I had addressed it to the chief imam of Cairo University. The trader was searched by Almoravids at the border and the letter was discovered. Karim heard of it and upbraided me for ingratitude and treason.

That night, before I could be arrested, I slipped away.

Boulders had covered the mouth of the cave, which was rippling again with prayer flags, but I was able to find my way through cracks as I had in boyhood. I still had the key that Paladon had given me for the mosque. I let myself in, and walked again under Paladon's pillars, lines of seven, representing the planetary gods. I saw the wires and globes silhouetted against the gap of stars where the dome had once been, all that remained of Paladon's celestial spheres. Slowly I made my way to the mihrab and twisted the Niche of Light.

And here I have been ever since, burning my books for heat, writing my manuscript and keeping always a little illumination in the lamp I took out of the Niche of Light (I will replace it before I leave), using as fuel the oil from the barrels that Paladon had thoughtfully stacked against the wall.

Any memoir should end with an account of what became of the characters within it. I cannot provide this. I never heard of Paladon, Yasin, Janifa or David again. They are lost to me, as Aziz, ibn Sa'id and innocent Ayesha were lost to me long ago. I like to think that one day Paladon or his son will return to build a new temple – mosque or cathedral, it hardly matters: it is the Idea it enshrines that is important. But that is only a dream, as inconsequential and probably as unlikely as my other dream that I will study philosophy again in Cairo.

Yet I have not entirely relinquished hope. I owe it to Paladon and Aziz to make something of the life that remains to me. For all our arcane vocabulary and attempts to plumb the depths of philosophy and knowledge, it was something very simple that our brotherhood celebrated. The God we were seeking was there all along – inside us. We found him that first moment under a fig tree when our hearts and minds bonded and we discovered our love for each other. The philosophy we learned together, the mosque we built, was mere dressing on a salad we had already tasted. Paladon was always much clearer-headed than I. *As long as we breathe,* he said to me during our last conversation, *as long as we see that God is life and joy, as long as we cultivate the best in us, not the worst, we're free . . . The idea remains.*

I originally set out to tell a tragedy. I conceived this account of our lives as a requiem to a world that was lost, but now I have finished it, I wonder if in the writing I have not performed some profound alchemy inside myself, turning the drab lead of my sorrow into a glistening new resolve. Last night when I recorded the events that I thought had broken my heart for ever – the death of Aziz, the death of Ayesha, Paladon's despair – my tears blotted each word I tried painfully to compose, but this morning I woke thinking only of what Paladon had also said to me in the hour before the end: *The world is rational and creative. It's a wonderful mystery for our minds to discover and celebrate. God's everywhere and we're all different. That's the beauty of it – the sheer diversity. What a tapestry to enjoy.* And I realised what a hypocrite and coward I had allowed myself to become.

The idea indeed remains – in me, while I live and can remember. I am not the caretaker of an empty mansion. Furthermore, if Paladon still lives, wherever he is, there are two of us. If he educates his son in what we learned, there will be three. An academy of three was how we originally started. Our Andaluz is destroyed, but there was always masonry in our philosophy. We can rebuild.

Such is the way of all things the Prime Mover has created. Mutability is inherent, but from corruption can spring new life. I should not allow the days I have left to be wasted in mourning. I have no Elijah to guide me, but I should set out as my father did, when tragedy befell him in Granada, trusting that he would find a better world.

I have decided to put aside the book of the past. I will leave it in one of the pillars in Paladon's mosque. And I will use the few days I have left before the caravan sets off for the sea to prepare for the future, whatever it holds. My departure will not be the exile I had thought it would be. It will be a journey into the unknown, and I will embrace whatever befalls me with curiosity and joy. There is a universe still to discover. And I am more fortunate than my father because the brotherhood has taught me what to seek.

Whatever befalls me, the journeying will be worth the effort. Paladon would approve. He would consider it to be another brave adventure.

I have a passage booked on a boat. If the man who said he would buy it for me is trustworthy, and if I can pass the Almoravid border guards and get to Cartagena, I will take it.

Or not. As the Prime Mover wills.

Acknowledgements

I would like to thank all the various people who so kindly shared their time and thoughts during the composition of this novel.

It was Ian Buruma (although I did not know him then) who gave me the germ of the idea when I read his *Murder in Amsterdam* on a ten-hour flight to China. Sitting in a garden overlooking the walls of Toledo a few months later, I opened a book on Moorish Spain, given to me by David Mahon, and read about the Christian 'suicide bombers' in ninth-century Cordoba: I had my historical setting. A year later, I was in a bistro in the Latin Quarter of Paris with Adeline Rucquoi, Reader in Medieval History at the Sorbonne. Over a delicious lunch and a walk down the Rue St Germain exploring book-shops, she tantalised me with tales of al-Andaluz, listened to my then flimsy synopsis and in her generosity helped me refine it so that my story made sense for the period; she also gave me copies of her lectures and an invaluable contemporary reading list. (I should thank my daughter, Clio, for finding some of these rare books for me in her university library in London.)

There were many others who helped me as I wrote my first draft, including, again, David Mahon, as well as Laurence

Browne, who both steered me through the maze of medieval Muslim thought and custom; Tony Galsworthy, who told me what trees and shrubs could be found in an eleventh-century Andalucían garden; Robert Sells, who guided me on the limits of ancient medical knowledge; Paul French, who gave me insights into the Spanish Civil War; Jeronia Clinton, Julio Arias, Peter Batey and Dylan Mahon, who corrected my Spanish patois; Barbara Alighiero, who told me where an Andaluzi king might find obsidian in the Mediterranean, and many others – Stephen Bradley, Helen and Robert Callender, Charles Collins, Leonora Collins, John Holden, Humphrey Hawksley, Hong Ying and Kit Naylor among many, who read my manuscript in its vestigial stages and gave me ideas along the way.

Finally I would like to thank my editors – Isabelle Holden in Beijing; my agents, Araminta Whitley and Peta Nightingale; my indefatigable copy editor, Hazel Orme; and of course my publisher at Hodder, Carolyn Mays, assisted by Francesca Best – who between them honed the novel from a first draft into what it is today.

The mistakes, historical and otherwise, are my own – although some I attribute to the ghostly Samuel himself, who certainly had an agenda of his own (as evidenced by his unflattering and certainly unconventional portraits of several historical characters who appear in his tale). For the humble scribe transliterating him, he sometimes took on a mischievous life of his own!

Adam Williams
Palazzo dei Piaceri Celesti, Force, Le Marche, Italy
27th June 2009

The Palace of
Heavenly Pleasure

ADAM WILLIAMS

'Indulge in a heady, passionate drama'
Sunday Express

China, 1899. A weakened Dynasty watches helplessly as western
powers encroach on its land. But driven by drought and hunger,
a secret society is preaching rebellion.

Unaware of the forces broiling around her, a young English girl
arrives in the city of Shishan. Life is picnics and tiger hunts for
the foreigners, but for Helen Frances there are other, more
dangerous delights.

For the Boxers are massing secretly in the forests and hills. Soon
Helen Frances and the other westerners will find themselves in
enormous peril.

At the end of the road, the Palace of Heavenly Pleasure beckons:
a brothel overlooking an execution ground, its scented rooms
offer safety – at a price few would be prepared to pay . . .

'Absolutely wonderful – a spellbinding novel'
Penny Vincenzi

HODDER

The Emperor's Bones

ADAM WILLIAMS

As 1920s China teeters on the verge of civil war, two Oxford graduates return to the land of their birth.

By the age of twenty-one Catherine Cabot has already witnessed more death and hardship than anyone should have to in a lifetime. A nursing veteran of the Great War and the Russian Revolution, she is beautiful, headstrong and complicated, just like her mother. Now all she wants is to lay the ghosts of her past.

Her friend, Yu Fu-kuei, is a revolutionary and communist spy determined to sacrifice herself and anybody else for her cause.

Caught up in a triangular love affair, Catherine is drawn into China's struggle. As warlords and nationalists tear each other to pieces, and Japanese militarists wait for an excuse to invade, Catherine becomes the pawn of two men who will stop at nothing to wreak their revenge. Meanwhile Yu Fu-kuei, betraying and betrayed, discovers that love might be her strongest weapon.

'This book is poetic and romantic in parts, harrowing and tragic in others . . . you'll be richly rewarded'
★ ★ ★ ★ *Heat*

HODDER

The Dragon's Tail

ADAM WILLIAMS

From the Cold War through the horror of the Cultural Revolution and into the bloody climax of Tianenmen Square, *The Dragon's Tail* traces a gripping adventure of modern China.

China is the land of Harry Airton's birth and privileged childhood – until the Japanese invasion leaves him orphaned and rootless. For twelve angry, disaffected years he has dreamed of returning.

When the British Secret Service sees in Harry the perfect spy to send on a dangerous mission to Beijing, he will finally get his chance. But under Mao's regime, nothing is what it once was. For Harry to achieve his mission he must compromise all he ever believed, and risk losing everything he holds dear.

'A true epic, spanning many decades and incorporating real events of magnitude. It is not easy to explain historical context entertainingly, but Williams pulls it off.'
The Times

HODDER